Butterfly on the Storm

Butterfly on the Storm

The Heartland Trilogy

Part I

WALTER LUCIUS

Translated from the Dutch by
Lorraine T. Miller and Laura Vroomen

MICHAEL JOSEPH
an imprint of
PENGUIN BOOKS

MICHAEL JOSEPH

UK | USA | Canada | Ireland | Australia
India | New Zealand | South Africa

Michael Joseph is part of the Penguin Random House group of companies
whose addresses can be found at global.penguinrandomhouse.com

First published in Holland by A. W. Bruna Uitgevers, 2013, then Luitingh Sijthoff, 2016
First published in Great Britain by Michael Joseph, 2017

001

Copyright © Walter Lucius, 2016

The moral right of the author and translators has been asserted

Epigraph credit: *Through the Looking-Glass, and What Alice Found There,* Lewis Carroll, 1871

Set in 13.5/16 pt Garamond MT Std

Typeset in India by Thomson Digital Pvt Ltd, Noida, Delhi

Printed in Great Britain by Clays Ltd, St Ives plc

A CIP catalogue record for this book is available from the British Library

HARDBACK ISBN: 978–0–718–18135–2

TRADE PAPERBACK ISBN: 978–0–718–18138–3

www.greenpenguin.co.uk

MIX
Paper from
responsible sources
FSC® C018179

Penguin Random House is committed to a
sustainable future for our business, our readers
and our planet. This book is made from Forest
Stewardship Council® certified paper.

'Well, in *our* country,' said Alice, still panting a little, 'you'd generally get somewhere else – if you ran very fast, for a long time, as we've been doing.'
'A slow sort of country!' said the Queen. 'Now, *here*, you see, it takes all the running *you* can do, to keep in the same place.'

– Lewis Carroll
Through the Looking-Glass,
and What Alice Found There

For Nicole – Her name embodies love

PART ONE

Dancer

He was making his way among the trees so quickly that he'd already stumbled twice. It was dark. He'd lost his sandals and was now running barefoot. The fallen branches cut the soles of his feet but he barely noticed the pain. And although he kept stubbing his toes on roots, that didn't bother him either. He'd never run this fast in his life.

He'd only just broken into a sprint, but already felt himself slowly lifting off the ground. He was floating, with branches sweeping past his face and lacerating his body. When a dangling earring got caught on a branch and was ripped from his earlobe, he felt no pain. The euphoria of the escape made him numb to pain, made him stronger, made him faster.

Everything in him was instinctively geared towards running. Every breath, every heartbeat, every movement served his flight. The direction didn't matter. Running, that's what it was about. As long, as fast and as far as possible.

He'd tried before, but he'd been caught. The injuries caused by the beating had kept him awake for weeks. Yet it didn't stop him from trying again. The man with the long black hair had planted a kiss on his glowing cheek, pressed his large hand against his back and yelled an order in an incomprehensible language.

He'd started running when he heard the shots. If he kept running he'd be safe. He ran towards the light that appeared behind the trees. All he heard now was his own breathing, his heartbeat. He wanted to embrace the rapidly approaching light as though it were salvation.

The light hit him with a dull thud.

I

Farah Hafez carefully placed her necklace with the silver-plated pendant beside her three silver rings and the black leather cuff. She looked into the bright-blue eyes of her naked reflection in the mirror and caressed the many tiny scars on her arms, breasts and belly. She'd scored them into her caramel-coloured body herself, back when it dawned on her that there could be no love without pain.

Time to get ready: sweep up her jet-black hair falling well below the shoulder in a cascade of curls and pull it into a tight topknot. Put on those loose-fitting, black satin trousers and fasten them around the hips. Place her arms into the wide sleeves of the jacket and then tie the red satin sash around it, so both ends fell across her left hip.

Farah took another look at herself standing there in her martial arts outfit. There may have been only an ultra-thin layer of fabric between her and the outside world, but she'd erected an imaginary suit of armour around herself. An invisible, yet impenetrable coat of mail. She took a deep breath, closed her eyes and tried to ignore the cheering of the audience that carried in irregular waves from inside the old theatre via the catacombs into her dressing room.

She bent her knees slightly and began the warm-up exercises she once learnt from her father. Soon all she heard was her own breathing. She was five years old again, standing in the walled garden at the back of her parental home, under the old apple tree in Wazir-Akbar-Khan, Kabul's affluent neighbourhood. Next to her father in his crisp white shirt and handmade linen trousers. He was counting out loud in what was to her an incomprehensible language, which he'd learnt from his Indonesian nanny as a little boy, *'Satu, dua, tiga . . .'*

Now Farah was whispering those very same words in a dressing room in Carré, an age-old brick circus building on wooden piles in Amsterdam. The same words after each exhalation, '*Satu, dua, tiga.*'

Just then the door swung open, revealing the silhouette of her coach. The deep voice of the emcee announcing the fight blasted in. She walked through the narrow corridors to the main auditorium, catching snippets of the introduction.

'Farah Hafez! An avenging angel with the body and power of an oriental tiger!'

Oriental? She'd been in the Netherlands since the age of nine. And though she obviously had an Afghan heart, she considered herself to be a Dutch woman in every other respect.

Blinking, she stepped into the bright glare of the spotlight, and climbed the steps to the ring. Her opponent in the other corner, a white-haired Russian woman, looked like a vulture. Cold and ruthless. Farah failed to detect any signs of respect in her. Farah felt a stab of confusion. She was doing this gala because she loved this martial art with all her heart. Besides journalism, it was the mainstay of her life. Pencak Silat, the noble art of war from the Indonesian archipelago. Her father had taught her, and for that reason alone she'd continue to practice it for the rest of her life. It was a lasting bond. But it was also a way of life: an ongoing mental and spiritual challenge focused on the positive and humane.

She closed her eyes and returned, one last time, to the silence in which she'd done her warm-up. Her father reappeared by her side. Back from the dead. He spoke with the calm voice of a spirit who'd left all cares behind.

'*Do you remember what you were doing when you first felt the fear?*'
She remembered.
'*You need to feel the fear to go through it.*'

She took up her starting position, only inches from her opponent. Her right hand open and held up as if about to hit an imaginary wall. The Russian woman formed her mirror image. Farah felt the electric charge when their palms all but

4

touched. She knew that strength alone wouldn't get her anywhere with this woman. She had to be quick and agile too.

When the referee yelled the starting signal, she reacted a split second too late. The Russian grabbed her left arm and pushed her back with all her might. The fear instantly paralyzed her. She had two opponents now: her assailant and herself. She ought to be like bamboo, bending and bouncing back hard, not like a tight string, snapping at the slightest touch. She had to focus. Breathe. Think.

Out of the corner of her left eye, Farah saw a punch coming her way. She blocked it and put her opponent in an arm lock. Tugging and pulling at each other, they spun around on the mat. All of a sudden, the Russian reached for Farah's head and began yanking at her hair. With tears of pain squirting out of her eyes, Farah kicked the Russian woman in the back with her right shin and made a scissoring motion that enabled her to throw her opponent on to her back and then clasped the woman's outstretched hand to her chest. The Russian was now lying underneath her, caught in an arm lock.

Suddenly she felt a searing pain in her left calf. Her opponent had sunk her teeth into it. The pain rushed through Farah's body, but instead of letting go she pulled even harder on the arm, so the hold tightened.

There they lay for a while, the Russian caught in an arm lock with Farah firmly on top of her, both screaming with pain, until the referee slapped their taut bodies with the flat of his hand.

'*Berhenti, berhenti!*' Stop, stop!

She released the hold, rose unsteadily to her feet and after brushing a hand across her calf noticed the smears of blood on her palm. As she stared into the Russian's squinting eyes she suddenly felt an overwhelming force take hold of her. These were the moments she feared most. Something or someone took possession of her and made her do things that were beyond her control.

Before she knew it, Farah had thrown a right uppercut at her opponent's chin. She pounded the woman's ribs with her left hand and then with a right kick sent her flying backwards across the mat. The Russian went down like a rag doll.

She heard someone calling her name from very far away. She looked over her shoulder. Her coach had jumped into the ring behind her. She could see the panic in his eyes. When she turned around again she saw the referee and the attendant kneeling down by the Russian's body, lying motionless on the floor.

It was dead silent in the hall.

2

The ambulance's bright-blue flashing light reflected almost fluorescent against the raindrops hitting the windscreen. Although the wipers were going like mad, visibility on the unlit wooded road was poor. But Danielle Bernson had complete trust in her driver who was in constant contact with police central dispatch. It wasn't clear where the victim would be lying.

The accident involved a child. The caller hadn't indicated much more. In the side-mirror Danielle saw a police car's emergency light rapidly approaching. When she glanced up again she shrieked. A pitiful heap of flesh was lying motionless on the road barely fifty yards in front of them. The driver, pumping his brakes to slow down, stopped the Mobile Medical Team ambulance alongside the body, diagonally blocking the lane. Grabbing her blue case and the resuscitation bag, Danielle jumped out of the vehicle into the rain.

It was a girl. She was lying face down on the wet tarmac. Her head was sideways, smashed against the ground. Her right arm was bent at an unnatural angle. Her left arm was limp and her right leg was twisted bizarrely, as if it wanted nothing more to do with the rest of her body.

Danielle knelt and together with the driver carefully lifted the girl's head and neck and slowly turned her over. She supported the neck with a brace. Judging from the child's dark-brown skin and jet-black hair she could have been Middle Eastern. Her eyes were darkly lined with kohl and greasy crimson lipstick was smudged around her mouth. She was dressed in a purple embroidered robe as if she'd just attended some kind of traditional festival. And she was hung with ornaments: in her ears, around her neck and wrists, even her ankles.

Jewellery with small silvery bells that tinkled faintly with the slightest movement.

The girl's eyes were shut. The only sign of life her distressed breathing. Danielle brushed a sticky lock of hair, clotted with blood, away from the head wound and began giving her oxygen.

Behind them a police car skilfully manoeuvred via the road's right lane and then, a good distance away and with its emergency light flashing, blocked the road. Meanwhile Danielle heard brakes screech to a halt behind the ambulance. A car door opened and was slammed shut again, followed by rapid footsteps. Seconds later a somewhat older Moroccan-looking man squatted down across from her.

'Give me room to work,' she said irritably. When she glanced up, she saw the look of disgust on the man's face.

'Detective Marouan Diba,' he stated without making eye contact. 'Any witnesses?'

'Nobody. She was lying here alone.'

A second detective had opened an umbrella above Danielle and was holding a torch to assist her.

The girl's lips were turning blue. Danielle grabbed her stethoscope and listened to both sides of her chest. On the right side she heard the faint sound of breathing; on the left side she heard nothing.

'Collapsed lung with tension pneumothorax.'

She knew the child was at death's door. No doubt a number of her ribs were broken from the impact of the collision and the pressure building up in the chest cavity made it hard for the heart to circulate her blood. Danielle took her thickest infusion needle out of the case, located the space between the girl's second and third ribs, slid the catheter over the needle into the chest cavity, then carefully removed the needle. She heard a hissing sound as the air in the lung decompressed. It sounded like a balloon deflating.

The detective muttered a curse, though it was obviously as a form of release. Danielle continued to ignore him.

'It must have been a serious blow to the head. She probably hit the windscreen first and then the tarmac,' Danielle said. 'In the best-case scenario, she's got a severe concussion.'

'And in the worst case?' the detective asked.

'Internal bleeding,' she answered as she checked the girl's breathing again and then instructed her assistant to prepare a drip. She examined the strange position of the left leg. She now saw a piece of bone jutting out of the thigh and noticed that the leg was starting to swell.

She carefully felt the girl's pelvis and was disturbed by what she found.

'There's a good chance her pelvis is fractured, meaning she could bleed to death internally.'

She removed a pair of scissors from her kit and began cutting away the girl's clothing so she could better evaluate the injury. Right away she saw that the girl wasn't wearing underwear.

And that she was a he.

The detective cursed again. He rose and walked away. Danielle took the pelvic sling from her assistant and together they stabilized the boy's hips.

'Bore needle,' she shouted.

Danielle had to drill into the boy's right shinbone to insert the needle. Fortunately, he groaned in reaction. That meant his brain was still functioning, but Danielle knew time was running out. She attached the drip and covered the leg wound with sterile gauze. Next, with the help of her driver and her assistant, she cautiously rolled the boy on to the yellow spinal board. She placed two blocks around his head to immobilize him.

'At three,' she called and began to count.

The detectives helped lift the board into the ambulance. Danielle leapt in beside the injured boy, the doors were slammed shut, and the driver contacted the hospital to provide their ETA. As the ambulance sped out of the Amsterdamse Bos along the woodland road, Danielle realized she wasn't prepared to part with this child until she was sure he was out of danger.

3

Back in the dressing room Farah came to her senses again. As if she'd woken from a nightmare.

She'd looked at her coach with a question in her eyes, and he'd started talking to her. Calmly.

'It's not your fault, Farah. I saw what happened. It's not your fault.'

She realized what must have happened. It had been too much. While she'd managed to stand up to the Russian's physical powers, she couldn't fight a force that was so much more intense and treacherous. The Russian woman's hatred had penetrated her emotional defences, and had sparked an uncontrollable fury in her.

She knew how important it was to check her temper, even in the most difficult situations. Self-control had saved her life on more than one occasion. Yet tonight of all nights she'd lost that control. For only a few seconds, but in those seconds she might have fatally injured another woman.

She rarely lost herself in rage during a fight. It was a lot more common in love, where she'd left a trail of victims. But they always lived to tell the tale – with or without a broken heart – whereas the woman who'd faced her in the ring this evening might not.

She heard the door opening. While the uproar out in the corridor came blasting in and her coach was having a whispered conversation with an official, Farah tried to find the silence inside her head.

She heard her coach approach with a heavy tread, pause right behind her and wait until she was ready to hear the outcome. She could hear him breathing. Tears trickled down her cheeks. *Father, where are you?* When she'd finally calmed her breathing, she got up, turned around and saw the composure in her coach's eyes . . . the reassurance. 'It's not too bad.'

Barely fifteen minutes later, Farah eased her black Porsche Carrera into the car park underneath the Waterland Medical Centre. She parked it close to the staircase and quickly ran up to the Emergency Department.

The receptionist looked at her with tired eyes that were devoid of all empathy. Farah told her that she was here for the woman who'd just been brought in with two broken ribs and a concussion.

'And you are?'

'The woman who did that to her,' Farah replied.

The receptionist looked shocked. Just then, a few doctors and nurses stormed into the corridor. They ran past the reception desk in the direction of an ambulance which had just arrived out front with its sirens wailing.

Farah saw a seriously injured girl being wheeled in on a stretcher. The shredded, colourful fabric covering her had once been a traditional robe. The girl was draped in jewellery and little bells that made a sound each time the stretcher shifted. Amidst the apparent chaos of doctors and nurses yelling at each other, Farah was transfixed by the girl's eyes. They were filled with terror. She also noticed the bluish lips moving slowly and noiselessly, trying to form a word.

Nobody seemed to see or hear this. And even if someone had heard, they probably wouldn't have understood, because it was said in a language that wasn't all that common here. But Farah had used that same word in her dressing room earlier in the evening. It had remained unspoken then, merely a thought.

'*Padar.*' Father.

She squeezed past the trauma specialists and bent over the girl on the stretcher. She spoke to her in Dari. 'Relax, sweetheart. He'll be here soon.'

The blonde doctor in the orange ambulance uniform looked up in surprise.

'Are you a relative?'

'No, but she asked for her father.'

'It's not a she. It's a boy.'

A little boy, in these garments, wearing jewellery and make-up . . . Farah understood in a flash. It had never occurred to her that this age-old tradition from her native country could crop up in a Western country. But the evidence lay bleeding on the stretcher in front of her.

'Is there an interpreter?' Farah asked.

'We're trying to contact one,' the blonde doctor said, raising her arm to stop Farah as the boy was wheeled into the trauma room.

'I can interpret!' Farah exclaimed as she watched how the boy was transferred, spinal board and all, to the operating table. She also heard the nervous tone of the consultations. She worked out that the doctor was refusing to surrender the boy to the care of the trauma team. Suddenly the woman gestured to Farah.

'Ask him who his father is,' she said as she began to cut the remaining clothes from the boy's body. Meanwhile two nurses removed all the jewellery and put it in a transparent plastic bag which they tied under the stretcher.

Farah approached the boy. She took him to be seven, eight at most. She began talking to him, softly, telling him that he was safe now, that he had to hang in there. She would stay with him.

When she gently took his hand in hers, the boy clutched her fingers.

'What's your name?'

He looked at her, bewildered, as if she came from another planet.

'*Namet chist?*' What's your name? She held her ear close to his mouth, but amidst the many loud instructions she couldn't hear, let alone understand his whispers.

She overheard the blonde doctor telephoning to say that a 'Priority 1' patient was coming through. At that moment a nurse rushed in, shouting. 'The surgeon is on his way.'

'I'm going to operate,' the doctor said, quite unperturbed, as she inserted a drain into the boy's chest cavity. Farah nearly passed out at the sight. She turned back to the boy and whispered in his ear.

'*Ma Farah astom, to ki hasti?*' I'm Farah, who are you?

She saw the tears rolling down his cheeks and felt an immense need to give free rein to her own tears, but she held them back and merely whispered some clichés.

'I'm here. I won't leave you.'

'Have you found out anything more about him?' the doctor asked.

'Not yet. By the way, where did you find him?'

'In the woods, the Amsterdamse Bos. A hit-and-run.' Farah picked up on the anger in her terse answer. The doctor immediately turned back to the nursing staff. 'Listen, everyone. We've got an open-book fracture and a femur fracture. Most likely internal bleeding in the abdomen and possibly in the skull as well. The boy's going to the OR. The fractures need to be stabilized or else he'll bleed to death. Then we're sending him for a CT scan. Is that clear?'

The boy was wheeled out of the trauma room. Farah walked beside him, still holding his hand. The doctor approached her as the lift doors opened.

'What's your name?' she asked once they were in the lift.

'Farah.'

'Listen, Farah, you can't go into the OR.'

'I wasn't planning to.'

'But please leave your name and number at the desk.'

'I'll keep in touch,' Farah said. 'Who do I ask for if I want to speak to you?'

'For Danielle. Danielle Bernson.'

The boy groaned. Farah stroked his hair while keeping hold of his hand. 'You're going to go to sleep soon,' she whispered. 'Then all the pain will be gone. And when you wake up, I'll be here again.'

He looked at her with something like resignation.

The lift doors slid open. They walked through an empty corridor and stopped in front of OR 12.

'Here we are,' Danielle said.

Farah held her head very close to that of the boy.

'The doctor's going to look after you now. I'll be here, waiting for you. All right?'

She caught a glint of mild despair in his eyes. Farah pressed a kiss on his cheek and gently released his hand.

'Thank you, Farah,' Danielle said as she wheeled the boy in.

Farah barely heard her. Once the boy had disappeared behind the slamming doors, all she could hear was the violent pounding of her own heart. She paced up and down the empty corridor for a while before coming to a decision.

4

At the exit for the woods, Farah slammed on the brakes and swerved off the A9. While carefully negotiating the bends in the increasingly ill-lit road, she realized she was doing something she'd long ago decided never to do again: she was acting on impulse.

What had drawn her to this place? The boy's eyes? His terror? Or was it his despair, which in that single whispered word had sounded like an echo from her past?

She slowed to a halt and parked the car by the side of the road with the engine idling. Her pulse was racing. She closed her eyes and tried to regulate her breathing.

'*Padar.*'

Farah had often heard the Dari word for father in her thoughts, in the silence that accompanies the dead. This evening the boy and his whispering had suddenly broken that long-standing silence. She had a suspicion that something had happened here this evening that was to have a far greater impact on her life than she could foresee. The thought scared her, but she was determined to trust her intuition this time around. Strangely enough, the decision to retrace the boy's route caused her pulse to gradually slow.

She saw emergency lights approaching from behind and refracting sharp blue lines among the trees. Soon afterwards, the shiny red metal of a fire engine whizzed past with clanging sirens. Without hesitation, she accelerated and pursued the fire engine. She stepped on her brakes when it turned left on to a narrow path. From there she could see flames shooting up into the sky, some hundred yards into the woods. A crash, at such a remote location? Unlikely. She decided not to check it out, but to keep going along the paved road. A couple of minutes later she was proven right. Two forensics officers were crouching down on the road, going about their business in the light of some big work lamps.

Farah got out of her car and paused in front of the red-and-white tape stretched across the road. That's when she realized that she wasn't dressed for the occasion. Not in the slightest. Her clothes had been chosen for tonight's festive closing gala: leather sandals with block heels under black trousers, loosely rolled up to just above the ankle. She'd left the second-hand, glossy black Versace jacket on the back seat. In her fitted, metallic shirt and with her tousled hair she looked like a dazed fashion model who'd been abandoned by the rest of the crew halfway through a shoot.

A little unnerved, she watched as one of the officers high-lighted skid marks some thirty yards further up on her side of the road. The tracks swerved to the right, off into the verge. A few yards away, still in the right lane, someone had used white chalk to trace the contours of a small body in a bizarre pose.

The skid marks were probably from the car that had hit the boy. Farah saw there was quite a distance between the spot where the boy had been lying and where the marks shot off into the verge. It suggested that the boy had been hit so hard he'd been thrown some distance by the impact. The other option was that the car had actually tried to avoid the boy and had *not* hit him: the driver had slammed on the brakes, yanked on the wheel and come to a halt against a tree. In that case the boy hadn't been standing there – he'd already been lying there.

In the left lane, level with the chalk drawing, Farah saw the second forensic scientist working on another set of skid marks. She slipped under the tape and walked towards him. He was young and completely focused on the wet tarmac, so it took him a while to notice her. He looked up in surprise.

'I'm sorry to bother you. I live nearby,' Farah said in her friendliest voice. 'Do you have any idea what happened here?'

The young officer glanced at her and then pointed at something behind her. 'Is that yours?'

'The Carrera?' Farah asked, turning around. 'Yes, it is.'

'Three-point-two litre rear-drive engine, 230 bhp, turbo body, lowered chassis and gas shock absorbers. You don't just want to drive it, you want to live in it,' the officer said with the admiring glance of an expert. 'And I bet it goes from zero to a hundred in less than six seconds.'

'I've never tried,' Farah said. 'It's from 1987, and I take really good care of it.' Sensing that she'd made it through his initial screening with some success, she decided to press him for more information. She gestured towards the shattered glass of a headlight. 'How fast was this car going?'

'My guesstimate: around eighty. Slammed on the brakes. You can tell by those thick marks over here.' He pointed at the tip of the skid marks, where the tyre print was most clearly visible.

'The boy was lying over there,' Farah said, indicating the chalk drawing. 'Is it possible that he was hit by this car?' It was out before she realized it and the man in front of her was immediately on his guard.

'The boy?'

'I'm a journalist,' Farah owned up straightaway. 'I'm trying to find out who's responsible.'

'Do you have any ID on you?' The young officer sounded rather tense all of a sudden. She could tell he was inexperienced and that he was trying to impress her with what little authority he had. Out of the corner of her eye Farah saw the other officer approaching them. She tried again.

'Look, you're doing your job and I'm doing mine. Are those marks on the other side of the road from the same car? What do you think?' The other officer, who was undoubtedly in charge, was only a few yards away now. 'I mean,' Farah rephrased her thoughts quickly, 'was there more than one car involved in this accident?'

'Ma'am, this is a crime scene. You need to stay behind the tape.'

Looking into the grim face of the second forensics officer, Farah realized she'd run out of credit.

'Of course, officer. I beg your pardon.' Feeling her emotions getting the better of her, she quickly turned around. As she walked away, she could hear the two men conferring with each other.

'Ma'am?' the officer in charge shouted.

She turned around again and saw him coming towards her.

'I understand you're a reporter.'

'That's right,' Farah said. 'I was at the Emergency Department when they brought him in. And to leave a child for dead, here . . . well . . .'

For a moment they stood facing each other in silence.

'I'm sorry, but we're not allowed to pass information to the press.' The officer gave her a conspiratorial smile. 'But you're right.'

'What do you mean?'

'More than one car was involved.'

'Thank you,' she said hoarsely.

'What for?'

'For your . . . help.'

'We didn't help anyone, ma'am. There hasn't been anyone who's needed it.' He turned around. 'Kevin, have you seen any-one around here in the past five minutes who wanted to know anything?'

The younger officer shook his head and smiled.

Farah got into her car, did a U-turn and drove to the spot where she'd seen the fire engine turn into the woodland path. Meanwhile she tried to make sense of what she'd just seen and heard. Skid marks on both sides of the road, from opposite directions. Two cars. At more or less the same time, in the same spot. And what linked them was the boy. Three pieces of what remained, for the time being, a sinister puzzle.

When she got to the woodland path, she looked over and there were those flames again. Could the fire have had anything to do with the accident? She was going on intuition now, and her intuition told her to find out.

5

It felt like driving into a tree-lined inferno. But it wasn't the fire or chaos that drew her in. More than anything, it was the growing awareness that what had taken place here might have something to do with what had happened to the boy not far from here.

As she approached a police officer who gestured for her to stop, she flashed her press pass from the driver's side in the hope of being mistaken for a detective, and accelerated without waiting for his response. She pulled up right behind a fire engine, opened her car door and hurried around to the clearing where helmeted firefighters were spraying white layers of foam on to the smouldering shell of a station wagon. Sudden shouting. She realized too late that she'd strayed within the reach of a water cannon used to keep the surrounding trees wet. Before she could jump out of the way, she was blown off her feet by the impact of hundreds of litres of water.

When, dazed and drenched, she tried to scramble up again, a stranger's hand quickly pulled her to her feet. Still tottering on her heels, she looked straight into the clear brown eyes of a young man with trendy stubble that accentuated the angular jawline of his face.

'Lost?' he yelled above the din.

'More unwanted, I think,' Farah said, while tugging at her shirt that was now stretched tightly around her body. But tug as she might, the soaked fabric slid right back around her braless breasts. She might as well have been topless.

'Detective Joshua Calvino. What's a lady like you doing in a wood like this?' He said it so mischievously that it made her smile in spite of the circumstances.

'Okay, detective, here's the score. I was at the WMC's Emergency Department when a seriously injured boy was brought in. He'd been hit by a car somewhere in the vicinity. And I wanted to know what had happened.'

'The boy was hit further up the road. Not here.'

'Hmm, I know. I've already been up there.'

'Then what are you doing here?'

'Two cars were involved. I thought maybe one of those cars was torched here.'

He took another good look at her. She could tell he was trying hard not to look at her breasts.

'You don't seem like the type who goes wandering around the woods at some ungodly hour just for fun. So what is it?'

'I'm a journalist,' Farah said and showed him her ID. Meanwhile they'd reached the clearing where the burnt-out car was, covered in foam. The ground was squelchy and the air thick with greasy smoke. Amidst the chaos of firefighters walking to and fro with their endless hoses, Farah noticed a somewhat older man, who was gesticulating angrily and having a go at their commander.

'My partner,' Joshua said, frowning at the scene. 'He's getting all worked up because those guys with their extinguishers and waders have probably wiped out all the prints. Most likely destroyed any evidence we might have had.'

'Any idea what caused the fire?' Farah asked tentatively.

'The car was doused in petrol and then . . . whoosh!' Joshua simulated striking a match and flinging it away.

The other detective came striding towards them. Farah could tell he appreciated her presence a lot less than his younger colleague.

'Those guys are bad enough,' he said, pointing to the firefighters behind him. 'So the last thing we need here are sightseers.' He was staring so blatantly at Farah's breasts as he said this that she took an instant dislike to him.

'She was at the Emergency Department when they brought in the hit-and-run boy,' Joshua said. 'She reckons this fire might have something to do with—'

He didn't have a chance to finish his sentence because of the sudden consternation among the firefighters grouped around the wrecked station wagon. He rushed over, with Farah hot on his heels. There she saw something she wished she hadn't seen: two blackened, contorted bodies coated in white foam in the back of the car.

Overcome by the sight and stench of the two charred corpses, she spun around and, clinging to the nearest tree, threw up the contents of her stomach in a couple of convulsive spasms. Even the smell of her own vomit was refreshing compared to the stench of burnt human flesh now stuck in her nose. With a handkerchief pressed to her mouth, she straightened up again.

Joshua Calvino put a hand on her shoulder. 'I think you've seen enough.' He sounded the way he was meant to sound in a situation like this. Someone with both authority and compassion. Someone she was prepared to listen to.

'Here you are.' He handed her a bottle of water which she drained in a couple of big gulps.

'Thanks.'

'I need to get on with things. And you've got to get out of here. Will you be okay?'

The almost sensual, dazzlingly white smile that accompanied his words was really quite inappropriate under the circumstances, but Joshua Calvino appeared to have the knack of shaking off the gravity of this kind of ghastly situation. Farah was half expecting to hear a backing track, a cue for Joshua to burst into song and for the firefighters to start dancing in the background, like you see in Bollywood films. She watched him as he walked over to the other detective, who was now venting his spleen on the phone.

When, a little later, she carefully manoeuvred her car on to the paved road, she felt dizzy, and, more than anything, intensely sad. That's why she opted for the fastest route around the

Amstelveense Poel, which would lead her straight to the big house with the thatched roof. Across the pond was the home of TV director and documentary filmmaker David van Rhijn, the man she'd been in a relationship with for the past six months. So far, it seemed to be bearing up despite her impulsive nature.

Earlier that evening David had arrived back from India, where he'd been making a documentary about the history of the national railway network that carried some eighteen million passengers every day. She didn't know if David was jet lagged and hoped he'd still be up. She thought of calling first, but changed her mind. If he was asleep, she didn't want to wake him. Instead she'd snuggle up to him, wind down after the day's events and fall asleep.

She thought of everything she'd been through that evening. The fight at Carré, its outcome, the hospital where the boy was brought in, the little help she'd been able to offer, the doctor who'd been so concerned.

All of a sudden she remembered why she'd gone to the hospital in the first place. Her opponent's injuries. By the time she could see David's house in the distance she was convinced that chance was a brilliantly orchestrated series of events. And for that reason alone she was desperate to believe in it.

6

David's house was infused with a spirit of sanctuary and harmony. As she climbed the wide wooden staircase in the dark, Farah remembered the first time she'd wandered around the place, six months ago. She'd felt like Alice in Wonderland.

This was the home base of a globetrotter who was in the habit of bringing back Asian dragons, African gods of thunder and Mexican skeletons along with Buddhas, Russian icons and pictures of American baseball legends.

When Farah and David first met, he was mourning the love of his life whom he'd just lost to pancreatic cancer. Farah was touched by the sincerity with which he told her about his loss and the remorse he felt when, despite the sudden emptiness, he found something of a new meaning in life – in her. Not once did he try to present himself as a victim, to arouse her pity to get her into his empty bed as a consolation prize. He simply told her about his life as it was now. Farah felt pain without pretence, saw grief without shame: mourning without any ulterior motives.

The key to Farah's unexpected passion for this stocky man with his head of dark curls and his boundless energy had been his melancholic eyes. They gave her a sense of security she hadn't known since her early years in Kabul. Two days after their first meeting, she turned up at his house overlooking the pond.

But she wasn't ready to move in with him yet, although David had said he was happy for her to give the 'whole freaking mess' a radical overhaul so it would feel like her home too. As long as David was around, it was his domain and she felt comfortable in it. But as soon as he'd gone off on one of his long trips, the big house suddenly felt crushingly empty.

In his absence she also missed the delicious smells emanating from the kitchen, because despite his rugged exterior David was a sophisticated chef. Out of a desire to please Farah he'd immediately started exploring Afghan cuisine and the first evening she came over for dinner he'd served up her favourite dish, *qabili palau*. But for now she was keeping her flat on Nieuwmarkt, in the centre of Amsterdam.

Tonight, however, she wanted to be with him more than ever. To feel his ample body, his aromatic breath mingling with hers. His huge hands on her. His embrace. Having reached the first floor, she tiptoed into the bedroom where she could hear his soft, irregular snoring. The bedside lamp was still on and reflected in the bottle of Campbeltown malt whisky which sat on the bedside cabinet among the opened *New York Times* and sections of the *Guardian*.

She slipped off her rings, removed her bracelet and necklace and undressed as quietly as possible before sneaking into the bathroom where she selected the massage setting of the shower. Under the wide, hot jet she could feel her body starting to relax and the resistance to her pent-up emotions gradually dissolving. She could stand there for ever, with her arms across her chest, her back slightly stooped.

When she turned around, she saw David in the doorway, naked, with dishevelled hair and somewhere between waking and sleeping, leaning against the doorjamb while absent-mindedly scratching his balls with his left hand.

'I saw this *Idols*-type show on an Indian TV channel,' he said between two yawns. 'It was called *Bathroom Singer* and the idea was that the candidates were afraid to sing anywhere other than in the bathroom. It was amazing, it really was. They've recreated entire bathrooms in the studio and it's a huge hit.' He sleepwalked over to her with a growing erection and in an exaggerated, honeyed Indian accent said, 'So, welcome to the show, Miss Hafez. What will you sing for us tonight?' He didn't notice she was crying until he'd come closer.

'Are these tears of happiness because you won tonight, or are you just happy to see me again?' he asked with an uncertain smile. He wrapped her in a tight embrace.

Farah snuggled up against his warm, hairy body and burst into tears.

He lifted her out of the shower cubicle, carried her into the bedroom and covered her wet face with tender, comforting kisses. Then he looked at her long and hard. Biding his time.

'Let's not talk,' she whispered. She pushed him away gently and as he landed on his back with a sigh, she bent over him, splattering his hairy chest with drops from her wet hair and kissing him long and deep.

Leaning over him like this turned her on. David's large hands grabbed hold of her hips as if to pin her even tighter against himself.

'Harder,' she begged when he thrust deeper inside her. It felt as if she was lifted by the force of a mountainous wave and suspended above the bed for several seconds, weightless, screaming with relief. Soon after David came inside her with a shudder.

Once she'd softly landed on him again, she could feel her body finally relaxing and her gloominess slowly ebbing away.

She wasn't sure how long she'd been by David's side. She felt all clammy. The flashing digits on the alarm clock told her it was five past four. She carefully extricated herself from his embrace and, without a sound, stepped past the swaying net curtains in front of the open window and on to the balcony.

Lost in thought, she stared across the pond. Her whole life, she'd been fascinated with things she didn't understand. Her first such experience had been the moment when, as a five-year-old looking out of her bedroom window, she'd seen her father doing those slow, unfamiliar punching and kicking movements under the apple tree. As if he was doing a non-existant dance to inaudible chords. The notion that he'd gone mad had briefly crossed her young mind. At the same time she'd been so intrigued by his calm, his strength and his control that she'd carried on watching, open-mouthed.

Afterwards, she'd spied on him from her room every morning and she'd soon discovered that he always followed the same pattern of moves. She began imitating him. Day in, day out. Until, one morning, she summoned up enough courage to go and stand under the apple tree and wait for her father to come out. And when he did, she began the first move, graciously, the way she'd seen him do it. When she was done, he was still standing there. Motionless. She looked at him, ready for any punishment she might get. But instead he folded his hands and, without a word, bowed to her. It was a magical moment she'd never forgotten. It marked the beginning of their soul connection, which transcended his earthly demise four years later.

Now that the wind had turned, the roar of the A9 tore the illusion of natural harmony to shreds. Farah walked back into the room and looked at David, who was fast asleep. She smiled. He'd be capable of vigorous sex even during his REM sleep. But the promise she'd made earlier that evening kept echoing through her mind, '*Buru khauw sho. Waqte ke bedar shodi mar peshet mebashom.*' Go to sleep now. When you wake up, I'll be here again.

In the walk-in wardrobe she found a pair of jeans, which she teamed with a plain white silk shirt. As she slipped into a pair of trainers, she took out her mobile phone and called the WMC. The operation was still underway. So far, nobody had inquired about the boy.

She walked back to the bed, leaned over David, pressed a kiss on his sweaty forehead and snuck out of the bedroom.

7

When Detective Marouan Diba left the Amsterdamse Bos around 4 a.m., en route to the police station, he was exhausted. He stunk of cigarettes and was sweating like a pig. Given his state, he hated that his youthful colleague Joshua Calvino, seated beside him in the decrepit Toyota Corolla, looked fresh as could be and was so revved up it seemed like their round of duty had only just begun.

'Didn't I tell you? Too many carbs, junk food and fatty meats,' Calvino scoffed as Marouan's intestines loudly rumbled. He mocked him further by demonstratively rolling down his window.

Marouan knew his well-groomed colleague was right. During tonight's shift he'd stopped three times to stuff his face with greasy kebabs drowning in sauces. Calvino had joined him once, but only snacked on some pathetic-looking lettuce leaves.

'But let me console you,' Calvino grinned as he gazed at his mobile phone display, 'it's going to be another gorgeous day, maximum temperature of 32°C with winds averaging force three on the Beaufort Scale, so that means . . .'

'You won't have any reasons to hassle me,' Marouan interrupted as he stepped on the accelerator and took the turns as fast as possible to get to a toilet as quickly as he could. Testing Marouan's patience even further, Calvino started singing 'Feeling Good', his favourite song, at the top of his lungs.

'You're a half-baked wiseguy, y'know,' Marouan retorted raising his voice, 'in need of serious help. You're suffering from a chronic case of confidence: like the Big C!'

'You're one to talk,' Calvino replied laughing, 'the man whose last name begins with the *D* for depressing.'

This constant bickering was a communication style the two men had developed over time, to make their collaboration tolerable. Calvino was in a position Marouan could only envy. It had been Marouan and the other young minority cops of his era who'd fought the barriers and prejudice in the police force in the 1980s to create opportunities for the next generation. Thanks to their lead, new youngsters like Calvino, right out of police training academy, could move up the ladder more easily. Being a detective meant the beginning of a promising career for Calvino, while years ago becoming a detective seemed impossible to Marouan, even as a final goal. The idea that he would never really profit from his groundbreaking efforts was somehow still unbearable to Marouan. But there were other unbearable things in his life, and he'd learnt to live with those too.

A heat wave in August . . . it had already lasted three days and during this stint on duty – which began yesterday at 10 p.m. and would officially end today at 6 a.m. – had led to a record number of calls. Okay, no serial killings, no bank robberies or terrorist attacks, but quarrels among neighbours, common brawls and domestic rows that followed in such alarming succession that Marouan had the feeling the masses were on the verge of total insanity.

When the call arrived just after midnight about a kid being run down in the Amsterdamse Bos, it felt as if the world stood still for a moment. The notion that a child could be left for dead on a deserted road in the woods turned Marouan into a vengeful racing driver pulling out all the stops, so he'd almost crashed head on into the ambulance blocking the road. He often thought he'd seen everything there was to see, that it couldn't get any worse, that he was used to it all, but there were still situations that tore him up. And this was one of them.

When he saw that child lying on the wet tarmac, close to death, with the blonde doctor who'd arrived at the scene performing an intubation, he got more than upset. But obviously nobody around him was the least bit in the mood for his cursing. He also understood the annoyance of the doctor, who demanded more space, because he was just staring at her and not helping matters at all. But what he couldn't understand was how his colleague Calvino managed to steal the show by simply opening his umbrella and shining his magic torch on the doctor's work. What gave this guy the presence of mind to take the initiative with such a subtle flair?

It had been an evening full of surprises. First the seriously injured Middle-Eastern-looking girl turned out to be a seriously injured Middle Eastern boy. This was immediately followed by a kind of explosion, not very far from them. The first thought that crossed his mind was an accident on the nearby motorway. But minutes later, when the ambulance carrying the boy had sped away, a call arrived about a burning car three kilometres up the road.

Marouan had instructed the two officers at the scene of the hit-and-run to cordon off the area and wait for the forensics team to arrive. Then he drove as fast as he could to the clearing in the woods where he and Calvino were the first to witness a station wagon going up in an inferno of flames.

Due to the excessive heat, they could only stand by and watch as one tree after another in proximity of the soaring blaze lit up like a candle. The fire brigade arrived with their entire arsenal. And what Marouan had feared also happened: in a matter of seconds the helmeted firefighters in their fluorescent uniforms turned the crime scene into a sea of white foam, this way destroying any possible footprints or other evidence. Protesting loudly he navigated the hose-happy bunch in search of the man in charge. When he found their commander, who tried to dismiss him with the lame excuse that they were only doing their job, he just about lost it. Marouan told him, in no uncertain terms, that by doing so they'd made it impossible for him to do *his* job.

In the meantime, Calvino was chatting up a soaking wet, sultry beauty who seemed to have fallen from the sky. And at this absurd hour of the night, when *nothing* seemed to be what it was, sure enough, Miss Wet T-shirt with her splendid breasts turned out to be a journalist. She was rather keen on connecting the boy who'd been run down to the burning car. But when the fire was extinguished and two charred bodies were discovered under the foam in the rear of the station wagon, she backed down a bit.

But Marouan shared her suspicions: his gut feeling told him that the two incidents had to be related. The locations were too close together and the station wagon was set ablaze less than twenty minutes after the hit-and-run was reported.

After the gruesome discovery he immediately rang police headquarters. The simple report of a car set on fire was updated with the info that a double homicide had taken place. Undoubtedly some kind of criminal retaliation. Then he called and woke up Chief Inspector Tomasoa. A few words sufficed: tomorrow, in consultation with the Public Prosecutor, Tomasoa would decide if the case of the gutted vehicle should be upgraded to MIT level. This meant an entire murder investigation team would get to work on it. Marouan hoped that his upcoming holiday – the yearly three-week visit to his native country and relatives – wouldn't have to be rescheduled because of this. His wife was already busy packing. Their flight was leaving the day after tomorrow.

Almost at the police station, Marouan, with his face contorted, was trying to keep his upset bowels under control. Deep in concentration behind the wheel, his thoughts wandered back to the journalist. She'd disappeared as quickly as she'd appeared.

Farah Hafez worked for the *AND*. Marouan was familiar with the newspaper but dismissed it as a periodical for students and left-wing intellectuals. He preferred *De Nederlander* – considered by some to be a tits-and-ass tabloid, a gossip rag at best, it still had Marouan's personal stamp of approval as a quality newspaper. No doubt this Hafez woman would change into a dry T-shirt and hurl herself into the case and report on everything in her own provocative and anti-authoritarian way. That was the *AND*'s style. And his colleague Calvino would undoubtedly stand there grinning in his own idiotic vegan way.

He instructed Calvino to call Forensics. Their findings on the hit-and-run needed to be on Marouan's desk as quickly as possible. It would be better if he, with his years of experience, got the investigation off to a good start before he went on holiday. So Calvino wouldn't cock it up.

A few minutes later, when he was finally able to relieve himself by quickly ducking into the visitors' toilet, he had to admit that the incident with the boy had upset him more than he'd expected. Moments later, munching on a chocolate bar, he located Calvino who was ringing the forensics department.

'This is the plan, kid,' he said with authority when Calvino had finished his conversation. 'We're going to the hospital to see if we can talk to the boy. Then to central dispatch. I want to find out where that hit-and-run call came from.'

'You're hopeless,' Calvino derided him as he glanced at the chocolate bar and caught the car keys Marouan tossed him. 'Utterly hopeless!'

8

'One, two, three, four... Count, keep counting,' Danielle instructed as the boy was lifted from the stretcher to the operating table as carefully as possible on a spinal board. Finally, at 'ten', he was lying in the right position for a body X-ray.

Danielle heard the anaesthetist calmly tell him what was going to happen next. 'I'm going to put you to sleep. Everything will be okay.' It sounded like something from a fairy tale. But most fairy tales had happy endings, Danielle reflected, while this child's life would undoubtedly turn out very differently. Perhaps he wouldn't wake up. She was completely overcome by the kind of empathy that is totally counterproductive in situations like this. She couldn't fight it off; it crept up on her and nestled deep inside her. She soon noticed that her hands were trembling and that her heart rate had gone up.

She bent over the boy as the anaesthesia took effect and looked at him as reassuringly as she could. And suddenly it struck her that this wasn't about the boy; she was the one who needed reassuring. The fear was back. The same fear she'd felt six months ago in the African night when she'd fled the soldiers wielding machetes and automatic rifles who'd forced their way into the field hospital. Fleeing had spared her a mad killing spree. But her escape had also meant leaving the children in the medical relief tents to their fate.

That was why she'd promised herself she'd never flee again. So at a moment like this one, she wasn't about to run from her responsibility for this boy.

Together with the OR assistant, she started to disinfect the stomach, pelvic area and thighs with iodine. She was busy marking the spots that needed to be drilled for the surgical pins when the senior trauma surgeon on-call entered. Nick Radder, in his early sixties, was entertaining enough to grab a drink with in your free time but the minute he put on those surgical scrubs he turned into a right old Machiavellian bully.

'What have we got here?' he asked impatiently.

'Open-book fracture to the pelvis. Using an external fixator to stabilize,' Danielle stated as she made her first incision.

'Bernson, you?' Radder said, taken aback.

'That's right, I'm doing this operation.' She remained focused on the task at hand.

'I don't think so,' Radder said in a tone one might use to deny a whining child an ice cream. 'I didn't get out of my warm bed to stand here like an idiot.'

'Not my problem,' Danielle said curtly. She hadn't made eye contact with him, but suspected he was doing his utmost not to grab the scalpel from her hand.

'I want a full status on this kid,' Radder said abrasively. 'And why wasn't a CT scan done first?'

'If this pelvic fracture isn't stabilized immediately, he'll bleed to death. No simpler way to say it.' She made her second incision and spread the tissue with a clamp. Meanwhile, the rest of the OR team went about their business undisturbed: totally concentrated on facilitating the operation.

'How was he was lifted?' Radder snapped.

'With the utmost caution,' she replied, finally glancing up at him. His forehead was sweating slightly. She heard the OR telephone ring.

'So his head, neck and back were still stabilized?'

'Right,' Danielle said, 'that's what utmost caution means.'

'So while you're pinning his pelvis back together, he can just bleed to death in his head?'

Radder's words were filled with contempt. In the background Danielle heard the OR assistant who'd answered the telephone say, 'Doctor Bernson is operating.'

'Step away, Bernson. I'll take it from here,' Radder said. She felt her newly regained composure begin to crumble.

'It's the MMT. There's another emergency call. What should I tell them?' the assistant asked with the phone still in her hand.

'Drill,' Danielle requested.

'Damn it,' Radder barked through his teeth.

Danielle looked at her team. It felt like *her* team. Their eyes assured her that she had their complete support. It gave her a sense of strength. The phone call ended with the message that Dr Bernson was still in surgery. The drill was handed to her and she positioned it at the first mark she'd drawn on the hip.

'Two centimetres higher, Bernson. You're too low.' Radder hissed like a poisonous snake.

'Perhaps someone could escort Dr Radder out of the OR?' Danielle said to her assistant with as much control as she could. Her whole body was tense. She tried to focus on the spot she was about to drill but had trouble estimating the correct depth. Her right eye twitched. The sounds of the heart meter, the anaesthesia equipment, the Cell Saver air filtering and the EEG monitor all merged into the rhythmic swishing of the wipers, the sound of the emergency siren and the thrumming of the raindrops against the ambulance's windscreen . . . and then blended with the ever-echoing screams of the children in the African hospital tent.

'Blood pressure's falling,' the anaesthetist warned. 'I can't keep it stable.' The sound of the metal drill rotating in the bone was shrill. Danielle drilled the next hole.

'His pulse is fading fast,' the anaesthetist shouted.

Even though a child's body has much less mass than an adult body, Danielle knew they bleed out just as quickly. She heard Radder's angry voice behind her, 'If he doesn't make it, this child's death is on your conscience, Bernson!'

At that moment she saw she'd drilled too low and that the acute bleeding just continued. Appalled, Danielle realized that Radder was most likely right. She'd have a dead child on her conscience.

Once again.

9

From the fifth floor of the Waterland Medical Centre, Farah looked out over a slowly awakening city. Viewed from up high, through glass, Amsterdam looked like a dream vision, like something from her youth.

As a child, she used to like nothing better than to immerse herself in a world in which everybody lived happily ever after, like in fairy tales. She couldn't get enough of the story of Layla and Majnun, the two lovers who, because of tragic circumstances, were united only in death. 'Only then,' Farah's mother read to her softly, 'did they no longer feel pain. And never would again for all eternity. For whoever must endure suffering, and bears it patiently in this world, will be full of joy and bliss in paradise.'

But Farah didn't want to wait for paradise after death. Despite everything she'd been through as a little girl, she decided that life here on earth was to be her only life. She'd witnessed enough death to know that it marked the definitive end.

To Farah it was all about life *before* death. And she wanted to make the most of that life. But that conviction was fraught with contradictions. She had a burning desire to experience everything as intensely as possible, and would do so by acting on her impulses and primal urges. But giving in to them was coupled with a fear of losing herself in licentiousness and rolling through life like a mere plaything of chance.

Whenever this fear struck, she would throw herself into a life of order with the same fanaticism, and cherish discipline like a sacred cow. Her chaotic apartment would be turned upside-down and given a cosy and domestic make-over. She would resume her daily visits to the gym, eat her greens, train and meditate, go to bed at a decent hour, get up early and submit her newspaper articles on time. Until this life, too, began to stick in her gullet. Next thing, fuelled by despair, she'd swing back to the other extreme.

And yet, throughout those tumultuous times, one mighty phenomenon always kept her balanced: her curiosity. From childhood, she'd been intrigued by everything that happened around her. The effort to come to grips with the world became her main priority. Writing down her thoughts about everything she saw, heard and experienced made her feel that, despite the many upheavals and setbacks in her life, she could still exert some control over herself and events.

Through the same process she later managed to find a delicate balance in her work as a journalist. Having learnt to control her own sometimes barely governable nature with words, she was now trying to master and understand the forces around her by writing about them.

Distractedly gazing out over Amsterdam, where more and more lights were now coming on, Farah clung to the thought that as long as they were still operating, there was hope for the boy.

She heard footsteps in the corridor behind her. They sounded different from the squeaking rubber soles under the shoes worn by the doctors and nurses who walked past every now and then. When she turned around, she saw the same two detectives she'd met a couple of hours earlier by the burning car in the woods. The younger of the two, the one with the trendy stubble, lavished a lovely smile of recognition on her. His older colleague seemed astonished, if anything, to find her here.

'Farah,' the younger detective said as he held out his hand. 'Are you feeling a little better?'

'Given the circumstances, yes. Thank you.'

In the way a beginning and an end are inextricably linked, these two men seemed to belong together, with the older detective no doubt symbolizing the end and his colleague the beginning. And like it has been since time immemorial, the negative force was trying to dominate its positive counterpart.

The older man, with his washed-out complexion, muscled in. He held out his hand and formally introduced himself as Marouan Diba.

Farah took him to be well over fifty. He must have been a good-looking man once but his weight, the random streaks of grey in his black hair and his jaded attitude suggested that he'd resigned himself to his own mortality, making him look older than his years. And his faint smile concealed elements of anguish – minute particles, all but invisible to an outsider. But Farah recognized them.

She recognized the pain of someone forced to accept the person he'd become. As for herself, she often thought back to who she'd been before she fled Afghanistan as a ten-year-old. That innocence, that idealism, she hadn't seen them in the mirror since. What she saw, more often than not, was a dark shadow in her pupils. That's what she saw in Marouan Diba. She heard it in the accusing tone he used with her.

'Why didn't you tell me last night who you were and what you were doing there?'

'You didn't ask,' she replied, on her guard.

'Can you tell me why you're so interested in the boy?'

'Interested is the wrong word, detective. I became involved. I happened to be in the Emergency Department when he was wheeled in.'

'And what were you doing there, if you don't mind me asking?'

'I went to inquire about the woman I'd just knocked out.'

Diba stared at her with raised eyebrows.

'I was taking part in a martial arts gala at Carré,' she went on to clarify. 'The fight didn't go according to plan. I injured my opponent so badly that she had to go to hospital.'

'So you went to the Emergency Department because you floored your opponent, and that's when the boy was brought in?'

'That's right.'

'Could you then explain to me why, shortly after this boy was wheeled in, you raced off to the Amsterdamse Bos?'

Farah felt anger bubbling up inside her. 'You do know the boy was found in women's clothing and that he was wearing make-up and lots of jewellery?' she asked as calmly as possible.

'We're aware of that.'

'And what do you think that means?' In spite of herself, Farah moved a step forward. Diba was silent. They were now standing so close to each other that their noses were almost touching. '*Bacha Bazi*, Detective Diba, does that ring a bell?'

'I beg your pardon?'

'It translates literally as "playing with boys". And I'm talking about boys aged five and up. Boys whose dirt-poor parents sell them to a warlord for a couple of hundred dollars. Boys dressed as exotic female dancers, but intended first and foremost as bedfellows for dirty old men.'

'Whatever it's called, Ms Hafez, what you're talking about happens in a totally different world from the one you and I inhabit,' Diba said stiffly.

'I'm sorry, but the world we're talking about appears to have found its way to ours,' Farah replied just a little more sharply than she'd intended. And when she saw the condescending look on his face, she added, 'Just like you and I found our way to this country.'

That's when the blonde doctor appeared in the corridor. On her face, the vacant look of a marathon runner who'd barely managed to cross the finishing line. The exhaustion after the lengthy operation seemed to have added years to her face.

Farah gazed at her without a word and felt the hope she'd nursed a minute ago evaporating. It had been an illusion. Of course. Happy endings only exist in fairy tales. And fairy tales can only exist in the shadow of death.

IO

Joshua Calvino stared at the bloody bundle of rags that together with some jewellery and ankle bracelets had been stuffed into a transparent plastic bag, which was now lying on his lap. He was with Diba in the Corolla on the way to police central dispatch, but he was oblivious to his surroundings.

Calvino couldn't stop staring at the bag and kept repeating, almost compulsively, the date and time handwritten on the label.

Friday, zero thirty hours.

Meanwhile, Diba was spouting off at the mouth. The last thing Joshua was in the mood for right now was listening to his clichés. He caught something about 'agreements' and 'media' and assumed Diba was referring to Farah Hafez. Diba was undoubtedly giving his standard rap about journalists, who according to him were only interested in one thing: namely their own thing. When he first met Diba, Joshua quickly concluded that his ideas about people and the world were so fossilized in his reactionary brain that it was pointless to even try to convince him otherwise.

Joshua was silent as he repeated to himself:

Friday, zero thirty hours.

It was the time the boy had been registered in the trauma room. Joshua pictured him again, lying on the wet tarmac in his girl's clothing. It was like looking into a bright light and then closing your eyes. The image lingered long afterwards. No matter where he looked or how hard he tried not to, Joshua kept seeing the boy's image. He also saw the face of the doctor, Danielle Bernson, who'd been first on the scene and had operated on the child.

Bernson had just told them that she'd repaired the boy's pelvis using pins which she connected to a metal frame in order to stabilize everything. She'd placed pins in his left leg as well. She'd operated on his spleen and inserted a drain in his lungs. Further examination had revealed a severe concussion and two broken ribs and they'd also tended to the rest of his external injuries. The result after hours of operating: he was stable but not out of danger.

Now he had to spend a minimum of five days in complete isolation in the ICU. Nobody except the nursing staff and his doctor could have access to him. This also meant that, for the time being, the boy couldn't be questioned, something Detective Diba – 'in the interest of the investigation' – had pushed for in his own less-than-subtle way.

Friday, zero thirty hours.

Stable, but not out of danger.

If he survived, what lay ahead for a boy like this? A displaced, possibly abused child, who was smuggled across several borders, finally to be left for dead in a foreign country? What would those who'd trafficked and left him there on the road do if they knew that he was alive? There was a lot to be said for keeping the case under wraps for now. Guarding him wasn't an option at this moment because they couldn't say if the boy had any vital information or not. Only if they could establish a link between the accident and the discovery of the two bodies in the station wagon would the boy become part of a larger whole. And that larger whole was a criminal retaliation. A completely plausible theory.

A few minutes later when they stepped out of the car at police headquarters, where central dispatch was located, Joshua could tell that it was going to be even warmer today than was forecast. Luckily the air conditioning inside the station was blasting. Otherwise the hot air coming from the computers in combination with the summer heat would have turned the whole department into a subtropical biotope.

The officer who'd taken the call was named Evelien. Joshua saw Holland in all its glory before him: blue eyes, rosy white skin and full red lips. Evelien had ash-blonde curls that fell loosely over the epaulettes of her immaculate white police shirt. She was a woman who loved sweets but loathed bullshit. In her case, the saying 'nobody fucks with Evelien' had to be taken quite literally, even if a heap of men on the force secretly desired her beautiful Rubenesque curves. Evelien was a long-standing proponent of monogamy and the doting mother of five children.

Whenever people called the central dispatch in a panic, she was the epitome of 'cool and collected'. She was purposeful when guiding her colleagues to the location where the call had originated. Last night she'd guided Marouan and Joshua through the Amsterdamse Bos with the same efficiency.

Now the three of them were sitting in a small room, listening to a recording of the call. Joshua took a sip of his aloe vera drink while Diba stirred the dregs of coffee at the bottom of his paper cup and brushed some biscuit crumbs off his lap.

'The caller was clearly in a panic. She indicated she was somewhere in the Amsterdamse Bos, she didn't know where, near water she said, so I thought near the Amstelveense Poel. She'd seen a child lying in the road. She didn't sound drunk and then abruptly hung up.' Evelien stated the facts in the level-headed way of someone who, through the years, had grown accustomed to all kinds of emergency calls.

'Okay,' Joshua said, 'let's hear it.'

Evelien pressed the play button and they immediately heard the voice of a woman who was clearly more hysterical than confused.

'*I didn't hit her. She was already there!*'

Then they heard Evelien's level-headed response.

'*Calm down, ma'am, tell us where you are.*'

The woman didn't seem to be listening to Evelien. She began to cry. '*She's just lying there. I think she's dead.*'

'*Do you know where you are?*'

'*The . . . the . . . Amsterdamse Bos. On the . . . a road. I don't know the name! Close to water.*'

'*Can you tell me what you see?*'

41

'*She's over there. She's bleeding from her head. I don't dare come any closer. Oh my God. I didn't hit her! I didn't hit her!*'

'*Ma'am, try to stay calm. I'll send an ambulance. Stay on the line.*'

The woman didn't respond. She continued to sob, was shrieking, kept crying. '*Oh my God, oh my God.*'

In the background Joshua could hear the rain in the woods; it sounded tinny. Then Evelien's voice again, calm but compelling. '*Ma'am, are you still there?*'

There was noise and what sounded like a clap of thunder. Then Evelien's voice again.

'*Ma'am?*'

No response. Only noise, as if the woman had dropped her phone.

'*Ma'am, are you still there?*'

Followed by a click. The connection was broken. They looked at each other.

'Let's hear it again,' Marouan said gruffly, in between bites of another biscuit. Joshua, who wondered if the thunderclap could have been a gunshot, looked at Marouan with embarrassment.

'They're boys you can play with,' Farah whispered. 'You know what I mean?' She and Danielle Bernson were looking through the ICU window as the boy was being hooked up to a myriad of tubes and machines.

'They're poor kids. Poor in the most literal sense of the word. That's why they're for sale. Their destitute parents are only too happy to part with them for money. They're boys with slender bodies. You drape them in women's clothing. You put make-up on them and teach them to smile seductively. You give them shiny jewellery with little bells that tinkle when they're dancing. Because dancing is what they're meant to do, to impress your guests. And those guests are other powerful men, usually warlords, wealthy businessmen and government officials. They're the men who get to enjoy these boys. First by just watching them, then by touching them ever so briefly as they whirl past. It adds to the excitement: the idea of your hand brushing past a dancing boy's leg, and the prospect of caressing that very same leg in your own bed later on. And you know the boy will let you do as you please because he's your plaything for the night. It's an ancient Afghan tradition, which has now been brought to the Netherlands by a bunch of bastards.'

'Now I see why those detectives asked us to keep things under wraps,' Danielle said.

'I suspect it's for his own safety as much as anything,' suggested Farah, who couldn't keep her eyes off the boy. 'The people who left him there must think he's dead. If they find out he's still alive and in this hospital, they'll want to silence him. As soon as the boy can talk, he's going to pose a very real threat.'

'But what I don't get is why they left him there. In the middle of the road. In that robe and all that jewellery. Why didn't they dump him somewhere else?'

'Something unforeseen must have happened.' Even as she said it, Farah recognized the truth of her theory. 'Something must have happened that threw everything into disarray.'

What that was remained a mystery, of course. But Farah liked mysteries. The bigger the mystery, the greater the challenge. She decided to go back to the scene of the hit-and-run and its immediate surroundings. The forensics team was probably done by now and had undoubtedly reopened the road.

She didn't usually cover this kind of a story. This was the work of detectives. But she wasn't looking for perpetrators. What she was interested in was unravelling cause and effect, following in the boy's footsteps and establishing a chronology of the night's events.

She was all too aware of the important role Danielle had played in the matter so far. She'd saved the boy's life. That in itself was an added incentive for Farah to delve into the case. Doctors save lives, journalists uncover facts, police arrest perpetrators. A highly functional trinity.

Farah understood why the boy had such a big impact on her. It had to do with her buried past, with the country and the culture she'd severed all ties with. Or so she thought. But what kind of emotional attachment could Danielle Bernson have to this unknown boy? What was behind her refusal to hand him over in the trauma room? Why hadn't she sped off to the next emergency with her Mobile Medical Team and let the trauma surgeon on-call operate on the boy? Farah decided to ask her as politely as possible.

'I gather you needn't have done that operation. You were on ambulance duty. So why did you?'

Danielle smiled, but it was a defensive smile and her tired features twisted into a grimace.

'I'm sorry, but I'd rather not talk about it.'

'But you saved his life,' Farah probed. 'So you must care?'

44

'Of course I do,' Danielle said. 'But it remains to be seen whether he'll pull through. The next few days will tell. And even when he does, what's to become of him? Are we supposed to keep quiet about him? What are his prospects? Does he have family?'

'For the time being we're his family,' Farah said.

Danielle looked at her with what seemed like genuine surprise.

Meanwhile, out of the corner of her eye, Farah saw the ICU nurse flashing Danielle a reassuring smile and giving her a double thumbs-up from behind the glass. The doctor visibly relaxed. 'One of our most reliable people,' she said. 'The boy's in good hands.'

'Last night I drove to the place where he was hit,' Farah said. 'The forensics team was working on the tyre tracks. It turns out that more than one car was involved. And not far from where you found the boy, a station wagon was torched. The fire brigade recovered two bodies.'

Danielle looked away and leaned against the window for support. 'Please spare me the details,' she said wearily. 'My sole concern is the boy.'

'I understand,' Farah said, 'it's your job and everything, but . . .'

'No,' said Danielle, her face now drained of all colour, 'you don't understand. This is about more than just my job. It's . . .' Her voice cracked.

That's what happens when you're a doctor, Farah reflected. She's so busy saving lives she's oblivious to her own pain. Danielle's pain must be considerable, and no doubt dating back much further than last night.

'Do you have children?' Farah asked.

'No,' Danielle said bluntly. 'I don't want any children. The vast majority of people seem destined to hurt each other as much as they can. I don't want to bring a child into this world who might grow up to become a victim or, God forbid, a perpetrator.'

You've experienced things you don't want to talk about, Farah observed. You've been places where you've seen things you'd rather forget. Like me.

They were silent for a while and just when Farah thought Danielle might walk away, the doctor put a hand on her arm.

'You're right, it doesn't make sense not to talk to you about what I saw. Tell me, what do you want to know?'

'What position did you find him in?'

'He was lying in the right lane, but most of his injuries were on his left side. He was hit by a car coming from the left, no doubt about it. The bumper hit his left leg. The impact must have thrown him on to the bonnet, after which he banged the left side of his head against the windscreen. He then rolled across the bonnet before ending up on the other side of the road, which is how I found him.'

Farah saw another look of doubt flash across Danielle's face.

'I'm only telling you this because . . .'

'I know,' Farah said. 'You'd better get some sleep. Your job is done for the night.'

'How about you?'

'I'm only just getting started,' Farah said with a smile. She turned around and walked to the lift. Before the doors even closed, in her mind she was already in the middle of the woods, searching for traces of the boy who'd run barefoot among the trees. She knew where he had fled to. Now she had to figure out where he had fled from.

I 2

At central dispatch earlier that morning, Diba had listened to the caller's message several times and had agreed that it wasn't a gunshot they were hearing but a thunderclap. Joshua, in the meantime, based on the caller's number, had discovered the probable identity of the woman: the phone was registered to one Angela Faber. He immediately went to tell Diba.

'Okay! When I say *The Game of Love*, you say?'

'That I'm not interested in your taste in music, Calvino,' Diba snapped at him. Which is when Joshua explained that perhaps it had escaped him that celebrity and TV host Dennis Faber was already in his third season putting the relationships of all sorts of couples to the test for an audience of millions. *The Game of Love* was a huge hit on IRIS TV, the commercial network. And Angela Faber, the woman who'd made that call last night, was none other than Dennis Faber's wife.

'The fact that Angela Faber reported the incident doesn't necessarily make her a suspect,' Joshua said, thinking aloud.

'No,' Diba grumbled, 'but what really looks bad is that she drove away; left the boy there all alone. And don't get me started on what she was doing in the Amsterdamse Bos in the middle of the night.'

'Not much, I think . . .' Joshua said.

'Is that what you think? Not much?'

'That's what I think.'

'Well, kid, good to know you've really thought this one through.'

'I haven't thought it through yet, but something tells me we shouldn't jump to conclusions.'

'And what exactly is that "something", Mr Mastermind? Perhaps you could enlighten us, the humble earthworms of this world, with your age-old wisdom?'

'I think Angela Faber happened to be driving by, saw that child lying there, and . . .'

'Go on . . .'

'I don't know. Something doesn't feel right. If you ask me, it seems much too obvious to just focus on this one woman.'

'Yeah, Calvino, but I'm not asking. You brought it up. What is that? Something they teach you at police academy? To run off at the mouth in the presence of others? Get a life, Cal. This is the real world! You're a detective, not a daydreamer, damn it!'

'Fine, and in the real world you just drove past the Fabers' house, you ill-tempered toad,' Joshua said. Once again he regretted sharing his thoughts.

After Diba had turned the car around, they drove through a gleaming wrought-iron gate into the grounds of a country-style residence with a thatched roof.

'Amsterdam School,' said Joshua reverently.

'I don't give a damn where you went to school,' Diba snapped at him again.

'The house,' Joshua said. 'The architectural style: Amsterdam School.'

'You chose the wrong profession, Cal, you should have been a professor in crapology,' said Diba while breaking somewhat too hard, causing a spray of tiny pebbles around the car.

Joshua got out and headed towards a carport supported by oak pillars to have a look. One car was parked there, a dark-brown Citroën DS in mint condition. Joshua walked around it. These cars hadn't been made in more than thirty-five years. They were collector's items, fancy 'magic carpet' models complete with semi-automatic gearbox and hydro-pneumatic suspension. Five metres in length. Literally rose to the occasion as soon as you turned the key in the ignition. A perfect specimen like this cost a tidy penny. It undoubtedly belonged to the man of the house.

Joshua jotted down the license plate number. As he walked back towards the house, he saw Diba peering through one of the curiously wide windows, which were supported in the middle by two carved arms. They seemed to be pushing the window further up.

'Hansel and Gretel, all grown up,' Diba muttered. 'They might have well-paid jobs and drive expensive Citroëns but they still live in bizarre fairy-tale houses. Get a load of those windows. Who in their right mind comes up with stuff like that?'

Joshua paused before the monumental structure and stared at the front of the house with the thatched roof moulded around it, like an over-sized pageboy hairdo.

Diba impatiently rattled the antique bell, while Joshua was reflecting on the fact that all the materials used to build this house were natural: brick, iron, wood and straw. In stark contrast, the woman who appeared at the door was anything but natural. She must have been young and beautiful once, with appealing imperfections. But by now all of these had been overly nipped and tucked. Resulting in a lifeless layer of plastic-looking skin, a dark veneer, tightly stretched over her face and body.

From the spiteful puckering around the corners of her mouth and the wrinkles on her manicured hands, Joshua could tell that Angela had to be well past forty. She had mid-length platinum-blonde hair and was wearing bleached jeans, Palladium sneakers and a low-cut pink T-shirt sprinkled with silver sequins that provided a perfect view of her supersized silicone knockers.

Tragic, Joshua thought. What was the point of fighting all of nature's laws, only to be 'the girl next door' for ever?

'Mrs Faber?' he said with the most reassuring smile he could muster.

'Yes?' she replied hesitantly.

'My name is Joshua Calvino and this is my colleague Marouan Diba. Police detectives. We're investigating an incident that

49

took place in the Amsterdamse Bos last night. We believe that you called it in?'

He saw that she was startled.

'Me? Call? About what?'

Diba threw Joshua a telling look. Then he turned towards Angela Faber and asked if they might come inside. It would be easier to talk. Joshua saw her catch a whiff of what must have been Diba's body odour because she recoiled slightly.

'I have no time,' she said, agitated. 'I've got to go.'

'Is that your car, ma'am?' Joshua pointed to the Citroën under the carport.

'Uh, well . . . No.' She nervously picked at her fingernails.

'Oh? It's not your car?'

'That's right.'

'May I ask where you were last night between eleven and one?'

'I was at home.'

'Alone?'

Angela Faber ran her fingers through her hair and Joshua glimpsed a bruise on the right side of her forehead.

'With my husband,' she said in a strained tone.

'So you didn't make that call?' said Diba, who now seemed to have discovered how badly he smelled and winced.

'I don't know what you . . . I don't know anything.'

'Ma'am, this phone is registered under your name.' While Joshua read the numbers aloud, Angela Faber stared at him as if she were being sentenced to death. But she stuck to her story.

'My phone was stolen a few days ago,' she said, as though prompted by someone.

'Fortunately by a thief who's a Good Samaritan,' Joshua said, smiling politely.

'What do you mean?'

'He steals your phone and then uses it to save a life.'

'Oh, after that accident,' Angela Faber blurted out.

'How do you know it was an accident?'

'You said so?'

'I said it was an incident, ma'am. Not an accident.'

'Oh, I must have misunderstood.' Her gaze drifted over his shoulder. When Joshua turned around, he saw a vehicle from a private security company driving through the gate. Joshua turned back to Angela Faber and gave it one last try.

'It would help if you were candid. It's important for us to know what you saw.'

'I'm sorry, but I haven't seen anything and I didn't make that call. I was at home.'

'Yes, with your husband,' said Marouan impatiently.

'He'll confirm that, right?' Calvino said.

'Of course he will,' Angela Faber said as she started to close the door.

'And where can we find your husband?'

'At the Westergas Studios,' she replied before shutting the door in their faces.

Out of the security van stepped two rugged tough guys with undoubtedly cast-iron tough-guy bodies, who puffed out their chests and approached Marouan and Calvino with purpose.

'Gentlemen,' said one of the tough guys as if he was a CSI TV detective, 'you do know you're on private property?' It wasn't so much a question, as a warning to a good listener.

'Do you have some form of identification we could see?' said the other tough guy who didn't want to be outdone in toughness by his colleague.

Joshua saw that Diba was about to lose his temper. He managed to get his partner's attention with a nod and indicated it would be better if he stayed calm. Meanwhile, he reached for his ID.

'Sorry we wasted your time, gentlemen,' Joshua grinned after flashing his ID and seeing the disconcerted reaction of the security duo.

'And what's more,' Diba added triumphantly, 'you're both guilty of obstructing a criminal investigation.' He glanced at Joshua with a mocking smile. 'What should we do with these two? Take them in for questioning?'

'It's certainly an option,' Joshua said, keeping a close eye on the security guys. 'But it won't look good on their CVs. Why were you called out?'

The two men looked at each other.

'C'mon! We don't have all day!'

'Complaint about two foreign types walking about on the property.'

'Foreign?' Joshua said. He pointed to his ID. 'You see what that says? Dutch, right? Or am I mistaken?'

'No, you're not mistaken,' said security tough guy number one with a look of dismay.

'I'll need the number of the caller,' Joshua said. 'And then we'll thank you for your assistance.'

The security guys contacted their dispatch, gave the number to Joshua and were relieved to be on their way a few minutes later. Diba decided then and there to call the Public Prosecutor. He wanted to arrest Angela Faber as soon as possible; they now had enough evidence. The phone she'd just contacted the security company with was the same phone used to report last night's accident.

13

This was literally the difference between night and day, Farah thought as she drove into the Amsterdamse Bos. Last night she'd driven through these woods like a woman possessed and had beaten a hasty retreat after the discovery of the two bodies in the station wagon. Now she was slowly traipsing around the same woods, feeling like a night owl blinded by the morning sun.

That changed when she saw a lorry pulling out of a narrow path and turning on to the road. She gasped when what was left of the station wagon, which had been loaded on the trailer, glided past like a dark, shadowy ghost ship. This had to be the lane that the fire engine had turned into last night.

From this point, it had taken her a couple of minutes to get to the section of the road cordoned off by the forensics team. How fast had she been going? Sixty, seventy maybe. With half an eye on her speedometer, she noticed that up ahead the road curved gently. Last night she'd seen the glow of the forensic lamps among the trees, thinking that maybe they were working in the middle of the woods. But having taken the bend, she realized she'd been wrong. Following that same bend now, she watched closely for anything familiar.

She slammed on the brakes as soon as she spotted a scrap of tape around a tree. The forensics guys had been a big help last night with their confidential information. And now the shoddy way in which they'd left the crime scene helped her out again.

Farah parked her car on the soft shoulder. When she switched off the engine, she could hear birds. A woodpecker rapping against a tree somewhere. Beyond it, the constant roar of the traffic on the A9 sounded like a distant ocean. This woodland didn't exactly strike her as the ominous setting where only a few hours ago a child had been bleeding to death on the road. But she soon stumbled across the chalk smudges on the tarmac, proof positive that it had.

She recalled Danielle's words. The boy had been hit from the left, banged his head against the windscreen, rolled across the bonnet before landing on the tarmac. The car that had hit him must have approached from the opposite direction on the left side of the road.

Looking around, she imagined the boy standing here last night. Where might he have come from? She decided to head deeper into the woods.

Here the terrain rose up gently while the trees were closer together, with an occasional low shrub. After a while she made out the contours of a house on top of the hill. She approached it with caution. It was an old manor house, half-covered in ivy and purple wisteria. Here and there, the coarse, once-white plaster was covered in green moss or crumbling, with small grey chunks falling off. The shutters in front of the big, tall windows were sealed tight. A balcony on top of the large bay at the front offered a view of the drive. All the paint had peeled off the rotten timber railings. At the top of the façade she read the date of construction: AD 1912.

A shiver ran down Farah's spine, as if the strips of sunlight that fell indirectly on to the walls and the closed shutters held no warmth, only coldness. Strange how the sound of distant traffic and the birds she'd heard earlier appeared to have faded here, swallowed up by a vacuum of silence. But this was an eerie silence. A muted cry, a soundless shrieking. It reminded her of the fearful figure in the Edvard Munch painting, opening his mouth in a grotesque way to utter a primal scream that was inaudible, yet so loud it penetrated every fibre of your body.

Farah knew she was a lot more perceptive than the average person. She registered things that others failed to notice. She also firmly believed that the things you saw or heard could be influenced by your subconscious. What you perceived was what you wanted to see, wanted to hear. All of a sudden she doubted whether the boy had actually spoken when he'd been wheeled into the Emergency Department. Had she perhaps heard her own voice when she'd seen him lying there helpless on that stretcher? Had the cry simply been her own cry? And was the chill she felt here simply something frozen inside herself?

She looked back at the grand manor house strangled by vines. If only she could grab a crowbar and pry open the shutters, lift the doors out of their frames and force her way into the dusty rooms where she expected to find silent ghosts aching to tell their stories. Once the boy was well enough to talk he'd tell her about this house. She was sure of it.

She was standing on the lawn in front of the house. The gravel on the drive was covered in moss. The world seemed to be holding its breath. But then the silence was shattered by a low-flying plane on its way to nearby Schiphol Airport.

She'd just made up her mind to head back down to the main road when she tripped over a tree stump. A low-hanging branch hit her face as she fell. About to scramble to her feet, she spotted something dark red on the mossy ground: a piece of shiny copper in the shape of a crescent moon. The red was dried blood. Her hand was trembling as she went to pick it up. It was an earring.

She looked around, taking in the dark outline of the house and the gentle slope down to the road where the Carrera was parked. She picked up the earring with a handkerchief and held it tightly in her hand. By the roadside, she rang Joshua Calvino.

14

Still on the grounds of the imposing Faber residence, Joshua tried to dissuade Diba from rushing into calling the Public Prosecutor to issue a warrant for Angela Faber's arrest. Diba was convinced Angela Faber was the prime suspect in what he now saw as vehicular manslaughter. As far as he was concerned there wasn't a man alive, let alone an individual atom, who could still have any doubt about her guilt.

Angela Faber had done it.

And Diba was a shark that smelled blood – obsessed, he threatened to strike out at his prey. In his anger, the only thing he knew for sure was that last night a woman had run down a child with her car and left the scene of the accident.

'And what's more, she's such a stupid cow that when she sees us snooping around her house, she uses her *stolen* phone to call her security firm!'

When Diba began to pant excitedly, Joshua interrupted him.

'She's probably not the only one involved.'

'What do you mean?'

'Exactly what I said, not the only one. In the sense of, "there are others!"'

'You're talking crap again, Cal. I want facts! Facts, not theories!' Faithful to form, Diba was spouting off while making theatrical gestures.

'What do you think? Did Angela Faber take this gas guzzler out for a spin last night?' Joshua asked, pointing at the DS in the carport.

'Highly unlikely.'

'Okay. At least we're in agreement about something. The vehicle involved in the accident must have been a different one. And that car was probably damaged during the collision or – now pay close attention, I'm saying "or" – during the evasive manoeuvre. Agree or disagree?'

'Uh, hello Cal, I'm not a moron and this isn't twenty questions!'

'Agree or disagree?'

'Damn it, I agree!'

'And did we come across another damaged car on the grounds? I don't think so. Or am I suddenly blind?'

'I agree with that too! I don't see any other car.'

'It could be somewhere else?'

'Somewhere else,' Diba repeated sarcastically. 'Good work, Sherlock. Very impressive. Only I don't see where all this is leading.'

'It's leading to the question of why Dennis Faber is so willing to back up his wife's story. Wanna bet he's going to lie through his teeth about everything?'

Diba stared at him with a glassy expression.

'I bet that's why Dennis Faber isn't driving his car this morning. He wanted to get his wife's damaged vehicle repaired as quickly as possible. Give me a few minutes and I'll prove my theory,' Joshua said.

'And then?'

'A few minutes,' Joshua repeated. 'That's all I need. If I don't come up with something substantial, you can go ahead and request a warrant to arrest Angela Faber.'

'Okay, five,' said Diba with an exaggerated sigh. He looked at his watch and strode over to a bunch of rhododendrons to wait.

Joshua rang the station and asked one of his colleagues to run a plate number. The Citroën in the carport was indeed registered to Dennis Faber and he'd been fined twice last year for speeding. Joshua inquired further about where Faber had purchased the car, called the dealership and asked if there were other cars registered to Mr or Mrs Faber. After Joshua had received confirmation that nine months ago a Citroën Picasso had been purchased for Angela Faber and that it had indeed been brought into the shop for repairs that morning by her husband, Joshua jumped into the Toyota and urged a flabbergasted Diba to do the same.

Fifteen minutes later the two detectives, waving their IDs, entered the Citroën dealership in Amsterdam-Zuid and headed straight for a bright-red Citroën Picasso, sitting on the ramp, with a substantial dent on the right side of the bonnet and a smashed headlight.

'That's what I'm talking about,' Diba said with a cheesy grin. 'You have to keep your eyes open, Cal, trust your instincts. Always be ready for the unexpected, so you can jump right in!'

Joshua recognized this as another amazing aspect of his older sidekick's personality. The entire trip to the dealership, he'd moped like a misunderstood child, but now that success was imminent, Diba wasted no time claiming responsibility for the action. Joshua had long ago lost interest in always pointing out Diba's shortcomings, not only because of how taxing it was, but also because he saw that Diba wasn't up to working as a detective much longer. The man was weighed down by his past. Calvino gave him six months at most. After that he would take early retirement for medical reasons or simply drop dead – without a single bullet in sight.

Diba, in the meantime, had the forensics guys on the phone.

'Immediately – no, now, immediately, you hear me?!' Over the years Diba had become more and more afraid that people weren't taking him seriously and often ended up shouting, which was counterproductive. When Joshua heard him ranting he walked out of the garage, called Forensics himself and calmly explained what was going on. Yes, Detective Diba's bark was worse than his bite, but they were this close to arresting two people possibly involved in the hit-and-run of that child. It was important to establish as quickly as possible that the damage to the red Picasso matched the damage that had been detected in the Amsterdamse Bos last night.

'You missed your calling, Calvino,' the forensics guy on the line chuckled. 'You should have been a diplomat. You'd undoubtedly get the Middle East peace process back on track.'

'Thanks for the compliment,' Joshua sighed. 'So when can I expect you?'

'We've already got one foot out the door!'

Diba came into the showroom with a self-satisfied expression on his face. 'Arranged! I read them the riot act. I'll wager a bet that we have this case wrapped up by this evening and then yours truly is on his way to Morocco the day after tomorrow.' He dragged Joshua in the direction of the luxury models. Big, shiny cars which neither of them could ever afford on a detective's salary.

'What is it about that place?' Joshua asked.

'Which place?'

'Morocco.'

'Why do I always go there? Jesus, man, homeland, do you know what that means, you poor excuse for an Italian? And three bloody beautiful weeks without you. That's reason enough. Get a load of this.'

They were staring at a black Citroën C6 Exclusive. Joshua checked the price tag. The amount was astronomical.

A young salesman came running towards them, rubbing his hands. Damn, they had no time for this nonsense. He returned to the shop to meet the forensics team and glanced over their shoulders as they compared their reports and the photos from last night to the damage on the Picasso.

They were all examining the glass fragments found by the tree in the Amsterdamse Bos against the Picasso's shattered headlight when Joshua felt the phone in his jacket pocket vibrate.

'Can you talk?'

Until now, Joshua had associated her with the shouting of helmeted firefighters among scorched trees in the night and the sterile silence of a hospital at the crack of dawn. Now he heard birds in the background and a summer breeze rustling through the trees. But she sounded glum. He paused.

'Shall I call back later?'

'No, it's okay. Tell me.'

'I'm at the scene of the hit-and-run. And I found something. Something that was no doubt overlooked.'

'What do you think we overlooked?'

'An earring.'

He had scrutinized the contents of the plastic bag containing the boy's things. Bloody rags, two anklets with bells. No shoes or sandals. Two bracelets, also with bells. A few rings. A string of beads. And one earring.

'Can you describe what it looks like?' he asked.

'A copper crescent with some sort of precious stone.'

'Where did you find it?'

'Halfway between the house and the road.'

'What house?'

'There's a manor house here. Very large and very old. It's boarded up but I have a hunch the boy was there last night.'

'You should be a detective, Farah Hafez,' Joshua said. He wondered how she did it. Apparently she'd gone to the scene of the crime and just like that, out of nowhere, had found evidence indicating that the boy had wandered about in the woods.

'How did you find the earring?'

'Well . . . I sort of stumbled across it.'

'But you didn't touch it?'

'I picked it up with a handkerchief and wrapped it up. There was blood on the earring.' She was silent for a second. 'It's his, right?'

Joshua hesitated. 'Sounds like it, yes.'

'He was in that house last night, I'm sure of it.'

'Listen. I can meet you later this afternoon. Then I'll take a look at the earring and we can talk. Okay?'

'All right. Can you leave that partner of yours out of this?'

With pleasure, Joshua thought, but he said, 'That's going to be difficult. We're a team, Diba and me. I have to tell him, even if you don't like him.'

'I understand.'

'And for the time being, let's not go announcing this to the world, okay?'

'We're only talking about an earring.' He could tell from her breathing that she was smiling.

'Meaning, you won't write a story about it?'

'Is that what you're afraid of?'

'I'm not afraid of anything, but it's far too early to get excited.' In more ways than one, he needed to remind himself.

There was a pause. 'You know where our office is located, right? The *AND* building on the waterfront?'

'I've got your number,' he replied. 'I'll call you as soon as we arrive.'

When he hung up, the senior forensics officer nodded in his direction. The initial results of their investigation showed that the Picasso was the same car that had left slivers of glass, traces of paint and a matching bumper impression on the tree in the Amsterdamse Bos last night. Secondary result: no traces of blood. The probability that the Picasso had hit the boy was next to nil.

Joshua nodded distractedly and thought of Farah Hafez. It was inauspicious that at the very beginning of an investigation a journalist was already one step ahead of him.

15

The first film Marouan Diba ever saw in a cinema was *Le Casse*. French actor Jean-Paul Belmondo steals diamonds from a Greek villain and is then chased by the Egyptian Omar Sharif, who plays the chief of police. Diba was just a kid, but from that moment on he was sure of the three things he wanted in life: wealth, Belmondo's bravado and a job as a detective.

Over the years he'd had to face the harsh reality that his first two wishes were rather difficult to combine with the last. Detectives weren't heroes, but cops with an average income. And since he couldn't accept the miserable status of his job, the dime-a-dozen lifestyle and the run-of-the mill house that came with it, he still steadfastly pursued wealth and the *je ne sais quoi* of a second Belmondo. An ambition that was as unrealistic as actually owning this Citroën, in which he had finally adjusted the seat correctly to fit his body.

The windows of the C6 Exclusive, which opened and closed without a sound, had a chromium-plated frame, said the salesman, grinning from ear to ear. According to him, scores of other innovations gave this car its unusual elegance and dynamic presence. Qualities Marouan would have loved to have attributed to himself.

And did the gentleman want to try the hi-fi system, which boasted six speakers and a subwoofer? From the passenger side, a CD was popped into the slot in the dashboard. My god, thought Marouan as he sank into the cushy beige leather, what a cheesy way to sell an expensive car.

The double-glazed side windows glided shut, turning the car into a soundproof bubble. With the first chords of a smooth, easy-listening jazz combo, he was suddenly wrapped in a majestic cocoon. Alone. He thought back in time and imagined himself once again behind the wheel of a luxurious rented convertible. Together with his brother and a few friends, cruising through Marrakesh on a summer's evening, with only the stars to light their way. His brother shouted at every passer-by that they'd been abducted by a *Khilqa*, a strange creature from another world. He pronounced the Arabic *q* gutturally as if to accentuate the contempt he felt for his westernized brother. Marouan Diba, a stranger in his own country.

Each time he returned home, he was treated with more and more respect by his family and friends, but also with increasing distance. Despite the fact that he felt just as Moroccan as he had forty years ago when he'd followed his father to the Netherlands. From the plane, Marouan, an illiterate boy of seven, saw an expansive Dutch polder landscape appear beneath him. With excitement he'd stared at the neatly defined fields and all the patchwork shades of green. In the arrivals hall of Schiphol Airport, he ran into the waiting arms of his father in a state of euphoria. As if this foreign country had welcomed him home.

To understand everyone and everything as quickly as possible, he'd immediately started rattling off all kinds of Dutch words and sentences, similar to the way he'd memorized texts from the Koran in Morocco. So in no time at all he spoke Dutch without an accent and could recite lots of synonyms and sayings and could even quote Dutch poetry. But getting to know the people was a whole other story.

The less he understood them, the more his hatred of the Dutch grew. He hated the indifference and arrogance of others. Those in life who'd acquired wealth and the self-confidence that goes hand-in-hand with that. A hatred of people who 'had it all' and therefore assumed they could cover up any transgression. People like the Fabers.

In the breast pocket of his jacket, his mobile phone trilled, beaming him back to the harshness of reality.

'*Diva*,' said a man on the other end of the line mockingly. He spoke English with a thick Slavic accent. 'What a festive tune I'm hearing. Is it because you're happy to hear from me again?'

'In your dreams,' Marouan muttered and immediately switched off the CD player. 'What do you want?'

He heard that arrogant laugh. 'Have I hurt your feelings, *Diva*? Am I treading on your tender soul? Don't act like a spoiled bitch! Though you do have the boobs for it.'

'Why are you calling me?'

'The boy. In the woods.'

For a moment, Marouan couldn't breathe. 'What does that have to do with you?'

'Everything and nothing,' said the voice on the other end of the line. 'How is he?'

'None of your business.'

'I'm asking nicely? How is he?'

Marouan took a few deep breaths. He had to say something. 'Out of danger.'

'Ah, good to hear! What do they say about the Prophet, my friend? That he's the bearer of good news. And now you're following in his fucking footsteps. Where is he?'

'Who? The Prophet? In Mecca.'

'Very funny.'

'Listen, I've been officially assigned to this case.'

'That's exactly why I'm calling you, *treplo*. I'm asking you nicely, where is he?'

Marouan heard tapping on the windscreen. He looked up and saw the fresh-faced salesman, who stuck his thumb up in the air with his eyebrows raised questioningly.

'I don't want to know anything about your role in this,' Marouan said as he waved the salesman away, 'just leave that boy alone.'

'Watch your mouth, *Diva*. I'm asking you – now pay attention – for the last time, where is he?'

Marouan felt an attack of heartburn coming on. He could feel his heart throbbing in his throat.

'In hospital. The WMC.'

'*Where* in the WMC?'

'Intensive Care.'

The salesman was now bent over the bonnet and was gesturing to Marouan like a professional mime artist to find out what was going on.

'And one last detail,' the caller said. Marouan was silent. He wanted to start the engine of the C6, press down on the accelerator and with a speed exceeding two hundred kilometres an hour crash head on into the caller and kill him.

'You're going to sweep this entire business under the rug for me.' His thick accent sounded slurred on the phone.

'What business?'

'What happened last night.'

'What? Everything? Do you have any idea how many detectives will be assigned to just the case with the station wagon? Two dead bodies, damn it!'

'Listen, friend. I'm only talking about the boy. Take care of it, you understand?'

Marouan thought of the journalist. 'Why?'

'Because I'm telling you to.'

'I'm not a miracle worker.'

'No, but I'm not asking you to walk on water or multiply loaves of bread. But this, you can manage. And why? Because I know you always do your stinking best for me. Understood?'

The click of the call abruptly ending made Marouan's ears ring and his head spin. He stepped out of the Exclusive and pushed the surprised salesman aside when he saw Calvino returning from the shop.

'And?'

'It's a match,' Calvino said, satisfied. And the Public Prosecutor had given them permission to arrest both Dennis Faber and his wife.

'But the question is,' Calvino grinned, 'are we going in our tin can or in this beauty?'

Marouan ignored him. He strode out of the showroom and started the Corolla. He barely gave Calvino time to get in. Car wheels screeching, he raced off to the old Westergas complex where IRIS TV's studios were located.

Farah was so preoccupied she almost missed the exit. Ten minutes later, she parked on a concrete platform alongside the IJ waterfront by a futuristic looking steel-and-glass building. The editorial offices of her newspaper, the *Algemeen Nederlands Dagblad*, had recently been relocated there.

She hurried across the bridge, into a glass lift that took her to the top floor. There she made a beeline for the office of her editor-in-chief.

Edward Vallent was standing with his back to her. His strapping body silhouetted against the cloudless morning sky made him look like a giant. The room smelled of espresso. He turned when he heard her enter. He was wearing beige wide-ribbed corduroy trousers and a charcoal grey sweater, and he had something of a beard. Edward was the sort of man who didn't consider his appearance, simply because he couldn't care less what others thought.

His steely blue eyes told Farah that something was seriously wrong.

'Did you see this, by any chance?'

He went to his desk and held up the front page of the newspaper *De Nederlander*. The headline of the article in the lower right-hand corner was catchy enough: JOURNALIST FARAH H. ASSAULTS OPPONENT DURING MARTIAL ARTS GALA. The article was written by Cathy Marant and included a photo of the Russian woman, looking more dead than alive.

Farah snatched the newspaper from Edward's hand and tossed it into the rubbish bin.

'That's where it belongs,' she said angrily.

'You're too late, Hafez. By now the gullible readers of *De Nederlander* will have eaten up this piece of fiction. I'm not going to let that rag get away with this.'

Farah was too shaken to react immediately. She finally asked, 'So what's your thinking on this?'

'Marant is on the warpath again. I want at least a rectification. And if they refuse I'm going after them for libel. But first I want to hear from you what went down.'

'To be honest . . .'

'Seems like a good place to start . . .'

'I can remember everything up until the moment the referee pulled us apart. Before that she'd scratched open my arm, literally pulled the hair from my head, taken a bite out of my leg. You know, when you're fighting, you're so focused that your perception of pain isn't the same as it normally is.'

'Do you think we can convince people,' Edward asked impatiently, 'that your actions during that gala fight last night weren't the actions of a woman who'd completely lost control and carried out –' he plucked the newspaper out of the rubbish bin and read aloud '– "*a ruthless act of revenge*" or should we just go with what eight hundred thousand of *De Nederlander's* trusted subscribers already believe?'

'What can I say, Ed? I really don't know.'

'This afternoon I'm going to have a couple of experts look at the fight footage, if that's okay with you, of course? If they confirm my suspicions, I'm . . . no, I mean *we* . . . we're going to go after them, agreed?'

Farah looked at him gratefully. 'It's a deal, boss. And now can we talk about something more important?'

'More important than this? Go ahead . . . you've got exactly one minute,' Edward said as he made a big show of looking through a pile of documents on his desk.

Farah dug into her pocket and then unfolded a handkerchief on his desk. Edward glanced at the bloodied, crescent-shaped earring.

'Seems you're missing one.'

'The other one is in an Emergency Department plastic bag, which the police have together with a pile of blood-stained garments and other jewellery.'

'So why do you have this one?'

'I found it some thirty minutes ago in the Amsterdamse Bos. Close to where a boy of seven, perhaps eight, was hit by a car last night and left for dead. Nobody knows where he's from or who he is. But one thing is very clear to me . . .'

In the meantime, Edward had gathered up all his files, intent on leaving the room. With a sweeping gesture of his arm he invited her to go first.

'The boy was used for Bacha Bazi, Ed,' she blurted out.

Edward froze in mid-step. Farah took this as an indication of interest.

'I was at the hospital when they brought him in. He was wearing a traditional dancer's robe, jewellery and make-up. As if he'd just been lifted out of a Bacha Bazi party.'

'Bacha Bazi?' repeated Edward. He sounded like he'd just been beamed to another planet.

'A big party where the boy has to dance for his, uh, owner's guests late into the night and then he's auctioned off to the highest bidder for the remainder of the night,' she explained.

'I know,' Edward mumbled, distracted. 'But it's been almost twenty years since I've heard those words. Not since Raylan Chapelle wrote about it.'

Raylan Chapelle.

Before she'd even started studying journalism, Farah had scrutinized every sentence, every word, every comma of his articles. Raylan Chapelle had a legendary oeuvre. Just like Albert Einstein was the father of relativity theory, Chapelle was regarded as the undisputed master of investigative journalism. It was Raylan Chapelle who'd proved as early as the sixties and seventies that the American government systematically deceived the American people about the war in Vietnam. Chapelle, an American by birth, spent years living in Kabul where he reported on the bloody coup in April 1978 that over-threw President Daoud's government: the communists attacked the presidential palace with planes and tanks and killed Daoud and his entire staff. Farah's father was among them.

Six months later Chapelle lost his life in Cambodia. The exact circumstances of his death never came to light. Rumour had it the CIA was responsible, in retaliation for his coverage of Vietnam.

Farah hadn't thought about Raylan Chapelle for the longest time. There had never been cause to do so. But now that Edward had mentioned his name, suddenly he was present. Farah could picture him in vivid detail: the way he slowly bent forward and stroked her mother's arm in the butterfly garden of the presidential palace in Kabul, almost thirty years ago . . .

'Farah?'

She flinched.

'Did you hear what I just asked you?'

'Sorry, I . . .' She didn't finish her sentence. Her mouth was dry and she had to sit down. Edward tossed his papers back on the desk and got her a glass of water, which she drank in one gulp. Across from her, he leaned against the edge of his desk. Suddenly he seemed to have all the time in the world.

'Should I be worried, or is it good news?' he said with something of a grin. 'And if so, does David know?'

She shook her head. 'It's not what you think,' she mumbled. 'I should have eaten something this morning.'

'Still, with symptoms like these, you should see a doctor. Unless you think it's normal to have the colour drain from your face and feel faint for no reason. But you didn't come here for advice from your boss, especially since you don't give a rat's ass about his opinion. Why write a story about this boy?'

She stopped thinking about Raylan Chapelle, jolted back to reality. 'Well, every year thousands of young Afghans are illegally smuggled into Europe.'

'That's nothing new.'

'Maybe not. But they're rarely as young as this boy, and they're certainly not all tarted up like this.'

'So you think he's the exception that proves the rule?'

'That's what I suspect. And another thing, if it's true and the boy was used for Bacha Bazi, what's he doing *here*? I mean here in the Netherlands?'

'Perhaps the market for these boys has gone global?' Edward suggested. 'An international network providing little dancing sex slaves? I mean, that lengthy war caused an Afghan diaspora of people fleeing to the West. Seems plausible that their traditions came right along with them.'

'I want to look into this further,' Farah said, determined. 'I think this boy is just the tip of the iceberg. A few kilometres from where he was found last night, a car was set alight, a station wagon. They found two bodies in it. The detectives believe it's a criminal retaliation. A whole team is being assigned to the case. You don't do that unless you suspect it's something big. This case is downright shady, Ed. If we can provide evidence of an international smuggling network that provides Afghan men in the Netherlands – and perhaps in other countries – with underage sex slaves, we will have exposed a worldwide crime ring.'

Edward looked at her long and hard. 'Why this sudden interest?'

'What do you mean?'

'You've never looked into child trafficking and international crime before, so why now?'

'Because it's big. Because it hit a chord. I mean . . . I can't get that boy out of my head.' She paused. Edward waited for her to continue.

'Something about the boy himself,' she said with a melancholy tone. 'Something about him. Perhaps not the best motive for an investigation like this, but I remember someone once saying that fascination is the best place for a discerning journalist to begin.'

Edward stood up. 'Have you talked to anyone else about this?'

'The two detectives investigating the case. I saw them last night at the crime scene. And this morning, when I was at the hospital waiting for the boy to come out of surgery. They want to keep the case out of the spotlight if they can.'

'Makes sense, given they've just started their investigation.'

'They're coming here this afternoon. For the earring.'

Edward started to pace back and forth in front of the large window, casting ominous shadows in the room.

'International child trafficking, sexual abuse of underage boys, two murders . . . and you have a hunch it's only the tip of the iceberg?'

'I think so, yes.'

'Then we'd better determine our position, Hafez.'

Farah loved it when Ed called her by her last name. It meant that he saw potential in a story. That he was going to let her run with it: head, tail, legs, the works.

'The question remains: do we conduct our own separate investigation alongside that of the police or do we try to cooperate with them?' he said, running his hand over the stubble on his chin. He stopped in front of her. 'That's a tricky one, considering you've effectively already started your own investigation.' He glanced at the earring. 'I think you're about to stir up a hornet's nest around here, Hafez. Best to give me some time to consult with management and our legal department.' He picked up the folders and marched towards the door.

'Now, go ahead and get the hell out of my office!'

Farah gently folded the handkerchief around the earring and smiled as she scooted past Edward into the corridor.

'Give me a call when they get here this afternoon to arrest you!' he shouted down the hallway.

She raised her hand in acknowledgement as she headed towards the cafeteria where she bought a bottle of mineral water and a big salad and then wolfed it down outside in the roof garden.

When she leaned over the railing a while later and looked out over the IJ, she felt Raylan Chapelle's presence again, very close at hand. Apparently, the injured boy was crying out to the spirits. Restless spirits who'd wandered the realm of the dead for years, and who would now seize the chance to reappear. She was afraid of such phantoms. But since last night she'd known that sooner or later she'd have to face them all.

17

On his better days, it filled Marouan with pride: knowing that even very important people were sometimes so off the mark that he, Marouan Diba, was just the man to expose their vile secrets. But now, on the way to arrest a national quiz show icon, only the Slav's cynical contempt plagued his thoughts. Hearing his voice on the phone had unleashed something in Marouan.

Bloody hell! Who'd spent years taking all kinds of shit from his superiors? Who'd met the unreasonable demands of those uniformed bastards? Who would one day get back at those boot-licking, ass-kicking shitheads? And who, with brute Belmondo bravado, would one day settle the score with all of them?

'DIBAAAH!'

Startled back to reality by Calvino's frantic scream, he saw they were about to crash into the studio complex's barrier gate with horrific speed. For a millisecond he felt the impulse to floor the accelerator, but the image of two headless detectives in a Toyota convinced him otherwise. They came to a standstill with the brakes screeching and smoking.

Calvino jumped out of the car, flashed his ID at the man in the guard booth and ordered him to open the gate immediately. After some heated negotiation – to which Marouan contributed by screaming from the driver's side window 'Police, dammit, police' – the gate finally opened. Calvino gestured for Marouan to keep going while he'd answer to the squad of security guards now hurrying towards them from every direction.

Marouan pulled the Toyota right up to the front door of IRIS TV's facility just as another guard came rushing outside. Damn, thought Marouan, they're like rats crawling out of the woodwork. But this one had been given a head's up by the gate.

Calvino apparently had the situation under control. This guy would escort Marouan to Studio 7, where the taping of *The Game of Love* was in progress.

As if in a feverish trance, Marouan followed the signs for Studio 7. His heart was racing uncontrollably. Sweat poured from his body and a dull, throbbing headache pounded his temples. He climbed the stairs and took the corners and curves at rapid speed, following the broad yellow line that finally brought him to a door that appeared to be hermetically sealed.

'Sorry,' said the guard who'd been talking constantly into his portable CB radio, 'you'll have to wait. I've got orders not to disturb the taping.'

'Is that so?' Marouan sneered and pushed at the solid door. To his surprise it gave way. Diba was immediately submerged in semi-darkness. He could see the contours of the technicians behind their large, rolling TV cameras and beyond them the audience in the stands and a towering heart-shaped backdrop. The spray-tanned man on the set, dressed in a glittery suit, had his arms spread like the statue of Jesus in Rio.

'Hello, all you wonderful people, welcome to *The Game of Love*, already in our third season. On today's show . . .'

Cameras as big as Hummers glided from one position to the next. Where the hell was Calvino? A looming figure materialized out of the darkness and was now facing Marouan. Not his partner, but a Shrek-like figure sporting a large headset with a single earpiece and a built-in mike on his bald head. Gesturing like a crazed conductor – as if this gatecrasher was the first violin in need of a good dressing down – he tried to stop Marouan.

Flashing his ID at Shrek, Marouan said the magic words, 'Police for Dennis Faber.'

The bald fathead with his cauliflower ears, his hand planted on Marouan's sweaty chest, whispered something into his microphone, listened intently to a voice Diba couldn't hear and then said, 'No way. Access denied by the director.'

'Is that so?' Marouan replied as he shoved the man aside and marched on to the set: past the cameras, fatheads, security men and confused audience. On the studio floor, which was so brightly lit he felt like he'd just landed on a tropical island, Marouan searched for the lowest-possible pitch in his voice as he went and confronted the astonished game-show host.

'Dennis Faber?'

A nervous smile appeared on Faber's heavily made-up face.

'I'm Detective Diba. You're under arrest on suspicion of being an accessory to vehicular manslaughter.'

As Marouan steered a shocked Dennis Faber past the cameras towards the door, he caught his partner watching him from the wings. With a deadpan expression, Calvino was clapping for him in soundless slow motion.

18

Right after lunch Farah had requested some archive materials on child trafficking and ploughed through these, searching for clues that might point to an international trade in boys used for Bacha Bazi. What she read turned her stomach. Slavery had long been officially abolished the world over, but in the twenty-first century other horrendous illegal practices flourished as never before. Girls from Nigeria, boys from the former Eastern bloc, babies from China – they were all for sale.

As soon as a hurricane wreaked havoc, some of the earth's tectonic plates shifted or civil war broke out in the poorer parts of the world, human trafficking was suddenly big business there. Thinking their child could have a better life thousands of miles away, desperate parents would go as far as to sell their last piece of land or even their house to pay the traffickers promising to transport their child.

And those traffickers were cunning. If the parents couldn't afford the passage, they could pay off their debt in small instalments. But if, in the end, they failed to cough up the full amount, the children would be used for other purposes. Crime usually. Prostitution and drugs.

And so desperately poor mothers and fathers would plunge themselves into even greater, lifelong poverty, unaware that on the other side of the world their children were being used as thieves and whores.

Farah had spent much of the past few years doing assignments for the city news desk. She'd made a name for herself with her stories about the murky goings-on around a huge building project, the so-called New Golden Age Project, the brainchild of property tycoon Armin Lazonder. Her recent three-part series about the country's asylum policy had also been well received. But setting up and carrying out a large-scale criminal investigation was completely new to her. Still, she'd never been so keen to throw herself into a story, especially since she had a hunch that it was something really big. She already pictured the first bold headline: THE LOST BOY OF AFGHANISTAN.

At the same time she was well aware that her eagerness to delve into this subject was disproportionate to the amount of time she'd be given. Because of the dwindling number of sub-scribers, the paper was cutting costs where it could and advertising revenue had become more important than ever. Unlike a few years ago, these days investigative projects were rarely given the go-ahead. After all, once journalists had been assigned to a long-term project, they were no longer available for the daily features. That meant bringing extra staff on board. So in effect you were pulling journalists off a job without the rock-solid guarantee of a scoop at the end of it.

The buzzing phone on her desk interrupted her train of thought. The second she heard Cathy Marant's voice she regret-ted answering.

'You've been a naughty girl, Hafez,' Marant said in a sugary voice. 'Beating the crap out of another woman and putting her in hospital. Anger management issues?'

Farah had known Marant since the time she wrote slick pieces for the *AND*'s media supplement. But that was years ago. These days Cathy Marant, who had the look of an Aryan camp guard in a Nazi porn film, could be seen showing off her trout pout and plunging neckline behind the presenter's desk of *The Headlines Show*, the hugely popular current affairs programme on commercial broadcaster IRIS TV. They didn't speak often, but when they did Marant got under Farah's skin, without fail.

'What are you insinuating?'

'You inflicted grievous bodily harm on that woman.'

'Two broken ribs and a mild concussion.'

'That's known as "grievous bodily harm". And you're responsible. Anything to say for yourself?'

'To you? Nothing whatsoever,' Farah said and hung up. It wasn't hard to work out what was going on. The entire editorial team of *The Headlines Show* was drooling at the prospect of getting a juicy quote from the *AND*'s punch-happy star reporter. 'No comment' wouldn't do.

'We were cut off,' Marant said when, ten seconds later, Farah answered the phone again.

'That's right,' Farah said drily. 'And it won't be the last time.'

The third time she rang, Marant sounded downright antagonistic. 'I think you're a coward. A high-handed journalist who's always going on about other people's misconduct but who keeps mum when she slips up herself.'

'I know, I know,' Farah said, 'you're just doing your job.' She hung up again.

A second later her mobile rang. Marant was a bully and her tenacity knew no bounds.

'I miss you,' a deep male voice now said.

Farah remembered the arms that had carried her into the bedroom last night.

'Where were you off to so early?'

'Hospital. Long story, David.' Her voice trembled.

'Is something wrong?'

'Not with me, no. Sorry. I'll tell you tonight.'

'I'll be having dinner at Hotel de l'Europe this evening. That's why I'm calling. No *qabili palau* at my place tonight, I'm afraid.'

'What's going on in Hotel de l'Europe?'

'A fundraiser for investors. And I'd like you to join me. All you need to do is smile, so I won't have to do too much sweet-talking and I can still rake in a load of cash for the Verne Project.'

These past few weeks Farah had given his project a great deal of thought. It was meant to be David's magnum opus. Taking inspiration from Jules Verne's fictitious trip around the world, he was planning to cross the continents in a myriad of ways and chart the huge changes the world had seen since the book's publication. All together, the expedition would probably take over a year.

David had asked Farah months ago if she might be interested in joining him as a reporter. She'd raised it with Edward, but he'd been dead against it. Not because he begrudged her an adventure like this, but because it meant she'd be unavailable for what could be eighteen months and it remained to be seen whether her travelogues would be a hit. However, surprisingly the paper's management team thought otherwise, and kindly suggested she take a sabbatical, David had included her in the budget as his researcher and line producer.

It all seemed too good to be true. As a child she'd fantasized about the big wide world outside her walled garden. Now, more than thirty years later, she was a Dutch journalist with the chance to travel the world and chronicle her experiences.

Her only reservation was the prospect of spending day and night in David's company. What would it do to their relationship? But it was such an amazing and challenging project that now wasn't the time to chicken out.

'What time are you expecting me?'

'I'll pick you up at eight, okay?'

'Fine.'

When she hung up, she felt lost in a hazy no-man's-land, suspended between two worlds. The wonderful promise of David's project clashed with the harsh reality of the suffering amassed in the files on her desk. She got up and went to the bathroom.

With her wrists under the cold tap she gazed at her reflection in the mirror above the washbasin. Two Farahs, two worlds. Were anyone to ask her which of the two she belonged to, she'd choose the world on her desk.

19

It had been Diba's idea to let Angela and Dennis Faber sweat it out in separate interrogation rooms. 'Cal, you've got the magic touch with women,' he'd said, so once again Joshua found himself face-to-face with the famous television host's wife. She was even more confused than the first time they'd spoken – frightened and distant at the same time. Her eyes were teary but appearances can be deceiving. Joshua knew that Angela Faber wasn't the dumb blonde that her face-lifted façade might suggest.

He spoke to her in a relaxed manner as if it was a routine conversation to which she'd freely lent her cooperation. Yet with his eyes he communicated a very different message. *You and I both know why we're here and now it's time for you to come clean.* He saw in her eyes that the message had been received loud and clear.

'Do you have any idea what happens when a child is hit by a car and just left for dead?' He didn't wait for her answer. 'It's literally and figuratively "all hands on deck". Ambulances race to the scene of the accident with police and criminal investigators hot on their heels. Code red alarm. Trust me. And meanwhile everybody involved is busy asking the question: What's a child doing alone in the Amsterdamse Bos? In the middle of the night? In the rain? Nobody seems to know.'

He paused to give her a moment to absorb his intro.

'Can I get you something to drink, Mrs Faber?'

'Water, please.'

After getting her a glass of water, he sat down again. He stared at her as he leaned forward with his elbows on the table and his fingertips touching each other.

'It's a boy.'

'A boy?' Angela Faber's eyes, swollen from crying, suddenly seemed to open wider.

'Surprised?' Calvino said drily.

'I thought . . .' Angela Faber's voice faltered.

'It was a boy,' Calvino continued. 'They dressed and made him up to look like a girl. It's tragic, such a young child. If the doctor hadn't intubated him, he would have died there on the spot. Then the person who ran him down would have the death of a child on his or her conscience.'

In the ensuing silence, Angela Faber blankly stared into her glass of water and her shoulders started heaving.

'Was he crossing the road?' Joshua asked softly.

She shook her head, no.

'He was already lying there,' she sobbed, and began to cry uncontrollably.

Calvino pushed a box of tissues in her direction. With faltering words, the whole story came out.

Angela Faber had been out dancing with friends. Something they usually did at least twice a month. What you'd call a sophisticated girls' night out: letting your hair down by drinking highly creative cocktails in trendy lounge bars. But she was 'a bit on edge' that evening and decided to head home early. When she got home, she understood why. The gods of fate had given her a heads-up: so she'd discover her naked husband in a rather unnatural, compromising position on the llama rug of their guestroom. Unnatural because he was on top of another man, whom Angela Faber immediately recognized as *The Game of Love*'s set designer, despite the fact that he was stark naked too. She couldn't get back to her car fast enough and then sped off in something of a blind panic. Going in the direction of the Amsterdamse Bos had been a completely unconscious decision.

At this point Angela Faber confessed – and here came yet another cliché – that she'd wanted to total the Picasso and herself in it. Then she mentioned a detail that aroused Joshua's interest. On the woodland road, she was blinded by the lights of another car speeding towards her in the other lane. And right after that she saw the girl, no, sorry, the boy, lying on the tarmac. She'd had enough presence of mind to brake, turn the steering wheel hard and come to a standstill against a tree. Only when she'd called the emergency number did she think about the consequences of her actions. The entire world would think that she'd run down this child.

Joshua tried to control his disgust. It took an immense amount of restraint on his part to not lean across the table and give this one-dimensional bimbo a good hard shake.

'You left a dying child in the middle of the road with the likely chance that another car would come along and finish off the job. Didn't that occur to you?'

Yes, Angela Faber realized it now. In hindsight. And she was extremely sorry about this, she said, with a big show of tears yet still an air of deception.

20

'I have nothing to say,' Dennis Faber said.

Marouan Diba entered the room where Dennis Faber was being interrogated and nonchalantly placed his wife's signed statement on the table.

'Suit yourself,' Marouan said. 'As long as you listen closely, Mr Faber. You're not here because we're curious about your sexual preferences. Or because you're cheating on your wife, for that matter.' He saw Faber's face turn beet red under his pancake make-up.

'You're also not here because in a rage your wife decided to speed through the Amsterdamse Bos and end it all in a spectacular fashion. No, you're here because when she returned home with the badly damaged Citroën Picasso, plus a hysterical account about possibly hitting someone with her car, you saw the chance to keep your adulterous adventure behind closed doors. And you made your wife play along, Mr Faber.'

'I don't know what you're talking about.'

Marouan pretended not to hear him. He leaned forward as far as he could and said in a hushed tone, 'I'll help you, if you help me. Don't make a fuss about the arrest and I'll make sure everything related to the collision is swept under the rug. Agreed?' He leaned back and patronizingly stared at the TV host, who was getting more agitated by the minute.

'Here's the gist, you deliberately tried to conceal evidence related to a serious crime. Am I warm, Mr Faber? Because if I'm not then your wife has been lying through her teeth, with this false statement as the upshot.'

As he said this, he slid Angela Faber's account towards her husband.

'And let me not forget to mention, for the sake of clarity, that your wife's story matches the findings of our forensics team. A significant detail, as you might imagine. If you cooperate and you're wise enough to corroborate your wife's story then we can wrap up this entire unfortunate incident quickly and discreetly, you understand? Give my offer some thought.'

Without waiting for an answer, Marouan shoved back his chair. He stood up and walked out of the interrogation room, with the knowledge that he had played bluff poker in order to save face.

They didn't have much to go on.

Angela Faber hadn't really been involved in the hit-and-run that injured the boy. Moreover, Marouan realized that even if he could locate the driver of that second car, he still had no idea why the child had been at that place at that point in time.

His phone rang in his jacket pocket. As he glanced at the display, he felt his legs go numb. When he heard that despicable, thick Slavic accent address him in English, his chronic heartburn immediately flared up.

'*Chort poberi!* So it's true what they say about Moroccans. You're a bunch of sheep-fuckers with the intellect of a pig's ass. The last thing I needed was for you to pull such a brainless stunt!'

'What are you talking about?'

'Arresting Dennis Faber, that's what I'm talking about. I asked you to keep this whole thing under wraps. But no, there you are in widescreen, you Moroccan fathead.'

'I don't understand . . .' Marouan stammered.

'Listen Diva, this bizarre behaviour of yours has to stop. You make damn sure that the mess you've created by arresting Dennis Faber is taken care of quickly. No more fuck-ups. There's no escaping this! Your line of credit is cancelled. Just do what's expected of you like the obedient family man you are. Because a good father makes sure nothing happens to his children, you hear what I'm saying?'

'You leave my children out of this! You hear me?' Marouan shouted.

He gasped. His legs were trembling so hard, he was afraid he might collapse. He thrust both his hands against the wall above his head to brace himself and, as he did this, imagined pushing down the entire building from the inside out.

21

'Yellow-bellied cowards! The lot of them!' Edward fumed as he approached her desk. 'You have to talk till you're blue in the face these days to get what you want. It's all about circulation figures and advertising revenues. Fucking "budgetary constraints" blah, blah, blah!'

'So the whole thing is off?' Farah asked.

'Don't be silly!' Edward snorted. 'Of course it's happening. But what really aggravates me is that I keep having to move heaven and earth to convince those spineless wankers that their bureaucratic nonsense isn't doing anyone any good. Goddamn, we're a newspaper, not a sanatorium. We've got three months for now. Granted, it's not enough, but once we're making headway with the story, hopefully they'll cough up more time.'

'But that's great news, right?' Farah jumped up to throw her arms around Edward's thick neck.

'Hold your horses, Hafez,' he said. 'There's one condition you have to agree to.'

'And that is?'

'A second reporter. Someone with experience.'

'They still don't have much faith in me upstairs, do they?' She couldn't hide the disappointment in her voice.

'It was my idea. You don't have enough experience with stories like these, and I can't keep a constant eye on you. It's still your initiative, but see it as a joint project; you, me and the person I've picked to cover your back.

'And who might that be?'

Ed stomped back and forth, stalling longer than strictly necessary.

'I want Paul Chapelle out there with you.'

After he finally spit out the name, Farah felt the restless spirits stir in her once again.

Edward had trained Paul. And apart from being his mentor, he was also his uncle. Paul had once been promising, but there wasn't much left of his potential. It was rumoured that Paul's previous posting in Moscow had turned into a fiasco, full of binge drinking and bad-tempered brawls. But Edward was a man who never gave up on people – he continued to believe in his nephew's journalistic career, despite the many signs that this was probably futile. He'd been instrumental in having Paul transferred to Johannesburg. But apparently things didn't go much differently there than in Moscow. Or indeed in Paris and London, where Paul had been posted previously.

Perhaps, Farah thought, Ed saw this project as a last-ditch attempt to bring his prize pupil aboard: give Paul a new chance at the *AND*. But why should she, in her first major assignment, have to put up with a self-destructive correspondent whose career was clearly on its way down the drain?

Ed's answer was simple. 'This is about a possible international network and Paul has international experience. You don't.'

She was too overwhelmed to reason with him. The dark clouds filling her head made it impossible for her to stand up for herself. 'And what if he says no?'

'He won't say no.'

'Wait a minute Ed. As you always say, what's in it for you?'

'What's in it for me? A top-notch team of journalists, of course.'

'How can you say that? We've never worked together.'

'Then it's about time. Listen, Hafez, how long have I known you? Since the first day you walked into the pressroom as an intern. Ambition in abundance. But let's be honest, you haven't exactly written exposés worthy of a Pulitzer. A few articles on asylum policy, some in-depth portraits of famous athletes, lots of regional news and finally that piece you're working on now about a general pardon for refugees. But what have you done to make a name for yourself?'

'Well, I certainly didn't put my head in a liquor bottle, like your nephew.'

'No, your claim to fame is beating the shit out of people so they end up in hospital.'

'God, that's a fucked-up thing to say, Ed!'

'Correct. But a journalist with as much talent and determination as you deserves better than what I just rattled off. And frankly, Paul also deserves better. And I'm not only saying this because he's family. His problem is that he doesn't have someone beside him to measure up to.'

'But why me?'

'Dammit, Hafez . . . because the two of you have more in common than you think. Trust me for once!'

Farah was reeling. 'I just need some time to get used to the idea, Ed. That's all.'

'You've got till tomorrow,' he said impatiently. He turned and walked away. 'And give me a heads-up when your coppers get here!'

22

Joshua Calvino knew for certain: his partner Diba was a carrier. A man who carried hate in his heart, a load on his shoulders: a Tempter of Fate. Weighed down by all the misery and setbacks he'd experienced in his lifetime. Diba, like a hardened homeless person, just kept filling his rusty shopping trolley. At the same time, he had a compulsive need to hide this burden from the outside world. As if nobody could see through his deceitful behaviour. But he couldn't fool Joshua.

On the way to the station, Joshua just sat there in silence. Diba didn't say anything either. There was no use talking. Their tin jalopy was practically shaking from the loud cursing of the arrested man in the back seat. Joshua took his partner's satanic grin as a sign that he was enjoying Faber's swearing. Just wait Diba, Joshua thought, until you hear what the brass has to say about your on-air arrest.

But during the interrogation of the Fabers, Joshua had suddenly felt sorry for him. It was the same feeling he got when he saw an elderly woman frozen with fear on the zebra crossing of a busy intersection, or a man in a wheelchair in front of an out-of-order lift. He couldn't *not* help them, because he was simply unable to abandon them to their fate. And even if Diba was fast becoming one of the most repulsive characters Joshua had ever worked with, he couldn't abandon him to his fate either.

This realization was strengthened when, after interrogating Angela Faber, Joshua walked into the canteen and glanced over at the television, where a handful of his colleagues were laughing at the image on the screen. There was 'Detective Marouan D.' in a brilliantly edited clip, complete with slow motion and sound effects – practically a film trailer – arresting a bewildered Dennis Faber as the TV host was about to greet his live studio audience. The clip was from YouTube. Diba's illustrious deed was being gobbled up by an audience of millions. Now their superiors finally had a legitimate reason to put one of their longest-serving detectives out to pasture. With immediate effect.

Joshua cursed himself for wanting to protect Diba from this apocalyptic event, but realized that this benevolent feeling was his own doing. Part of the baggage in his shopping trolley: a soft spot for the ultimate underdog.

Outside the station he saw an army of press – with bright lights flashing and cameras rolling – gathered around the newly released television personality and his wife. He heard Dennis Faber say how the police had made a colossal mistake because of the stupidity of a detective with dual nationality. The moron had claimed his wife was guilty of a hit-and-run when in fact she was the one who'd reported the accident. Faber ended his statement by expressing the hope that this detective would be sent back to where he'd come from. And that in Morocco they were probably chomping at the bit to hire police of his calibre – to guard the king's harem.

Joshua felt a less than mild-mannered desire to force Faber to swallow every word, but he managed to control his temper. He walked down the hallway and ran into Diba by the interrogation rooms in a posture that resembled stretching. Perhaps it was just Diba wishing he could literally crawl into the wall and disappear.

When Diba turned towards him, Joshua recognized the fraught gaze of a kamikaze pilot in his eyes.

'The chief wants to see us,' Joshua said.

'When?' Diba asked without emotion.

'Now.' But as Diba set off towards the lobby, on his way to the boss's office, Joshua stopped him.

'Wait. Not a good idea.'

'Why not?'

'Everybody's going to want your autograph.'

'My head, you mean?'

That's reserved for the chief, Joshua thought. Then he said, 'Best to let me do the talking.'

'Why?'

'The whole arrest was my idea.'

'But I'm the one who screwed up.'

Perhaps that's the story of your life, Joshua reflected. And then he impulsively did something even he found surprising: he put a friendly hand on Diba's shoulder and gave it a pat.

23

As she left the *AND* building, Farah started walking towards the two rust-coloured giants with butterfly-shaped shields, watching over the northern riverbank of the IJ. Two impassive steel warriors. They'd recently been placed there as a symbolic protest by opponents of the so-called New Golden Age Project. Farah had just penned a series of articles about the megalomaniac scheme of Armin Lazonder, a business tycoon intent on putting Amsterdam back on the map.

Here in Amsterdam-Noord, on what used to be industrial terrain, he was planning to build three office towers as well as a marina, a sprawling cinema and theatre complex, restaurants, hotels, a luxury shopping arcade and an immense museum for ancient and modern art. The intention was to restore the capital to its former Golden Age glory.

Farah was heading towards the crowds, to Het Fort, an enormous early twentieth-century shipyard which was now occupied by a squatters' collective which enjoyed the support of the local people.

The steel giants marked the entrance to what looked like an almost medieval spectacle. Makeshift tents, old caravans, converted fire engines and army trucks were arranged in circles. The place was teeming with backpackers, pop-punks, dark ambient fans, Goths and neo-folkies, all rubbing shoulders with Japanese and American tourists who'd been spat out by tour buses and were now gawking at the many stalls. Besides plenty of organic fruit and vegetables, the vendors were selling aromatic oils, hemp clothing, Tibetan bread, prayer wheels, second-hand books and guitars, jewellery and crystal balls, T-shirts, jeans and a choice of textiles with Eastern patterns. The lingua franca was broken English.

The colourful crowds reminded Farah of the open-air bazaar in the Kabul of her childhood, where traders from the four corners of the world, tourists and hippies seemed to mingle quite happily. She came almost every day, usually around lunchtime, to savour the atmosphere, watch the people and stock up on fruit and vegetables.

She paused in front of a tiny stall where a Goth girl was displaying delicate jewellery, hand-made books of haikus and origami angels. Among all the other keepsakes she spotted a butterfly. It was made of fabric, paper and rope. The wings, which were almost as big as the palms of her hand, were tied together in the middle with fluffy rope to form a fat body with two bristly antennae on top. Each wing was made of layers of paper with oriental symbols and Chinese linen.

'A good-luck butterfly,' the girl with the mysterious smile said in English. 'It only works for people who are open to it.'

'Open to what?' Farah asked.

'Luck,' the girl said drily.

'You'll have to explain that one to me.'

'The thing about luck is that you shouldn't try to hold on to it. Just enjoy it as long as possible and then let go again.'

Farah wasn't a big fan of new-age speak. 'It's beautiful. Did you make it?'

'No. It's really old.'

'How old?'

'No idea.'

'How much?'

The girl named her price. Farah didn't haggle. When the girl handed her the butterfly she held Farah's hand for a moment.

'Take good care of it, will you?'

Farah left her shopping for what it was and made her way to a quiet spot along the waterfront where she took a closer look at the butterfly. Gently, very gently, she blew on the wings. A breath of wind did the rest. The butterfly seemed to be dancing just above her hands. She could hear the rustling of other wings. They were fluttering all around her, taking her back to when she was a seven-year-old girl in the courtyard garden of Kabul's presidential palace.

She looked at her mother who was nearby, talking to a man. He was touching her arm, Farah noticed. And then she saw the blond boy with the cheeky look in his eyes. He was standing very close to her.

'Yours are blue too,' he said, as if he was the first person to ever remark on this. A whole raft of people had assured her that with those eyes she must be a descendant of the Greek general who'd invaded the country thousands of years ago. She was quite proud of this. And then some random brat had the nerve to tell her 'yours are blue too'. His use of the word 'too' was particularly annoying. She took an instant dislike to him.

The butterflies were still whirling around her. The boy said nothing, just sneered at her.

'They're not coming anywhere near you,' Farah said, 'because you've scared them with your dark soul.'

This seemed to strike a chord in the boy.

'Do I scare you too?' He sounded sincere.

'No,' she said. 'You can't scare me, because I can do this.'

Farah demonstrated a few of the Silat moves her father had taught her, very slowly and very confidently. He stood and watched her sheepishly, until long after she'd finished.

'That's not fighting, that's dancing!' the boy said eventually.

Farah tried to stay calm. 'Every single movement has meaning.'

He slammed his fist against the palm of his hand like he'd seen her do. 'Hitting your own hands. What's the point of that? Hurting yourself?'

'No, blocking your opponent. Go on, attack.'

He looked at her, clearly unnerved.

'What?'

'Go on then, attack me. Or are you afraid?' She saw he was angry.

'I don't fight with girls,' he said irritably.

'Why not?'

'Because you're the weaker sex.'

She slapped him in the face. 'Hit me. Now!'

At that, he lost his cool. He clenched his fists and took a swing at her. She parried his first blow with her left arm. It hurt, because he swung hard. She not only blocked his second blow, but immediately followed it up with an arm lock and held him tightly. He tried to wriggle free, but couldn't.

'I'll let go of you now,' she said to him.

He stood facing her and tried to swallow his frustration. But instead of getting more angry with her, he asked, 'How did you do that?'

'Using the same moves I just showed you,' she said proudly and repeated the sequence she'd demonstrated earlier. 'This is how I blocked you. And with this move I put you in an arm lock. It's not dancing, it's fighting. Now do you believe me?'

'I believe you,' he said. 'Let me try again.'

'Go ahead.'

He took another swipe at her, but a controlled one this time because he was keen to see how she would react. Again, she put him in an arm lock. And there they stood for a while, very still, until she realized how intertwined they were. She'd never been this close to a boy before. She could feel his body, his tense muscles, and hear his breath in her ear. She'd like nothing better than to stay like this a while.

'Farah?'

Her mother had disappeared with the man for a few minutes, but now the two of them were back and standing in one of the arched openings between two columns. Farah saw the man run his hand down her mother's arm.

The boy let go of Farah, turned around and walked towards the man, who was just bringing her mother's hand to his lips and pressing a kiss on it.

The man put his arm around the boy's shoulders. When they were gone, Farah could tell a change had come over her mother. She seemed softer, rounder. Her eyes were prettier and her laughter clearer than usual. She thought about running after the boy and telling him that she wouldn't mind teaching him some more. But that would be silly. She looked up at her mother.

'Mum, who was that man?'

'A journalist, a friend of your father's,' her mother said in the tone she reserved for bedtime stories.

'And the boy?'

'That's Paul. His son.'

The bellowing horn of a cruise liner docking at the port across the IJ jolted her back from her daydream.

The butterfly was lying in her hand. As if it had finally found its way home.

24

Marouan Diba wasn't mistaken. He hadn't been touched by God, but by the hand of a half-baked Italian. Yet, Calvino's reassuring pat on the shoulder had provided the calm he needed, even if it was simply a reprieve for a man who knew he was about to be handed his head – the chopping block was waiting.

Marouan couldn't read the eyes of his executioner. Whenever anyone entered Chief Inspector Tomasoa's office, the man had the habit of surrounding himself with an aura of impenetrability. With his Indonesian head shaved clean and his rugged jawline, he reminded Marouan of the actor Yul Brynner. He'd seen his films as a child. Brynner as the King of Siam, Brynner as a Wild West hero – all in black – who'd rallied a gang of fearsome gunmen on horseback in *The Magnificent Seven*. Brynner always played winners and heroes. Brynner never broke a sweat and needed few if any words, similar to the Chief Inspector. It occurred to Marouan that things could be worse. After all, it was practically an honour to be suspended from duty by Tomasoa.

'I was in Carré yesterday,' Tomasoa stated calmly. The chief could pronounce a death sentence and still make it sound like a haiku. 'At the Pencak Silat Gala.'

Unexpected lead in, Marouan thought. It instantly threw him off. He looked at Tomasoa, poker-faced.

'Heard of it, detective?'

'Carré? Of course,' Marouan said offhandedly. 'Used to be a circus with prancing horses.' When he caught Tomasoa's weary reaction he quickly added, 'Pencak Silat is a martial art. Oriental, from South East Asia, I believe.'

'More than a martial art,' Tomasoa corrected him. 'Pencak Silat is a way of life. Developed centuries ago by Sumatran monks. They studied the survival techniques of tigers, monkeys and even wasps. They mingled those techniques with the ancient spirituality of their people. So a martial art was born in which not only the body but also the spirit of the fighter are central.'

Tomasoa looked alternately at Calvino and Marouan, who both kept staring straight ahead. 'And that brings me back to last night's gala,' he continued after sipping his tea. 'The women's exhibition fight.' He stood up and paced back and forth with controlled steps, underpinning his storytelling with his huge hands, attached to a brawny Indonesian body.

'On the one hand,' announced Tomasoa, as if he was covering the fight from ringside, 'an elegant woman, type crane. On the other, a heartless fighting machine, type vulture. The referee gives the signal. The vulture starts to spew hate, pounces on her opponent, straightaway goes for the jugular, drags her across the mat by her hair, claws deep into her skin. And the minute her opponent gets her in a leg grip, the vulture sinks her venomous teeth into her rival's calf. Blind rage. And what's the upshot?'

Marouan braced himself for the moral of the story, which Tomasoa was going to pull out of his hat any moment now.

'A loser, gentlemen. Because our vulture is not a winner, not a master of her situation. She's let her herself be enslaved by her passions. And that's why *she* was taken down. You could say, heartlessly taken down.' Tomasoa chuckled at the thought. 'It's the law of nature. Simple, effective and centuries old. *Tenaga Dalam*, inner strength. Followed by *Kanuragan*, magical self-protection.'

Okay, the hatchet man has massaged my neck, Marouan thought, and now he's going to swing his axe?

'What I expect of my investigators,' Tomasoa continued, 'is that they are masters of the situation, always and anywhere, and they don't let their passions get the better of them.' His eyes fixed on Marouan. 'Is that unreasonable, Detective Diba?'

'No, sir,' Marouan said, as self-possessed as possible. The hairs on his neck were standing on end; his skin tingled from the chilly wind of the axe whooshing by.

'Then I must have been hallucinating,' Tomasoa said sarcastically. 'Because wasn't that you I saw on television? In the guise of a ravenous vulture, with your claws in a Dutch celeb?'

Calvino cleared his throat. The axe slowed . . .

'In a way, it was my fault, sir.'

'I'm referring to your partner's charming television performance, detective. Not your hand in this.'

'I know,' Calvino brazenly continued, 'but based on a conversation Detective Diba and I had with Mrs Faber, we quickly got the impression that she and her husband had tried to cover up last night's hit-and-run. Once we had enough evidence it seemed only logical to us, and to the Public Prosecutor, that we should also question Mr Faber.'

'It's about your approach here,' Tomasoa barked. The axe accelerated again. Marouan saw the Chief Inspector was having trouble controlling his growing irritation. What's with Calvino and all the interruptions? Marouan thought, almost cringing with astonishment at so much unexpected loyalty.

'Get this,' Tomasoa said, raising his voice. 'You can go to a football game and enjoy the match along with the other supporters. But it's something else to run out on the field, moon the public from the centre circle, and then belt out the team song. Bit of a crooked metaphor, made up on the spot, but hopefully you get my gist.'

'You're right, sir,' Marouan hesitantly said, 'I take full responsibility for this, uh, shitty situation.'

'Oh, don't worry, Diba, I'm going to hold you responsible,' Tomasoa said. 'But not before we clear up a few matters. Number one: what do we really know about the hit-and-run victim?'

Calvino continued to jump in and Marouan understood why. He'd already stuck his hand in the fire for him. That damn Italian would make him cry if he kept this up.

'Sir, we believe there were several cars involved,' Calvino said. 'One of them, we've concluded, belongs to Mrs Faber. But she didn't run down the boy. And the only thing we know for sure about the other vehicle is that it was *blinding*. In this case, a literal description, given it sped past Angela Faber from the opposite direction with its glaring full beams on.'

'Right,' said Tomasoa. 'Typical needle in a haystack. Next matter. What's the story with the burnt-out station wagon?'

'Working on it,' Calvino said. 'Determining the license registration is extremely difficult and the identification of the two bodies is practically impossible. The fire did a number on the car.'

'So not much chance of a quick breakthrough. Matter three: the relation between the two? Yin and yang. Boy and station wagon. Is there a connection?'

'No,' said Marouan, too definitively.

'Haven't established one yet,' Calvino corrected him.

'Right,' said Tomasoa again. 'But can I infer from what you're telling me that a relation between the station wagon and the hit-and-run hasn't been ruled out? And if there is a connection, then the focus of our investigation is lying in intensive care. When can the boy be questioned?'

'They expect in about a week. Assuming he makes it,' Marouan answered.

'Then the moment has come when you're going to have to step up, Detective Diba. I'm counting on you and your overly devoted sidekick to resolve this matter as quickly, and as efficiently, as possible. Because I can hold press conferences until I'm blue in the face, I can do damage control to quiet the sneering reviews of your nationwide television debut, and to limit the conceivable annoyance and even anger your colleagues are rightfully feeling, but at the end of the day, you're the only one who can set this right. Namely by escorting the actual perpetrator into this station. And as far as I'm concerned, the sooner the better.'

In a flash Marouan realized the hatchet man had changed his tactic. He wasn't going to swing the axe himself, he was handing the axe to Marouan's wife who'd react hysterically when he told her that their holiday this year would have to be postponed until further notice.

As if Tomasoa could read Marouan's mind, he asked, 'Naturally, I'm very curious about how far your sense of responsibility goes, Detective Diba? I ask, of course, in light of your approaching yearly return to your beloved homeland.'

'My sense of responsibility goes so far that I will completely throw myself into this case in the coming weeks, sir.' Marouan had the feeling he'd taken a free-fall nosedive out of an airplane, without strapping on a parachute.

'Then it's settled, gentlemen,' Tomasoa lightheartedly said. 'Anything else I need to know? Particular aspects of the case that could possibly complicate the rest?'

Marouan saw Calvino biting his lip. Damn it, that poor excuse for an Italian knows more than he's saying.

'Nothing we can't handle, sir,' Calvino replied.

And before they knew it, they were back in the corridor.

'Merci,' Marouan blurted out matter-of-factly. 'But it wasn't necessary.'

'What?'

'Jumping in to help me.'

'That's what partners do,' Calvino replied.

'But there's something you're not telling me?' Marouan said.

'We're off to visit the crane woman who took down her rival – heartlessly, as we were informed.'

'Spare me the jokes. What's going on?'

'I'm serious. We've got an appointment. To pick up an earring from her, covered in blood.'

'Blood? Whose?'

'The hit-and-run victim's, who else?'

25

The man who'd taken the seat opposite Farah was the same man she'd seen last night beside the burning station wagon, having a go at everything that moved. It was the same man who'd tried to impress her with his boorish behaviour in the hospital this morning. The same man she'd seen on YouTube this afternoon, interrupting a live taping by slapping handcuffs on a television presenter as though he were a serious criminal.

The same man, yet somehow different.

It looked like Detective Diba had fallen to pieces somewhere along the line, had been hurriedly pasted back together and was now trying to pretend nothing had happened. She studied him closely, looking for the cracks. She found them in his eyes. While his body language sought to exude control, those eyes were quietly screaming 'mercy'.

'I understand you've got something for us,' Detective Diba said.

His voice also sounded different to Farah. Almost mechanical. As if he was being remotely controlled.

She couldn't stand sitting opposite this man.

Edward, on the other hand, seemed to feel perfectly at ease in this company. A bit too much, in fact. The man who was supposed to determine the strategy, the man who refused to be impressed by anyone, this very man now appeared to have fallen like a brick for Calvino.

Farah found it quite endearing to see Ed so wholly overwhelmed by the young detective's virility. The way they'd stood there beside the glass wall, shooting the breeze with those self-assured smiles some men have. As if they'd been friends for years. Farah was familiar with it. It was something she noticed a lot in the men at the gym, in between their weight training sets. Laid-back, easy-going encounters, but extremely masculine. Pats on the back, smiles. Idle chit-chat. Circumscribed cruising. Farah wondered if the attraction between Edward and Joshua was mutual.

Five minutes had passed. The discussion got underway.

'Perhaps this is only a misunderstanding, Detective Diba.' Edward made the opening move from behind his desk.

Diba turned towards her boss, seemingly exasperated, while Calvino kept gazing stoically over the IJ through his Gucci shades.

'I assume nobody's on trial here,' Edward remarked.

'Am I insinuating otherwise?' Diba asked politely.

'*C'est le ton qui fait la musique,*' Ed chuckled.

'I'm not here to make music or friends,' Diba replied. 'I'm here to retrieve a piece of evidence.'

'You see, that's exactly how misunderstandings come about,' Edward said cheerfully. 'You want to retrieve something. But was it ever yours to begin with?'

'I'm not here to play word games, Mr Vallent. You have something that belongs to the police and it's a vital part of our investigation.'

'In the meantime it's also become part of a story that one of my investigative journalists is following up.'

'Obtained by traipsing around the scene of a crime before Forensics got to it. If it turns out that this has undermined the ongoing investigation in any way, then . . .'

But Diba didn't get to finish his sentence. Calvino, who appeared to have had his fill of the view and regained his power of speech, jumped in.

'We really appreciate that you're prepared to hand us the missing piece of evidence, and that you've specified exactly where you found it.'

Farah threw him an amused look.

'And we hope, Ms Hafez,' added Diba, as if he'd rehearsed this two-hander with Calvino, 'that from now on you'll leave your police ambitions to us and stop getting in the way with those lovely legs of yours.'

Calvino froze.

'Misunderstanding number two,' Edward cut in, 'has nothing whatsoever to do with Hafez's legs, but more with the fact that we have a mutual interest here. Why should we get in each other's way? Hafez used her expertise to locate something that's of value to your investigation. Since she's prepared to share this information with you, I think it's only reasonable that you provide something in return.'

'Pardon?' Marouan looked as if he'd just had abuse hurled at him.

'We all have our interests,' Edward clarified. 'The question is whether we can bring those interests in line with each other?'

'So what you're saying,' Calvino summed up, 'is there's no such thing as a free lunch.'

'A simple way of putting it, but yes.'

'We get a dangly earring from you,' Calvino summed up. 'What do you get from *us*?'

'To begin with, infinitely more credit than your colleague is giving us right now,' Edward replied, smiling his most charming smile.

'Speaking for myself, I have no trouble at all giving credit where credit is due,' Calvino said while peering at Farah over his shades. His gaze instantly revealed that he was as gay as the pope is Protestant. 'But as a detective, I have some serious reservations. We don't collaborate with the press during ongoing investigations: matter of principle. Surely someone with your degree of experience is aware of that, Mr Vallent?'

Edward's smile was now forced. He shifted in his seat, as though a thumb tack was sticking him in the butt. Farah, too, had picked up on Calvino's sarcasm. As far as she was concerned the conversation was going in the wrong direction.

'Based on that experience,' Edward reacted guardedly, 'I know that principles, however firm they may be at first, can shift as soon as other interests come into play.'

'The interests are clear, Mr Vallent,' Diba said with the exaggerated conviction of a politician in the run-up to an election. 'And we're not reneging on our principles.'

Farah regarded him with contempt. She had a sneaking suspicion that he might be heading for a heart attack if he carried on like this. But Diba clearly couldn't care less about her suspicions.

'I understand damn well that as a journalist you want to cover the boy's case,' he continued angrily. 'But do you have any idea what you might be stirring up? Are you prepared to accept responsibility for the boy's safety once the story is splashed across the front page of your newspaper, purely for your own journalistic gain?'

'Your contemptible clichés are as offensive as the way you keep staring at my breasts,' Farah said coolly. 'Not to mention your rude remark about my legs.' From the corner of her eye she spotted an incipient smile on Calvino's face. 'What I'm trying to bring to light,' she resumed, 'is who can be held accountable for the state in which the boy was found and who's guilty of trafficking children like him. It's absurd to think that you and I have completely different interests in all this.' No mercy for a man intent on elevating insensitivity to an art form, whatever his position in the police force.

'Besides, what right do you have to judge others after making such a spectacle of yourself in the IRIS TV studio this afternoon? Who do you think you are? Rambo?' A good note to end on, she reckoned.

The blood drained from Detective Diba's face and he turned ashen. Joshua Calvino went and stood behind his colleague's chair, as if to give Diba literal backing. Or perhaps to stop him from having a go at her in his next angry outburst.

'As you rightly said earlier, Mr Vallent,' Calvino spoke soothingly, 'nobody's on trial here. Why don't you give us the earring and we'll call it a day?'

'Do you think it's possible that the boy was being used as a sex slave over here, Mr Calvino?' Edward asked calmly.

'That's an interesting hypothesis, Mr Vallent. What makes you think that?'

'The way the boy was dressed and made up.'

'The boy was indeed dressed unconventionally. But if clothes and jewellery were sufficient proof for whoring, our prisons would soon be overflowing, don't you think?'

'What are you trying to say?' Farah asked.

Calvino pushed his shades up on his head and turned to her with a smile.

'What I'm saying, Ms Hafez, is don't judge a book by its cover.'

'Gentlemen.' Having risen to his feet, Edward was now dangling a sealed plastic bag containing the earring in front of Calvino's face, like the pendulum of an old-fashioned hypnotist. 'It's been a real pleasure. I see we're not getting anywhere, and that we can forget about potentially collaborating on this matter.'

'This is the first and probably the only time I agree with you.' Detective Diba's voice sounded strangled, like solidifying lava. He stiffly rose from the leather chair.

'I do hope you understand that the whole affair involving the boy continues to be newsworthy for us. So whether you like it or not, we're planning to really sink our teeth into this case.' Edward held out his hand to Diba.

'We've got press freedom in this country,' Diba replied, placing a limp hand in Edward's.

'Thank goodness,' Edward responded, 'because if it were up to you, I'd probably be out of a job.'

26

Edward lay the blame for the difficulty of the negotiations squarely on the visiting party.

'We were dealing with a common street fighter and a professional slimeball, damn it. We didn't stand a chance. You're up against it, Hafez. Really up against it. Have you made up your mind about Paul, by the way?'

'No,' she muttered.

'Is there something you want to tell me? Come on, Hafez! Out with it!' Edward was playing Freud, or Jung, or both.

'Stop it, Ed! I saw two charred corpses last night, escorted a seriously injured boy from the Emergency Department to the operating table and on top of it all I barely slept. What do you want from me?'

'I want you to go home.'

'That's exactly what I'm planning to do. Bye, Ed, speak to you later.'

As she walked down the corridor, she received a phone call from Danielle.

'Sorry to bother you, but could you make your way over here? To the hospital, I mean.'

Farah's heart skipped a couple of beats.

'Have things taken a turn for the worse?'

'No, but we're planning to wake the boy up. Someone will have to tell him what happened to him and where he is. Would you mind doing that?'

Without a moment's hesitation, she set off and twenty minutes later she exited the lift on the ICU floor. Danielle, who was there waiting for her, immediately took Farah through the anteroom to the boy's bedside.

'Let me talk you through the procedure,' Danielle said as they entered the room.

Farah halted in her tracks. There, asleep in a big bed, bathed in artificial light, was a little boy. His body was intertwined with all kinds of tubes that were attached to a stack of machines and monitors. Seeing the tubes in his nose and mouth, she realized just how vulnerable he was.

'We're keeping him sedated because of the pain.' Danielle's voice sounded muted. 'But we have to wake him up so the neurologist can test his brain function. He won't realize what happened to him, and he won't be able to talk because of the tube down his throat. There's a very real chance that he'll panic. You can help him with that.'

'How?' Farah asked.

'By calmly talking him through what happened and why he's hooked up to these machines. Explain to him why he can't talk right now.'

'Okay,' Farah said. 'When?'

'As soon as the neurologist gets here.'

Danielle exchanged a few brief words with the critical care head nurse. Then she introduced her to Farah.

'This is Mariska, she's looking after the boy.'

'Thanks for helping us,' Mariska said, shaking Farah's hand.

'My pleasure,' Farah replied. 'Can you tell me what this is for?' She pointed to a complex construction of tubes which had been inserted into the boy's carotid artery.

'We use it to administer medication that could be a strain on his regular veins,' Mariska said. 'We're giving him propofol, a sedative, and fentanyl, so he's not in any pain.'

At that moment the neurologist entered. The tall woman with glasses greeted Farah with a quick, professional handshake. 'Let's get started,' she said.

'We'll discontinue the propofol in a minute,' Mariska said to Farah as she began tying up the boy's hands. 'He'll come to very quickly. The first thing he'll want to do is pull this tube out of his mouth. As soon as you've had a chance to tell him what's going on, I'll untie his hands. It's only a precautionary measure.'

Farah was getting nervous. She wiped her palms on her trousers and took a couple of deep breaths.

'I'm stopping the propofol now,' Mariska told the neurologist.

All four of them were standing around the bed, waiting for the boy to open his eyes. But nothing happened. Not a single reflex. He didn't wake up.

The neurologist's impersonal voice came as an anticlimax.

'It's not unusual, but if there's been no response in the next hour or so, we'll have to do a CT scan and an EEG.' She checked her watch. 'Notify me as soon as there are any signs.' And off she went.

Farah saw the boy's chest rising and falling with mathematical regularity and heard the sinister sound of the mechanical bellows providing him with air. Instinctively, she reached for his hand. It felt cold to the touch.

'What could it be?' she asked.

'He has a head injury,' Danielle said. 'When the car hit him, his head slammed against the windscreen. There's probably some swelling and this in turn can cause bruising of the brain and slow his reactions down.'

'Will he pull through?'

'It's impossible to say with any certainty at this stage.'

Farah could tell that Danielle was trying to put a professional face on it, but underneath it all, she was highly emotional.

'I've been thinking about what you told me this morning,' Danielle said, her head turned towards the boy. 'In recent years, I've only worked in war zones. The moment they're brought in, the children with severed limbs, the mothers and fathers with bullet wounds, the soldiers with fatal injuries, I really don't think about who's fighting who, why and how unjust it all is. I set to work. I dive in head first. I start cutting, I open a chest, I amputate a leg. I try to save a life, because that's my job.' She brushed her hand across the boy's forehead. Farah was silent.

'The world knows next to nothing about these wars,' Danielle said. 'And when you're in the middle of them, you don't really think about it either. But since I've been working here these past couple of months I've been doing so all the more.' She gave Farah a penetrating sideways look. 'This morning you said "I haven't even started yet." What did you mean by that?'

'The investigation into what happened,' Farah replied. 'This is an extremely complicated case.'

'I want as many people as possible to finally see what's happening to these children. You could play a key role in this. The case is topical right now,' Danielle said. 'There's plenty of interest, especially after that television couple were arrested. And tomorrow something could happen that overshadows this story.'

Last night Farah had seen a capable doctor at work. The way in which Danielle had taken the initiative in the midst of a crisis had commanded everybody's respect. The woman in front of her now was guided by personal motives, trying to turn the situation to her own advantage. She shook her head.

'I'm afraid it would be counterproductive to write a story about it at this early stage,' Farah explained. 'The story would be punctuated by "maybes" and "possiblies". I'm after certainty. Solid evidence that the boy was smuggled into the country and that we're really dealing with a Bacha Bazi ritual. As long as I don't have that evidence, I won't write about it. I'm sorry. We'll have to wait.'

They both looked at the boy, who was still not responding.

'How long?'

Farah heard the disappointment in her voice. 'Longer than you'd care to, I suspect.' She caressed the boy's cheek. 'I hope it wasn't the main reason you asked me to come here.'

She didn't want to hurt Danielle's feelings, out of admiration for what she'd done last night, but then again she didn't want to spare her either. 'The thing is, I'd rather not feel like I'm being manipulated.'

'That sounds rather harsh,' Danielle said coolly. 'I thought we were on the same side.'

'We are. I'm going to investigate this. But it may take months. The boy is probably only the tip of the iceberg.'

'I see.' Danielle sounded downright hostile now. 'You're only interested in the boy because he can lead you to something else. That's all.'

'That's quite a lot,' Farah said, her feelings hurt.

'I should have known better. I'm too naive for my own good. Sorry to have brought you over here for nothing.'

'Not for nothing. I want to help you in any way I can, but not with this kind of publicity.'

'This kind of publicity?' Danielle echoed cynically, but at that moment a slight shudder passed through the boy's body. His eyelids trembled and slowly parted. Danielle immediately called for Mariska.

The boy seemed to be staring into nothingness. But when Farah leaned into his field of vision their eyes met and it all came back. The recognition, the fear, the loneliness.

'*Shokr e Khoda.*' Thank God, she said, 'you made it. Do you remember me?' She felt his hand stirring feebly. 'You pulled through. And now they're going to patch you up.' She looked at him so intently that she barely noticed the neurologist entering the room.

Suddenly the boy began rolling his eyes and frantically trying to move his limbs.

'His feet!' Danielle yelled at Mariska when the boy began to kick. 'Fasten his feet!'

Farah saw the boy's panicked gaze darting around the room, and tried to re-establish eye contact with him.

'*Ma inja hastom, peshet astom.*' I'm here, I'm with you. Look at me.

'Heart rate!' she heard Danielle shout. Mariska responded with a figure.

'Calm down now. You were hit by a car. You've got very serious injuries. That's why you've got all of these tubes sticking into you. Even in your mouth, so you can't talk. But it's all to make you better. Do you understand? Can you hear me?'

The boy kept thrashing about and rolling his eyes. Unable to get through to him, Farah was close to tears.

'If you hear me, if you understand what I'm saying, please nod. Or squeeze my hand. *Khahesh mikonam.* Please . . .'

She wrapped her fingers around his tiny hand and felt him squeezing back, his eyes suddenly fixated on her.

'Tell him everything,' Danielle urged her. 'From the beginning.'

'You're safe here. I'm with you,' Farah began. The boy kept looking at her.

'You were in the woods. Then a car came. And hit you. You've got a lot of injuries, to your legs and to your stomach. You've had surgery. And so that everything that was broken will grow back together again, they've put some clever things into your body. Things made of steel. They'll be taken out again after a while. And then you'll be able to walk again. Do you understand?'

The boy nodded. He was starting to look less frantic.

'All those tubes in your body, including the one in your mouth, are there to make you better again. That's why they must stay in for the time being. When we untie your hands in a minute, you mustn't pull them out. Do you promise?'

He gave her an intensely sad look before nodding again. She wiped away the tears rolling down his cheeks.

'*Sha-bas.*' You're very brave, Farah whispered and gave him a kiss.

'You can untie his hands now,' she said to Mariska. 'And his feet too.'

They stood by in silence as Mariska did her job. All were poised to react instantly if, in a reflex, he were to yank at the tubes, but he remained calm.

'You've got beautiful eyes,' Farah said. Although she was smiling, the tears were now rolling down her cheeks too. She heard Danielle's voice.

'How do I say "hello" to him?'

Farah told her: *salam*.

The boy looked at them with question marks in his eyes.

'She found you,' Farah said. 'She brought you here and operated on you. She saved your life. Her name is Danielle. And my name is Farah. I can't be with you all the time, because I don't know much about all these machines.' She turned around and asked Mariska to come and stand next to her for a moment. 'This is Mariska. She's here for you. Around the clock.'

Mariska smiled reassuringly at the boy and asked Farah to explain to him that there was no need for him to be in pain. If he was, he should press the button.

As Farah told him this, she could feel the pressure of his hand in hers weakening slowly. His eyes closed briefly before opening again.

Danielle placed a hand on her arm.

'We need to do some tests.'

27

From the monumental Blauwbrug, Marouan looked out over the River Amstel towards the Magere Brug – the bridge's thin wooden structure clearly delineated by small lights. Five white swans in stately formation steered clear of an approaching tour boat that glided almost silently through the dark water.

From his vantage point on the bridge, he gazed at the tall canal houses and Carré, the old theatre. After sundown this part of Amsterdam had the timeless allure of the early port city it had once been. The decorative use of lights and the old street lanterns gave you the feeling you'd stepped into the seventeenth century, the Dutch Golden Age.

He'd also stood on this very spot in the middle of the bridge on a lovely spring evening some nineteen years ago, alongside his new bride, Aisha. He wanted her to feel at home in Amsterdam so he took her to visit the heart of it. With the hope of reaching *her* heart.

He'd pointed to the lit-up wooden bridge, 'The Dutch queen comes here every year when we commemorate the end of the Second World War,' he'd whispered as if telling her a fairy tale. 'Then, on a float in front of the theatre, a full orchestra plays for her. And people come and moor their small boats to listen to the music.'

She was silent and looked at him at that moment as if an orchestra also began playing for her.

She crept closer to him, and he knew then that what they shared *must* be love. And that this love would work miracles. Move mountains. Build bridges. Break down boundaries.

He'd been coming here for nineteen years. The bridge felt like his anchor against all that was transitory in this life.

As the tour boat passed beneath the bridge, his thoughts drifted back to this afternoon's encounter with the journalist and her editor. It was their first undertaking after being reprimanded by Tomasoa, and Marouan had been determined to show Cal he was worthy of his loyalty. But basically he'd blown it. He'd let himself be provoked by a woman with breasts that *no* man could resist staring at. And what for? He convinced himself it was exhaustion. But he knew better. He was in need of solace. He knew he could find it there, where he'd riveted his eyes.

Cal had given him another sturdy pat on the shoulder. 'Go home, take a shower, talk to your wife. And get some sleep!'

Aisha was already busy packing when he got home. Everything was straightened up and the house smelled of disinfectant. After taking a shower, he went into the kitchen wearing only his boxers to tell her what was going on. But nothing had to be said. She already knew the story. In recent years she'd long since made up her own story. A story he wasn't interested in. One marriage. Two stories. And however contradictory these two stories were, they had one thing in common: mutual resignation. The knowledge that there could be no other outcome except sitting opposite each other in a kitchen that smelled of Dettol.

Marouan stared at his wife from across the table. She had the elusive look of someone who was used to burying her feelings, her thoughts, even her personality on a daily basis. Thinking about the future for her meant thinking about the next day, filled with the same rituals and self-sacrifices.

He knew it and she knew it too. When she arrived tomorrow late in the afternoon, tired from the flight, and embraced her family, all of the words and emotions, everything she had bottled up for the past year, would erupt. A three-week long torrent, a litany. A long, bittersweet lament.

After his short monologue at the kitchen table – *I'm sorry, problems at work, don't believe everything people say, it's been shown on television, you go ahead with the kids, I'll come later* – he'd staggered off to bed. Then came a brief, coma-like sleep. The smell of dinner woke him. For a second he thought he'd dreamt what had happened that day and the night before. But at the kitchen table Jamila and Chahid's faces suggested otherwise.

'Did Mum tell you?'

They nodded. He could tell from their uneasiness that they'd seen the whole thing on TV. Also, they could tell he was embarrassed. Therefore nobody had much of anything to say. They ate in silence. Then he announced he had to go back to work.

He'd left the Corolla in the Bijenkorf department store's car park. He crossed the cobblestones in front of the Oude Kerk and stopped beside the church to watch her from a safe distance away. The way she stood there. In red lingerie. Behind the street-level glass door. He'd seen her for the first time weeks ago. She reminded him of Aisha when she was young. She recognized him, smiled and waved. He'd continued on his way.

Now he was in the middle of the Blauwbrug. Alone. Nineteen years ago, on this very spot, he promised himself that he would protect his young, shy wife for ever. He would give her everything within his means. He would kiss the ground she walked on. He'd done his best. Given her two children. Bought her a house in a better neighbourhood. Paid for redecorating; let her furnish it how she saw fit. Made the yearly holiday to Morocco financially possible. Paid her monthly phone bills. Set aside funds so Jamila and Chahid could study later on. All of this with only one purpose: to make sure she was happy in life.

He walked on, across the Blauwbrug, in the direction of Rembrandtplein. He entered the Golden Game Casino on the square, bought some chips, headed directly to the large round table covered in green felt – surrounded by all-too familiar faces – where 8-Game Mix, Blind Man's Bluff and Ace to Five Draw were his preferred choice of poker games.

Nineteen years gone – having already lost so much, it felt like there was nothing left to lose.

28

Before she'd even left the hospital car park, Farah was playing U2 at top volume in the car. She flew along the ring road and into the Zeeburgertunnel, heading downtown. It wasn't until she reached Nieuwmarkt that she stepped on the brakes and continued at a crawl among the crowds. The square was teeming with tourists and locals who'd all been drawn to the summer festival.

Long after she'd found a parking space she remained seated in the Carrera.

The meeting with Danielle Bernson continued to haunt her. The look she'd given Farah as they said goodbye was the provisional low point of an intense twenty-four-hour sequence of events and confrontations.

Names from a remote corner of her past had been dredged up. The spirit of a dead man had stood silently beside her this afternoon. She thought of the cold hand of the boy in intensive care. Of the eyes of Paul Chapelle in the butterfly garden.

Standing in her apartment, she noticed the orderly line-up of the cushions on the large dark-brown sofa, the symmetrical arrangement of the three sanded tree trunks she used as side tables and the careful composition of the photos on the cork board. It put her on edge. After making a pot of herbal tea and slipping an Anoushka Shankar CD into the player, she took an enamel bowl from the china cabinet in her fifties-style kitchen and mixed two tablespoons of honey with three tablespoons of yogurt. She carried the mixture through to the bathroom where she turned on the hot-water tap, undressed, lit some incense sticks. Then she went back into the living room to get *Vogue USA* and sprinkled a few drops of almond oil into the bathwater.

Using gently rotating movements, she massaged wild rose scrub on her face, rinsed it off and then carefully daubed the honey-yogurt mixture on her cheeks, chin and forehead. She'd once seen her mother do this and even now, many years later, she still tried to perform this modest ritual twice a week, in tribute to her. Lying in the bath with her tea, she leafed through *Vogue* while the plaintive chords of Shankar's sitar drifted through the apartment.

After about fifteen minutes, she wiped off the mask with a flannel, showered, dried herself and rubbed body lotion into her skin. She put on a cardinal-red lace bra with matching knickers and appraised herself in the mirror. Thinking of her surprise appearance at Hotel De l'Europe later, she pulled a long-sleeved black lace top out of her wardrobe and a red pencil skirt reaching to just above the knee. She'd team it with gossamer-thin black tights and black stiletto heels with pointy toes. Her long black hair would look great in a messy bun.

As she lay the complete outfit on the bed, the music and laughter from outside, on Nieuwmarkt, slowly filtered through. She could hear, smell and taste the excitement of the summer festival and suddenly realized that after everything she'd been through she really didn't relish spending the evening being an exotic accessory and squeezing money from the pockets of potential investors. She left a message on David's voicemail to say that she wasn't coming and ten minutes later she joined the crowd at the summer festival.

The many music stages produced a loud and irresistible mix of salsa, jazz and schmaltzy Dutch songs. There was also a small faux-vintage 'culinary Ferris wheel' with old-fashioned red leather bucket seats, which rotated so slowly you could easily finish your paella in a single revolution.

Enjoying the lively atmosphere, she came to a halt in front of the 'Swing', a mid-twentieth century carousel ride with wooden seats. The Swing was an annual feature. In the three years she'd lived on this square, she'd been on a couple of rides every day of this August week. Soon, in about half an hour or so when she was feeling a bit better, she'd nestle on one of the wooden seats again and briefly float away from all the negativity.

She entered an old-fashioned Spiegeltent with brightly coloured stained glass windows.

The heat inside was the kind more commonly associated with tropical rainforests. Exhilarated locals and baffled foreigners were packed in tight, listening to two brassy blondes dressed in sixties skirt suits performing hilarious renditions of old, sentimental Dutch ballads. Tragic songs about girls of ill repute, of poverty-stricken origins or a combination of the two, who met with tragic and premature ends.

Farah barely knew the lyrics, but after her third beer she was quite happily hollering along when she spotted Joshua Calvino in the spirited crowd.

She elbowed her way through the sweaty mass until she was standing right in front of him and with a great deal of feigned surprise tried to make herself heard about the noise.

'You HERE?'

'I live NEARBY.'

'No!'

'YEAH! Where do you live?'

She steered him out of the Spiegeltent and pointed to the flat above Café Del Mondo.

'You win,' Joshua said with a grin. 'Fancy another drink?'

They ordered bottles of Mexican beer and Spanish tapas from a large Mercedes-Benz truck with 'Cantina' written across it in red letters.

'You have no idea what you turned down this afternoon, Mr Detective,' she said half-jokingly after they'd found a seat.

'I think I do.' He squeezed half a lemon into his beer glass. 'It's not every day you meet someone who finds lost earrings for you.'

'I reckon your esteemed colleague has a lot to answer for,' she said between sips. 'You know what he reminds me of?'

'Tell me.'

'The "Fat Man".'

The "Fat Man"?'

'The atomic bomb dropped over Nagasaki.'

Joshua shook his head, but smiled.

'He's my partner,' he said simply.

'Your *partner*,' she said cheekily while chomping on a stuffed olive. 'Is he now? You mean you're taken. What a shame.'

The look he gave her now was the same as when he helped her up in the woods. Remembering his firm hand, she could feel her heart racing.

'Now I know what you think of my colleague,' he said, grinning broadly, 'but not what you think when you picture me.'

'There's no need to picture you, since you're sitting right in front of me.'

'Okay,' Joshua said. 'That gives us two options. Either I'm out of here like a shot and you picture me and tell me about it later, or I stay right here and you tell me now.'

On the other side of the square someone started ringing an ear-splitting bell. 'The Swing!' Farah exclaimed delightedly. She grabbed hold of his hand. 'Let's go!'

She pulled him along and together they zigzagged through the crowd to join the long queue which had formed in front of the carousel. Joshua laughed as he let himself be led by her. Farah called out to the man who'd rung the bell. He gestured for her to walk around the back, where he pushed a fence aside so they could slip unseen on to the platform and take the last available seats.

They sat with their backs touching, which felt like a reverse embrace. He rested his head on her shoulder, his mouth close to her ear. 'I have a confession to make. I can't stand going backwards.'

They burst out laughing.

The steel cables produced a squeaking noise as the carousel slowly chugged into motion. People on the ground waved at them as though they were embarking on a long journey. With each rotation they went a bit faster. Farah could tell by the way the people and the lights on the square started blurring; she could tell by her hair, which was blowing about wildly; she could tell by the tears in her eyes and her difficulty breathing as the wind took her breath away. She could tell by the sounds which were breaking up into snippets, the cheering of the spectators which tightened into high-pitched squeals and cut ever sharper through the spinning sky.

And then the lights on the ride were dimmed. Farah allowed herself to drift away into the hazy eye of a hurricane made of fragmented light and sound. Then came the smoke. Billowing like an ancient genie out of a magic bottle, the artificial mist spread among the whizzing seats. It felt as if they were flying through fluffy clouds. Given the speed they were going at, all the seats were now listing so badly that the square, the people on it and the buildings around it appeared to have been tilted out of true.

Amorphous, forbidding shadows came crawling out of the dark recesses of the sky, hitting Farah in the face like cold gusts of wind. She felt the fear penetrating her body and her eyes dilating. She opened her mouth to scream, but no sound came out.

She saw someone free himself from the crowd on the square and float towards the Swing as if there were no such thing as gravity. It was the boy in his beautiful robe. After each rotation he was a little closer. Farah gestured to him wildly, trying to tell him to stay where he was so he wouldn't be crushed by the fast spinning carousel, but still he came closer and closer.

She began screaming at the top of her lungs, but the boy took no notice of her.

As she charged at him at full speed, he raised his right arm and brought the little bells back to life by stamping his right foot. She uttered a cry of great anguish the moment she hit the boy head-on.

29

Farah had no idea how she'd escaped her spinning hell. All she knew was that she was standing on the square again, closely entwined with Joshua. She could feel his hands going up and down her back. She was trembling and crying like a child who'd just been jolted awake by a nightmare. And yet she knew that what she'd just experienced had really happened.

'It's okay,' she heard Joshua say. 'It's over.' He tenderly took her head in his hands and forced her to look him in the eye.

She knew there were a couple of things she had to do to calm down. The first was to accept that Joshua kept hold of her as they left the square and crossed the street. The second was to let him escort her up the steep wooden staircase. The third was to allow everything he proceeded to do next.

She let herself be laid down gently on the bed. She heard the shower running. Then he pulled off her boots and whispered to her, 'Trust me.'

She allowed him to take off her trousers and help her sit up. He lifted her arms, so he could pull off her long-sleeved top. Then he carried her to the bathroom and placed her under the hot water jet in her underwear, holding on to her all the while. Without a word, she let it all happen. She just kept breathing.

In and out. In and out.

While in the shower, unable to fight the flood of tears, she began crying again. It made her angry. She grabbed hold of Joshua and her open mouth slid across his face and found his mouth. Sweet excitement replaced bitter sadness.

Suddenly she saw herself, as though she'd left her body and was now watching it from a distance. Standing there, half-naked, passionately kissing this detective who was pressed up against her in the shower. The thought of David carrying her into the bedroom last night instantly returned her to her body. She abruptly freed herself from the clinch.

'Sorry. This isn't . . . what I want. I'm fine now.'

He looked as though she'd slapped him in the face.

'I'm sorry,' he said, and she didn't doubt him. 'I'm sorry.'

'Me too,' she replied. 'You'd better go now, Joshua.'

'What about you?'

'Go, Joshua. I mean it.'

Farah couldn't help but smile at the formal way in which he tiptoed backwards out of the bathroom, as if he'd just had an audience with the queen.

'Joshua?'

'Yes?'

'It's okay.'

'I'm going, all right.'

She stood there, in her soaking wet lace underwear, until she heard the door of her apartment slam shut. Only then did she move again. She wrapped a large bath towel around her, retrieved her mobile and keyed in the hospital's number. While waiting for someone to answer, she walked across to the open window. The smells of stale beer and grilled meat wafted in on a slight breeze.

As soon as she saw Joshua look up at her from the square, she stepped back from the window. She was in the middle of the room when she was put through to the ICU and was told what she'd feared all along after her panic attack.

30

Danielle groped around for her mobile phone after a ringtone of chirping birds disturbed her dream. She was fleeing in the darkness through knee-high grass, as the sound of exploding grenades drowned out the screams of the children she'd left behind.

When, in her drowsiness, she finally located her phone under the pile of clothes lying beside her, it felt as if a whole flock of birds flying in every direction in a blind panic had splatted against the freshly-painted walls of her spacious rented house in Amsterdam-Noord.

She muttered a hoarse 'Hello?' and heard the agitated voice of Mariska, the ICU head nurse whom she'd asked to call her immediately if any problems arose.

'The boy's blood pressure dropped suddenly.'

Danielle responded instinctively. 'Give him saline!' She sat up and turned on the bedside light.

'It's already been done.'

'How does the blood gas read now?'

'Listen, Danielle. I shouldn't even be calling you.'

'Take him for a CT scan!' Danielle shouted as she grabbed her jeans.

'This is out of your hands. The trauma surgeon's in charge now. You know that?!'

'I'm on my way!'

Mariska was of course right. According to hospital protocol Danielle had nothing more to say, but she'd promised herself that she'd be there for the boy whenever necessary. As she stumbled down the stairs, all kinds of possibilities of what might be wrong with him rushed through her head. What had she overlooked that she shouldn't have? Within a few minutes she was speeding along the ring road at 150 kilometres an hour headed for the WMC.

At this hour of the night the road was practically deserted. A few kilometres further she heard the birds in her handbag go again. She swerved to the right, pulled on to the hard shoulder and slammed on her brakes. She left the engine running and rummaged in her bag on the passenger's seat looking for her phone. When she finally found it, she was too late picking up.

From the distance came the menacing honking of a lorry that had also swerved right. Hadn't she turned on her hazard lights? Damn, she had no time for this. She quickly hit 'missed calls' on her phone, while pressing down on the gas, and raced off before the truck overtook her.

She steered with her right hand and held the phone to her ear with the left. She was transferred to Mariska, who told her that the surgeon on-call had immediately sent the boy for a CT scan because he suspected his spleen was ruptured.

Danielle cursed aloud in exasperation. She'd missed something: the damage to the spleen was worse than she'd thought, but had only come to light once his blood pressure improved over the course of the day. As soon as it returned to normal, the spleen ruptured.

'Who's the surgeon on-call?' she asked.

'Radder,' Mariska said.

Tears of frustration welled up in Danielle's eyes. Of all people, Radder. Radder was a butcher. He'd make a fifteen-centimetre incision left under the rib cage and remove the whole spleen. Her body was overwhelmed with despair.

'Call me as soon as they know for sure it's the spleen. Radder shouldn't be doing a splenectomy. Under no circumstances!'

'I'll do what I can,' Mariska said, sounding less than convincing. Danielle knew that none of the nurses was prepared to confront Radder. But as long as she was still on her way and couldn't actually speak to Radder in person, it was best to exert her influence on Mariska.

'If it's the spleen, then the boy needs to go to the angiography suite,' she said forcefully. 'He mustn't be taken to the OT. We need to get an interventional radiologist in. The spleen needs a coil embolization, but it shouldn't be removed!'

'You know I don't have a say here, and neither do you,' Mariska said reproachfully. 'Radder's in charge.'

Danielle knew Mariska was right. She was out on a limb.

'Put me through to the OT.'

'Fine,' said Mariska. She sounded relieved.

Meanwhile Danielle had driven two exits too far without having noticed. Her temples throbbed and she was drenched with sweat. She'd just rolled down the window a crack when she heard the voice of Gaby, the OT assistant who'd helped her during the boy's operation.

'Gaby, it's Danielle. Was an emergency operation called in?'

'Correct, a ruptured spleen.'

'It's the boy!' Danielle exclaimed. 'The child we performed surgery on last night. Radder will no doubt go for a splenectomy. But I want the interventional radiologist consulted first.'

'I'll let Dr Radder know that you called with this request.'

'Explicit request!' Danielle corrected her.

'But unfortunately there isn't much more I can do right now.'

'I understand. Please ask him to call me back immediately? I'm on my way.'

It seemed like her whole body had gone numb. Although she was clutching the steering wheel, she couldn't feel her hands. She had no idea how hard she was pushing down on the accelerator, it could just as well have been a pillow. Even the wind on her face at 150 kilometres felt like a faint caress.

The outline of the WMC appeared in the distance. She was pulled back and forth between feeling invincible and being afraid. Without reducing her speed she exited the ring road and drove through two intersections with a blinking yellow traffic light. It was increasingly clear to her that Radder wasn't going to call her back. He would rely on his own inimitable style of butchery, blind to alternatives and deaf to better advice.

When she sped into the parking garage, she was too agitated to find her pass quickly enough to open the gate. She shouted her name into the intercom and indicated she was there for an emergency. She then hurried to the service lift in the main lobby. Moments later, in the dressing room, she threw on OT scrubs and clogs and grabbed a cap and a mask on her way into the operation.

'Anyone we know?' Radder said without even looking up as she raced into the OT.

Danielle caught the helpless gaze of Gaby, who was standing beside him.

'Please not a splenectomy,' Danielle said desperately. 'If you do that, the risk of pneumonia or an infection is too great. His body can't withstand a second operation in just two days! And if he makes it, he'll be susceptible to infections for the rest of his life. You could try using a coil.'

'Seems to be all the rage these days,' Radder coldly replied. 'I'm dealing with spleen tissue here that's significantly torn apart. Stitching it up is almost impossible.'

'Almost,' Danielle interjected. 'At least consider the other options!'

'No time!' Radder snapped. 'I have to keep this patient from bleeding to death. Sorry, Bernson.'

It sounded like he was enjoying himself. The dictatorial smugness in his voice when he asked for the scalpel, which Gaby placed in his open hand, was intolerable for Danielle. She wanted to cry, but restrained himself.

She went and stood on the other side of the table directly across from him and did her best to exude calm.

'You know as well as I do that the risks of living without a spleen still aren't clear. And this child has a whole life ahead of him.'

'Not if I don't do something soon,' Radder replied impatiently.

Danielle could only look on helplessly as Radder made the incision and exposed the ruptured spleen. Gaby suctioned the blood while Radder examined the damage.

'In itself a disappointing turn of events that the rupture was only discovered after the fact.' Radder sounded like a judge sending her down for life.

'I suspect it was a subcapsular hematoma.'

'You didn't take his low blood pressure into account,' he said sharply. 'The consequence of you going it alone, against my express advice to operate on the boy. And lo and behold, the result.' He said this with such gloating triumph that Danielle felt sick to her stomach.

'What I wouldn't do to change this,' she heard herself say.

Her words popped out so spontaneously that her sudden shift in attitude had an immediate effect. Radder looked up at her and she saw the coldness ebb from his eyes for a moment. It was only a fraction of a second, but she was certain of it.

He felt the spleen from all sides. 'Maybe we can salvage a piece of it.'

She wanted to jump for joy. He evidently felt his authority was no longer being questioned, which confirmed his apparent feeling of superiority.

'Bernson,' he said, motioning for her to take a closer look. 'We're going to have to remove this piece.' He pointed at the most damaged part of the spleen. 'This middle tear is beyond repair. But we might be able to save these bits left and right.'

Danielle was silent and nodded obediently. She knew it was important for her to play the role of dutiful student. In the interest of the boy, she had to give the master the floor.

'If they're both viable, then we can push the pieces together, surround them with a net. What do we think, Bernson?'

'Perfect solution.'

'My feeling exactly. And let's just hope the bits grow back together,' Radder said in the arrogant tone he seemed to have a patent on. He immediately began to cut away the damaged part of the spleen.

Within half an hour, the two remaining halves of the spleen were joined using a bio-absorbable net.

'Since you're here anyway, Bernson, why don't you close him up?' Radder grumbled.

A while later, as she escorted the bed with the boy in it through the almost deserted hospital corridors back to the Intensive Care Unit, Danielle felt like she was floating. She helped Mariska reconnect him to all the ICU machines.

'There's someone in the waiting room for him,' Mariska said. 'The same woman who was here yesterday morning.'

Danielle immediately felt herself tense up. The way Farah had made it clear to her this evening that she needn't count on her if she went public with the boy's story was bewildering. Farah *was* involved, she definitely wanted to help the boy, yet at the same time refused to use her resources to reveal the abuses suffered by a victim of child trafficking.

'You have to take a step back, Danielle,' Mariska said. 'Don't let it become an obsession. It's not good for you, not for him either.'

She gazed down at the boy and realized Mariska was right. Because of the immense obligation she felt, she hadn't managed a proper diagnosis during the first operation. A less emotionally involved doctor wouldn't have made such an error.

Perhaps taking the boy under her wing was a big mistake. Less than six months ago she'd deserted panicked children in their beds to save her own skin. Was she just using him now to prove she wasn't a coward? As a way to clear her conscience?

'Did you contact her?' Danielle asked Mariska.

'Who?'

'That journalist.'

'Is she a journalist?'

'Yes, she writes for the *AND*.'

'No, why would I call the newspaper?'

'Then how does she know what's going on?'

'No idea. Why don't you ask her?'

Danielle left the room. She massaged her throbbing temples with her fingers. When she saw Farah Hafez's silhouette in the waiting room, she couldn't help but shiver.

3 I

For the second time in barely twenty-four hours, Farah found herself looking out over nocturnal Amsterdam from the fifth floor of the WMC. She thought of the boy as if he were her own child. A child she hadn't asked for, but who'd entered her world so forcefully that now she couldn't possibly abandon him.

She also thought of Danielle and her urge to go public with the story. Danielle was a doctor, she'd sworn an oath, but now she wanted to go beyond that oath. She was keen to show that it wasn't about saving his life, but about preventing it from being necessary in the first place. The cause needed tackling, so no more children would be left for dead, anywhere in the world.

As far as the boy was concerned, Farah suspected that her own objectives didn't differ all that much from Danielle's. However, their ways of realizing those objectives were miles apart. Given her strong emotional involvement, Danielle opted for the quickest route. But haste makes waste, as they say, and that could well be true in this case. You never know what forces are unleashed by courting publicity without due preparation. But Farah had no say over Danielle's life or, for that matter, her choices.

She heard muffled footsteps behind her back. Reflected in the window, she saw a woman dressed in scrubs. Farah turned around.

'Hello, Danielle. What's happened to him?'

'His spleen ruptured, so we had to remove part of it. He's stable. For now.'

Farah detected a note of detachment in her voice and saw Danielle scrutinizing her.

'How did you know what was happening?'

'I didn't. I phoned because . . .' Farah hesitated and then decided not to tell her about the carousel. Since their previous encounter, the distance between her and Danielle had grown too big for the complex truth.

'Did one of the nurses phone you?' Danielle inquired, suspiciously.

'No.'

'Then who did?'

'I phoned off my own bat. I just told you.'

'Why?'

'Is this a cross-examination?'

'I want to know why you phoned, that's all.'

'I wanted to know how he was doing.'

'After midnight?' As Danielle pursed her lips, her eyes narrowed and her voice shot up. 'So just as he's taking a turn for the worse, you think to yourself, hey, let's give them a call.'

'I'm not going there,' Farah said calmly.

'I just want to know who told you what was happening.'

'Okay. But then I'd like to ask you something first. And I'd like you to give me an honest answer. Did anything go wrong the first time you operated on him?'

Danielle blanched.

'How would you know?'

'I have this strong suspicion and I'd like to know if it's true.'

Again, an ashen veil spread across Danielle's face.

'You can't fool me. You've spoken to someone. Why are you being so secretive about it?'

The woman now standing before her didn't look anything like the calm, self-assured doctor who'd saved the boy's life. This woman was seething with suspicion.

'It's simple. I saw him. It happened twice. The first time was last night, after I'd driven to the woods to take a look at the spot where he was hit. About thirty minutes after you wheeled him into the operating theatre, he suddenly appeared before me. In his dancing clothes. Wearing all of his jewellery. Incredibly lifelike.'

The disbelief on Danielle's face was all too apparent. Against Farah's better judgement, she decided to tell her the rest.

'The same thing happened earlier tonight. But it was even more realistic this time. It felt as though I'd hit him myself.'

The disbelief in Danielle's eyes made way for fear.

'It sounds stupid, but I think the boy is trying to communicate with me,' Farah said falteringly. 'I don't know what it is and I can't explain it either. It must sound rather strange coming from a journalist's mouth.'

She felt she'd laid herself bare and could only hope that Danielle was prepared to take her seriously. Being more candid than this wasn't possible.

'Strange is not the right word,' Danielle said, her voice trembling. 'It's downright bizarre. You know what I don't get? You're not a relative, yet you keep showing up here. You're a journalist, but you don't want to write about him. What are you doing here? Why the interest?'

'The first time was a coincidence. But now I think he may be trying to tell me something. Tell *us* something. Maybe we ought to think less about ourselves and more about him. I don't know.'

Danielle stared at her. 'I don't get you. Why are you bothering me with this nonsense?'

'I was hoping . . .' But Farah didn't get the chance to finish.

'Spare me the rest of your new-age claptrap. Go home. There's nothing you can do for him. In fact I don't even *want* you to do anything for him. Is that clear?'

Farah realized that there was no point arguing.

'Whatever your thoughts are on this, I hope he'll be all right,' she said softly. 'You've done amazing things for him. You saved his life. But what you have in mind is dangerous, Danielle. It could turn against you.'

As she walked down the corridor she felt the blonde doctor's eyes burning into her back.

32

In the car park Danielle waved her ignition key in every direction, but didn't hear the clicking of her car door locks anywhere. She'd spent another hour in the ICU with Farah's warning echoing through her head the entire time. Publicizing the boy's story might be dangerous. It could very well turn against her.

It gradually dawned on her that it wasn't so much a warning, as it was an indirect threat. She now distrusted Farah to the bone. In retrospect, it couldn't have been a coincidence that Farah showed up at the Emergency Department at exactly the same moment the boy was brought in. Danielle needed to share her suspicions with the detectives working on the case.

She anxiously walked up and down the rows of cars in the garage when behind her she suddenly heard door locks open. She was startled, just like she was startled by every random noise these days – a door slamming, a ringing telephone, the click of door locks opening. Her door locks.

Before getting into the car, she instinctively looked around. Since returning from Africa, this had also become part of her routine. A nervous obsession that told her to scan her sur-roundings before going inside anywhere, whether it was a lift, a pub or a car. She didn't see anyone in the car park. Yet, she had the distinct feeling someone was there. This was fuelled by a fear nestled deep inside her. A fear that festered like a virus.

On the ring road heading towards Amsterdam-Noord she stared straight ahead and began to recite her daily mantra. A pep-talk meant to keep her from panicking.

'I'm a doctor. People need me. I'm not spineless!'

Just a few months ago she'd run for her life, through knee-high grass. But she was still fleeing, constantly short of breath, always looking over her shoulder as if death was hot on her heels. The children she'd left behind in the camp kept shouting her name, and not only in her dreams. She heard their cries even when she was awake.

She constantly had to convince herself.

'I'm here. I'm safe. I'm brave.'

In the airplane returning to the Netherlands, she'd suddenly remembered a poem about a gardener. While weeding early one morning, he sees Death taking a stroll and in a panic flees to another city, believing he can outwit the Grim Reaper. But Death, surprised, just wonders what the man is doing in the garden early that morning when he has to pick him up some-where entirely different that same evening.

During that night flight Danielle wondered if the same might happen to her. She'd escaped Death, but perhaps it was just patiently waiting for her thousands of kilometres away in the arrivals hall at Schiphol Airport.

That thought had triggered all the obsessive-compulsive neuroses that would plague her. It was also the first time in her life that she really felt frightened. And for months now that fear reared its ugly head at the most unexpected moments.

She had to circle her neighbourhood three times before she found a parking spot. As she got out, she looked around again. She forced herself not to race to her house. Despite her pound-ing heart, she tried to walk to her front door as calmly as possible. As she rummaged in her bag for her keys, she heard a car slowly approaching in her dead-still neighbourhood. Trembling, she dashed into her house and bolted the door behind her.

In the hallway she braced herself against the wall for a few minutes so she could catch her breath. She had to do some-thing. No mantra was a match for this. She had to take control – overcome her anxiety attacks. She walked up the stairs to her living room, turned on all the lights and poured herself a whisky. She decided she would go for a run the next morning. She'd even done this while she was in Africa. She was athletic and running always made her feel better. She was pleased with this decision. At least it was a start.

After three gulps of whisky she was trembling less. She collapsed on the leather sofa and zapped past inane TV stations until she saw Cathy Marant, in a low-cut shiny blouse, sitting behind a desk hosting *The Headlines Show*. She understood that it was a repeat broadcast from earlier that evening. With the on-air presence of a hyena, Cathy Marant talked about an incident during a martial arts gala in Carré, where according to several sources someone had been seriously injured.

To Danielle's amazement, she was watching the same woman who'd just tried to convince her that she'd had paranormal contact with the badly injured boy mercilessly slamming a defenceless woman against the mat. In the meantime, Cathy Marant looked directly at the camera and, piling on the pathos, stated that Farah Hafez's victim was doing well under the circumstances, but that a journalist, especially one who thought that all illegal immigrants living in the Netherlands should receive a general pardon, needed to be punished for violently battering others in public, and behaving rudely, for that matter.

'There can be no question of a pardon here,' Marant argued. 'Also not a general pardon, Ms Hafez! What will become of our democracy if we allow such things to happen?'

Danielle discovered one amazing thing after another, because in the following item she saw the same detective who'd sternly spoken to her in the hospital the other morning arresting Dennis Faber in the middle of his live TV show and hauling him away like a common criminal. The reason for his arrest, Marant reported, was that the police initially suspected Faber and his wife of being guilty – directly or indirectly – of a hit-and-run involving an underage boy in the Amsterdamse Bos.

Marant denounced the heavy-handed ineptitude of the police. What made it even worse, the detective who'd swooped in appeared to be drunk. Witnesses declared that they smelled something suspicious. Luckily the police quickly realized the magnitude of the mistake they'd made and immediately released the popular presenter and his wife, after it came to light that

Mrs Faber had only seen the boy lying on the road and had called emergency services without delay.

Danielle watched Dennis Faber and his wife coming down the police station steps. Cleared of any alleged involvement. Beleaguered, traumatized celebs who must be buckling under the weight of all this bad publicity.

At that moment, a light went on in Danielle's head. She gathered her thoughts and her plan began to take shape. The Faber couple would be the key to getting the boy's story out into the world. With a starring role for Cathy Marant as well.

She felt the fighting spirit that she thought she'd lost after returning from Africa. This plan would finally allow her to shake off all her obsessive thoughts.

'I'm here. I'm safe. I'm brave.'

33

David was a man who thought about the future, who was forward-looking and had faith in promises. Farah would love to be like that too, but to her promises were like soap bubbles that could burst at any moment. Lies and death were a constant threat.

She was approaching the exit that would take her to David's house. He'd left a message saying that he'd be waiting for her at home. 'However late it gets, darling,' he'd said, before adding something about 'an unexpected breakthrough' he wanted to celebrate with her. When she passed the exit she told herself that at that moment in time she had no control whatsoever over her destiny in life.

The former ship's cabin exuded a warm, inviting glow. Via a wooden gangway she reached the deck of the steel barge where she heard the muffled tones of a jazz combo and, after she'd rapped on the door, the sound of feet on the steps. Joshua Calvino appeared in the doorway without an inkling of surprise.

'I'm sorry,' Farah said, 'for turning up here unannounced.' She knew she was talking to herself more than anyone. 'You know, I'm not normally . . .'

'I don't believe in normal,' he cut her short and led her down the steps to the living quarters below decks. The floor was polished wood and paintings of clouds dotted the boat's walls. 'I love clouds,' Joshua said as he handed her a glass of red wine, 'but I'd rather not have my head in them. Cheers.'

They clinked glasses. She took a sip, put her own glass down, took his out of his hands, pulled him close and began to kiss him long and hard. Although she felt like ripping the clothes from his body, she refrained and carefully unbuttoned his shirt first and then his trousers. She continued to do everything extremely slowly to curb her own excitement. She was the one taking the initiative and she wanted to be as careful and meticulous about that initiative as possible.

She pulled off her top in one fluid movement and unhooked her bra, and in the narrow space between their bodies his hands groped her breasts and massaged her nipples. When she pushed him down, he first slid his tongue across her breasts before moving further down her belly until his head was between her legs and she felt his tongue entering her.

With John Coltrane's *A Love Supreme* playing on vinyl in the background, Joshua was on his knees, as though worshipping a half-naked statue of the Madonna. Farah let herself be worshipped. She felt he was liberating her from the nightmarish twilight that had enveloped her and, feeling light-headed, she grabbed his hair with both hands when he made her come with his tongue.

She could taste herself when she proceeded to give Joshua a long and intense French kiss. Then she took his hand and led him to the bed, lay down on her back, pulled him towards her and lovingly ordered him to fuck her as hard as possible.

Tears came to her eyes when, with both arms resting on the mattress and with a yell from somewhere very deep down, he came inside her.

She didn't want to let go of him. If necessary, she'd lie here for the rest of the night, with his still-shuddering body on top of hers. But he slid off and lay down next to her, his eyes on the ceiling. Farah turned on her side, caressing him. But the smile on her lips was full of doubt, as the boy slipped through the vents of her subconscious and she knew that sooner or later he'd make another appearance. Not quietly, like Raylan Chapelle, who'd simply sidled up to her in the afternoon, but suddenly and forcefully. The way he'd suddenly appeared before her in the carousel, giving her no choice but to hit him head-on.

'Joshua?'

'Yes?'

'I'm scared.'

He sat up and turned to face her. 'There's no need. I'm with you.'

The needle of the record player had been circling the final groove of the LP for ages. She sat up and felt dizzy.

Joshua put his hand on her shoulder. 'What's wrong?'

'From the very first moment I laid eyes on that boy, something quite extraordinary happened. I looked at him and felt – apologies if this sounds stupid – I felt as if he was a part of me; a forgotten part. As if I were his age again and recognized him as the little brother I never had but used to fantasize about.'

'Do you remember what that forgotten part looked like?' he asked tenderly.

As she thought about the afternoon she felt a burning sensation in her eyes. She looked at him long and hard and thought that maybe this is why she'd come to him. After all the unexpected ghosts and echoes from the past, here was a chance to open up her heart to someone who'd marvel at it.

'I don't really know, to be honest,' she said. 'I don't know what I've made up about my former life in Kabul and what really happened.'

'How old were you when you came to the Netherlands?'

'I must have been nine. But I gave a different date of birth.'

'Why?'

She swallowed a couple of times before she replied.

'Because I was scared. My father was Aadel Gailani. He served as Minister of Interior Affairs in President Daoud's cabinet for three years. When the communists attacked the presidential palace with planes and tanks in April 1978, he and the President were assassinated, along with thousands of others.' She spoke slowly, as if trying to convince herself that this was how it had all happened.

'My mother was a lawyer. Her name was Helai. Helai Durani. The communists arrested her during the coup too, but eventually released her. She'd been tortured. We fled together, a couple of months after the Russians invaded the country. That was late 1979. The coldest winter I've ever experienced.'

'What happened to your mother?'

'She didn't survive the journey. She . . . I don't want to talk about it now, Joshua.'

He caressed her. 'So you were alone when you arrived in the Netherlands?'

'Ultimately, yes. To begin with, there was a small group of us. A family with two children. I didn't know them, but I was supposedly their third child. They stayed behind in Germany. I continued on to the Netherlands.'

'And then what? Where were you given asylum?'

'In a refugee centre in Drenthe. That's where I fell ill. Seriously ill. Double pneumonia. I was taken to a hospital, where I spent two months. The doctors told me it was a close call. One day I received a visit from an older man and his wife. He was a physician and a friend of the doctors at the hospital. The couple had no children, and when I got better I moved in with them. The months in hospital were almost like a form of quarantine but it allowed me to slowly get used to the life and language here. As soon as I was on the mend again, I began reading. Adventure stories. *The Secrets of the Wild Wood. The Letter for the King. Nobody's Boy. The Brothers Lionheart.*'

She showed him the photograph she always carried in her purse: a strapping little girl with pale-brown skin and startlingly blue eyes, thick, dark-brown hair that fell well below her shoulders and a bold look in her eyes. On the back it said, FARAH, 12 YEARS OLD.

'I was an anxious child.'

'It doesn't show.'

'I kept it hidden. Even from myself.'

She got up and walked naked across the wooden floor to the half-open porthole.

'It didn't matter where I was,' she resumed softly, 'in school, during the day, halfway through dinner at home, and very often in bed at night. It would feel like I was plucked from reality and dropped in a cinema where I was forced to watch the most gruesome things. And then I'd panic. Because no matter what I did, the film kept playing and I had no choice but to keep watching. Except I knew it wasn't a film. It all really happened.'

Recounting the story had worn her out, but she wasn't ready to stop yet.

'Between the moment they assassinated my father and detained my mother and the moment I arrived in the Netherlands, I'd seen and experienced so much I couldn't understand that I didn't have the words to tell others about it. All I could do was try to forget.'

Joshua gazed at her for a long time, a sad look on his face. 'Was there anything you did want to remember?'

'My father showing me martial arts moves in the garden. My mother in a beautiful gown reciting the wisdom of Rumi at a picnic, "It is time for you to go out into the world and learn from it what you can."'

She stopped there, sought his mouth, his tongue. She sought everything that might give her comfort.

34

Until late in the night, consumed by his desire to win and under the influence of the beating he was taking, Marouan had been unable to pull himself away from the poker table. When he finally staggered outside, he did so as the pathetic owner of a larger debt. With much difficulty, he restrained himself from hurling both his shoes at the statue of Rembrandt van Rijn, peering down at him with pitying eyes from his marble pedestal on the square.

He crossed back over the Blauwbrug with only one desire. To dissolve into thin air. To disappear. For good. He slowed his steps for a moment and gazed across the Amstel. People were largely made of water. He could throw himself into the river here. Escorted by a pair of swans he would float away into oblivion. Fish and crabs would first nibble at the soft tissue of his face. His skin would wrinkle and soften and eventually fall off his bones. And once the decomposition gases were expelled, his bloated body would end up somewhere at the bottom of the Noordzeekanaal. Cruise ships, pleasure yachts and barges would pass over him while eels slithered around in his body cavities.

Instead of jumping he walked back along the cobblestoned streets to the Oude Kerk. He pretended that time had stood still. That he hadn't walked away from here earlier that evening. That he hadn't gambled. That he'd stood here the whole time. From a distance he watched the younger version of Aisha still standing there in her panties and bra behind the large window, luring male passers-by inside with a smile, a seductive wink and her delicate hand gestures.

Enough interest. They all wanted her. Just like all the men of his village had wanted Aisha at the time. But *he* had been given her. He, Marouan Diba. With the promise that their children would grow up in a new world, he'd won the heart of the most desirable girl in the village.

It was wintertime when he left the arrivals hall at Schiphol with her. He thought she'd be impressed, just like he'd been when he first landed there. But she didn't say anything. He interpreted her initial silence as astonishment. Not as numbness, an unfeeling acceptance of fate, as it later turned out to be.

He had no idea how accustomed she was to living according to how others dictated. Aisha didn't live the way *she* wanted to, but the way she was expected to live. By her father, her family, by Allah. Her feelings were not taken into consideration. Just like her marriage to the policeman was ultimately not part of her story, but that of her parents.

During their wedding night Aisha had let go of her reticence for the first time. She'd given in to his every wish. And blinded by sexual desire he'd mistaken obedience for passion.

If it had been Aisha's own wish to obey him, perhaps the story would have turned out differently. But her obedience stemmed from a fear of deviating from the path that her family had mapped out for her. Aisha married out of fear, not out of love. She gave Marouan two children and raised them guided by the same fear. It was too late by the time he realized that Chahid and Jamila weren't rebellious because they were teenagers, but because they wanted to free themselves from that fear.

He began hitting them: his beloved wife and his children. He beat all three of them, just like he'd seen his father do, and he only stopped on the day Chahid finally hit him back. It was too late now for atonement, or for questions about the whys of everything. Any kind of regret and all possible answers were long overdue.

He finally ended up back in the car park to pick up the Corolla, and he aimlessly rode around the city for a time. Hours later, when he drove on to the ring road, the early morning sun glared in his windscreen.

Aisha and Chahid were already up when he parked the car in front of the house. He woke Jamila, silently grabbed the suitcases and bags from the hallway and piled them into the trunk. He estimated that he'd have to pay a hefty overweight charge. They drove to Schiphol without speaking. Jamila listened to music on her iPhone with her eyes closed and Chahid stared out the window with a disinterested gaze. Aisha's eyes were focused straight ahead.

At the check-in desk Marouan paid for all the excess baggage. He handed Chahid the tickets and escorted them to Customs. Every step felt like a stabbing pain. He said he'd call them every day.

He watched them disappear into the large departure hall. They didn't look back.

35

When Farah woke up, Joshua was no longer lying beside her. She thought of how he'd held her with the canal water splashing softly against the boat. The gentle movements of their bodies. He'd caressed her small scars, kissed them without asking questions. And amidst the murmur of his reassuring words, the calming timbre of his whisper, her eyes had slowly closed.

'Go to sleep. I've got you.'

She put on her T-shirt and walked past Joshua's digital weather station with its flashing green weather symbols and red numbers. It reminded her of the monitors on the Intensive Care Unit where the boy was being treated. Last night she'd given the staff at the WMC her number, but her mobile display didn't indicate she'd missed any calls.

She found Joshua crouching on the afterdeck. Some swans were gathered around him in a semicircle, like a group of disciples. He spoke to them warmly as he fed them, and the swans actually seemed to be listening. But as soon as one of them spotted her the magic evaporated. Joshua turned around. His smile betrayed that he'd known all along that she was standing there. He beckoned her closer.

'Will they be okay?' she asked warily.

'Sure, as long as you don't pull any Pencak Silat moves on them.'

'In your fantasies,' she teased. 'What do you know about Pencak Silat?'

He slowly pulled her close. She didn't put up any resistance and allowed his hand to find her breasts underneath her T-shirt, while the fingers of his other hand played with the string of the thong between her buttocks. She closed her eyes and was about to kiss him passionately when she felt they were being watched.

On the bridge across the canal a man was training his telephoto lens on them. He looked like he'd stepped straight out of a Marlboro commercial and didn't even seem embarrassed about being spotted. When Farah showed signs of wanting to run after him he quickly snapped a few more shots before striding away.

Joshua stopped her.

'Just about every foreigner thinks of downtown Amsterdam as an open-air museum, and of us as the extras,' he said calmly. 'I'm used to it.'

'But what we were doing . . . he's got pictures of it.'

'And back home he'll show them to his mates and tell them just how liberated we are here in the Sodom and Gomorrah of the Lowlands. Allow a tourist his illusions. Or would you like me to arrest him?'

'He didn't look like a tourist to me,' Farah said suspiciously.

Joshua shrugged. 'Probably an American from one of the cruise ships, doing a tour of the historic city centre first thing in the morning. You've no idea how often I've been photographed on deck by the Chinese, Arabs, Americans, you name it. I bet I'm world famous without even realizing it.'

In the tiny shower cubicle Farah tried to rinse away her discomfort while listening to Joshua humming along to a Vivaldi violin concerto. When she reappeared above deck fifteen minutes later, she was practically bowled over. A large fold-down table boasted a festive selection of Japanese bowls filled with consommé, porridge, pressed cucumber salad, jam, ginger and miso soup with steamed pak choi and lemon.

It was all too wonderful. Too light. Too carefree. Her vibrating phone and the appearance of Edward's name on the display brought her back down to earth. She gestured to Joshua that she'd be back in a couple of minutes and walked to the afterdeck.

'Hafez? I want you at the press conference this afternoon,' Edward said as soon as she answered.

'Good morning to you too, Ed. I'll be in The Hague this afternoon. Parliament is debating the general pardon.'

'Hafez, at times I think our dear Lord put you on this earth for the sole purpose of tormenting me. Speaking of which, is it true you haven't been in touch with that Russian since you landed her in hospital?'

'Says who?'

'Marant on *The Headlines Show* last night.'

'It was on TV as well?!'

'Of course. When Marant has something spectacular to report, she exploits both *De Nederlander* and *The Headlines Show*. Kills two birds with one stone!'

'After the fight I actually went to the hospital to see how the Russian was doing. That's when the boy was brought in.'

'Good to know. Because we need to keep the boy out of this. Otherwise things will get tangled up. And we can't let Marant get wind of our investigation. What if I move that press conference to five o'clock? Will you be able to make it then?'

'Do I have to, Ed? Can't it wait?'

'I've got a bad feeling that Marant is up to something. That woman will go to any lengths to throw mud at us. I'm eager to nip it in the bud. Especially now that we've launched the investigation. By the way, what's that I hear in the background? Are you on the water?'

'Yes, er . . . Ed, I need to go and finish breakfast.'

'You never eat breakfast, Hafez.'

'Mind your own business. See you later.'

'One more thing: Paul? You've got until this afternoon to make up your mind. If you haven't decided by then, I'll decide for you. Call me, all right?'

For a split second, everything seemed to stop. She realized that she couldn't put off making a decision forever. Her past had needed a long run-up, but finally it was about to catch up with her. Paul was the one who'd raise the dead. She wanted to tell Edward that she wasn't ready yet, that she'd never be ready.

'I'll be in touch, you old grouch.'

The instant she hung up she felt a familiar despair take hold of her. The morning's earlier lightheartedness was gone.

'Bad news?' Joshua asked, sounding worried.

'My boss.' She forced a smile. 'He wants to organize a press conference in response to my fight at Carré the night before last, and the way I was portrayed in *De Nederlander*. He reckons they're waging a smear campaign.'

'Who are "they"?'

'*De Nederlander* and IRIS TV. It's actually not aimed at me specifically, it's more of a vendetta against the *AND* in general, if I'm not mistaken.'

'I don't get it. What's a martial arts gala got to do with a vendetta against the newspaper where you work?'

Farah took a sip of her tea. 'Armin Lazonder is the owner of IRIS TV.'

'Lazonder, the property tycoon?'

'That's right. Two years ago he set his sights on the *AND*. He wanted a broadsheet as part of his media conglomerate. One of the fiercest opponents of that impending takeover was my boss, Edward Vallent. He waged an impassioned campaign against it, both in the paper's editorials and in the media at large. He wanted to avoid at all cost that "his paper", the *AND*, one of the last remaining independent quality newspapers, would fall into the hands of someone he considers to be one of the most crooked property tycoons this country has ever known. Ed's no stranger to a bit of melodrama. But it was partly due to his efforts that the *AND*'s management refused to get on board. The sale never went through.

'In the end Lazonder bought *De Nederlander*. Since then he's been trying to buy up our best people and *De Nederlander* is out to screw us every time we make a mistake or slip. But they've never stooped to personal attacks before. Now, after the incident at Carré, they're doing so for the first time. They want to make their readers believe it was assault. By putting me in a bad light they're hoping to cast doubt on the credibility of all of the *AND*'s journalists.'

'And is it working? Do people believe this kind of claptrap?'

'Lots of people hang on Cathy Marant's every word. She can make them believe anything.'

Farah looked at her breakfast. The small dishes and bowls looked like something from a dream, just like the entire boat felt like something from another world – and she didn't belong here. She thought about David and what she'd say to him.

Without a word, they sat opposite one another. Neither of them ate anything. The sight of Joshua's inquiring gaze made her feel sad.

'Do you have any coffee?' she asked tentatively.

36

The editorial assistant Danielle was transferred to sounded just as bored and arrogant as the other people from IRIS TV she'd had on the line up until then. It took some effort to stay calm as she explained yet again that she was calling about the case related to Dennis and Angela Faber.

'Are you from the police?'

'No, I'm a doctor.'

'What do you have to do with the case then?'

'Everything.'

'Can you be more specific?'

'I have important info.'

'What kind of info?'

'Confidential info. I'm only interested in talking to the person in charge.'

'Hold on.'

Muzak.

'This is Jessica speaking.'

'Who?'

'Jessica Zomer, from *The Headlines Show*. With whom am I speaking?'

'Danielle Bernson. I'm a traumatologist at the WMC and I . . .'

'Sorry, ma'am, but does this have anything to do with the item in today's broadcast?'

'No. Uh, well. I . . . '

'Could you be a bit clearer, ma'am?'

Danielle exploded.

'Listen, Jessica, I think it's best if you put me through to your editor-in-chief!'

'Hold on.'

By now Danielle was like a tightly strung violin, and rather nervous because she realized what she was about to do was morally reprehensible. But she saw no other way.

'Alexandra Mons, editor-in-chief, *The Headlines Show*. How can I help?' This was the resolute voice of a woman who was used to doing ten things at a time, or so it sounded. She probably had a phone to each ear and two laptops in front of her, while she was also keeping an eye on eight screens in the control room.

'You're speaking to Danielle Bernson. I'm calling you in connection with the hit-and-run of an unidentified boy in the Amsterdamse Bos and the arrest of Dennis Faber. I'm the doctor who was first on the scene.'

There was a long silence. On the other end of the line she heard the rapid ticking of a keyboard, an instruction to zoom in and a schedule being communicated. Followed by a mechanical 'Yes?' directed at Danielle.

'Mrs Faber was picked up as a suspect in the hit-and-run of the boy.'

'Mrs Faber was released,' Alexandra Mons replied curtly.

'That's right. But what everyone has overlooked is the fact that her emergency call made it possible for me to save the boy's life.'

The ticking on the other side of the line suddenly stopped. It sounded like people were whispering in the background. Alexandra had muffled the phone with her hand, but Danielle thought she heard her say 'wait a minute' to somebody. Then the conversation took a more positive turn, 'Continue, Ms Bernson.'

'Reputations have been damaged by the erroneous intervention of the police. I think the record needs to be set straight.'

'And what would you suggest?'

'I'm no PR expert. I'm a doctor. But I could arrange access for the Fabers to visit the ICU, with a camera crew in tow. Perhaps a short item about how Mrs Faber heroically performed her civic duty and thanks to this a boy's life was saved. As far as we know the boy has no family.'

There was a pause on the other end of the line before Alexandra Mons asked the obvious question.

'What's in it for you, Ms Bernson?'

'I'm only interested in the truth. Ever heard of something called Bacha Bazi?'

'No. Does it have something to do with the boy?'

'The boy was probably abused by older men. It's some kind of traditional Afghan ritual. The boy is a victim of a child trafficking network. You ask what's in it for me? I want the story made public.'

'So it's a matter of killing two birds with one stone. Angela and Dennis Faber are rehabilitated and the boy's story gets out. Is that what you've got in mind?'

'Precisely.'

'Well, Ms Bernson. It's very clear to me. In fifteen minutes I have a meeting of my editorial staff about tonight's broadcast. I'll certainly run your idea by them. As soon as I know more, I'll call you back. Later in the morning. Agreed?'

Danielle's mind was racing.

'There's also interest from other broadcasters. So if you think it's something for your viewers, best not to waste too much time,' she bluffed.

Less than fifteen minutes later, her phone rang.

'Dr Bernson, you're speaking to Cathy Marant. I'd like to discuss a few matters with you, and then I'm prepared to make you an offer.'

37

Joshua Calvino tailed Farah's Carrera into the woods and followed her example by parking on the right shoulder, the same spot where she'd left her car the day before. He blamed himself for not returning to the scene of the crime earlier. But the previous day's developments, the apprehending of the Faber couple, the commotion caused by this, the overtime and all the paperwork related to questioning them simply delayed this part of the investigation.

He hadn't slept last night. Not because he couldn't, but because he didn't want to. He wanted to spend every second looking at her. At her body, which couldn't lie still for a minute. He just wanted to keep listening to her irregular, at times rushed, breathing. She slept as if constantly switching from trotting to sprinting. He'd felt her relax when he drew nearer and carefully put his arm around her. And as he lay beside her, he realized it was best not to delude himself. Everything told him that Farah Hafez was a woman who was only passing through.

She stepped out of her car and he did the same. The early morning sunlight cut through the trees. There was no traffic on the woodland road. Joshua crossed to the other side a few paces behind her. Silent, but with his head awash with emotions and snap decisions. The most important of these was pure self-preservation. He wasn't about to lose himself in a relationship that would leave him marked for life. He wasn't going to fall for this woman who was traipsing through the woods a few steps in front of him. He would arm himself, protect his independence. Even more so than in past years.

She turned around.

'I rang you from here yesterday.'

He suddenly felt like he was approaching an inevitable end, a point where everything from their very first meeting until this moment would be erased and he would return to being his old predictable self.

When he'd bumped into her last night in the Spiegeltent at the festival downtown he'd been surprised by his own behaviour, his openness and lightheartedness. It was such an inexplicable moment that Einstein would have probably had a theory about it. Time, gravity and energy had played on his feelings. All his positive particles had collided, taken over, and he'd become a better version of himself.

His instincts, his inherent need to control a situation, hardly ever allowed this. He preferred to avoid surprises in his everyday life; he believed in the logic of cause and effect. This didn't mesh with a scenario filled with unpredictable developments. Immense, disruptive emotions were not allowed. Control kept him sharp. That's why he was so good at his job: he was a pro at analysing. Everything had a reason, nothing happened just like that, and everything ordinary mortals considered coincidence was nothing more than an uncommon, but not necessarily inexplicable, collision of unique circumstances.

So the boy injured in the hit-and-run hadn't ended up here by a quirk of fate. There were explanations for this turn of events. Vile but logical explanations. And he would find them, even though he didn't have a convincing explanation right now. Barely twenty-four hours ago there was a burnt-out station wagon with two charred corpses here, and then this woman appeared – he immediately knew she'd turn his life upside down. Now the latter frightened him. He couldn't find any more logic in what had happened between them since they'd first met.

She stood still. 'This is the spot.'

'Are you sure?'

'Very sure.'

He took out his handkerchief and tied it at eye level around a low-hanging branch to mark the spot where she found the earring.

Some of the branches nearby appeared to be broken. There was blood on the earring. Someone had made the boy's earlobe bleed, or perhaps a branch had wounded him. That must be it. The boy had been running. And when he was fleeing, the earring got caught on something and was ripped from his earlobe. The forensics team should be able to find traces of blood here.

He suddenly realized how foolish this whole morning expedition was. Besides the fact that he and Farah were currently contaminating the forensic evidence in the area where the boy had probably run with their own footprints, he'd soon be obliged to explain in one way or another *how* the earring had ended up in his possession. Finding the earring had made Farah an official witness in this case, and if that wasn't bad enough, she was also a journalist. He didn't want her to become caught up in this whole affair in this way. It had to be prevented, only he wasn't sure at this moment how.

'You can see the villa from here.'

He followed her guiding finger. Semi-hidden by the foliage was the dreary outline of a dilapidated building with closed shutters.

'Can you show me how you walked to get here?'

She nodded. At the top of the hill, about fifty metres from the villa, she stopped again. She shivered.

'What is it?'

'Don't you feel it?'

He looked at her questioningly.

'You go ahead without me,' she said. 'I've been there once; that's enough.'

He walked on alone, slowly looking around. On his guard. In front of the villa was a patio with black and yellow tiles. Is that what he thought it was? He squatted to get a closer look. Drag marks mixed with streaks of dried blood. He carefully took a step back to avoid contaminating the evidence on the patio with his footprints. In the fine gravel beside the house, he saw that the trail continued and met up with other marks, which seemed to originate from the side of the villa. At the point where the two sets of marks came together, the gravel was scattered. Joshua could tell that a car had been parked here. This was where the two bodies had been lifted into a vehicle.

Joshua saw the burning station wagon again, in living colour in front of him. He kept an eye on Farah, who was following his every move from a distance and he nodded in her direction. Had she simply over-reacted to the chilly atmosphere surrounding the building? Maybe she had a sixth sense for things that other people don't normally pick up. With a gift like that and his analytical ability, they'd make the perfect investigative team. He immediately put the thought out of his head and walked back in her direction.

'Someone was dragged out of the house,' he said. 'Someone who was injured. A second victim collapsed there. They were dumped into a car.'

'The station wagon?'

'There's a number of tyre tracks running through each other. One of them could certainly be the station wagon.'

'So it's related to the boy?' she asked.

'It seems to be,' Joshua said as he looked around. 'I have to put some things into motion here.'

'What things?'

'The forensics team needs to go over this entire area. We also need to find a way to get into the house. It wouldn't surprise me if it was full of evidence.'

'Do you still need me now?'

Of course, he wanted to say, not only now, but for always. Except he could only muster a detached, 'No, not for now.'

'Then I really need to go,' she said with something of a tired glance. 'I've got a busy day ahead of me.'

He wished he could do something, could say something to show he didn't want her to go. Or that he'd go with her and leave that cursed house for what it was. But she beat him to it.

'This is much bigger than we actually realize, right?'

He wasn't sure if she was talking about what had happened between them, or about the investigation.

'You could be right. In any case, I'll have to indicate in my report that you found the earring.'

'Of course,' she replied with a frankness that made it clear to him that they'd been talking about the case the entire time.

'This also means the police will want to officially question you. About what brought you here in the first place and what you found,' he added somewhat sternly.

'Damn it, Joshua, is that really necessary?'

'Standard procedure,' he answered uneasily.

'That's some way of saying, "thanks for all your help."'

He felt every muscle in his body tense up. Why hadn't he said something to Tomasoa yesterday? He'd acted on impulse, which had resulted in a stupid mistake. He'd concealed the fact that a journalist was also involved in the case and that she was the one who'd discovered an important piece of evidence. He'd never hear the end of this once Tomasoa knew. Diba had gone along with him, but when push came to shove he could blame Calvino.

He felt threatened and he knew why. Normally he had a good overview, knew exactly what he was doing. But since he'd literally stretched out his hand to a sopping wet journalist in the middle of the night, he hadn't been himself. Even yesterday, during their visit to her editor, he'd played the cool cop in his Gucci shades. An exaggerated form of showing off. It's one thing to do that as a teenager, but as a seasoned detective? He'd gently stood her under the shower last night, to make her feel like he understood what she was going through. But at the end of the day he wasn't interested in the woman's troubles as much as the woman herself.

38

The Carrera sped down the A4 at 130 kilometres per hour, on its way to The Hague.

Farah was driving on autopilot. She was thinking of Joshua Calvino and wondering whether there was a significant other. She hadn't asked. In fact, she'd asked very little. She knew hardly anything about him, and certainly not what he felt for her. If it had been a combination of pity and lust, she'd certainly not felt any pity, more a respectful compassion. And as for the sex, she was the one who'd taken the initiative. At most, she could reproach him for responding so highly efficiently.

It surprised her that the owner of that beautifully restored barge wasn't only an inventive lover, but also a good listener. He felt like a soulmate. She'd never experienced anything like it before, and it made the memory of her first encounter with Paul, thirty years ago, all the more vivid. She'd only been a child, but she clearly remembered the intense confusion she'd felt afterwards.

Paul had been the very first boy she'd had erotic fantasies about. After that encounter, her thoughts and emotions stirred until they found release in an explosive rush. Her young girl's body had started burning and every movement hurt. She was confined to bed with a fever for three days and three nights. The doctor thought it might be a virus. Her mother sat beside her, dabbing her forehead and wrists with damp cloths. Farah remembered the look of despair in her mother's eyes and the words she muttered that first night. '*To kho ne bachem, ami tu kho ne.*' Not you too, sweetheart. Not you too. Farah didn't know what she meant, but the words resonated with an intense sadness. It took a whole week before she'd fully recovered and she was able to rejoin her father under the apple tree in the early morning. She'd decided not to reveal the real cause of her 'illness' to her parents, but somehow or other her mother seemed to know. It was the look in her eyes. A look of recognition.

She started at the sound of her ringtone. David. In an impulse to confess everything that had happened last night, she answered straightaway.

'Where were you last night?' He sounded hoarse.

'I'm sorry. I really am,' she said dejectedly.

'You really missed something, darling. We've been given the green light for the Verne Project. It's a done deal!'

Thank God, she thought to herself. No awkward questions, no reproaches or melodrama.

'That's great, love,' she reacted, sounding forced. She tried to muster a little more enthusiasm. 'Congratulations!'

'What's up?'

'What do you mean?'

'You sound different.'

He was on to her. David had crossed the ball, now all she needed to do was head it in. *Tell him. Tell him!*

'I didn't get much sleep.' At least that wasn't a lie.

'Why? Feeling guilty?' He still sounded upbeat.

'I spent practically half the night at the hospital. The boy suffered a ruptured spleen.'

'Heavy. Now what? Are you on the road?'

'Yes, I'm on my way to The Hague. For the general pardon.'

'Please drive carefully, I'd like to have you in one piece tonight. We'll celebrate. I want to set off in three months' time, so we've got some decisions to make. You can sublet your flat now. We're off!'

She'd never heard David sound so elated before. Oh darling, she thought, I need to tell you something. I screwed another man last night and it was divine.

'Edward wants me to do a press conference this afternoon. I don't know what time it finishes.'

'That's fine, sweetheart,' he said happily. 'We've been blessed by the gods. What matters now is that we make the right

decisions, you and me. Keep me posted about your whereabouts. Hey, Farah?'

'Yes?'

'I've really missed you. I've become something of a Farah
junkie. And I want to be hooked on you for the rest of my life.'
He laughed exuberantly.

'I love you too,' she replied mechanically, and then hung up.
All of a sudden she felt like stepping on the gas and overtaking
everything and everyone at full throttle, faster than the speed
of sound, faster than the speed of light, to arrive somewhere
without memories, without sweet temptations and, above
all, without betrayal.

PART TWO
Ghost

Everything around him seemed to be spinning while he himself remained still in the centre. But perhaps that was just an illusion too.

For some time it had been very dark and very quiet. He felt like he was lying in the palm of a giant hand, which kept rocking him back and forth, gently, somewhere nobody could reach him, somewhere between heaven and earth. But he wasn't dead yet.

Noises began trickling through an invisible crack in the darkness.

At first they were distant and distorted, like the faint signal of a radio station: market sounds, people shouting at each other, clothes being washed in the river and then beaten out, the engine of an old diesel truck which got stuck in the mud. But gradually the sounds became clearer. Human voices in a strange language. Men yelling harsh orders, alternating with female voices that sounded firm and occasionally tentative.

Next, he detected the faces, as if his eyes were slowly getting used to the dark. In the beginning the faces were indistinct blurs with lifeless eyes. He briefly thought he saw himself, that he saw his own *eyes. But they were set in the face of a naked woman studying the many small scars on her body in a mirror.*

It got him thinking: if I recognize my own eyes in a face, it means I can still see. And if I'm thinking, it means I still have my thoughts.

That's when the stars emerged from behind the clouds. He saw them through the window of the car driving him through the rain. And he saw his own reflection in the steamed-up glass. This time his eyes were set in the face of a girl who could pass for his twin sister. The girl had black kohl around her eyes and greasy lipstick on her mouth. As he traced his mouth with his fingers the girl did the same. Then the girl pulled at the crescent moon earring and he felt pain in his earlobe.

The sequinned sandals pinched his toes. After each faltering step in the unfamiliar house the grip around his upper arm tightened. The hand forced him further down the corridor, through doors and rooms that were dead quiet save for their footsteps.

The man who stepped from the shadows had his father's eyes. His gun was shiny, as was his black suit. Then he heard a thumping sound and the man who'd escorted him down the corridor hit the floor beside him. The sound was that of his own heart. The man in the black suit grabbed hold of him and ran outside. The hammering in his chest and his panting alternated with shots, breaking glass, yelling and finally with a dull metal thud when he was hit by the white light.

He was floating in the light. There was something wrong with his body. He couldn't move. For the longest time, a blonde woman was hunched over him. He felt cold. The pain wore him out. His eyes fell shut. Out of the darkness, the woman he'd seen naked in front of the mirror appeared. Her eyes were blue. Unlike all the men earlier, she didn't speak a different language. She spoke his *language. She said his father would come and collect him. He just had to wait a while.* 'Aram bash bachem. U alan miyaya.' *Keep calm, sweetheart. He'll be here soon.*

She also wanted to know his name, but he was too tired to even try to find the words. Still, what she said lessened the pain. Maybe he was dead after all. And she was his angel. A beautiful Angel of Death.

'Ma peshet mebasham,' *she said. I won't leave you.*

I

Downtown Johannesburg teemed with honking minibuses. Groups of children in their school uniforms ran along the pavement, past high-rise residential flats filled with immigrants who'd travelled in huge numbers from all over Africa to Egoli, place of gold, as Johannesburg is referred to in Zulu.

Despite the bustle of activity, the obvious security on the street and the urban conversions that were meant to make this part of the city more attractive to everyone, you primarily saw black faces. And as a white man – here in 'Mugger's Paradise' – Paul Chapelle knew you were still asking for trouble. All the same, by now he'd worked as a freelance journalist in Jo'burg for three years and he'd simply ignored this from day one.

Most of his articles were published in *The Citizen*, one of the few South African newspapers that hadn't yielded to the temptation of splattering the most heinous of crimes across the front page. Paul found this repeated accounting of crimes without any context completely pointless. He was interested in writing in-depth pieces; stories that provided insights. *The Citizen* offered him that opportunity.

He went to live in the black township Alexandra, among its half-million black residents, to report on the daily misery there that sharply contrasted with life in neighbouring Sandton, Johannesburg's affluent and mainly white business centre. Mandela had once said that South Africa was a rainbow nation, but in between the slums and the glass and steel skyscrapers Paul saw primarily the black–white disparity. Although the ANC had improved the living conditions of many poor blacks, the South African middle class had also acquired a better standard of living and therefore, on closer inspection, the glaring gap between rich and poor in Mandela's rainbow nation had basically remained the same. It's true, you saw a fair number of wealthy blacks scattered among the wealthy whites, but for most poor blacks, the location and possibility of mingling remained inaccessible, a pipe dream.

And that was precisely what led to pent-up frustration and growing hatred, not only directed at affluent whites, but also against the ANC, whose leaders were suspected of lining their pockets. It was just a matter of time before a populist leader, a political demagogue, would mobilize an army of frustrated blacks and put an end to South Africa's fragile democracy.

This feeling of doom pervaded the air, but despite all of the city's troubles and contradictions Paul loved Jo'burg: its beating heart of traffic jams, the endless honking, shouting and feverish activity. The city was like a blender where hope and hate, visions of the future and harsh realities, lies and truths were shaken up every day anew.

From afar he saw the kiosk owner waving the international edition of the *Algemeen Nederlands Dagblad* in the air. It appeared every Friday.

'Same as usual, Mr Chapelle?'

'Same shit as usual,' he replied with a laugh.

Moments later, with the *AND*, *The Guardian* and *The New Yorker* tucked under his arm, he entered Stella's Coffee Bar— where he always ordered his macchiato mixed with a double espresso – and started to thumb through the *AND*. He closely followed the path his uncle Edward Vallent had set out for the paper and, he had to give him credit, it was still a successful one. Edward had managed to attract a stable of young journalists who really threw themselves into their work, even if they were still wet behind the ears.

But today Paul was having trouble concentrating. His eyes glanced at the bold headlines and the black-and-white photos on the front page, but his brain wasn't registering anything. His thoughts constantly wandered back to the emptiness that had taken hold of his life in recent months. He hadn't found a way to rid himself of the feeling, and he couldn't stop obsessing about it either. It was like constantly running your tongue along a rotted tooth.

Until six months ago, Paul had lived in Jo'burg just like he'd done before in Istanbul, Athens, Paris and Amsterdam. Always on the lookout for the next story.

Paul had inherited his father's genes and with that came an acute and unrelenting distrust of authorities, state institutions and multinational corporations. Whenever the opportunity presented itself to write a related story, he sunk his teeth into it with the ferocity of a great white shark.

The commitment with which he threw himself into an investigation starkly contrasted with how capricious he was when it came to love. Although there were always women, nothing ever lasted. Paul was usually long gone before they realized that he lacked any need for intimacy. Or before anyone meant so much to him that he'd get hurt by them leaving first.

He had dedicated himself to this lifestyle, until one parched evening he ran into Susanne. Literally. Paul had thrown himself into jogging ten kilometres three times a week and he regularly passed through Alexandra, usually followed by a pack of children shouting excitedly. He'd stopped that night in an unfamiliar neighbourhood at the intersection of five roads because he was lost. He saw her in a cloud of dust with her own group of little followers. It was a funny situation and he laughed at her. But with an annoyed expression, she just kept running. Paul picked up his pace and came up beside her. He had to speak rather loudly because of the shouting children behind them.

'Where are you from?'

'None of your business.'

'Where's that?'

'Where's what?'

'That place called None of Your Business.'

She stopped abruptly. 'What do you want?'

'Nothing, I'm just interested. And I seem to have lost my way,' he answered in Afrikaans. She looked at him, taken aback.

'And frankly, it isn't every day I come across a jogging South African in a township,' he said, with his most charming smile.

She gave him a wry grin. 'Get used to it.'

'Okay if I join you?'

'If you can keep up.' And she took off.

Later that evening, while drinking lots of ice-cold beers at an outdoor café, she told him about her work with the Be Aware Foundation. She'd already spent six months in Alexandra helping children who, because of poor sanitary conditions, were at an increased risk for tuberculosis. Susanne became Paul's jogging mate, his confidante, his drinking buddy and – thank heaven for running girls – not long afterwards his passionate lover.

In that same period, Paul was investigating the South African Minister of Defence, Jacob Nkoane, who'd apparently spent billions of dollars purchasing weapons. The deliveries originated in the Ukraine and went via Egypt to Johannesburg. At least two planes registered in the Ukraine had each delivered thirty tons of weapons via that route. And then there were all kinds of questionable transactions as well. Part of the money from his ministry had almost certainly been pocketed by Nkoane himself. A flow of funds, efficiently channelled into overseas accounts, was traced back to his bank account.

The sources at Paul's disposal were so reliable that *The Citizen* dared to prominently publish his article on the front page. In reaction, a government spokesman claimed it was libel, but the paper wasn't sued. Responding to the article in a television interview, Nkoane said if there were problems, they were South Africa's problems and would be resolved by South Africans and not by foreigners.

Strengthened by the fervent denials and reactions, Paul felt himself grow in his role as David, the tireless journalist going up against Goliath, the ANC political party – so deeply rooted in the country it seemed untouchable. He'd undoubtedly find more officials in high places who'd used their power to enrich themselves at the expense of their constituency.

He became obsessed with the investigation. At last he'd make history with his reporting and follow in the footsteps of his respected father Raylan. Paul became something of a fanatic, rushed from one mysterious appointment to another while Susanne, after her daily work in the slums, craved his presence but hardly ever found him at home.

Shortly thereafter, Susanne was told that her work for the Be Aware Foundation was ending with immediate effect. The ANC wasn't prepared to fund an organization who let their doctor associate with a subversive journalist. She had to choose.

Paul was furious. That very same day he'd slammed his fist on the table during an editorial meeting at *The Citizen,* after the editor announced that in view of the pending national elections, more positive news needed to be reported. News that should express a 'will to transformation'. Another way of saying that any follow-up articles Paul wrote about fraud in high places wouldn't be printed.

'I won't be stopped,' Paul barked at Susanne that evening. 'Not by anyone!'

'Did you hear me, Paul? I'm being forced to quit my job,' Susanne said.

'Yes, too bad. But of course there was no other option.'

'Of course there *was* another option!' she cried angrily. 'Doesn't that even occur to you? And what about me? I'm being forced to abandon my children, because you always need to go off on a crusade!'

He hated blackmail and especially detested the emotional variety.

'Sorry. I didn't know it was about you. Or "your children". You're not some goddamned Mother Teresa!'

Her eyes flashed. 'No, this is not about me. It's about you. About your life with those ghosts you're always chasing. You think about them when you wake up. And at night you dream about them. You can't think about anything else. Until you've found something you can use to nail them to the cross. And why is that? Because you want to make the world a better place?

Or is it because you want to prove to everyone you're as brilliant a journalist as your father?'

He had let her speak her piece. On the outside he looked calm, but he was fuming on the inside. She had no idea who he was or what was important in this world.

'And you don't want to live with a ghost any longer. Is that it?'

'What do you want from me, Paul?' Her response said it all. She didn't want to make the decision herself. He would have to do it for her.

'I want you to see me for who I am,' he said as calmly as possible. 'It's very simple. Without my work, I'm nobody. A nobody without a purpose. And without that, I have no life.'

'And without me?' she asked with tears in her eyes. Relationships. The equivalent of opium. First, the blissful intoxication. Then, the hangover and the inevitable loneliness.

'I'll survive just fine without you.'

He didn't hear anything from her for a week. He'd called her. Left messages that he was sorry. But the answering machine didn't respond. Once in the middle of the night, when he couldn't sleep and he knew she was at home, he went and stood on her doorstep and hurled a torrent of abuse at her.

Then his phone finally rang, but with the news that Susanne had been murdered during a violent burglary in her flat. In Hillbrow, the downtown district of Jo'burg where she lived, the hotels and flats had once been inhabited by the upper middle class. Now they were home to people from the countryside and lands bordering South Africa. There was no street watch, and she didn't have a dog or gun at home and certainly didn't have a burglar-proof cage protecting her bedroom. She was attacked in her sleep, raped and beaten to death. Just another one of Jo'burg's many unsolved murders.

Consumed by guilt, Paul was too upset to even start looking into the facts of the case. As if finding the murderers would solve the problem. So he threw himself into betting on illegal fights as a remedy, and with the money he made drowned his sorrows in a bottle. His research into the corrupt Nkoane came to a standstill.

Then one evening he got a call from an unidentified man who, with the soft, cultured voice of someone who undoubtedly belonged to a better social class, said he could provide Paul with information that would lead to a breakthrough. Information that would definitively tie Nkoane to the Russian mafia.

By now it had become busy in Stella's Coffee Bar. Paul's macchiato was lukewarm and the headlines still danced before his eyes, unintelligible. After Susanne's death, he'd come here countless times by himself, like he had before he'd met her. But he still couldn't stop himself from looking up every time he heard the cafe's door open.

He cursed himself and the inane fantasy that it would be her: He'd get up and place his hands on her smooth, powerful body. With a flying start, they'd end up in his bed, where groaning from pleasure and sweating heavily, biting, grabbing and clinging to each other, they'd make love. Then they'd lie awake together, listening to the sounds of the city.

He glanced at his watch, realized he was going to be late arriving at the location of the appointment with his unknown informant. He paid the bill and hurried outside, where he immediately tried to hail one of many minibuses. It would take a long time before all that emptiness inside him could be filled again. Susanne was still in his head, his heart; she was in his whole body and it hurt like hell.

2

Decked out in oversized sunglasses, wearing a flowery scarf on her head, Angela Faber emerged first from the car that pulled up at the WMC staff entrance.

Given the woman's appearance, Danielle straightaway had serious doubts about the plan she'd devised with Cathy Marant. But she couldn't back down, not now.

Dennis Faber, also in shades, stepped out behind his wife. From his faltering movements, it seemed like he was attached to the car interior with elastic: at any moment he might snap back inside the vehicle. He was barely recognizable without that fake TV grin plastered on his face, Danielle thought. Faber seemed disoriented. He clung to his wife, who melodramatically peered over the rim of her enormous glasses.

It wasn't every day that the Faber couple was dropped incognito at the rear entrance of a hospital.

The third, unfamiliar person whose rugged face jutted out above the car roof – armed with a photo camera and a case full of lenses – seemed to be the only one of their group who understood they had to enter through this door here.

He stuck out his hand, and Danielle responded by gripping it firmly.

'Eric Sanders, photographer.'

'Wait here, Eric.'

Danielle walked over to Angela Faber, who looked utterly lost, and introduced herself to her.

'Oh, you're Dr Bernson, the one who saved his life!' Coming from her mouth it sounded like she was complimenting Danielle on her mascara brand, her hair colour, or the model of her white lab coat.

'Dr Bernson?'

Danielle turned and saw the sea-green eyes of Cathy Marant – hardly any make-up and a perfect complexion. Tight-fitting red lace-up boots under Pepe jeans, light-grey jacket, expensive-looking handbag and a piercing look that said, I'm in charge here.

'Please, just call me Danielle.' It was her attempt to break the ice. Women like Marant got right down to business, but kept their distance, and Danielle needed her close, at least for a while.

'Well, Danielle, thank you for giving us the chance to tell this wonderful story and to put things right.' Her handshake felt like the confirmation of the alliance they'd agreed to previously on the phone.

That morning, Danielle had quickly realized that the plan Marant was proposing was much more realistic than what she'd suggested herself. She'd wanted a news item in which Angela and Dennis Faber would have a walk-on role and she would take the lead with her story about child abuse. But the hard-nosed Marant immediately saw the likely pitfalls. She didn't think a camera crew in the ICU was a good idea. Too realistic, too little space, too much of a hassle. She immediately came up with a tear-jerking alternative, a newspaper and TV scoop rolled into one. After all, she not only presented *The Headlines Show*, but she also had her extremely popular 'Headlines' column in *De Nederlander*.

Marant briefly explained her two-stage plan. Stage one consisted of rehabilitating the Fabers in the newspaper. With a headline like: FORMER SOAP STAR SAVES LIFE OF UNKNOWN CHILD, she could entertain her devoted public with a heartbreaking tale, complete with full-colour photos of Angela and Dennis Faber at the boy's bedside. The story would be about how Angela saw him lying on the road in the middle of the night and had the presence of mind to avoid hitting him. Via emergency services, she'd immediately involved the doctor who successfully operated on him. This was then followed by a lunatic detective dragging her and poor Dennis into the police station for questioning under suspicion of running down the boy. A shocking, tragic article with a happy ending. Little boy rescued: the Fabers' exclusive story as a means to exposing the failings of the police. All of this splashed across the pages of *De Nederlander*.

Then came stage two. The story about the severely injured victim who was found in the middle of the night on a woodland road. Told by the doctor who saved his life, because the boy was still in intensive care and unable to talk. A story about a child trafficking network, the abuse of young Afghan dancing boys, the mystery of where he came from. Who was he? An exclusive broadcast by *The Headlines Show*. Danielle would have to sign an exclusivity agreement, promise she wouldn't share this story with any other media.

Danielle agreed immediately. Initially, out of sheer inexperience, she had set her hopes on journalist Farah Hafez. But Hafez had her own reasons for refusing the offer. Fortunately, Cathy Marant saw it in the exact same light as Danielle: a tragic story for a broad audience. In retrospect, Farah's refusal had been a blessing.

And now here she was at the staff entrance of the WMC and somehow it didn't feel right, but she attributed this to nerves and her inexperience with this kind of media circus. She hadn't informed any of her colleagues about her intentions; hadn't brought a single hospital manager up to speed on this. She knew damn well that the hospital would have never consented beforehand, so she hoped for a teeth-gnashing approval later on – because of the glowing publicity the WMC would receive.

'Let's do this quickly and efficiently,' Marant said, hastily checking the display on her phone. 'I have another appointment I need to get to. We've talked it through, everyone knows exactly what to do.'

I certainly don't, thought Danielle to herself, but instead said, 'Follow me.' She led the four along the corridor to the service lift. With a theatrical gesture, Angela Faber covered her nose and mouth with a hanky. 'Oh, what an awful smell! The place reeks of disease!'

Her husband responded pointedly, 'It's a hospital, dear, what do you expect?'

'Yes, all right,' she pouted, 'but does it have to smell like this?'

They were jammed into the service lift. Angela Faber smelled of Joy perfume; Dennis Faber reeked of liquor.

When the lift doors opened, Danielle quickly invented a story that Management had given her the authority to stop everything when it threatened to get the least bit out of hand.

Cathy Marant didn't seem impressed. 'We'll be out of here in fifteen minutes, Danielle.'

When Angela Faber entered the room and saw the boy lying on the bed, she threw herself at him, moaning and whimpering like an opera diva. Eric started clicking and encouraged Dennis Faber to go to the other side of the bed and take his wife's hand as he bent over the boy. It was the cheapest display of melodrama Danielle had ever seen, and the realization that she'd initiated it herself filled her with disgust.

3

She'd forgotten about the roadworks that make the A4 from Amsterdam to The Hague so prone to traffic jams. Farah badly wanted to step on the gas, but right now she couldn't go much faster than fifty kilometres per hour. It meant she'd arrive late at the home of the man she'd known since her childhood in Kabul. Although he wasn't related, she called him *kaka*, uncle, often adding *jan*, which meant 'dear' as well as 'soul' and 'life force'.

Parwaiz Ahmad, to give her *kaka jan* his full name, had been in the Netherlands for more than ten years. Today, Parliament was set to vote on whether refugees and asylum seekers who'd been caught up in all kinds of legal procedures for years would be eligible for permanent residency. If so, Parwaiz would finally become a citizen of his adopted country. Not long ago, she'd written a lengthy article about him, and today that article might finally have a happy ending.

Back in the seventies, Parwaiz had been the director of Kabul's National Museum. As a little girl, Farah had spent hours wandering among the treasures with her art-loving mother. And whenever he could, the distinguished and courteous Parwaiz would keep them company. He always had a good anecdote, she recalled, inspired by a small ivory statuette, an old painting or an antique vase.

When the Russians invaded Afghanistan in the winter of 1979, it was the prominent figure of Parwaiz who organized a protest march to the presidential palace. Unfurled at the head of the procession was a seven-metre-wide banner with a likeness of Malalai, Afghanistan's mythical resistance heroine. Legend had it that Malalai was a water carrier for the soldiers of the Afghan Liberation Army when it went into battle against the British colonial troops on 27 July 1880. The British artillery looked close to crushing the Afghan troops. When Malalai saw the standard-bearer taking a hit, she grabbed hold of the flag herself, began waving it about and from the top of a hill spurred the demoralized Afghan soldiers on to victory.

Malalai's likeness sent out a clear message. And to underline it, Parwaiz addressed the protestors with the words, 'Now and in the future, sovereign Afghanistan will always belong to us Afghans.' Afterwards Parwaiz was arrested by the Khad secret police and thrown into prison where he was subjected to lengthy interrogation. It was widely known that 'interrogation' by the Khad was a euphemism for torture.

Parwaiz was incarcerated for days but never talked about it. Later, Farah learnt from reliable sources that a respected Russian archaeologist had personally intervened to secure Parwaiz's release. Thanks to his intervention, Parwaiz not only retained his directorship, but was also invited to put together a Soviet-Afghan team tasked with analysing the countless jewels and other art objects in the National Museum of Kabul from the burial tombs of Tillya Tepe.

For ten years, Parwaiz managed Afghanistan's cultural treasures at the museum, thereby implicitly conveying the message that the Afghans ought to be proud of their national, historical and cultural heritage. But his efforts were not universally appreciated. Those who continued to oppose Russian rule viewed him as a first-rate traitor. In their eyes, Parwaiz was an ostrich who buried his head in stuffy art so he didn't have to see how the Russians had claimed two million Afghan victims during their ten-year occupation, all but devastated the economy and plundered the museums in other cities including Hadda and Jalalabad.

Everything was to change after the Russians left Afghanistan in 1989. The Mujahideen fighters entered Kabul victoriously, but instead of forming a harmonious new government after collectively driving out the Russians, the power-hungry warlords now began to fight among themselves.

The civil war was fought with grenades, mortars and tanks. Kabul was the central battleground and within months the ancient city was reduced to rubble. Parwaiz secretly had a large number of artworks transferred to a safe in the presidential palace. The museum itself was hit by a rocket and after it caught fire the roof collapsed, destroying a room full of frescoes. Plundering ensued and the Mujahideen officially accused Parwaiz of colluding with the former Russian enemy. Amidst the chaos of rampant anarchy, he managed to escape. He and his wife fled the country and eventually ended up in the Netherlands.

However, the Dutch government held that every refugee who'd worked for the Afghan government during the Russian occupation was a potential war criminal. And because Parwaiz had been on the government's payroll as a museum director all that time, he was denied a permanent residence permit in the Netherlands.

Uncle Parwaiz a war criminal. It was tantamount to the idea of Gandhi propagating the atom bomb.

The peace-loving Parwaiz decided to tempt fate and to remain in the Netherlands, hoping justice would prevail. In his home country he'd buried both sons. One had been killed by a Russian machine gun, the other by an American-made bazooka. In the Netherlands his wife died of a cardiac arrest, and while still mourning Parwaiz could do nothing but sit back and watch the Taliban on television blowing Afghanistan's historic masterpieces, the towering Buddhas of Bamiyan, to smithereens.

In spite of everything he remained hopeful that the future would be better, both for himself in the Netherlands and for the people in his home country. He was active in the Afghan community, gave frequent talks at schools about Afghanistan's cultural history and even helped set up a large exhibition about ancient and modern Afghan art. It was at the opening of this exhibition that Farah bumped into him.

Parwaiz had been just as stunned as Farah. With tears in his eyes, he had embraced her and called her *dokhtar jan*, a heartfelt compound of 'girl' and 'daughter'. Farah was overjoyed.

All that time, *Kaka* Parwaiz had been the only one who knew who Farah really was. But her secret was safe with him. He was also the only one who knew that Farah had been forced to let go of her mother's hand on a snowy mountain pass on the Turkish–Iranian border. Parwaiz was the only living link between herself and her past.

She parked the Carrera right in front of the door. When she looked up, she spotted Parwaiz's slender frame on the balcony. There he stood, with both arms spread wide, and for a brief moment it looked as if he was about to leap towards her.

4

On the way back from Schiphol, Marouan took the exit to the police station. Thanks to his action yesterday in the television studio, a series of humiliations would undoubtedly be awaiting him there. He would swallow them all.

The morning heat crept into the car. Marouan switched the car ventilation to the coldest setting and thought back to the first time he'd walked into a Dutch police station. As an eager eighteen-year-old, with a lot of Belmondo bravado and with trembling knees, he'd approached the mistrustful duty officer behind the counter.

'What do you want, kid? Here to turn yourself in?'

'I'm Moroccan. And you're looking for Moroccans. I saw this.' He pulled out a newspaper advertisement and he slid it across the counter. The duty officer put on his reading glasses and peered at the recruitment ad.

Five minutes later, Marouan was back outside holding a stack of forms to fill in, with the duty officer's words ringing in his ears, 'Until you all piss off back to your own country, we need a few of you who can communicate in that gibberish of yours. So if you're willing to put on a uniform, wear a cap on your ridiculous head and do your bloody best, then you too – alas! – could qualify for a job as a cop.'

And the more Marouan's family and friends tried to convince him that it wasn't something for him, the more convinced he became that he'd found his calling. During his years at the police academy, he regularly studied in his bedroom late into the night. Hoping that his father would one day tell everybody how proud he was of him. Alas! Still, his uniform looked good on him. He was the handsome, ambitious young cop patrolling neighbourhoods where his Moroccan countrymen, especially, eyed him with great suspicion.

His Dutch colleagues kept a close watch on him too.

Today, as always, Marouan resisted the urge to drive right through the wall of the car park, directly into the service lift. One day he'd simply do it. As an ultimate tribute to Belmondo. Then, with a big cigar and a broad grin, he'd step out of the smoking wreck to receive not only the applause of his colleagues, but his walking papers as well. He was already looking forward to the big day.

There were more cops around the coffee machine in the hallway than on the entire ring road circling Amsterdam. More than ninety per cent of the uniformed folk roaming these halls were caffeine junkies. Marouan, with a big mug in hand, joined the end of the line, where the first clown started in on him. He held an image under Diba's nose of Dennis Faber, standing against the backdrop of *The Game of Love*, but with Marouan's Photoshopped face.

'Are we going to lose you to showbiz, Diba?' the clown sneered. 'There's a multimillion dollar contract on the horizon for you, man. And nationwide fame. My mother-in-law wants your autograph.' One of the cops then pinned an enlargement of the same photo-montage on the wall, to the immense amusement of his colleagues. Chuckling all around.

Marouan's phone vibrated in his jacket pocket. It was Calvino. He was probably still busy salutating the sun on the afterdeck of his houseboat, or he was fishing some algae from the Amstelveense Poel to add to a salad.

'Cal. Where are you?'

'In the woods. That journalist took me to the spot where she found the boy's earring. And I've discovered a few other things, Diba.'

In the meantime, Marouan walked over to the enlarged photo, tore it from the wall and left the coffee corner in search of a quieter spot. He was on edge.

'So you're romping around in the woods with Miss Afghanistan?'

'Just stop with the stupid jokes, okay?'

'I see that she's wrapped you around her little finger.'

'Shut your trap, Diba. I'm just doing my job.'

'Your job? If you wanted to do your job, you'd have taken me with you! Get my drift, partner? I should have been there!'

'You were busy saying goodbye to your family.'

'You should have waited, come here and we'd have gone together! So, what did you find?'

'An old villa. Seems to be boarded up. But it looks like something has been dragged from the house. And out front there are more traces of dragging. And there's blood. I asked Tomasoa to send the forensics guys. And we need to do a walk-through of the woods.'

Marouan felt himself break out in a sweat. Not from anger, but out of fear. He was caught between two fires and the heat was being turned up on both. The case involving the boy was dodgier than he'd initially thought.

'Damn it, Cal,' he snarled. 'You arranged all of this behind my back. We're partners, remember? We do things together!'

'What about those arrests yesterday?' Calvino retorted. 'That was some show of cooperation! Think for a moment, Diba. Look at it from where I'm standing, you see there's a trail from two different directions. Suddenly both stop because a car was parked there. Then you also see the words STATION WAGON written in glaring neon letters. You still with me? We're no longer dealing with a traffic accident, but with a double murder, if you ask me. And the boy probably witnessed it.'

Marouan steadied himself against a doorframe and saw Tomasoa striding towards him.

'I gotta go, Cal.'

Tomasoa looked sharply at Marouan, with his Yul Brynner eyes.

'Good work,' he said. Not a hint of cynicism, no ironic glance. He sounded serious, like he meant it. 'Calvino brought me up to speed. I'm going to give a short briefing in the squad room. You get the men you asked for.'

Marouan just stood there, stunned. If he'd done such a good job, he'd also like to be brought up to speed about exactly what he'd done. And for which men had he asked? And why? But Tomasoa was already way down the hallway and, in passing, was informing the chief of Forensic Investigation, Dick Park, about the case. Conspiracy theories reared their ugly head. What had Calvino been up to behind his back?

Wherever he looked, his own image was staring back at him. In that same 'glamour' photo taken on the set of *The Game of Love*. Dennis Faber's suit looked good on Marouan. That had to be said. And he'd slimmed down quite a bit. But his head was too big. Clumsy job and anonymous as always. His spineless colleagues were having a good laugh at his expense. The image was pinned to the noticeboards in the hallway, on the door-posts of all the offices, even taped to the screen of the PC on his desk. It was nauseating.

As he knocked back his coffee, Marouan noticed the Post-it in Cal's handwriting. All of yesterday's case reports were already processed in the system. One thing was clear, Calvino was really putting himself out. And Marouan racked his brain, to no avail, about the reasons why.

5

'Good to see you again, *kaka jan*,' Farah said softly as she looked Parwaiz in the eye and held his wizened face with both hands.

He regarded her gravely.

'Has life confounded you again, *bachem*?' There was no escaping it. She couldn't keep secrets from Parwaiz.

'More than that, dear uncle. Everything's been turned upside-down.'

'Excellent,' he said with an enigmatic smile. 'That means there's still plenty in store for you.' He escorted her into his two-room apartment, which was littered with art books, half-finished gouaches and charcoal drawings. The living room was sparsely furnished: a chair, a table and a large, hand-woven Bokhara carpet. The table had originally been a workbench. Farah had transported it in a minivan from a dilapidated factory in the Belgian Ardennes. Whether it had been used by a blacksmith or a butcher was unclear, but that didn't matter. If need be, a war could be fought on the eroded worktop. The thing rested on heavyweight metal legs and had two large drawers in which Parwaiz stored his sketches and the rest of his artistic paperwork.

One entire wall was dedicated to what Parwaiz described as his 'life's work in the making'. Anything he came across in newspapers or magazines and that he associated with Afghanistan he would cut out and glue on before priming the surface and frantically drawing all over it. And so it grew into a historic panorama that went back to the invasion of Alexander the Great and covered the centuries until the arrival of the US Air Force. Shards of exploding Buddha statues were everywhere. Whatever befell his country, Parwaiz always managed to find it a place in his detailed mural.

They drank tea and ate the dates that Farah had bought in a Turkish cornershop. Then she retrieved the parcel with her gift for Parwaiz. 'A special day calls for a special gift,' she said with a tentative smile.

His fine long fingers caressed the gift wrap.

'Open it carefully, *kaka jan*, it's fragile,' she said, eager to see his reaction.

He removed the sticky tape, unfolded the parcel and looked at the paper butterfly as though it were the world's most precious diamond.

'Ah, a lucky butterfly.' He brushed his fingers over the wings and then over the paper body and smiled at the two enormous antennae on its head. 'I'm putting it in the same drawer inside my heart where I've put you, *dokhtar jan*.' He blew her a few kisses.

'Are you nervous about today?' she asked in an effort to keep her emotions at bay.

'Today is a special day. Special days stimulate the nerves,' he said with a smile. 'But let's talk about you, *bachem*. You've been through a lot and you haven't had much sleep,' he said as he scrutinized her. 'Your forced cheerfulness worries me.'

She stared at the floor for a while, the tea glass untouched in her hands. Finally, she looked up at him.

'*Kaka jan*, what do you know about Bacha Bazi?'

'I don't know much about it.' If he was surprised because she brought this up, he certainly didn't show it. 'It's a tradition that goes back a long way, it originates in rural areas. Owing to the strict Islamic moral code, women were practically unattainable for men. Before marriage, they always lived completely separate lives. But the men still had needs. It's a common phenomenon in monasteries, in prisons, in virtually all places where men live without women. In those communities, other men are often forced to assume the role of the woman. And the younger and more feminine the man is, the more desirable he becomes to the others.'

He drank some tea and chewed on a date.

'Boys without beard growth,' he muttered. 'Boys with a girlish face. I once found myself at such a party, Farah. I'd been invited, but I didn't know that's what it was. And then suddenly she appeared. I say "she", because that's what he looked like. A boy tackily made up and laden with jewellery by other men. I left. It was disgusting. Why are you asking me this?'

'Such a boy was found in a wood outside Amsterdam the other night.'

This time Parwaiz was unable to hide his surprise. He stared at her in disbelief.

'Impossible,' he muttered, 'impossible.' And what he then added would stay with Farah as a prophecy of everything still to come: 'We live in a world in which the hell that is our past always catches up with us.'

6

Tomasoa kicked off his briefing with the manipulated image of Dennis Faber.

'Nice try, but we're not letting Detective Diba go off to TV land so easily. While all of you were still snoozing, he and his partner Calvino delivered a good piece of investigative work this morning on a hit-and-run in which a boy was seriously injured.'

There was an immediate commotion in the room. Marouan couldn't believe his ears. Had he ended up in some insane collective joke that even Tomasoa was involved in, or had his colleagues put something in his coffee and he was hallucinating? After putting his wife and children on the plane, followed by a sleepless night of gambling, he'd aimlessly driven around the city. When had he supposedly done all this top-notch detective work?

But Tomasoa continued unperturbed.

'There are strong indications that this case involves more than just an accident. In the immediate vicinity of where the boy was run down, evidence has been found suggesting the likelihood of a multiple homicide. Drag marks and traces of blood were discovered at an old, empty villa a few hundred metres from the site of the collision. After extensive deliberation between the Public Prosecutor and the Examining Magistrate, the go-ahead has been given for a detailed technical investigation of the area around the villa and the villa itself. The purpose of this investigation is to secure evidence and to reconstruct what might have happened there, and to determine if the boy was present.'

The commotion had died down and been replaced by an impressed silence. Tomasoa took a moment to treat his men to one of his inscrutable glances.

'What complicates this matter is that the villa in question appears to be the property of the Dorado Group. As you may already know, it's a billion-dollar business divided into real estate, shipbuilding and media, and the kingpin of that conglomerate is none other than Armin Lazonder, who also owns *De Nederlander* and IRIS TV, and is the man behind the New Golden Age Project.'

Tomasoa had pointedly glanced in Marouan's direction when he mentioned IRIS TV. Nobody said anything.

'The fact that we're going to focus part of our investigation on a property belonging to Lazonder will certainly cause a stir in the media,' Tomasoa continued. 'That's why I'm asking you to avoid all contact with the press. Our PR department will make the appropriate announcements and arrange any necessary contact.'

The colleague who'd shoved the manipulated photo in Marouan's face at the coffee machine raised his hand. 'So for the time being no more live arrests on television, chief?' The men started laughing. Tomasoa swiftly raised his hand. A small gesture, but big enough to silence the laughter in no time.

'Let me put this plainly, Dennis Faber was arrested on suspicion of complicity for withholding evidence in a hit-and-run case. The prosecutor, based on the available evidence, issued an arrest warrant. Therefore, the action of detectives Calvino and Diba was completely justified.'

Tomasoa paused, a tactical silence – every second that it lasted confused Marouan even more. He stared at his boss and did his utmost to follow his arguments as unemotionally as possible.

'I spoke with both detectives yesterday,' continued Tomasoa. 'They agreed that their choice of location for the arrest was unfortunate.' He held up the Photoshopped image of Marouan as the host of *The Game of Love* again. 'So if anyone else here has something to add, or has whipped up yet another manipulated masterpiece, he can now stand up and give us all a chance to enjoy it. If not,' he stared into the room and gave his sovereign ruling, 'I consider the incident around Dennis Faber closed.'

Moses probably had a look like this on his face when he parted the Red Sea, Marouan thought.

'Back to the business at hand,' Tomasoa continued. 'As already mentioned there are two different investigations underway. Forensics is going to do an extensive search in and around the villa, and there will be a "walk-through" starting from the location of the villa to the spot where the boy was hit. The reason being: we want to determine whether the boy came from the villa before he crossed the road. Detective Diba will lead this investigation. He has asked for some volunteers, which I will now democratically appoint.'

Marouan kept his eyes glued to the ground. Regrettably, among the names called were a number of men who'd in the past given him a hard time for various reasons. Alas!

'Given the nature of this investigation, I expect everyone to do their utmost today,' Tomasoa said after announcing the last of the names. 'Are there any questions? Comments?'

One of those present raised his hand.

'Is it possible that what happened at the villa and the hit-and-run involving that boy are both related to the case of the burnt-out station wagon the MIT is currently working on?'

'At the moment, it's simply speculation. We can only start thinking about this once the results of our own investigation are in. However, at this stage we shouldn't rule anything out.'

You could feel an undercurrent of excitement among the men. They were starting to grasp that there might be something huge, even sinister, behind what at first glance looked like an ordinary traffic accident. The men whom Tomasoa had appointed to comb the woods with Marouan assembled. Marouan knew that Tomasoa's briefing hadn't changed anything about their attitudes towards him, but these men were professional enough to realize they had to put their personal feelings aside and get down to business.

Tomasoa motioned for Marouan to come over to him.

'Keep the upper hand. If there are problems, please let me know right away, understand?'

'Crystal clear, chief,' Marouan heard himself reply, but the only thing really clear to him at that moment was the enormous and mounting chaos that was his life.

7

Despite the glorious summer weather, a dark cloud had slipped into Parwaiz's apartment. Farah regretted mentioning the Bacha Bazi boy. She'd been determined to push aside her own troubles and to really be there for Parwaiz *jan*. This was supposed to be *his* day. But she was bewildered and, however much she wanted to, she couldn't hide her emotions from him. He was a sensitive man. The minute she'd walked in, he picked up on her state of mind. The cloud wouldn't simply lift, that much she knew.

'How did you come in contact with him, *bachem*?'

She was startled. For a split second she thought he meant Joshua. But while Parwaiz might have many talents, so far she'd failed to detect any telepathic powers.

'I was at the hospital when he was brought in, *kaka jan*.'

'What were you doing there? Is anything the matter with you?' he asked, worried.

'No, I . . .' Remembering that Parwaiz didn't read any Dutch newspapers and never watched TV, she decided to spare him the story about the martial arts gala. 'I'd gone to the Emergency Department for someone else when the boy arrived. He was seriously injured. A hit-and-run. I helped interpret for the doctors.'

'Was he able to tell you anything?'

'He was in really bad shape. They operated on him. The operation went well, but last night he took a turn for the worse. And no family has come forward to claim him. I suspect he's the victim of child trafficking.'

'No doubt about it,' Parwaiz said. 'Bacha Bazi is never voluntary. It's a form of forced prostitution.'

'I'm sorry I mentioned it, *kaka jan*,' Farah said.

'I'm glad you're telling me what's bothering you, *dokhtar jan*,' he said with a smile. He leaned forward and whispered, 'So why don't you tell me everything?'

Farah could no longer hold back her tears. She started off by apologizing, saying that she'd really wanted this to be a festive day for him. And now she was spoiling it. But Parwaiz dried her tears the way a worried uncle would and very gently told her to start at the beginning. He wanted to hear the whole story.

And so she told him, haltingly, about the dramatic way the dancing boy had entered her life, and about her conflict with Danielle. Parwaiz listened intently to the obviously abridged version of her meetings with Joshua Calvino, the appearance of Raylan Chapelle's ghost and the story of Paul's return, more than thirty years after their first meeting in Kabul's butterfly garden.

'Some people claim the future has all kinds of secrets in store for us,' he said, while lovingly touching the lucky butterfly. 'But as long as you don't know the secrets of the past, you can't really focus on the future.'

'But I don't know what to do, *kaka jan*. What to choose?'

'In your heart of hearts, you know what choice you're going to make, *bachem*. Follow your heart.'

'Even when it frightens me?'

'*Especially* when it frightens you. I won't be able to offer you much more help, my child. I'm an old, worn-out man. I don't have much time left.'

'You mustn't say that, *kaka jan*,' she said with a smile breaking through the tears. 'Apparently, as a freshly minted Dutchman, you have the right to a brand *new* life. And I bet it will be a long one.'

'That's sweet of you, but you know, Farah, my old life is too precious to me. I think and dream in Dari. However pleased I am to become a Dutchman, my heart will always be Afghan.'

'I understand, *kaka jan*.'

His lips curled into a solemn smile.

'*Dokhtarem*, you've always been candid with me. You've always confided in me. And I've always treasured your visits. Your support has helped me through difficult times. But while you've been up front about what you've been going through, as you were just now, that's more than I can say for myself. I've never spoken to you about some of the things that happened to me, like my imprisonment in Kabul. Even now I can't talk about the unspeakable things people inflict on others. Not even to you. But it's time for me to be frank and share a secret that I've kept to myself for far too long.'

He fell silent, searching for words. Farah's heart was in her throat.

'I promised someone dear to us both to keep this secret as long as I deemed necessary,' he continued. 'I only wanted to share it with you when I thought the time was ripe. That time has come.'

Parwaiz struggled to his feet and walked over to the workbench where he pulled the top drawer open with some difficulty before removing a bulky parcel wrapped in tissue paper and tied together with frayed string.

Farah thought of her mother and father. Had either of them left her something?

Parwaiz stood with his back to her, looking at the parcel in his hands, his head bowed, lost in thought. Then he turned around.

'I'd like to ask you, *dokhtarem*, not to jump to conclusions about what you find in here. In their quest for the true meaning of life, people should be allowed to walk paths you perhaps don't want them to go down . . .'

'You speak in riddles, *kaka jan*.'

'But you like riddles, don't you, Farah *jan*?' he said with a knowing smile as he came towards her with the parcel. 'Look, some people betray their political ideals to protect art, like I did . . .'

'Wholly justified,' Farah said encouragingly.

He stood right in front of her now. She was tempted to reach for the parcel, but stopped herself.

'I'd like you to be just as forgiving of your mother Helai after you've laid eyes on this.'

A wave of sadness swept through her at the mention of her mother's name. She couldn't utter a word.

'Helai experienced more doubts than she cared to admit in her quest to be true to herself.'

'I'd never judge her, *kaka jan*, whatever she did or whatever she felt. Is it painful, what I'm going to see?'

'Her story has some parallels with what you've told me about yourself,' he said tentatively.

Suddenly her mind jumped. To the unthinkable. It was out before she knew it. '*Kaka jan*! Don't tell me you and mum . . .'

Parwaiz shook his head, shocked.

'No, your mother confided in me before she decided to flee with you,' he said firmly. 'Other than that, I play no role in any of it. She handed me this with the words, "If you can protect defenceless works of art against bombs, you'll know what to do with this." She told me what you'll read here. But I won't disclose what it is. That's for you to find out. I hope it will give you a better understanding of why certain things in your life are the way they are.'

He handed her the parcel. It burned in her hands, because she knew that as soon as she removed the tissue paper she'd forget the world around her and lose herself in its contents. And they would no doubt be explosive. She had to control her emotions. This was supposed to be Parwaiz's big day and so it would be. She gave him a grateful smile.

'I'd like you to store the parcel in the same place for now, *kaka jan*. We mustn't be late. When we get back, I'll take it home with me. Let's get going.'

Parwaiz put the parcel back in the drawer and walked to the balcony doors to close them. When she saw him standing there, his slender silhouette against the sun, she suddenly felt as if the time had come to say goodbye.

'*Kaka jan*!' she exclaimed, with mild panic in her voice.

'What is it?' Worried, he walked over to her and put his hands on her shoulders.

'I . . . I love you very much,' she said, feeling sad.

'I know, *bachem*. I love you too.'

8

Marouan Diba thought of the rising star he'd once been. In spite of, or perhaps due to the antagonism of his colleagues. He was Moroccan and they'd known it, inside as well as outside the police force. He'd been stationed in Amsterdam-Oost because he knew the young Moccros who hung around on the street corners. He'd grab them by the neck and get them talking. Because they respected him, they showed him their true selves. And if they talked back, they might get a smack from him. Then they sat there moping with a bloody nose or a fat lip. 'Go file an assault report,' he'd say. Because he knew that they wouldn't do it. Filing a report was the same as yelling for your mummy or daddy. The ultimate humiliation. And so they fell. One by one. Out of respect.

Respect was a rarity nowadays. As rare as that pat on the shoulder Calvino had given him yesterday, just before they were going to have their heads handed to them by Tomasoa.

Marouan had been confused by Calvino's gesture. He'd climbed the executioner's scaffold but got a pat on the back. Had Calvino done it out of some sort of misplaced pity? Marouan couldn't imagine. His confusion had only increased when the half-baked Italian claimed during their talk with Tomasoa that he and not Marouan had initiated Dennis Faber's arrest. Calvino was as sly as a fox. He knew better than most that if Marouan kept bungling the case, he'd be blamed too.

People would always associate Calvino with this case. 'Weren't you the guy who worked that unsolved hit-and-run involving a young boy with that blundering Moroccan?' Calvino, who was only interested in success, couldn't risk this, of course. He'd undoubtedly devised a plan to prevent it.

He clearly had something up his sleeve. *Think it through.*
Analyse. What had Calvino done? What had he said? What had
he *concealed*?

He saw Calvino biting his lip again when Tomasoa had asked
at the end of his monologue if there was anything else he
needed to know. He remembered Calvino's more than cunning
answer.

'Nothing we can't handle, chief.'

Clever how you could combine a denial and an affirmation
in a single sentence. Nobody could get Calvino on this one.
But in fact he had concealed from Tomasoa that less than an
hour later they would be given an earring with DNA. Marouan
had asked Calvino why he hadn't revealed this. 'Wouldn't have
looked good for us if the chief had found out we'd received the
evidence from a journalist,' Calvino had answered.

'But how the hell are you going to handle this one?' Marouan
had asked. 'Are you going to keep avoiding the truth?'

'I'll think of something,' had been the answer. The dumbest
answer possible. Because detectives didn't just invent any old
thing; they were interested in facts. And they reported those
facts very factually: exactly the way the facts were. And when
detectives took liberties with the facts, or even concealed them,
they ended up filing an official report based on a story they'd
made up, effectively committing perjury. And that was the
direction Calvino was headed.

Had Calvino, behind his back, perhaps told Tomasoa this
morning that it was Marouan who'd found the earring? Was
that the 'good work' Tomasoa was referring to? No matter how
Marouan looked at it, that was the most logical scenario he
could think of.

Well, if that's how things were – and nobody was going to
convince Marouan otherwise – it meant his partner Calvino
was a dirty backstabber. Marouan had always suspected as
much. You couldn't trust Italians, even if half the blood running through Cal's veins was Dutch, enough cells were infected
with the mob gene.

It seemed like Calvino, in the name of their partnership, was arranging as much as possible on his own. Otherwise, how could you explain Calvino heading straight for the woods early in the morning with that Hafez woman, without first coming to the office, without consulting his partner?

Damn, he'd almost fallen for it. Calvino had entered into an alliance with Hafez. It was therefore in Calvino's interest to keep Marouan at a safe distance. Meanwhile, of course, he had to keep up the appearance that they were working as partners and indicated to Tomasoa that it was Marouan who wanted a line search of the crime scene. As if Marouan had been to the spot himself. Naturally that bastard Cal thought he could kill two birds with one stone this way. Act supportive to his partner while he pulled a fast one behind his back.

Marouan began to smirk. Naturally Calvino wasn't aware of the double role Marouan was playing. He'd have to keep his cards close to his chest, make sure Calvino didn't get wind of his suspicions. Meanwhile he'd lie in wait for a chance to catch Calvino and Hafez in the act, to use this as his trump card. Because if Tomasoa was urging them to stay 'under the radar', to avoid the media like the plague, he would certainly be surprised to hear that Detective Calvino was messing around with a journalist. And the fact that this messing around wasn't going to be limited to the crime scene was obvious.

Now it dawned on Marouan that he was out there on his own, as always. Didn't he have enough problems on his plate?

The large-scale forensic investigation today clearly put his secret mission at risk. Marouan dialled the number on his prepaid phone. Just thinking about the conversation he was about to have made his heart pound.

The voice on the other end of the line sounded as nasal and glum as always.

'Diva. You have one minute.' The Slavic accent, broken English and deadly complacent tone of the voice made Marouan's hands and forehead break out in a clammy sweat.

'This is no time for joking,' he heard himself say.

'I'm not joking,' the voice on the other end of the line replied. 'Why would I waste a good joke on an Arab, Diva? You've got exactly fifty seconds left.'

'They're going to comb the woods.'

'I wish them a lot of luck. Forty-five seconds.'

'They're going to turn the house inside out.'

There was a pause, a kind of icy breathing.

'How did they find out about the villa?'

'How many seconds do I have left?' Marouan asked recklessly.

'Damn it, remember who you're talking to, sheep-fucker! Tell me what you know.'

Marouan swallowed hard. 'A child was run down in the middle of the night. And he didn't just fall from the sky. Otherwise they'd have found a parachute or angel wings.' Marouan couldn't help himself.

'You should be doing stand-up, Diva. So they don't know where that child came from? So what?'

'So they're going to investigate the scene of the crime,' Marouan said. 'They've called out the forensics experts. To analyse the traces of blood they found for DNA. You don't have to wonder where that's going to lead them.'

Marouan tried to bluff his way through his fear, but from the reaction he got, he wasn't very successful.

'You're going to delay their case. Waste their time.'

'You're obviously not familiar with the police system. If my boss arranges something with the Examining Magistrate, do you think they're going to listen to a detective who suggests they send everyone out for a long lunch?'

'Just keep them away from that villa.'

'Impossible! How the hell can I keep this case under wraps if I'm repeatedly surprised by this shit? I can't fucking work like this if I'm constantly a step behind the facts. If you don't want it to get out, I need to know what it is!'

'Listen, *ty parshiwaya skotina,* you little shithead. Your job is to be my eyes and ears. That's what I fucking pay you for. So I'm telling you to muck up this case, and you're getting cocky with me. Are you telling me that *you* can't work like this? You worthless piece of shit!'

By now Marouan was a complete wreck.

'I'm asking you something, asshole!'

'No . . .' muttered Marouan.

'No? What no?!'

'No, that's not what I mean.'

'What did you mean then?'

'Never mind.'

'I'll decide that too. You just do what I tell you to. I repeat: waste their time. And now you're out of time!'

Immediately the line went dead. Marouan hurled the phone through the car and, ranting and raving, took a sharp turn in the woods, which hurled the car into a ditch.

He continued ranting and raving. He banged the flat of his hands on the steering wheel, threw the car door open, paced back and forth cursing, and then slammed the flat of his hands on the Corolla's roof, over and over again, as hard as he could.

Until he no longer felt any pain.

9

With Susanne still nestled in his head, his heart and every muscle of his body, Paul rushed to Ponte City, the round, ramshackle tower near Highland Hills. Constructed in the seventies as a luxury residential high-rise to attract whites, over the years it had fallen into disrepair and literally rotted away from the inside. On the fiftieth floor he'd meet the informant who could tell him more about the new name that had surfaced during his inquiries, that of the Russian oligarch Valentin Lavrov.

After the collapse of the Soviet Union, Lavrov, with a sophisticated organization, had become an international player in the market for gas and mining companies, whereby billions of dollars in profits were funnelled through a complex network of international banks. Lavrov's AtlasNet was based on a worldwide system of highly influential contacts that reached into the topmost circles of business and government.

During an official three-day visit to South Africa a few months earlier, the Russian president Potanin announced that cooperation between the two countries would be strengthened. This seemed to relate especially to the exchange of nuclear fuel and technology for future nuclear energy projects. In the meantime, behind the scenes, there were intensive discussions between government officials led by Nkoane and a team from AtlasNet, which of course was headed by Valentin Lavrov. These negotiations concerned the rights to develop uranium mining on South African territory. AtlasNet wanted to acquire these rights from the South African government.

Paul knew that enormous sums were at stake with the sale of mining concessions to foreign enterprises. It was highly likely with this deal that many of these concession dollars would be misappropriated by Nkoane himself. That's why he expected a lot from his upcoming meeting. Apparently there was now inside information that would enable him to prove a thing or two.

The only question was whether he was going to make it on time. Paul detested being late and cursed himself for losing track of time in Stella's Coffee Bar. The man who could almost certainly give him more information about Nkoane had probably already taken off.

When he finally arrived at the deserted high-rise, he was immediately struck by the metre-high heap of discarded furniture and debris dumped in the building's indoor courtyard. As he looked upwards, the smell of rot penetrated his nostrils and he could hear the sounds of the city echoing and mingling with what seemed to be screaming in this tubular concrete amphitheatre. It came from above. Paul saw that windows and walls on some of the upper floors were completely broken away. His common sense told him it would be wise to turn around and leave. Right now. But since he believed that journalists shouldn't always listen to common sense, he took the only remaining working lift which, jerking and rattling, carried him to the fiftieth floor.

Once there, the noise of the city seemed to have ebbed away, transformed into a steady and dark murmur, as if he could hear his own blood pulsing in his veins in the menacing silence. Because many of the walls were gone, he had a view of a large part of the dusk-shrouded fiftieth floor, but he didn't see any movement. Then suddenly he heard a dull thud from close by, as if someone had fallen down on the concrete floor and quickly tried to stand up. Paul didn't move, listened attentively, and heard the sound again. It was coming from behind a thick column about ten metres in front of him.

Cautiously circling the pillar, he discovered a black man on the other side – firmly bound, but in a makeshift way – who was trying to free himself with spastic movements. The man was unrecognizable. His face was a bloody mess; he'd been beaten to a pulp. He was still conscious, but couldn't utter a sound because of the black tape across his mouth. His eyes were wide open in anguish.

Paul was about to help him when he heard sharp commands barked in Russian behind him. Before he knew it, he was being punched, beaten and kicked in places that he'd never known could hurt so much. He'd also never realized how long a person could tolerate such a beating without losing consciousness. They kept hitting him. The men who were going at him knew exactly what they were doing and how far they could go. They employed exactly the amount of force needed to beat him bloody and break his bones in such a way that he was fully conscious during this thrashing from start to finish.

A stocky, bald man with a goatee appeared from behind the pillar. He was wearing a white shirt with short sleeves, under which tattooed spiders walked towards the tattooed stars on his forearms. His bald scalp gleamed with sweat and an oversized pair of mirrored sunglasses were resting on his hawkish nose. A man in his sixties with the look of a condor and the build of a gladiator.

Now positioned in front of Paul, the man grabbed an inhaler, took a deep breath and held it seconds long, while in the reflection of the glasses Paul watched the two baboon-like brutes who had just given him a good beating. After the condor exhaled with a deep sigh, he casually nodded in the direction of the struggling man tied to the pillar and then turned to Paul.

'Do you know this man, Chapelle?'

He asked this in a heavily-accented English that left you with the aftertaste of home-distilled vodka. Paul was amazed that the man knew his name. He shook his head.

'But you did have an appointment with him?' whispered the condor, leaning even closer to Paul. 'And you don't seem the type for a blind date.'

Now he began humming a melody, something classical. He walked over to the man against the pillar, stood right in front of him with his legs spread wide, then turned his bald head towards Paul.

'I'd guess classical music isn't your thing. You strike me more as a jazz lover. Like your father. You don't know what you're missing, Chapelle. Mozart, Goddammit! *Don Giovanni.*' He clumsily sang a few notes, waving his arms theatrically. The man bound to the column began to thrash about involuntarily.

'*Pentimento, pentimento.* Repentance, repentance! Remorse after sinning. But that remorse usually comes too late. Look!' The condor pulled out a USB stick, which he then dropped back into his shirt pocket.

'This bastard wanted to give you this. Do you know why? Because he'd forgotten our agreement. Agreements are not made to be forgotten. Because when you forget, you can't fulfil them.' He chuckled. 'Agreements – no, these are laws. And if you violate an agreement, you break the law. Could it be any simpler? A moron could understand it.' He nodded towards the man against the pillar. 'But this *balbes* here simply forgot.'

The condor casually snapped his fingers and while one of the baboons restrained Paul, the other untied the black man and dragged him to the edge of the floor where the wall was broken away.

'For God's sake, why?' Paul mumbled, foreseeing what was about to happen. As he spoke, blood dripped from his mouth.

'There are penalties for breaking the law, Chapelle.'

The condor gave an order in Russian and the battered man was pushed over the edge like a sack of rubbish. Seconds later Paul heard the thud of his body landing on the rubbish pile a hundred metres below.

The bald head with the trimmed goatee and mirrored glasses now loomed over Paul, who was trying not to hyperventilate. The man ran his right hand across Paul's forehead – almost fondly – down his cheek into his neck, which was covered in sweat. Paul shuddered as the wheezing condor threateningly whispered in his ear.

'Fascinating to see how sons follow in their fathers' footsteps. As if it's a biological imperative.'

He clutched his inhaler again, eagerly sniffed up the oxygen, and then grabbed Paul's face with both hands, as if trying to compress it with all his might.

'I like clear agreements, Chapelle. Your father knew that. And whenever I hear bells ringing somewhere, I know there's treachery in the air. So I'll say it only once. Don't write about things that are none of your business.'

Paul couldn't move a muscle. His body was being restrained with the force of a pneumatic tool and his face was completely immobilized between the condor's hands. When he suddenly let go, lightning struck his lower back, as if a steel fist wanted to drill a hole right through his spine. He collapsed on to the ground like a rag doll and gasped for air. He immediately felt a stabbing pain, this time in his upper back. He couldn't breathe and his surroundings began to spin around dizzyingly fast.

He was pulled upright and subjected to a new round of punches and kicks with the force of a freight train. When the sole of a shoe hit him full force in the face, he heard an eerie cracking. Then came the liberating darkness.

10

From a distance, Farah and Parwaiz could see the fluttering celestial bodies made of kite fabric hovering above downtown The Hague. Blood-red, canary-yellow and bright-green fighter kites with small tails whooshed around them. Farah remembered them. Their next-door neighbour in Kabul used to make them out of bamboo and ricepaper. These were their modern incarnations, kite fabric made of ripstop nylon and frames of flexible fibreglass.

As they drove up Prinsessewal and past the Palace gardens, Farah glanced sideways at Parwaiz. His age-ravaged face had transformed into that of an astounded boy. Open-mouthed and all eyes, he peered at the colourful kites in the sky. Farah was touched by his vulnerability. Despite everything he'd been through, Parwaiz could still be moved. Naive is what most people would call it. Genuine was the word Farah was thinking of.

She manoeuvred the Carrera cautiously through the traffic on Lange Vijverberg as slowly as possible to allow Parwaiz a good view of the Dutch parliament buildings.

'Splendid, splendid!' he said. 'Those beautiful buildings have been the home of democracy for centuries!'

Democracy, my arse, Farah caught herself thinking. The mere thought of the Dutch government's treatment of refugees like Parwaiz over the years infuriated her. First they were branded potential war criminals, next they were denied any chance of a fair process. Under the legal system in the Netherlands you were innocent until proven guilty, but the Immigration and Naturalization Service played by different rules. If someone was found guilty after its own investigation – without being consulted – that person would then have to prove otherwise! All by themselves. Justice turned upside-down. It was too bizarre for words.

As her anger mounted, Farah raced into the underground car park at such speed that Parwaiz uttered a cry of distress and clutched her arm in a reflex.

'I'm sorry, *kaka jan*,' she apologized. She parked the car, helped him out, rang for the lift and in no time they were standing in the August sun at the foot of the William of Orange statue. Her anger dissolved.

For several minutes they looked out over the tree-lined square which had filled with enthusiastic kite-fliers, protesters and baffled tourists. The atmosphere was animated, festive even.

Farah noticed that despite his fragile body Parwaiz walked over to a kite-flier with something of a spring in his step. The man was trussed up in leather straps, which in turn had been attached to kite ropes.

'Look!' Parwaiz exclaimed delightedly, and when Farah followed his finger pointing to the sky she discovered the large banner high above the square: a replica of an age-old image depicting a young woman waving an Afghan flag.

'*Malalai!*' Parwaiz called out her name at the top of his lungs, as if he'd just bumped into an acquaintance he hadn't seen in years.

Farah recognized the painting of Malalai from her childhood visits to the National Museum. Suddenly she remembered the prediction Parwaiz had whispered in her ear at the time.

'*Dar ayenda to mesle u mashhur khahad shodi.*' One day you'll be just as famous as her.

Thinking of the old days and seeing the large banner gliding through the air had the unexpected effect of making her feel like the timid little girl she'd once been, especially when Parwaiz's long arms enveloped her in a fatherly embrace.

'Thank you, *dokhtarem*, for all of this,' he said softly.

'No, no, don't thank me, dear uncle. *Tashakor az shoma!*' I ought to thank you! she stammered.

'Would you believe,' Parwaiz began as they carried on walking, 'that in the sixties and seventies Kabul was known as the Paris of the East? There was a sense of promise in the air. Nobody can imagine it these days, but that's how it was.' He turned around. 'The people who organized the get-together this afternoon must have known.'

They had now reached the entrance to Parliament. Farah looked at the mostly young men and women around them. The majority of them were Afghan, sons and daughters of Afghan fathers who'd been civil servants during the Russian occupation. Like Parwaiz. Fathers who'd sought asylum in the Netherlands with their families and who'd found themselves caught up in all kinds of legal proceedings. Like Parwaiz.

What was it like for a child to see its own father branded a war criminal? She hoped that the young adults around her were just as proud of their fathers as she was of hers. She cherished the memory of him as her hero.

Farah was jolted from her thoughts by the sudden appearance of a blond cameraman. He peered through his viewfinder with his left eye squeezed shut and with the other eye shot some footage of her and Parwaiz. Behind him stood a thick-set sound engineer, bald as a coot. He was recording the ambient sounds using a microphone with a grey plastic popper on a long boom pole. Farah smiled at the camera and then glanced at a flustered Parwaiz. She was curious to see how she looked alongside *kaka jan* on this special day. Maybe the festivities would even make the evening news.

Having taken his shot, the cameraman spun on his heel like a professional dancer, bent his knees a little and walked away from them, into the crowd, holding the camera steady and straight. The soundman followed right behind.

The television crew was headed in the same direction as most of the bystanders, as though pulled by a magnet. At the same time, she sensed a growing excitement sweeping through the crowd like a gust of wind. At the entrance to the Parliament building people were crowding around a man in his forties with cold blue eyes and a square jaw. Dressed in a well-fitting navy pinstripe suit, he looked like he'd stepped straight out of a fashion spread. Farah immediately recognized Vincent Coronel, the most controversial leader of the opposition in the House of Representatives. The frontman of the right-wing Democratische Partij Nederland was firmly opposed to the introduction of the general pardon. Several camera teams and photographers had gathered around him, and flanked by two burly bodyguards Coronel spoke passionately into the extended microphones. The vast majority of the onlookers tried to drown him out by jeering and chanting slogans, but Coronel took no notice and continued, illustrating his argument with firm gestures. Whichever way you looked at it, Coronel was no coward. He wasn't doing this in a little pressroom somewhere, or at an inconspicuous back entrance. No, he was standing here, as he put it himself, 'in the heart of democracy, on the square where William of Orange, this country's founding father, now faces the sorry sight of multiculturalists frittering away our national heritage!'

Farah thought that Coronel's behaviour didn't show courage as much as boundless arrogance and she hoped the people around her would have the good sense to refrain from doing anything stupid in response to his provocation. It only took a single unhinged person to give Coronel the ammunition to start harping on about the 'lack of respect for our Dutch values in most immigrant circles'.

She noticed that Parwaiz was starting to feel uncomfortable amidst the jostling, and decided to return to the relative peace and quiet of the square. She was about to cross the road when Parwaiz grabbed her by the arm. It was immediately clear why: an approaching silver Bentley. Although the car wasn't going very fast, it moved the way she'd once seen Russian tanks moving through the streets of Kabul, without any intention of stopping.

'*Bachem*, watch out.'

She saw that the Bentley, which glided past majestically, was driven by a chauffeur in a dark-grey uniform. As the car passed,

Parwaiz's paternal grip suddenly turned into a painful, cramped grasp. Horrified, he stared at the unfamiliar man in the rear. He clutched his chest with both hands, as if wanting to tear his shirt to shreds, and uttered an almost animalistic yell, which cut through Farah like a knife.

As his knees buckled, Parwaiz's face drained of colour and he started retching. He panted for help. He seemed absolutely horror-stricken, and when Farah broke his fall, he felt as fragile as a glass sculpture splintering from within. She managed to gently lower him on to the pavement, where he lay writhing in pain and began vomiting.

She rolled him on his side to prevent him from choking. His brown skin had turned ashen, and he could barely utter a word. Farah wiped the vomit from his face and supported his head with her other hand. Then she sat up and yelled as loud as she could for someone to phone an ambulance.

Very few people had a clue what was happening. It was too busy. The band on the square kept playing and the kites were still dancing up in the air.

Although he was now barely breathing, Parwaiz tried to pull her close. As Farah bent over him, she brought her ear as close as possible to his mouth. He produced some soft, incoherent sounds.

'Don't talk, *kaka jan*. Don't try to talk.'

But he pulled her close again and whispered hoarsely in her ear.

'Mi . . . ka . . . lov . . .'

Practically emotionless, like a statement. As if those three sounds could explain what had happened.

'Mikalov? *Kaka jan*, what do you mean?'

He looked at her without reacting.

With eyes that were devoid of life.

I I

In the last light of the setting sun, Paul saw a bloody hand appear above the edge of the fiftieth floor. Then the second hand appeared, and a moment later he was staring straight into the eyes of the man with the smashed-up face.

His yelling alerted the night nurse who ran into the room where Paul, connected to tubes, was lying amidst the beeping hospital monitors. When he opened his eyes again, it was morning and there was a young black man in a white shirt beside his bed looking at him as if he'd just been told a bad joke.

The man introduced himself as Elvin Dingane, Homicide detective. He was curious about what Paul had been doing in the dilapidated Ponte City tower complex.

Paul wasn't sure he could trust Dingane, although everything about him suggested he was an extremely committed and conscientious detective. Somebody who was used to getting down to business. A man who radiated confidence, with even a bit of empathy in his eyes – something you rarely saw in men who performed the thankless job of detective.

'Does the name Thaba Zhulongu mean anything to you?' Dingane asked.

'Who?'

'Thaba Zhulongu, Senior Defence Official.'

From a brown leather folder, Elvin Dingane pulled a black-and-white photo of a civilized-looking black man with a friendly smile.

'Is this Zhulongu?' Paul asked.

'When he was still in one piece,' said Dingane. 'He leaves a young wife and three children behind. We found what was left of him splattered on the ground-floor rubble in Ponte City.'

Paul felt the panic race through his body again and his head began to throb violently.

'The Scorpion Unit doesn't consider you a suspect, Mr Chapelle,' Dingane calmly said. 'It's clear to us that you walked into a trap; you should count yourself lucky that you survived.'

The Scorpions were considered the most successful opponents of organized crime in the whole of South Africa. Paul gave Dingane another inquiring once-over and decided not to beat about the bush with him.

'If it's the same man,' Paul said, looking at the photograph, 'then, when I found him tied to that pillar, there wasn't much left of him.' He let out a laboured breath. 'He'd been tortured. Then they hurled him to the bottom of the tower to show me what they do to snitches.'

'It was Zhulongu,' said Dingane. 'We were able to identify him by his dental records. Because of his murder, we've been ordered to launch a full-scale investigation into the affairs of Jacob Nkoane's ministry.'

'Damn,' Paul said, grinning. 'It gets better all the time.'

'The good news is that the majority of the ANC's leaders are trustworthy people, Mr Chapelle, who've all demanded that the corruption be investigated and fought at the highest levels of government. The bad news is that we're unable to offer you any form of protection. That beating you got in Ponte City was a warning. If you carry on with your inquiry, after the next article we'll probably find you somewhere in an alley, under a bridge, or in a landfill. And I can assure you there will be far less life in you compared to now.'

'So you're asking me to abandon my investigation?'

'I'm asking you to leave the investigating to us now.'

'I'll have to give that some thought,' Paul said curtly, as he sunk deep into his pillow and closed his eyes.

12

Walking the line on a crime scene required the utmost in concentration: a kind of tunnel vision. You had to continually scrutinize the few square metres right in front of you, until you saw something out of the ordinary. The detectives formed a line and slowly walked in formation from the hill where the villa was situated through the woods towards the road. A controlled march of silent men with their faces pointed downwards, no further than an arm's length apart from each other, their eyes searching for possible variations in colour, different shapes and footprints. Any evidence to corroborate that a young boy dressed as a girl in traditional Afghan attire had possibly run for his life here.

Joshua Calvino was walking the line on the right, alongside Marouan Diba. He was having trouble concentrating on the matter at hand. In twenty-four hours he'd seen his partner change from a bitter but reliable colleague into an out-of-control, bad-tempered enigma. Suddenly Diba was a shadow of the detective he'd once been.

From the very first moment Joshua had started working with him, he knew he'd need to be tough as nails. He'd have to be able to endure Diba's moods and get used to the underlying threat posed by his partner's pent-up anger. Joshua had been forewarned. Yet, as a junior detective he was determined to learn a lot from the renowned Marouan Diba, who'd scored on several fronts early in his career.

Diba's reputation preceded him. As a policeman, he'd ended up in the limelight by carrying out an impressive number of heavy-handed arrests of Moroccan youngsters in Amsterdam. Remarkably, because of this, these youngsters grew to respect him, and eventually made him their confidant. If there was something or other in the air, police command sent Diba to check it out. And nine times out of ten he managed to put to rest yet another conflict about to erupt between the neighbourhood's immigrant and Dutch residents.

A few years later, he even shot to national attention. He led an investigation team at Schiphol Airport to eleven boxes in the hold of a cargo plane arriving from the Caribbean, an unprecedented achievement. The estimated street value of the 600 kilos of cocaine hidden in those boxes was in the neighbourhood of forty million euros, making Detective Marouan Diba responsible for the second largest drug bust ever at the airport.

Joshua certainly wanted an icon like this as a mentor, at least for a while. So he'd resigned himself to the inconveniences that came with the package, like the fact that Diba more often than not started his shift reeking of alcohol, that he tended to sweat like a pig, and his manners and eating habits were like those of a pig too. Joshua, headstrong as he was, continued to believe in the good intentions behind the unruly and sometimes revolting behaviour of his one-time hero.

Yet even Joshua couldn't deny that Diba's best days were now behind him. He was a man entangled in what appeared to be a web of depression. Joshua read it in his eyes, heard it in his voice, he even saw it in his step. Diba carried a heavy burden.

There was intense speculation behind his back about what that burden might entail. Alcohol addiction, a failed marriage, manic depression or an impending burnout were just a few of the variations on the topic. But despite all the speculation no one spoke to Diba directly, not even Joshua. Talking about these kinds of things was not what you did as a member of the police force. You just kept going.

In one way or another Diba's decline made Joshua feel a moral obligation to protect his colleague for as long as he could. For that reason alone, he wanted nothing more than for this whole affair with the boy to be solved as quickly as possible. Hopefully then he'd be able to put Diba on a plane to Marrakesh for a much-needed holiday.

By now the line had reached the spot Joshua had marked this morning because Farah had found the earring there. The detectives continued in silence. Only the rustle of the low bushes brushing against their trousers and the crackle of twigs beneath their shoes were audible, while behind them came the occasional shout of the forensics team who were setting up a perimeter around the villa.

Suddenly one of the detectives to the left of the line raised his hand. On an overhanging branch hung a torn piece of blue fabric stitched with gold thread. The detective marked the spot by tying a piece of police tape around the tree.

Joshua could hear Diba breathing heavily, but resisted the urge to glance at him. Instead he scanned not only the ground in front of his feet, but also secretly focused on Diba's area. And this paid off. Out of the corner of his right eye he saw something. It was a dull shade of red and half hidden by the dark moss on the ground. He was counting on Diba to also spot it; after all, it was lying right in front of him. But Diba kept going as if he was sleepwalking.

When Joshua himself gave the sign to stop, he thought he'd caught a glimpse of despair in Diba's eyes. Or was it anger?

Joshua left the line and walked past Diba towards the red object, which looked like a slipper or a sandal. He tagged the spot with a piece of tape. He gazed back at the place where they'd all entered the woods, and he imagined the zigzagging path the boy must have taken. As they got back into formation, Joshua didn't dare ask himself the obvious question: had Diba really missed it?

When they were finished, based on the spots they'd marked, they would be able to reconstruct the most probable route the boy had taken and give the area another once-over for more trace evidence. The question still remained if the fleeing boy had been chased by anybody. They needed to find footsteps, but unfortunately the forest ground was very dry. In the past few weeks it hadn't rained much to speak of. At least not enough to soften the ground, therefore making it easier to detect footprints.

*

Joshua walked the course again, together with a forensic detective who was snapping photos and placing additional markers on the spots they'd investigate later in the day. But while he was doing this, Joshua had only had one thing on his mind. What the hell was going on with Diba?

The forensics guys in their white suits were still busy on the patio and around the villa. Joshua saw Diba watching from the other side of the police tape with a worried expression. A bigger contrast with the man who just a day ago had gone berserk at the firemen hosing down the burning station wagon was hardly conceivable.

One of the forensic detectives shouted to his colleagues that he'd found something by an oak about fifteen metres from the villa. Joshua thought he saw him holding a bullet casing in the air. He wasn't entirely sure, but he thought he heard Marouan cursing under his breath.

'What's going on, partner?' Joshua asked casually.

'What did they say again?' Diba replied without even looking at Joshua. 'It's all a lot of smoke but no fire.'

'Sorry, I didn't see any smoke.'

'Keep your jokes to yourself, Cal. How many detectives are working this crime scene right now? And what are grown men like you and me actually doing, with all this senseless line-dancing through the woods? Maybe we should all hold hands too? And why? Because you and your squeeze went romping around the woods early this morning and don't dare to tell anyone.'

'What's your friggin' problem, Diba?'

'What did you tell Tomasoa this morning?' Marouan asked crossly. 'That you were here with me?'

Joshua threw him a harsh look. 'And you're telling me that you didn't see anything on the ground just now?'

'Let me tell you what I see,' Diba angrily replied. 'Here, right in front of my nose, I see a hypocrite who's chasing his Italian dick.'

Joshua had to keep himself from punching Marouan in front of all their colleagues.

'Hey, I'm talking to you, asshole!' Diba shrieked in a high-pitched tone. He was panting.

At that moment, the Examining Magistrate arrived at the villa. He gave Dick Park, the head of Forensics, permission to go inside using an old pass key. Joshua thought back to what Farah had said to him earlier that morning. 'This is much bigger than we actually realize, right?' He turned around and saw Diba slip into the woods and decided to follow him.

Diba seemed distracted, and looked as if he'd put on an impenetrable coat of armour. Joshua tried to reason with him.

'Diba, listen. Yesterday, I didn't say anything to Tomasoa because I wasn't sure if Farah Hafez really had something for us. And yes, I was concerned about the fact she's a journalist. But she agreed to come to the office to give a statement. And if you want to interrogate her, you go right ahead. And for the record, I put everything in my official report, except for the fact that I just saw my partner ignore a piece of evidence he practically stumbled over.'

'Dammit, Cal!' Diba cried out like a caged animal. 'Shut your trap and piss off!'

Diba walked off, leaving Joshua looking around, worried that someone had seen or heard them. But they were alone and hopefully beyond earshot of the rest. He'd often seen Diba angry, but he'd never seen him so exasperated, so unsure of himself and so unpredictable and destructive. While what just happened here took on a grimmer and greater significance for Joshua, the role of Marouan Diba in all this became more and more puzzling.

13

It had been over five hours since the paramedic had gently prised Farah away from Parwaiz's lifeless body. A policeman had briefly questioned her, wanting to know who she was, what her relationship to the deceased was and what she thought might have happened. Farah had not mentioned the passing car. She couldn't imagine a connection between the two. How on earth could a faceless man in his forties in the back of a Bentley have caused the heart attack of an old Afghan man? Yet she kept hearing his feeble whisper, 'Mi . . . ka . . . lov.' And again she felt his powerful grip on her arm.

She was jolted from her thoughts by the bright-red brake lights of the car in front of her; they were approaching rapidly. A few seconds later she was stuck in traffic, with trembling hands, a throat as dry as dust and throbbing temples.

For the past couple of hours she hadn't allowed herself to feel how Parwaiz's death had affected her. The blond cameraman and his sound engineer had offered to follow the ambulance and take her to the hospital. But Farah had instantly put herself into 'modus practicus'. Action, she hoped, would help her outrun the panic and the sadness for as long as possible.

She'd driven to the hospital where she was taken to a cold, tiled mortuary room. Parwaiz lay there like a wax likeness of himself. When she told the hospital worker that he was a Muslim she was given the phone number of an appropriate funeral company. The friendly woman she got on the line assured her that Parwaiz's body would be collected for a ritual washing in the evening.

Then she returned to his apartment. Some time ago, Parwaiz had given her a key for what he termed 'unforeseen circumstances'. This was the first time she'd used it. She opened the front door, quietly hoping she'd see him sitting in his Chesterfield as usual. He'd get up, with a surprised look, and their embrace would confirm that what had happened this afternoon was simply a delusion.

But the Chesterfield was empty, and a grim silence pervaded the apartment.

She walked over to the large table and carefully opened the top drawer. The paper butterfly lay on top of the tissue-wrapped parcel Parwaiz had given her. She picked up the butterfly and held it aloft in both hands, in front of her face, like she'd done at the market yesterday.

She looked at the paper wings and felt the sorrow of the past and present merging. Slowly but surely it took complete possession of her body. Each movement, each action felt gruelling. But she had to keep going.

Feeling numb, she wandered through the apartment for a while. Then she did something she hadn't done in a very long time. In the middle of the Bokhara carpet she knelt down, bowed to the east and began praying. 'Allah, You may doubt me just as I doubt You at times, but please admit Parwaiz *jan* to Your Paradise.'

She sat down at the sturdy workbench, picked up a sketching pencil and on the back of a drawing jotted down a list of all the practical things she wanted to take care of today. She looked for and found insurance documents in the drawer, phoned the housing association and told them to cancel the tenancy agreement owing to the death of the tenant, checked the gas and water meters, made a note of the readings and passed them on to the relevant companies with the request for disconnection.

She planned to store the contents of the two large drawers in boxes at home, and would arrange for the old Chesterfield, the workbench and the carpet to be taken to her own apartment. They were the most tangible reminders of Parwaiz *jan*. She'd donate the rest of his sparse furniture, the curtains and lamps to the Salvation Army.

After locking up the apartment she got into her car. By the time dark-grey clouds came rolling in from the west, the heat had become stifling. And now she was stuck in a tailback stretching for ever, unable to stop thinking about what had happened. Her whole body started shaking and it felt like her throat was being choked.

The first big, fat raindrops splashed down. She threw open the door, ran past the stationary vehicles and on to the hard shoulder where, leaning over the crash barrier, she started retching.

She had no idea how long she'd been there when she heard loud honking behind her. As she turned around she saw that the Carrera was the only car standing still in the middle of the three lanes. Some of the drivers who were manoeuvring their vehicles around it made angry gestures in her direction. In tandem with the pouring rain, the blaring horns and furious name-calling from the lowered windows produced a cacophony of noise.

Farah took a deep breath.

She stuck both hands in the air, waving them about to create the firmest stop sign she possibly could, and stepped out on to the motorway. In the full glare of braking cars she dashed into the Carrera. The engine started straight away. She stepped on the gas and drove deeper into the torrential rain.

14

It was approaching five in the afternoon when Marouan Diba hesitantly knocked on his boss's door; he got the feeling he'd had to wait a bit too long before being asked to 'come in'.

Upon entering the room, he felt as if he'd interrupted a secret meeting. Calvino, the head of Forensics, Dick Park, and Tomasoa looked at Marouan as if they'd been talking about him at great length, but hadn't yet decided if they'd immediately tar and feather him and ride him around in a cart, or they'd do it as soon as they were finished talking.

'Have a seat, Diba,' Tomasoa offered. 'As you already know, via the Examining Magistrate, I've asked the forensic lab to put a rush on examining all the evidence Dick's team collected today. To my surprise, this has already delivered a number of possible clues that we can cross off the list.' Just like a bingo card, Diba cynically thought.

First off, Tomasoa wanted to know what they'd found during the line search. Marouan saw Calvino sternly nod in his direction as if to say, *Go ahead, you tell them.*

Marouan wondered what he was even doing there. Since being snarled at and ordered about early this morning, he'd had the same feeling as thirty years ago, when he took the bus from Tangier to Marrakesh to bring his youngest brother, the baby of the family, home. Marouan had boarded that bus while everything in him screamed not to. He'd ignored that warning, a warning similar to what he felt this morning when his clandestine associate with the Slavic accent had ordered him to stall the investigation, while he knew there was no way he could do that. He wanted to put on the handbrake but there wasn't one. And besides, if there had been a handbrake, it probably wouldn't have worked. Just like the brakes on that bus which also hadn't worked.

He'd acted impulsively this morning in the woods: pretended he hadn't seen anything. An impulse that suddenly felt like treason when Calvino gave the stop sign and walked over to something red that looked like a sandal. After that altercation in the woods, Marouan spent the entire day trying to avoid his partner. Partly out of embarrassment for his petty behaviour and partly because he sensed that by now Calvino had to have at least a vague suspicion about his double-dealing.

Calvino coughed. Marouan was jerked back to reality and saw the three men impatiently looking in his direction.

'There were three items found,' he stammered. 'An earring with blood spatters, a piece of cloth from the boy's robe and a sandal.'

Tomasoa gazed at photos of the three items, which the senior forensics officer had taken at the location.

Marouan threw Calvino a compelling glance, as if to insinuate, *And now you. Tell, them, asshole!* Calvino looked away.

Park broke the silence. 'The lab confirmed that the blood on the earring is the boy's. There are no further DNA matches in our system.'

'Anything else in particular to report?' Tomasoa routinely asked.

'Yes, about the earring,' Calvino muttered, 'that is, uh, it wasn't our find exactly, chief.'

'Then who exactly found it?' Tomasoa looked at him as if he knew he wasn't going to like the answer. The chief could see right through people, Marouan thought.

'A journalist,' said Calvino, sounding like a choirboy who'd been up to something naughty. 'It's a bit bizarre: she's the same person you saw the night before last in that fight at Carré.'

'The crane lady?'

'Yes, her.'

Here we go, thought Marouan.

'What does she have to do with this case?' Tomasoa asked in an icy tone.

'Long story, chief. She was in the ER to check on her opponent at the moment the boy was brought in. She's Afghan and interpreted for the medical staff. Then she went to the scene of the accident, walked through the woods and found the earring.'

'So she got there before you?' Tomasoa now asked, clearly irritated.

'That's right. Afterwards she called us, sorry, called *me* to report her find and we went to see her immediately.'

'We? Calvino? Is that the royal, plural "we", or . . .?'

'Detective Diba and myself.'

'Obviously. And when did that visit take place?'

'Yesterday afternoon.'

'And how do you know exactly where she found the earring?'

There was an awkward silence. Calvino stared at Marouan and this time it was Marouan who looked away.

'I went with her this morning to the spot she'd indicated,' Calvino replied softly.

Tomasoa looked at them individually. 'This morning? I had the idea that you were there together. And by "you", I mean the two of you.'

'I was there, chief,' Marouan suddenly heard himself lying aloud. 'Then I came to the station.' He ignored the surprised look on Calvino's face.

Tomasoa had laid the photos aside and was rummaging through the piles on his desk for something. 'And I understood that . . .' he said, still searching, 'based on the clothing, jewellery and make-up that the boy was used for something called . . .'

'Bacha Bazi,' Calvino said.

'Afghan dancing boys,' Marouan clarified for him.

'In other words,' said Tomasoa while he hurriedly read through the document he'd found, 'a boy whore.'

Nobody responded. They were used to hearing pretty crude stuff, but when Tomasoa uttered these words, it somehow sounded like someone swearing in church.

'Is that why the journalist is so caught up in this?'

'Without a doubt,' said Marouan.

'But I'd like to hear it directly from her,' Tomasoa said. 'When is she going to be questioned?'

'As soon as possible, chief.'

'Tomorrow,' said Tomasoa. 'Not a day later.' He looked at the document again.

'Bacha Bazi. A new phenomenon. That brings us to the question of what on earth went down at that villa.'

'From the different tyre tracks found, we can deduce that the villa was possibly used as a meeting place,' said Park, who took his time to elaborate. 'At this stage we don't have any evidence that we're dealing with something like child prostitution, but we can conclude that it got rather out of hand when the parties met up at the villa. There were shots fired both inside and outside the place. We found bullet casings, blood and drag marks at both spots. Based on those casings, while performing the autopsy the pathologist found a match with the calibre bullet in the sternum of one of the men from the burnt-out station wagon. In the case of the second victim, two bullets passed right through the body, but the entry wounds were compared with those bullet casings too and also indicated a match.'

'Can we deduce that the two men in the station wagon were both victims of that shoot-out?' asked Tomasoa.

'That's the most likely scenario,' agreed Park.

Tomasoa straightened his back – Yul Brynner-style – and looked at Marouan, who again felt more and more like the helpless passenger he once was in a fast-moving bus, as a lorry full of asphalt barrelled towards it from the right.

'I'm trying to reconstruct the scene,' Tomasoa said, glancing at Calvino. 'A number of parties come by car to the villa. The boy was probably part of the entourage. Then something goes wrong. What exactly, we don't know. Shots are fired. At least one of the shootings takes place inside the villa. So we can make an educated guess that there is at least one victim now. Shots are also exchanged outside. Another victim. Somewhere in that chaos the boy manages to escape.'

As he summed up, Tomasoa shifted his gaze to Park. 'Our first victim was then dragged from the villa. The other victim who was shot outside was also dragged away. They were dumped in a car and found a short time later a few kilometres away. What do we know about the car?'

Park fumbled through some papers and handed Tomasoa a document. 'Via the chassis number we've determined that it's a Russian car, delivered by the manufacturer in Odessa to an importer who leases cars to a letterbox company, owner unknown.'

'So it's a dead end,' Tomasoa concluded.

Marouan's mouth went dry as he recalled the final seconds before the lorry rammed the bus. He'd wrapped his arms around his younger brother and pressed him to his chest to protect him.

Tomasoa shifted uncomfortably in his chair.

'We've reached a point where I feel like we're groping around in the dark. And let me assure you, I can do without this. So gentlemen, enlighten me!' He began drumming his fingers on the desktop, impatient for answers. 'Why so close by? Why set fire to the station wagon on a spot that can be connected to the villa so easily?'

'Maybe it was an unplanned rush job,' Calvino said, pausing to see if Tomasoa approved of him continuing.

'Go on,' said Tomasoa with a wave of his hand.

'What if it was one man?' Calvino suggested.

Marouan sat up. Since that morning he'd had the same suspicion.

'One man?' asked Tomasoa.

'That would explain a lot.' Calvino glanced at Park. 'I understand that more than two trails of blood were found?'

'Correct,' Park verified.

'Suppose our man himself was injured during the exchange of shots. If he was alone . . . We're dealing with a pro. He knows that if his victims are identified the evidence will lead us directly to him. He uses the station wagon fire to make sure we can't identify them. But he doesn't want to do this at the villa. Because that immediately places the primary site of the crime in the spotlight. So he torches the wagon somewhere else. However, he can't go too far from the villa because he's alone. He has to go back because he's left his car there.'

Marouan was stunned by Calvino's astute analysis. It suddenly dawned on him why he'd perceived Calvino as a threat for such a long time. The man had qualities that helped a detective rise above the poor slobs who were just trying to do their very best. He had command of the job in the way a chess master controls the board. He looked ahead, considered all the possible moves and made his choices.

Marouan could only conclude that Calvino had long since passed him by. And he hadn't done that with a lot of bravado, it had happened quietly. Marouan had completely missed it. And now he could only listen dumbfounded to Calvino presenting his brilliant theory about the case.

'Our man uses the station wagon to transport the bodies to the clearing a few kilometres away. He removes the plates, along with rings, watches and any other personal belongings of the victims, pours petrol over the vehicle and lights a match. Boom!'

Marouan felt dizzy. After more than thirty years, he could still feel the bus skidding at an angle at the moment the lorry rammed it. Once again he heard the deafening racket of tearing metal, splintering glass and the screams of the passengers who were launched through the spinning vehicle like live projectiles. His brother included.

'Everything okay, Diba?' Tomasoa threw him a concerned glance.

'I'm okay, boss,' he lied.

'And then,' said Calvino, 'our man still has to return to the villa. And he's not about to call a taxi.'

'So you're saying . . . that's why he stayed so close by,' Tomasoa mumbled.

Calvino nodded enthusiastically. 'Exactly. And that's also why we found all that trace evidence. By the time he gets back to the villa it's dark, the area is swarming with police because the boy has been found on the road, and our suspect is also wounded. No opportunity, no time and too badly hurt to cover his tracks.'

Marouan could tell them exactly who they should go to in order to verify Calvino's story. An impulse told him to just give up the name of the man he now pictured. A man who liked to dress in tight-fitting Armani suits, wore a bizarre sort of ponytail as if he'd just stepped out of a kung fu film and spoke English with a thick Slavic accent. But Marouan also realized that as soon as he revealed the man's identity, he'd be the victim of his own honesty. The mere mention of the name would have the same impact as the blow with which the lorry hit that bus in Marrakesh thirty years ago.

In the meantime, Tomasoa had given his undivided attention to Calvino and seemed impressed. Marouan knew that Calvino would one day be sitting in Tomasoa's seat. And Tomasoa didn't look like a man who felt threatened by this. Only true masters respected each other, because of the talent and qualities they recognized in one another, thought Marouan. He saw Tomasoa studying him again.

'Could the collision with the boy be related to the shooting, Diba?' Tomasoa asked.

Marouan was amazed at his quick response. 'If they intended to run down the boy on purpose, they wouldn't have hit the brakes,' he said. 'And even if this was their plan, they would have never left him there on the road like that.'

'Anyway,' said Tomasoa, 'in no time at all that poor child has been upgraded from the victim of a traffic accident to the chief witness of a criminal retaliation. That means that the hit-and-run investigation is no longer an isolated case.'

'What does that mean for us, boss?' asked Marouan, who already knew the dreaded answer.

'That this case will be coupled with the double murder that the MIT is investigating,' Tomasoa said, 'and that both of you will probably be added to that team.'

Here we go again, thought Marouan, realizing what this meant. He would be strapped into the straitjacket of a hierarchically led team. If he was lucky he'd be sent out now and then to fetch coffee for the experts. He'd have zero control over anything that happened. Every movement or action that deviated from protocol would immediately stand out. Marouan's hands were tied. He'd no longer be of any use to the menacing voice with his orders and threats.

Marouan wiped the sweat from his forehead. He realized that little had changed in his life since he'd crawled out of that bus to Marrakesh, the only survivor.

15

A can of iced coffee, two hummus wraps, a snack pack of baby carrots and two cans of Golden Power comprised the haul of Farah's quick raid on the first service station she came across. With the energy supply in her arms she was queuing at the till, waiting to be served, when her eye fell on the newspaper rack and the black-and-white photo gracing the front page of *De Nederlander*. She saw a man who looked vaguely familiar and a woman holding a large bouquet of flowers. They stood on either side of a hospital bed and looked into the camera with sad eyes and regretful smiles.

Farah's heart skipped a beat when she recognized the boy in the bed.

He looked just like he did when he was brought into the Emergency Department. With the eyes of someone who appeared to be caught in his own nightmare.

She snatched a copy of the paper, paid and rushed across the car park. Less than a minute later she was sitting in the Carrera with *De Nederlander* folded across the steering wheel. As she sank her teeth into the first hummus wrap, her eyes darted across Angela Faber's emotional account in the article accompanying the photo, headlined 'My Day in a Police Cell'. Angela Faber recounted how, in the middle of the night, she had seen a seriously injured Middle-Eastern boy dressed as a girl lying in the road, and had saved his life by immediately alerting emergency services.

Farah read about the 'appalling blunder of the detectives' who subsequently arrested Angela as a prime suspect in the hit-and-run.

But that was not all.

Under the heading THE PRICE OF MY FAME, Angela's husband, Dennis Faber, aka 'star presenter and frontman of IRIS TV', revealed the drama of being 'handcuffed and carted off like a notorious criminal' in front of the cameras while taping *The Game of Love*. 'A traumatic experience', according to Faber, all the more so because he was charged with complicity when, by his own account, he'd been nowhere near the scene of the accident. Faber did not mince words about the police's actions. 'You do wonder where this country is headed when two immigrant detectives can get away with making a laughing stock of our legal system with their primitive, un-Dutch behaviour.'

Furthermore, the 'deeply affected couple' let it be known that 'obviously' they would be filing an official complaint against the police for unlawful deprivation of liberty.

However, 'an emotional Angela Faber' stressed that 'the greatest victim of this sorry affair' was the little boy himself. 'So we've set aside our own problems to really be here for him today.' Whereupon Dennis Faber said 'with immense compassion' that there was nothing they could do for the 'poor little mite' except 'hope and pray he would be all right'.

Not only did Farah find the hypocrisy insufferable, but she wondered why in God's name Cathy Marant, of all people, was suddenly looking into the boy's case. Was Marant aware of Farah's involvement and was she now trying to incriminate her in this way? Farah got the answer to this question when she turned to the paper's media section, where the article continued. On seeing Danielle's name and photo, all the pieces of the puzzle fell into place. This article had come about on Danielle's initiative, no doubt about it. Exploiting the Fabers' story to her own advantage was a brilliant idea. If Danielle ever decided to leave medicine, there would be a PR job waiting.

According to Danielle, 'the seriously injured boy was given specialist care and treatment at the ICU of the Waterland Medical Centre.' Only the visiting hours were missing. How could she be so stupid? She even went on to say that the boy 'had been the victim of a ruthless gang of child traffickers who had left him for dead in the woods'.

Had it not occurred to Danielle that with this article she was effectively rolling out the red carpet for those very same 'ruthless' characters, so they could shut him up for good? But the real shock came at the end of the article when Farah read that Danielle would give her own 'blood-curdling account of the boy's discovery' on *The Headlines Show* tonight.

Farah's fury at Danielle's self-serving behaviour got the better of her grief for Parwaiz. She remembered what Danielle had told her earlier. 'The case is topical right now,' she'd insisted. 'There's plenty of interest, especially after that television couple were arrested. And tomorrow something could happen that overshadows this story.'

Should Farah have reacted differently to Danielle's proposal? She'd explained quite clearly why she couldn't and wouldn't help her. Was there anything she could have done? Should she have argued her case more forcefully, stressing that it was unwise to attract public attention to this case so soon? Either way, she had refused to be part of Danielle's plan. Because she'd felt exploited. Now she was paying for this refusal.

She also realized that Danielle's appearance on *The Headlines Show* would attract far more media attention than her investigation needed. Her boss Edward wanted her to work 'under the radar'. Perhaps he'd call off the whole investigation?

Dog-tired, she stared into space, chewing some carrots without tasting them and leaning on the steering wheel so the pressure of her elbows slowly tore the newspaper in two. She tried to make sense of it all, to find a satisfactory explanation for this sequence of bizarre events.

Again, she pictured the boy looking at her after waking from the sedation. Again, she felt Parwaiz's tight grip. She saw his eyes the moment life left them. The two faces merged with one another. The face of the boy fighting for his life and the face of Parwaiz losing his.

Then suddenly it dawned on Farah that she was the link between two events that were seemingly unrelated.

She checked her watch. She had lost all sense of time. It was past four o'clock. If she hurried, she would just make it to the press conference. Then afterwards she could persuade Edward of the importance of continuing the investigation. No matter what. Even if it meant collaborating with Paul.

16

With one hand Danielle adjusted the tap as she held her other hand under the streaming water to test if it was a good temperature for her bath.

This morning hadn't gone as smoothly as she'd hoped for. She'd asked Mariska if it was okay for Angela Faber to pay a brief visit to the boy. 'One minute, no more . . .' Mariska's hesitation turned into a resolute refusal upon seeing the entourage following Angela Faber into the ICU.

'They're going to hand me my head for this. It's not okay!' Mariska cried as Danielle hastily escorted her illustrious company into the boy's room. 'You've gone too far, Danielle. Get these people out of here or I'm going to call Security.'

Seeing the boy made Angela Faber stiffen and she couldn't manage more than a pathetic 'Oh my God, my God, what have they done to you?' Dennis Faber couldn't contain himself. 'They saved his life, that's what they did to him!' he snorted. 'And let's leave God out of it, because God doesn't have a damn thing to do with this.'

Meanwhile, in the corridor, Mariska was calling Security, loud enough for everybody to hear.

This fleeting visit would have been a complete fiasco if Cathy Marant hadn't directed the Fabers to stand on either side of the bed and look into the camera as seasoned actors, smiling sadly and filled with compassion.

Marant quickly pressed a bouquet of flowers into Angela's hands and ordered the photographer, Eric, to take up position so the boy was lying right between Angela and Dennis Faber. It was meant to be about the boy, Danielle reassured herself, but in this photo shoot he was reduced from the main character of his own personal tragedy to a non-speaking extra in a third-rate drama about two celebrities concealing their guilty consciences and empty marriage.

Fortunately, everything was over in no time. Immediately after the obligatory pose, Dennis Faber hurried out of the room again without giving the boy another glance. Cathy Marant grabbed Angela Faber, who was now a puddle of tears, and as quickly as possible manoeuvred her back into the corridor.

'Now you,' Eric had said to Danielle, positioning her in front of the apparatus that provided the boy with the medications he needed. 'We need to stop now,' Danielle said to Eric, who just kept on clicking.

When she came out of the room with Eric, Danielle caught a glimpse of Mariska's punishing but above all disappointed expression. 'I can explain, Maris,' Danielle tried, but it had little effect. Mariska was fuming.

Danielle and Eric shot into the right lift at the very moment the left lift doors opened and Hospital Security stepped out.

'That was a close call,' Eric said with a smile, standing a bit too close to her in the descending lift.

Danielle thought of the boy. She felt like she'd betrayed him.

Only after she saw Marant and her entourage driving away from the staff entrance was she able to breathe a sigh of relief. When she returned to the ICU Mariska was still busy talking to the two security guards. 'It's all fine,' said Danielle to soothe the tension, 'they're gone, it's over,' and she returned to the boy's room.

She leaned over him and stroked his fine black hair. He looked through her as if she wasn't there.

'I'm sorry,' she said, 'but I had to do that. One day I'll explain it to you and I hope you'll understand.'

She felt much guiltier than she'd anticipated. She doubted whether her intentions were quite as sincere as she'd previously thought. However, with this brief visit she'd earned herself a place in the spotlight tonight. And on that stage she would tell his story. If he couldn't, she would. She'd let him speak through her.

It felt like an eternity since Danielle had stood beside the boy's bed. As soon as she'd left the hospital car park earlier this afternoon, she'd picked up a copy of *De Nederlander*. At home she read the article with her heart racing and happily concluded that it had gone exactly as she'd imagined. She'd actually put together a circus act, she thought to herself, smiling. She'd positioned the Fabers together in the limelight first, but then she unexpectedly climbed on their shoulders and in one fell swoop grabbed all the attention.

The tub was almost full and she poured big drops of Energy bubble bath with ginseng into the water, sniffed its sweetness and began to undress.

She heard the chirping birds of her mobile go, grabbed her phone from under her clothes, hesitated when she saw it was Farah, but finally answered.

Farah sounded agitated. 'I read the article in *De Nederlander*, Danielle. Is this what you meant by informing the public?'

'It's exactly what I meant,' Danielle replied coldly.

'But you've used that poor child! And what do you get in return?'

'What I get in return,' Danielle said, 'is that I can tell eight hundred thousand viewers that his story symbolizes all the horror stories of millions of children who don't have a voice.'

'Is that what you've arranged with Cathy Marant?'

'Why are you asking me that?'

'Because Cathy Marant isn't interested in stories like this. Marant is all about sensation, broken marriages, celebrities who end up in the gutter and journalists who land people in hospital after a good beating. She only goes for heart-wrenching stories about children when it's the child of a celebrity, or a goddamn child star. Did that even cross your mind? You're making a very big mistake trusting her!'

'What should I do then? Trust you? You're not going to help me. But Marant is.'

'Have you even considered the boy's safety? Or even your own safety? Why are you doing this? What are you trying to prove?'

'I don't owe you an explanation. We could have done this together. You didn't want to. So you'll just have to deal with the consequences.'

'Danielle, you're underestimating the consequences. Don't do this. It's going to turn against you.'

'You know, Farah, I can see right through you. You're just like the others. It's all about you. I won't mention your name tonight, so you don't need to worry. I'm going to talk about the boy tonight. He'll finally get the attention he deserves. I'll see to it. Take care, Farah!'

She hung up, wrapped a towel around herself, walked into the room and noticed how tense she'd become in those few minutes. What if Farah was right? That she'd compromised the boy's safety? She saw herself fleeing for her life through the knee-high grass in the middle of the night. She heard the screams of the children again. Whatever she did, wherever she went, she'd always hear their cries. For ever echoing in her head.

17

As a boss, Edward Vallent prided himself on his powers of empathy, but as Farah tried to keep up with him on her way to the escalator these were in short supply.

'So you're telling me that someone you called uncle suddenly passed away this afternoon, and that's why you vanished from the radar until now. Is that right? You never even bothered to phone me!'

'Sure!' Farah fumed. 'That's my first impulse when someone dies in my arms. Let's phone Ed.'

'It may not be your first impulse, but a second or even a third one might be nice. Jesus, your tenth impulse, for all I care, but get in touch! You burst in here, just minutes before we're doing a press conference, while I haven't had a chance to go through it with you. And as I'm about to tell you what we're planning to do, you try to shout me down with the improbable story that the man's death this afternoon had something to do with the Bacha Bazi kid who got run over! Got any other crazy theories, Hafez?'

'Damn it, Ed. Put like that, it does sound like shit.'

Edward came to an abrupt halt and, seriously pissed off, turned to face Farah.

'It *is* a shit story!'

For a moment they faced off like two frozen gladiators. Then the colossus moved again and Farah followed him.

'No doubt we're all connected in an I Ching, Ying Yang or Feng Shui kind of way, and all living cells form one big cosmic web of cause and effect, but that's not something a driven journalist bursting with talent ought to go by! If that's a path you want to pursue, I suggest you take the first available plane to the highest Himalayan peak and have fun clinking the singing bowls in a Tibetan monastery. But here in the real world we're still all about facts and analysis. *Facts and analysis*, Hafez. Ever heard of those?'

Ed was about to walk away but Farah stopped him.

'You're a bastard, Ed. A man died in my arms this afternoon, someone I loved like a father. You only give a shit about your newspaper and precious little about the people around you, but that still doesn't give you the right to act like this.'

Suddenly the fury in Edward's eyes died down.

'Okay, Hafez, calm down.' Again, he was about to walk away, but Farah blocked his path. It felt like positioning herself in front of a revving Hummer.

'I demand trust and respect,' she said. 'Without it I can't do the investigation, and I'm desperate to do it, Ed. If only to prove you, with your big opinions, wrong, you arrogant dickhead.'

'I love it when you talk dirty to me, Hafez,' Edward said with a grin, 'but we have to go downstairs now and present a united front! If only to keep up appearances. We'll talk more later. Come on.'

She turned around and felt the flat of Edward's hand pressing against the small of her back, an antiquated gesture men still regularly used since they saw women as children who needed to be pushed.

When they reached the escalator, they could hear the impatient hum of the gathered journalists and photographers in the central atrium downstairs.

'Let's get one thing straight, Hafez: you behave yourself and I do all the talking,' Edward said.

'Be my guest, you overbearing jerk,' she agreed.

As they glided downstairs next to one another, Edward leaned towards her and whispered in her ear. 'I'm sorry to hear about your loss today. And apologies for earlier.'

She pretended not to hear and kept staring straight ahead.

18

'Good afternoon, ladies and gentlemen!' Edward exclaimed jovially, as though about to buy a round for the journalists and photographers who had gathered in front of the large screen. Meanwhile he cursed himself for his bad habit of antagonizing those he cherished. It wasn't until Farah had a go at him that Edward realized just how fond he was of this woman. Perhaps it was the very reason he kept provoking her. To keep feeling how, underneath the heavy armour of his workaholism and professional autism, his small heart continued to beat unconditionally for her.

In the course of the afternoon, when Farah had failed to respond to his text messages, he'd started worrying. She was as meticulous in her day-to-day business as she was quick to respond to calls and messages. Later he heard from a political correspondent in The Hague that right before the debate in Parliament one of the bystanders outside the building had been taken away in an ambulance. This had triggered a bizarre urge to leave a string of messages on Farah's voicemail.

Edward couldn't stand being concerned without knowing exactly why, and the more messages Farah left unanswered the greater his concern got. In the end, he could barely concentrate on his work. So when she finally burst into his office, shouting 'sorry, sorry', he'd welcomed her with frenetic patriarchal barking when all he'd wanted to do was hug her.

Why did Farah Hafez have this effect on him?

She first barged into his office more than ten years ago. Late, even then, and with an enthusiasm bordering on hysteria.

To his question of who or what had motivated her to go into journalism, she'd named her great inspiration.

Raylan Chapelle.

He had been touched by Farah's fascination with his deceased brother-in-law. Raylan Chapelle's writing about the Vietnam War and his later coverage of the run-up to the Saur Revolution in her former home of Afghanistan bore witness to great insight and courage, Farah had said.

'Without insight and courage you don't get anywhere,' she'd added. Whereupon Edward had asked her what *she* wanted to achieve at the *AND* with her courage and insight. The response of the dark-haired idealist with the striking blue eyes hadn't been a surprise.

'I'd like to empower people. It's up to us, journalists, to keep reminding them that our leaders and social institutions are dependent on our support.'

'Have you ever considered going into politics?' Edward asked with a patronizing smile.

'I became a journalist so I could keep an eye on every kind of authority, and that includes politicians,' she'd responded.

He'd hired her and helped her to the best of his ability to link razor-sharp intuition to crystal-clear analysis, although in the heat of the moment he'd just denied her those qualities. Farah had been right to demand trust and respect. It was time he admitted to himself that as the person in charge he found it incredibly difficult to have so little control over Farah and her work.

In the case of the hit-and-run boy she'd exhibited the qualities of a seasoned pro. Not only should he have given her the trust and respect she asked for, but also the freedom to conduct the investigation the way she saw fit, not the way he prescribed. Edward had made the same mistake with Paul. It had cost him his most talented pupil.

The question wasn't so much about Farah being ready for the major league, as it was about the big boss being able to handle it. He looked at her, sitting next to him at the large table beside the big screen, completely at ease, by the look of it. No trace of the stress she'd shown ten minutes earlier. No trace of the sadness he'd seen in her eyes as she told him about her uncle's death.

He briefly rested his hand on her shoulder before turning to the array of print journalists, photographers and the conspicuous team of reporters from IRIS TV.

'I would like to take this opportunity to introduce you to Farah Hafez,' Edward said in an informal tone. 'Farah has been working for us for over ten years and alongside her journalism career she has dedicated herself to the noble martial art of Pencak Silat. She's been so successful this year that she was chosen to round off a major martial arts gala at Carré.'

He took a sip of water.

'Why a press conference on a martial arts gala? Before I answer that question I'd like to invite you to watch how *The Headlines Show* chose to report on this fight yesterday,' he resumed, and pressed the play button on the remote.

Cathy Marant appeared on the large screen, wearing a shiny purple blouse.

'Pencak Silat is a martial art which originates in Indonesia,' she said with a generous dose of pathos, hinting at impending disaster. 'But this evening it was no Indonesian warrior who stood out, it was the Afghan "Farah H", in daily life a journalist with the *Algemeen Nederlands Dagblad*, who so badly manhandled her opponent in the ring that she was taken to hospital with serious injuries.' Marant paused a moment and stared into the camera. 'Let's take a look!'

The fight footage was shaky and grainy and shot from some distance away. Yet its impact was dramatic and Edward knew why. It had been manipulated. The event had been officially documented in a steady wide shot. In the montage, however, it had been digitally altered in such a way that it looked as if someone with a mobile had made an illegal recording from the stands. It camouflaged the vile tricks Farah's opponent had pulled. As soon as Farah began meting out her final few kicks and blows, the picture switched to a second camera which recorded the fight from nearby.

Then there was something else that Edward had noticed earlier in the day. At the moment Farah's right uppercut hit her opponent's chin, its dull impact was inexplicably loud. When Farah's left fist hammered her opponent's ribs, he heard something snap. And the kick with which Farah landed her rival on the mat was accentuated by a nasty whizzing sound and a dull thud, like an axe brought down hard on a lump of meat. And to top it all off, each of Farah's kicks and thrusts were relayed in slow motion.

Edward faded the picture to black after Farah's opponent had gone down – in slow motion, of course, and with the sound of a heavy sandbag hitting the ground.

'As you've no doubt seen,' he said nervously, 'the better part of the fight was filmed in wide-angle. What you're about to see are the images from the camera that actually shot the close-ups. Unlike the footage you've just seen, these images haven't been cut, edited or enhanced with sound effects.'

After he pressed play again it was plain to see how her opponent grabbed Farah's head, pulled her across the mat by her hair, and when held in an arm lock, bit Farah's calf so hard it started bleeding, causing Farah to scream in pain.

Edward pressed the pause button at the moment the referee intervened.

'These images were reviewed today by members of the international Pencak Silat Association,' he said dispassionately. 'Based on their conclusions, Farah Hafez's opponent has been banned from all national and international competitions for a minimum of two years.'

He took another sip of water, ignored Farah's look of surprise and concluded by showing Farah's final kicks and blows again without any of the image manipulation and sound effects. Although it still wasn't a pretty sight to see her opponent go down like that, it all looked a lot less shocking and brutal than in the cut broadcast on *The Headlines Show*.

'The Association has unanimously decided that Farah Hafez has won this fight on forfeit,' Edward resumed as he held the contested article from *De Nederlander* in the air. 'But apparently Cathy Marant is a martial arts expert: she claims this was, and I quote, "Ruthless Revenge by Afghan Farah H."'

He straightened his back. The time had come to put his authority as well as his strapping size to good use.

'I wonder,' he said, raising his voice, 'why a journalist who was born in Afghanistan, but has had a Dutch passport since childhood, has suddenly become an "Afghan". And, let me ask you, why is Farah Hafez referred to as "Farah H."? Simple. Somebody's last name is reduced to their initials when we refer to serious criminals!'

He realized he was getting carried away in reaction to the indignation he was generating among the gathered press in the atrium. He paused a moment before launching into his final argument.

'In our view, the reporting on this fight, both in *De Nederlander* and on *The Headlines Show*, shows that Cathy Marant not only manipulates the facts but then takes it all one step further by making false accusations, thereby both slandering one of our journalists *and* casting criminal aspersions on her!'

Edward glared into the camera of the IRIS news team. He remembered an incident years ago, when he'd taken a blind drunk Cathy Marant, who was still working for the *AND* at the time, back to her home after an office party that got out of hand. Because she was completely legless, he'd carried her inside and put her down on the bed. Before he'd had a chance to react, she'd unzipped his trousers and panted in his ear, 'I want you inside me, now!' But no sooner had Edward pushed her off than he witnessed an instant transformation. From a lusty lass she changed into a hate-spewing dragon. 'So it's true what they say, you're a queer.'

The air seemed charged when Edward uttered his final few sentences.

'Ms Marant asks what's happened to the values espoused by our nation if we tolerate the conduct of "Afghan Farah H.". *I* would like to know what's happened to the values of journalism if we continue to tolerate the libellous reports of Cathy Marant?'

The reporter with the IRIS TV team raised his hand. 'Marc Combrée for IRIS TV,' he said pompously. 'I have a question for Ms Hafez.'

Edward glanced at Farah, who nodded to indicate that it was okay.

'If it's true, Ms Hafez,' Combrée began, 'that you're the peace-loving angel your boss claims you are, then why didn't you just give your version of events when Ms Marant asked you about it? In fact, why didn't you issue a denial?'

Edward felt a surge of panic. He imagined Farah flying across the table and lunging at poor Marc with an outstretched leg.

'I'm familiar with Cathy Marant's work,' Farah said calmly. 'As you know, Marant was let go by this paper because she didn't exactly excel at checking her sources, and that's putting it mildly, believe me. Cathy Marant draws her conclusions before she begins writing the story. She isn't interested in what people actually have to say. She simply uses their accounts to confirm her own ideas. I didn't want to do her bidding when she asked me for my opinion. I only cooperate with journalists who respect the ethics of our profession.'

Edward could barely believe it. The same woman who'd just held a dying man in her arms was now sitting here like a tower of strength.

'How do you intend to follow up on these allegations, Mr Vallent?' Combrée asked in an insinuating tone.

'Our legal counsel will ask for rectification of both the article in *De Nederlander* and the item on *The Headlines Show*, and if our request is not honoured we'll sue for slander,' Edward said, pretending to be perfectly calm and trying to suppress the triumph in his voice. 'That's all, as far as we're concerned. Thank you for coming.'

He waved authoritatively at the journalists as if to say: there's no point in shouting questions over and above the crowd in the noisy room. Then he and Farah tramped off together and took the escalator without saying a word and without looking back.

'Does Marant know about our investigation into the boy's case?' he asked when they got to the top. 'In other words, does she know you're involved?'

Farah looked at him in surprise. Edward grinned.

'I glance at *De Nederlander* from time to time.'

'I don't know how much Danielle has told Marant,' Farah said.

'What does Danielle know?'

'Yesterday morning, after the operation, we swapped information. She brought me up to speed on his medical status and gave me her thoughts on the accident, while I shared my suspicions of child trafficking with her.'

'That's it?'

'That's it.'

'Then why is she making such a fuss?'

'Because she wants to tell her story.'

'What story?'

'Danielle Bernson spent years working as a doctor in war-torn African countries and I'm guessing she's suffering from post-traumatic stress disorder. So one night she sees a seriously injured Middle-Eastern boy in the woods and suddenly all the anguish of the past years comes back to haunt her. To her, the boy is a symbol for all the suffering children she's tried to help over the years. Her literal words to me were, "I want as many people as possible to finally see what's happening to these children."'

'Danielle Bernson thinks that Cathy Marant will give her a platform for her story? She'd be better off reading *How to Deceive Yourself for Dummies*. Marant isn't the least bit interested in poor kids in the Third World. Unless, of course, it involves a national fundraising event with lots of razzmatazz and a bevy of celebs.'

Meanwhile they'd reached Edward's office. He closed the door behind them, swallowed and tried to put as much empathy in his voice as possible.

'So how are you feeling now?'

'It's kind of creepy, Ed, when you pretend to have emotions,' Farah said, but her smile suggested she was just poking fun at him.

'It's a straightforward question,' he said in a conciliatory tone. 'But if it's too much . . .?'

'I can handle it, Ed, you know that. There's a lot going on, but I can handle it.'

'I know,' he said warmly.

'Are you going to call it off?' she asked.

'Call off *what*?'

'The investigation.'

'Why on earth would I call off our investigation?'

'Because of all the unwanted publicity, because of Cathy Marant.'

'Why do you think we just did that press conference? Nothing is being called off here, Hafez. I've done my damnedest to secure the necessary clearance and funds for our investigation! Now it's your turn. What's your decision?'

'I'm buying a one-way ticket to the Himalayas to join a monastery.'

'Seriously, Hafez.'

'I'm fine with Paul,' she said curtly. 'Can I go now?'

'As long as you keep me posted about your whereabouts and your antics,' Edward said with a grin.

'Would you like to fit me with an electronic ankle tag?'

'I wouldn't dare. Make sure you send me a postcard with a bunch of smiling monks.'

And with that she strode out of his office again. Edward stared into space, pondering his plan. It was almost certainly doomed to failure, but he still wanted to give it a try. He just hoped Farah would never discover his true motive.

19

It was by sheer luck that Farah managed to park the Carrera right in front of the brick façade of De Hallen, a former transport depot in the west of Amsterdam. Once upon a time, all the trams serving the capital were parked here for the night. In addition to housing a cinema and a photography museum, it was now home to all manner of graphic and audio-visual enterprises.

During the press conference Farah's mind had mostly been on what had happened in The Hague that afternoon. She kept seeing the Bentley gliding past, the horror in Parwaiz's eyes and the silhouette of man, indistinguishable because of the sunlight reflecting off the car windows.

But then something occurred to her. She'd been so preoccupied with breaking Parwaiz's fall and coming to his aid that she'd all but forgotten about the camera that had been circling them earlier that day. After leaving Edward's office she managed to track down the cameraman, whose name was apparently Sander, and asked to see the footage. She was more than welcome to drop by, he told her.

She entered De Hallen and thought about the brainwave that had brought her to the Amsterdamse Bos the previous morning. Just like she knew then that she was going to find something, she was convinced there was something for her here.

Daylight came in through the raised wired-glass skylights. A narrow lane of artificial plane trees ran parallel to the old tram tracks. At the end of it, Sander was waiting for her. He took her through the adjacent hall, past a panoramic artwork of brightly coloured reels and wheels rotating non-stop with interminable rattling and squeaking.

'It represents old, interconnected film reels,' Sander said with a hint of irony. 'It's an ode to the film business. Rather old-fashioned of course, since everything is digital these days. It's supposed to symbolize that our profession doesn't stand still.'

Farah thought of death and gave him a wry smile.

'Was he a relative?' Sander asked.

'Kind of. He was like an uncle to me.'

'It's hard either way, I imagine.'

They'd arrived at a large orange door labelled THE BOYS in hand-written black capitals. 'That's Tom and myself,' Sander explained as he ushered her into the small studio, where Tom emerged like a bald Colossus from behind a stainless-steel bar and walked over to Farah with two enormous arms spread wide.

'Hello, lass,' he said, and his sympathetic tone came as such a surprise that she accepted his two smackers without protest. 'What would you like to drink?' he asked next.

'What's the strongest on offer?' she replied, much to her own amazement.

'I can make you a batida,' he said with a grin.

'Tom is our caipirinha champ,' Sander said, smiling.

'A caipirinha for this lass then, please,' Farah responded, a little forced.

As she looked around, her eye fell on a metal wall, which looked like it was made of white enamel and that boasted five portholes of different sizes and colours. The set-up reminded her of the exterior of a fantasy submarine.

'I suggest we go and sit over there,' Sander said as he escorted her to the other side of the room, where a pale wooden caravan with a large picture window was parked. Inside, both the floor and the three walls were clad in thick orange-red fabric. The mahogany work table boasted two flat screens and a keyboard flanked by large black speakers. A gypsy boy with a shiny tear falling from one of his eyes graced the wall.

'That's how we feel right now,' said Tom, who entered carrying a tray with three large caipirinhas. 'Like you, we can do with a stiff drink after what happened this afternoon,' he said, and handed her a glass. 'We're glad you dropped by.'

Farah felt tears roll down her face. She couldn't help it. 'I could join the boy on your wall,' she smiled. She took her first sip and felt the comforting combination of the lime, cachaça, ice and sugar going down like a treat.

'What programme were you there for?'

'We were doing an item for the eight o'clock news,' Tom said. 'After you went to the hospital, we carried on filming and did a couple of interviews and a few mood shots.'

'Would you like us to stick around, or would you rather watch it on your own?' Sander asked, after opening the first video file.

Farah liked these men. Judging by the photos in the studio they had travelled half the globe, but hadn't lost their consideration for others. Of course she wanted them to stick around.

'Yes, please,' she replied. 'Kind of you to ask.'

Sander pressed play and soon after she saw herself walking alongside Parwaiz on the sun-drenched Haagse Plein. She shuddered. She'd last seen him in the mortuary this afternoon. It felt like a cruel reunion, like a macabre trick.

'Please pause a moment,' she said, as tears rolled down her cheeks again. She took a large sip of her caipirinha, swallowed the wrong way and felt Tom's hand gently patting her on the back.

'Potent stuff, right?' he chuckled. She knew what he meant, then nodded and gestured to Sander that she wanted to carry on watching.

This time she was better prepared. When the frozen image of Parwaiz moved again, she noticed that even at that stage he hadn't looked at ease. She also saw herself. It was shortly after she'd seen the large flying portrait of Malalai and she'd felt so happy. When she spotted the camera she smiled at it, a naive smile, it seemed to her now, the smile of a woman captivated by her own happiness and oblivious to what was really happening around her.

The camera swerved, wobbled a bit and jerked about in search of faces in the crowd which had thronged together in front of Parliament.

'This is the rough material,' Sander said.

'Unedited, he means,' Tom clarified.

Farah saw smiling as well as serious faces. The camera closed in on a girl eating an ice cream. The band on the square was clearly audible in the background and suddenly she heard Tom, off-camera, yelling something at Sander, at which point the camera instantly panned 180 degrees. Now she saw Parwaiz from the back as his knees buckled. The camera jerked closer and registered how she caught him gently, almost as if they'd rehearsed this move together. She saw Tom's sound boom plunge across the picture, but the camera remained focused on her. She saw herself bent over Parwaiz.

Suddenly, the camera swerved again and she saw herself staring at the back of the Bentley, which drove at a leisurely pace past those championing the general pardon and the tourists on the square, none of whom seemed to realize what had just happened. Then it looked as if the camera itself was dropped and the picture went black.

She drained her glass in one gulp.

'Can you show me the end again?' she asked numbly.

Sander rewound the image extremely fast to the shot of the girl eating ice cream, and then everything unfolded again. Holograms re-enacting the same events time after time. Bizarre how quickly you get used to it. Now she understood why photographers and cameramen in war situations managed to keep registering everything despite the horrific events taking place right in front of their eyes. Peering through a lens gives you the illusion of safety.

Once again, she saw Tom running towards her and Parwaiz and kneeling down. She knew what she would be seeing when, shortly, the camera would pan, and when she saw it she immediately yelled, 'Stop!' She pointed to the Bentley in the distance.

'Could you enlarge this?' she asked.

'It's digital,' Sander said. 'It can be enlarged until there's nothing left but pixels.' He began tapping away at his keyboard, creating a frame around the Bentley which he then magnified.

'What are you looking for?' Tom asked.

'The number plate,' Farah said nervously.

'Cool,' Sander said with a grin, and created a new frame around the number plate which he enlarged until it filled the screen. Halfway through this process the digital pixels emerged, rendering the number illegible.

'Hang on,' Tom said as he walked off. Before long he was back with a magnifying lamp which he placed in front of the screen, so when Sander reduced the size of the number plate the letters and figures were just about readable.

'Write this down,' Tom said as he peered into the lamp and read out the number.

It was quiet after Farah had jotted it down. She stared at the collection of figures and letters and softly repeated Parwaiz's final words.

'Mi-ka-lov.'

'I beg your pardon?'

'That's what my uncle whispered right before he died,' she said.

'Let me guess what you're thinking,' Tom said, grinning. 'You think that figure in the back seat of the Bentley is a certain Mr Mikalov. Am I right or am I right?'

She smiled feebly.

'Would you like another caipirinha before we all start Googling?' Tom asked, clearly up for a challenge.

'Not just yet,' she said. 'Could I make a phone call in the other room?'

'Go ahead, we'll keep ourselves occupied,' said Sander, who had already typed Mikalov into his laptop.

Farah walked over to the studio next door. When Joshua answered, she told him straight out, 'I need your help, Joshua.'

His ensuing silence annoyed her.

'Joshua?'

'Help with what?'

She outlined the afternoon's events in The Hague as briefly as possible. 'It looked as if he saw a ghost,' she concluded.

'And that "ghost" was sitting in the back of a chauffeur-driven car? Why didn't you tell the police?'

'Because it struck me as too absurd for words. I simply couldn't believe there might be a connection.'

'But you do now?'

Farah hesitated. 'I still believe it's absurd, but I keep thinking about it. How could he just have a heart attack? Something had to bring it on, right?'

'Do you know the expression "if looks could kill"?' Joshua asked. 'It's a figure of speech. Looks can't kill. A secret US military unit had men stare at goats till they dropped dead. But looks can't kill. So someone in the back seat of a car can't stare someone else to death, do you understand? Even if you manage to identify the man, what do you think you'll achieve?'

'I don't know. But I still want to know who it was.'

Joshua was silent. She heard his breathing in between the pounding of her own heart. 'Okay, give me the number,' he said with what sounded like a note of resignation in his voice. 'But let's get one thing straight: if you're planning to write about this, we never had this conversation.'

'It's known as source protection, Joshua,' she said to reassure him and immediately texted him the licence plate number.

'I'll be in touch,' he said in a business-like tone, and hung up.

She returned to the caravan in the studio where Tom and Sander had started Googling frenetically.

'You don't want to know how many hits we've got,' Tom chuckled. 'Here we go: Doctor Abraham Mikalov, boob-job doctor, I mean breast specialist in Ohio. But then there's also Lauren Mikalov, editor of the *Rockland Jewish Reporter*.'

'And how about this?' Sander turned his screen to show her a video of a singer belting out '*Doom, da da-di da-di, doom, da da-di da-di*'.

'Mika – '*Love Today*'!' Sander exclaimed enthusiastically.

'Then there are the Mikalofs with an "*f*",' Tom said. 'Have a look: *10 Historical Documents & Family Trees for Mikalof.*'

'A myriad of Mikalovs,' Sander joked.

Farah's phone rang. It was Joshua, still sounding all business-like and detached.

'The Bentley with the number you gave me is registered to Elite Drive, which leases chauffeur-driven limos.'

'That doesn't get me anywhere,' Farah said. 'I want to know who the company leased that car to.'

'Of course you want to know that, but I'm not going to tell you. Not now. Not over the phone.'

'Why not?'

'There's more. Can you come to the Sky Lounge at the DoubleTree Hotel? It's by the river. In fifteen minutes?'

Farah sighed. 'I'm on my way.'

Tom and Sander had become completely absorbed in their digital quest. They barely seemed to hear when Farah said she had to go.

'Does that mean you've got no time for a second?' Tom asked, holding up an empty glass.

'Not now, but I know where to find you,' Farah said with a smile.

'Do you mind if we carry on for a bit?' Tom asked solemnly.

'Of course not,' Farah said. She walked over to him and gave him a hug. 'Thank you for everything.'

'Okay, lass, chin up and stay in touch.'

She could tell he was touched.

'Can we have your email address?' Sander asked as he escorted her out, past the perpetually turning film reels and down the lane of artificial trees. 'In case we find something significant.'

Farah gave him her office email and held out her hand to him. After a slight hesitation, he shook it. She got in her car and drove off. In her rear-view mirror she saw him standing there. With a broad smile and two big thumbs-up. She stepped on the brakes, turned around, drove back, got out and gave him a kiss on each cheek. Then she sped off again.

20

Joshua Calvino stared past his own reflection in the large plate glass window separating the DoubleTree Sky Lounge from the darkening sky above downtown Amsterdam. On Wednesday evenings he was a regular here: in this post-modern glass structure with its magical incandescent lighting, where you could eat a trendy lunch or brunch or have dinner among other trendy types. The glimmer of lights was an effective way to soothe a lurking depression.

He cherished the rituals that he used to give meaning to his life. The certainty of weather forecasts. The conviction that by taking a sip of spring water every fifteen minutes, he'd preserve the sixty per cent water make-up of his body. The confidence that he could always steer his emotions in a positive direction as long as he kept smiling. The certainty that he would always be able to solve the most difficult of cases as long as he continued to keep his mind sharp. Despite all the rampant negativity in the people and the cases he investigated, Joshua was still convinced that he had a soul. And deep within, he longed for the presence of Farah Hafez – wanted to solve the mystery that was her.

She sat down and with a brief 'I don't have much time!' shattered Joshua's illusion.

'I understand, you've been through a lot today,' he said, sounding as if he could read her every thought.

'Why am I here?' She said, impatiently waving an approaching waiter away.

'I wanted to warn you.'

'What?'

He pulled out a printed list of vehicles Elite Drive had rented out that day, complete with chauffeur. The Bentley

Farah had seen in The Hague was circled. He gave her a knowing look and read aloud the name of the firm that had hired it.

'AtlasNet. A Russian energy conglomerate which annually delivers 3.8 billion cubic metres of natural gas to the Netherlands. They recently opened an office on the fourth floor of the De Bazel building, the former office of the Netherlands Trading Society here in Amsterdam.'

'Why the Netherlands?'

'A number of reasons. AtlasNet is interested in a depleted gas field in North Holland: to convert it into one of the largest gas storage facilities in Europe. But the Provincial Commissioner who represents that province is blocking the plan. Such a Russian multinational firm is of course viewed with great suspicion. People immediately think of mafia practices and black-market money. An official business address in a prestigious location in our nation's capital never hurts.'

'You said there were a number of reasons?' Farah asked with irritation.

'Yes. There's also the tax-related reason. The Dutch tax system makes it possible for international players to channel their profits to the Cayman Islands, St Maarten or other tax havens via trust companies in Amsterdam. AtlasNet will of course benefit from this construction too.'

He pushed the paper towards her.

'Such a company doesn't appreciate a journalist digging around in their backyard, if you know what I mean.'

'Hmm. You don't know who was in the car?'

'Undoubtedly one of AtlasNet's hotshots.' He caught her angry gaze. 'You seem disappointed.'

'Joshua, after everything that's happened today, you ask me to come all the way here so you can hand me a piece of paper with the name of a Russian natural gas company ... you could've just told me on the phone?'

'I could have done that, yes. But I also wanted to see you.' He thought he saw her gaze soften a bit, or at least it felt like there was less distance. 'Let me get you something to drink.' He gestured to the waiter without waiting for her reaction.

She ordered a mint tea and he another dry white wine.

'Can you come to the station tomorrow?' he asked hesitantly.

'Tomorrow I have a funeral in The Hague,' she replied impersonally. 'Muslims, as you know, have to be buried within twenty-four hours.'

'Why don't you tell me more about what happened today?'

'Not now, Joshua. Didn't you see today's newspaper?' From his questioning look, she realized he hadn't. 'There's an article about that couple you and your utterly charming partner arrested yesterday. They went to the hospital this morning, photos were shot, now everyone knows where the boy is being treated and in less than an hour, Danielle Bernson is going to elaborate on the story in *The Headlines Show.*'

'Sorry, you're way ahead of me,' he said, surprised.

'Maybe you should get up to speed then. Because right now I don't have time to give you a blow-by-blow account of this afternoon while that boy's life might be in serious danger. Isn't it possible to post a police guard outside his hospital room?'

'Possible, but difficult if there's no specific threat.'

'The boy was purposely run down and left to die! Isn't that specific enough?!'

The din of voices at the tables around them stopped for a moment and inquisitive glances were thrown in their direction. Joshua ignored them. He stared at Farah and realized to his dismay that she was right again. Tomasoa had already said it: the boy probably witnessed a liquidation, and the fact that he was still alive meant that his life might be in danger. Why was everything happening so slowly? How was it possible that Farah Hafez was always one step ahead?

She'd found the earring that led to the investigation at the villa. That investigation had brought about a breakthrough. Now she was insisting here in the Sky Lounge that the boy needed protection. He should be grateful to her, and he was –

somewhere deep in his mind — but more than anything he felt annoyance because she'd portrayed him as a typical civil servant instead of the incisive detective he wanted to see himself as.

'What else did the investigation uncover?' Farah asked eagerly, blowing on her hot tea to cool it down.

Joshua sighed. 'You know I can't discuss an ongoing investigation.'

'C'mon, Joshua, I helped you, now it's your turn to help me. You know how that works.'

'No, actually I don't know how that works, why don't you enlighten me.' He felt hurt and needed to give her some of her own medicine.

'Tell me how big the case is,' she said compellingly.

'Big. The villa is owned by Armin Lazonder's Dorado Group. In fact, very big. In any case, so big that the investigation now falls under the MIT.'

'The same team investigating the station wagon case?'

He nodded.

'So there's a connection?'

'I'm not free to say, Farah.'

'Yes or no, Joshua?'

He took a sip of wine, gently put down his glass and looked at her, determined this time not to fall into her seductive trap. She answered his action by standing. The murmur of the tables around them quieted once more.

'When am I going to see you again?' he asked as neutrally as possible.

'I don't know.'

'What does it depend on?'

'A lot of things. Too many to mention now. Why can't you tell me what you've found out?'

'I can't tell you about an ongoing investigation,' he repeated.

'Then it looks like we're done talking for now.'

Her eyes misted over. He didn't know if it was because of what she'd been through or if he was the reason. Perhaps it was a combination of both.

'Then I suppose we are.'

Out of the blue, she leaned towards him and stroked his face.

'Don't' he said. 'Just don't.'

He couldn't shake the image of the boy. There was something elusive about the entire case. Just when you thought things were coming into focus, the shadows in the background moved, clouding over or distorting the overall picture again. He'd underestimated the boy's case from the start. Even now that there was a clear connection to the station wagon murders and the boy was a potential material witness. He simply hadn't realized how vital it was for the boy to be given protection.

Lost in thought, Joshua crossed over a bridge without paying attention to the traffic and was almost run down by a woman speeding by on a bike. In a flash he thought he recognized the blonde doctor from the WMC.

21

Detective Elvin Dingane had slipped into Paul's room at St Helen Joseph Hospital and poured him a glass of water, while Paul was studying his black-and-blue swollen face, partially covered with bandages, in a hand mirror.

'Water bearer, what a noble profession,' Paul whispered as he took the glass from Dingane. 'They who quench the thirst of the screaming needy in the desert – those who are never heard.'

'Maybe you're needy, even difficult, but you'll certainly be heard,' Dingane said with a smile.

'I can't wait.' Paul banged the glass on the bedside table. 'But first tell me how you found me.'

'Ponte City is guarded by a group that works with the local police,' said Dingane. 'They're called the Stockbroke Boyz. There are lots of illegal Africans living in that building.'

'You don't say,' Paul mumbled.

'They have to pay exorbitant rents to gangs who control many of the floors. The Stockbroke Boyz patrol there. One of them saw a man taking a dive off the fiftieth floor.'

'I'll have to thank those boys, 'Paul said. 'If they hadn't got to me so fast, they probably would've found me lying on top of Zhulongu.'

'Murdering foreign journalists isn't a good strategy. Too much of a ruckus, politicians wanting to stick their noses into it, ministries sounding the alarm and, again, loyal colleagues delving into the whole thing. It was a warning, Paul. I'm interested in the man who gave you that warning in Ponte City.'

'Ah! *El condor pasa*! 'Paul said, grinning.

'We fed your description of him into our system,' said Dingane, 'and we came up with a profile of Arseni Vakurov.'

'Okay, and what's his story?'

'Vakurov is the right hand of Valentin Lavrov.'

'Lavrov,' Paul muttered. 'So Zhulongu must have had some seriously incriminating material with him. But he slipped up at some point. Someone got wind of our appointment.'

'That's for sure,' Dingane said. 'What do you know about Valentin Lavrov?'

'He's a Russian tycoon with more than twenty billion euros socked away in the bank. He came to South Africa with a shovel and suitcases full of black-market dollars, intent on digging for uranium. He negotiated with Nkoane in secret about this.'

'And what kind of info did Zhulongu have for you?'

'Probably about the deal the two of them made. A deal that was not only favourable for Lavrov.'

There was a silence.

'We're not out to get Valentin Lavrov,' Dingane finally said.

'I understand,' Paul said, closely following Dingane, who was now pacing around the room. Paul could feel that more was coming.

'Ever heard of Grigori Michailov?'

'Michailov was a prominent figure,' replied Paul. 'He received the *Medalj zolotaja Zvezda*, the medal of the Gold Star. If they pin that on you, you automatically become a Hero of the Soviet Union. When I lived in Kabul as a boy, the Saur Revolution took place. It was an uprising of the communist army units predominantly supported by leftist students at the universities. Russia wanted Afghanistan as a buffer state. America had its sphere of influence in Persia and Russia feared that the Americans would pull the same stunt in Afghanistan and gradually close in on Russia. It's claimed that Grigori Michailov was the Russian genius behind that coup. I know all of this because my father was conducting an investigation at that time.'

'Raylan Chapelle, the American Vietnam journalist?'

'You've done your homework, Dingane,' Paul said with a grin. 'But what does this Michailov have to do with Lavrov?'

'Grigori Michailov is the link between Lavrov and Vakurov,' said Dingane. 'Vakurov once served in the Russian 40th Army.

A legendary corps because during the Second World War they drove the Germans out of the Soviet Union. The army was re-established in May 1979 in the Turkmenistan Military District on the border of Afghanistan. The 40th Army was commanded by General Grigori Michailov. Vakurov was his second in command. After their return to the former Soviet Union, Michailov benefited considerably from his glory and along with a number of political and mafia pals caused the fall of Gorbachev. And Vakurov was always nearby, in the wings, the ever-reliable assistant. When Michailov was killed in a bomb attack in the middle of Moscow, Vakurov went looking for another boss. He apparently chose the much younger Valentin Lavrov. If Vakurov came to Ponte City personally, it means that Zhulongu must have had incriminating information not only about Valentin Lavrov but also about Jacob Nkoane.'

Paul stared straight ahead. He remembered the condor with his mirrored glasses standing in front of him on the fiftieth floor of Ponte City and heard the echo of his words. Paul repeated them to himself under his breath.

'I like clear agreements.'

'Sorry?'

'That's what he said.'

'Who?'

'Vakurov.'

'I like clear agreements,' he'd said. 'Well, that beating was more than clear.' Paul sighed. 'Besides that, he knew my father.'

'Who?'

'The condor. So it must have been Vakurov.'

Elvin Dingane was standing at the foot of Paul's bed, his hands clutching the steel frame. 'Leave the matter to us. Leave Jo'burg for a time. Don't stay in South Africa. Not only is Nkoane your enemy now, but there is also a wealthy Russian who has a notorious hitman at his beck and call.'

'First you tell me to stop doing my job and now you're telling me to bugger off.'

'It's your choice, Paul.'

'It certainly is, yes! So mind your own business.'

Dingane remained remarkably calm. 'Your life is in danger here, Paul. Anyway, for the time being no major newspaper is interested in your articles.' He hesitated a moment, then headed towards the doorway. 'Hope you're up and about soon.'

'Oh really?'

Dingane stopped and looked at Paul as if he'd just done him a great injustice.

'Yes, I mean it.' Then he strode out of the room. Paul called him back.

'You'd better stay clear of politics,' he said when Dingane stuck his head back around the doorframe.

'Why do you say that?'

'Because you're too honest.'

A smile appeared on Dingane's face and then he disappeared behind the wall with its peeling paint.

22

Danielle was now on the ferry, travelling from the north side of the River IJ back to the heart of town. She gazed up at Centraal Station's elongated glass dome with the huge letters AMSTERDAM increasing in size as the boat got closer.

After her phone call with Farah, Danielle had no longer been in the mood for a relaxing bath. She'd put on her sports gear and gone out for a run. It was the only way to clear her head. As she covered ground, she weighed her options. To what extent had publicizing the boy's story compromised his safety? Was her upcoming media appearance in line with her principles, that as a doctor you had to tackle people's problems and not try to save the entire world – or start a revolution, for that matter? Did she have a clear conscience when it came to the boy and was she sure she wasn't using him to compensate for her guilt feelings about Africa?

By the time she'd reached her front door again, she had her answers.

It was dusk and the muggy wind wafted from the IJ through downtown. The ferry docked and she biked at rapid speed along the quay, past the new DoubleTree Hotel, across the wide bridge, towards the Schreierstoren. In her haste, she almost ran down a man who unexpectedly stepped on to the road. For a split second she thought he was one of the two detectives she'd met yesterday morning in the WMC. After passing the grand Victoria Hotel, she turned on to Haarlemmerstraat and rode straight to the former Westergas complex where IRIS TV's studios were located. As she crossed the small drawbridge, a woman jumped out in front of her bike. She braked, cursed and seconds later realized it was Farah, completely out of breath, now grabbing her handlebars with trembling hands.

'I promise to help you if you don't do this,' Farah gasped.

'How the hell are you going to help me now?' Danielle exclaimed. 'Do you think there's a way back? That I enjoyed seeing those two idiotic celebs hovering over the boy this morning? With their so-called compassion! You think I like appearing on a TV programme like this? I can't go back, Farah. Not after this morning. If I do that, Faber and his hysterical wife will have their story and I'll be left empty-handed!'

Farah had caught her breath. 'You're making a mistake, Danielle.'

'Maybe. But then at least I tried!'

'But have you considered all the consequences?'

'No, I haven't, but neither have you. So let go, Farah, I'm late.'

'Wait. I have a proposal.'

'They're waiting for me. I really have to go.'

'An entire article about you, your motivations, your experience, the injustices you've seen.'

'Isn't it a bit too late for that? Let go of my bike!'

Farah released the handlebars. She shook her head.

'I hope it goes well, Danielle. Good luck. I mean it, really.'

At the entrance of the Zuiveringshal someone else jumped in front of her, this time an exceedingly hyper young woman.

'Dr Bernson?'

'Am I very late?' Danielle asked, as she locked her bike, still slightly out of breath.

'Thank goodness!' the girl exclaimed, laying on the pathos. She had such white hair that it looked like someone had emptied a carton of yogurt on her head.

'We were getting worried. I texted you quite a few times. Wrong number or you don't do it? Send texts, I mean?'

Danielle now remembered that she'd put her phone on silent after talking with Farah earlier in the day. She could have kicked herself.

The girl stuck out her hand. 'Karlijn,' she panted her name. 'I'll be assisting you this evening. The other guests have already arrived!'

Another thing Danielle hadn't taken into account. There were always several guests on *The Headlines Show*, mostly people from politics, culture and entertainment. Given she wasn't from any of these three fields, she wondered what other surprises awaited her. She didn't have much time to worry because Karlijn, wearing boots with ridiculously high heels, strode into the studio ahead of her. An army of cameramen, lighting and sound technicians, along with the rest of the crew, had assembled for the camera rehearsal. She shouted, 'She's here!'

As everybody turned towards her, an embarrassed Danielle focused her attention on the jumble of bulky cables, cameras the size of small tanks and colossal lamps on the iron grating above her head.

'Danielle! Wasn't the article wonderful?' As if she'd been pulled out of a magician's hat, Cathy Marant was suddenly right there in front of her. She shook her hand and showered her with the proverbial clichés. 'So super that you're giving us this opportunity. Glad you're finally here. Break a leg.' And she was gone again.

A bit overwhelmed by it all, Danielle let Karlijn drag her into a room where a weary make-up artist grabbed a tiny sponge and routinely covered her face in a thin layer of brownish foundation. Meanwhile, on a small monitor without any sound, the camera rehearsal unfolded in front of her. It was total chaos.

'Is it always like this?' she asked.

'Nervous?' asked the make-up artist while rubbing some gel into Danielle's hair. 'Don't be. It's no big deal. Just sit at the table and don't forget to open your mouth. It's like being at the pub.'

With one difference, Danielle thought, there's a million viewers watching my every move. She wished it wasn't too late to still take Farah's advice, so she could run outside, jump on her bike again and at breakneck speed race home to sink deeply into the pillows on the sofa and see how the live broadcast would go without her.

'I'll check you one more time before you go on,' said the make-up artist after she'd made her look like someone who'd just returned from a week-long cruise in the Caribbean. Karlijn then coaxed a reluctant Danielle to the studio floor.

'Who are the other guests?' Danielle asked, somewhat uncertain. Karlijn mentioned a name that sounded like 'DJ Maestro', who according to her made a 'super-cool' comeback. Another guest was a model and former football WAG, who was apparently battered for years behind closed doors so her husband could refine his footwork.

When she suddenly bumped into a security guard wearing an earpiece at the entrance to the studio, Karlijn fell silent. Behind the bodyguard Danielle saw an attractive man in his forties wearing a fashionable pinstriped suit. He looked familiar, but she couldn't place him. They shared the same artificial brown tint.

'Are you also a guest?' she asked a bit timidly.

'Yes,' he said, sounding almost apologetic as he extended his hand.

'Vincent.'

'Danielle.'

In the studio itself there was no trace of the earlier rehearsal chaos. Only the chaos in Danielle's head remained. As she stepped on to the platform to take a place at the table, it felt like she was ascending the executioner's scaffold. With a shrill buzzing in her ears, she sat down in the seat the floor manager pointed to and a sound techie started to fiddle with her blouse to pin a microphone on it. Danielle held her breath while he was doing this – the man had bad breath – and looked around anxiously, like a cat up a tree. She caught Vincent standing a bit too close to Cathy Marant, consulting with her. They were both looking in Danielle's direction.

When she heard the floor manager call 'one minute', she suddenly remembered where she'd seen Vincent before: behind the rostrum in parliament, where he'd sharply spoken against the Cabinet's immigration policy.

Danielle braced herself, as if she was sitting in a plane with roaring engines that was ready to take off. There was a reason this image popped to mind. It had just occurred to her that she wasn't only afraid of flying, but also of speaking in public.

As she wiped the first beads of sweat from her forehead with the back of her hand, she caught Vincent Coronel's icy-blue eyes gazing at her from across the table, and under her breath she repeated the mantra that reminded her never to flee from anything ever again.

23

Straight after her meeting with Joshua in the Sky Lounge, Farah had hurried over to the Westergas Studios in the hope of averting any potential disaster that Danielle might bring down on the whole affair. She had a new proposal. She would offer to write a profile, homing in on Danielle's experiences in various war-torn African countries and her fight against the injustice done to children there. The focus on Africa would relegate the boy to the background. But she hadn't counted on Danielle's icy stubbornness.

Farah watched her go and then went to lick her wounds at Grand Café IRIS where the evening's edition of *The Headlines Show* would be shown on large screens. She ordered mineral water and a tuna sandwich and checked her messages. According to her iPhone she had an email from Sander, the cameraman.

Hey Farah, we continued our Mi-ka-lov quest over here and I may have something for you. See att. Gr, Sander. P.S. Let me know if it's useful.

She opened the attachment. It was a Wikipedia article about a certain Grigori Michailov, who was born on 23 October 1943 in Saratov, Russia, and who died in 1996 after being blown up in his limo right outside his flat in Moscow.

How's this relevant, Farah wondered. She was about to close the attachment when it became clear why Sander had sent her an article about this particular man. Michailov, it turned out, had been a prominent Afghanistan veteran, widely decorated for his 'services' as commander-in-chief of the Khad, the dreaded secret police at the time of Afghanistan's communist regime between 1979 and 1989.

So Parwaiz may have had a brutal encounter with Michailov in Kabul. But even if that were the case, why had Parwaiz whispered his name? What connection was there between the name of a dead Russian and the man in the Bentley in The Hague? Farah knew that ghosts from the past could manifest themselves. They were always there, floating around you unseen, and at the most unexpected moments they would assume their former human forms and scare the living daylights out of you. But it was absurd to think that Parwaiz had seen the ghost of his long-deceased torturer from Kabul sitting in the back of a passing limo.

It was high time to inform Edward of her failed attempt to stop Danielle and tell him about the link to AtlasNet Joshua had told her about.

She hit the speed dial on her phone.

'How do you do it, Hafez?' he said after listening to her findings.

'What do you mean?'

'Not only do you get a detective to give you confidential information, but that information turns out to implicate AtlasNet. And when you say AtlasNet, you're saying Valentin Lavrov. And when you say Valentin Lavrov, you're saying . . . ?'

That's when another piece of the puzzle fell into place for Farah.

'Armin Lazonder!'

'Well done, Hafez. And in no time at all. Ten points!' Edward said, laughing. 'Lavrov is the chief investor in Lazonder's New Golden Age Project. I don't know how you pull it off, but I feel like I've ended up on a giant rollercoaster with you. But I never ride the things because they make me sick!'

'And that's not all,' Farah said, and told Edward about Sander's email.

Edward whistled through his teeth. 'Michailov was the last Soviet soldier to leave Afghanistan, did you know that? Before the eyes of the global media he walked from Afghanistan to Russia via the Friendship Bridge across the Amu Darya river. Michailov was a fierce opponent of the pull-out. But he had no choice. President Gorbachev had ordered it. Raylan Chapelle actually clashed with him once after the Saur Revolution. Raylan said he had proof that Russia was behind the coup and that Michailov was the puppeteer controlling the Afghan officers and their troops.'

'But Michailov is dead,' Farah replied. 'The Chechens blew him up in the nineties, car and all.'

'Yes, that's correct. You won't find him driving around in a Bentley any more,' Edward agreed.

'And yet there must be a reason for Parwaiz mentioning his name before he died. Assuming he was referring to Michailov, that is.'

'It's too bizarre for words,' Edward said. 'There's this little Afghan boy who was left for dead, which is all we know about him, and yet we're already juggling names from the extreme other end of the spectrum. A Russian billionaire with world-wide connections, a Dutch property tycoon with global ambitions and a dead commander-in-chief of the Russian army who, if he hadn't died in a car bombing, would have collapsed under the weight of his military decorations. But whatever it all amounts to, we mustn't get carried away, Hafez.'

'I'm not, Ed.'

'Excellent. Where are you now?'

'Grand Café IRIS, right outside the studio, waiting to see what *The Headlines Show* is going to dish up.'

'I don't know what Marant is planning, but our gal Bernson is in for a rude awakening, trust me.'

'I take it you'll be watching too?'

'You bet. Of course I'll be watching.'

'I'll call you back after the show, okay?'

After ending the call, Farah suddenly felt vulnerable and alone. The lead-in for *The Headlines Show* was shown, but she kept seeing Parwaiz's eyes as the life drained from them.

Those eyes would be etched in her memory for ever.

'Mi-chai-lov.'

After Sander's email she couldn't shake off those three syllables.

24

Edward Vallent was pacing around the spacious front room with the fireplace and the broad wooden rafters that had supported the old farmhouse for generations. Cows were once stalled here, but Edward's brother-in-law Raylan Chapelle had literally broken with that practice by converting the former cowshed into the house he'd promised his wife Isobel when they left Kabul after the Saur revolution of 1978. The house where they would spend their lives together, where they would watch their son Paul grow up and where their two worlds would continue to converge. The world which Isobel painted on panoramic, abstract canvases in melancholic shades of red and gold leaf; the world of international wars and political conspiracies that Raylan documented in his investigative journalism.

Edward looked through one of the small windows across the polder, and saw the setting sun, half-hidden behind clouds, highlighting the skyline of Amsterdam with its blood-red brush. He decided to go outside.

Walking in the fading light, with the perfume of flowering honeysuckle and petunias all around him, he briefly felt as if a burden had been lifted off his shoulders. Earlier that evening, he had carried his sister Isobel up the narrow staircase and put her to bed after she had collapsed with fatigue in her studio. Isobel worked too hard. Since Raylan's death in the autumn of 1978, Isobel had thrown herself into reimagining their years together in Kabul. Her studio had become the permanent meeting place of past and present, where the dreams of a young woman in love merged with the abject loneliness of an ageing widow.

For Isobel it proved to be an effective way of dealing with her solitary reality. Travelling back in time by painting, to the years when Raylan was still alive, not only gave her the necessary comfort, but it also guaranteed her an exceptionally good income because her melancholic canvases appealed to a growing number of buyers worldwide.

Edward pondered the bitter irony of it all. As Isobel increasingly withdrew into her studio and locked herself away in her romanticized memories, her son went out into the world and threatened to throw away his future by behaving like a cheap imitation of his father. Less than that, even. Like his son, Raylan may have been a volatile man, someone who frequently lost his temper, but he also had a sharp tongue and a ferocious journalistic insight so he could hold his own in even the trickiest situations. And that's exactly what his son couldn't seem to manage.

Edward had been powerless in the face of Paul's decline. The offer he was about to make would be his last. A lifeline, wrapped in a promise. Because Paul didn't accept lifelines.

He walked back to the farmhouse and switched on *The Headlines Show*. Marant, whose breasts looked like they were about to pop out of her shirt, was just introducing her guests. Edward heard the name of a certain DJ Maestro and caught something about a comeback following a near-fatal crash in Ibiza. Sitting beside him was former top model Vera Hilbrand who, given the identical bosom, probably had the same plastic surgeon as Marant, but who didn't look in great shape otherwise because her husband had battered her for years. Edward instantly recognized the third guest as the right-wing populist politician Vincent Coronel, leader of the Democratische Partij Nederland. It was a public secret that Marant shared more than just political sympathies with Coronel, and a large percentage of the country's TV viewers and tabloid readers relished the combination. Edward didn't see what Coronel was doing on this particular edition of the show, unless it was to say that he fiercely opposed the general pardon which Parliament had in the works.

Finally, Edward saw the woman he had heard so much about and who, in Marant's words, 'had been able to save the life of a badly injured boy-dressed-as-a-girl thanks to Angela Faber'. It all sounded as sordid as a freak show at a village fair.

But Edward's repulsion assumed truly spectacular forms when he heard Marant mention his own name.

'Edward Vallent, editor-in-chief of the *Algemeen Nederlands Dagblad*, was quick to react to last night's broadcast in which we discussed the working methods of one of his journalists. Someone who beat another woman so badly she had to be taken to hospital.' Suddenly it was no longer about a martial arts gala, but about 'his journalist'.

'Let's see what Mr Vallent had to say,' Cathy Marant said, and before he knew it, Edward saw himself on the screen. Red-faced, he looked into the IRIS TV camera.

'*I* would like to know what's happened to the values of journalism if we continue to tolerate the libellous reports of Cathy Marant?' he heard himself fume. Somebody must have fiddled with the colour balance in the editing suite, because he looked shockingly bad. Red-faced, with bulging cheeks and drool coming out of a mouth distorted in anger.

Marant appeared on screen again. 'You may well ask what Mr Vallent is getting all worked up about. The indisputable fact remains that Farah Hafez didn't bat an eyelid when she dispatched another woman to hospital. But that's not all.'

Edward gasped for breath. Projected on the screen behind Marant was a crystal-clear photo of Farah, looking like she was about to lay into a paramedic.

'It may be a coincidence,' Marant exclaimed in mock-surprise, 'but here's the same Farah Hafez, the journalist who we now know as a woman who packs a mean punch. This photo was taken this afternoon by an onlooker at a demonstration of illegal Afghans in The Hague. It looks like our girl has a thing for hospitals. Here she apparently wants to stop a paramedic from doing his job. I've got this to say to Ms Hafez, assaulting your opponents is one thing. But keep your hands off our paramedics!'

Edward hurled the remote control with such force that it shattered against the wall. Enraged, he keyed in Farah's number again.

25

Whenever Farah was overcome by emotions, she instinctively switched to her mother tongue. Sorrow, rage or triumph were all expressed in Dari. She couldn't help it, and nor did she want to. It was part of her nature.

Marant was in every respect like the opponent Farah had brought down at Carré the evening before last. A seasoned vulture who was out for the blood of her kill and the kudos of a scoop and was prepared to pull the nastiest tricks to get what she wanted.

When she saw Edward's picture on the display of her vibrating iPhone she knew what to expect.

'I thought we'd agreed to speak after the broadcast,' she sighed.

'Is there something you forgot to tell me this afternoon, Hafez?'

'I didn't know photos were taken this afternoon.'

'Clearly there were and you've seen them now, so why don't you tell me about what happened!'

'I spent a long time trying to resuscitate my uncle . . . and when the ambulance arrived to take him to hospital, he was already dead. I wasn't allowed to accompany him . . . I was in a real state, true. But I didn't touch the man, Ed.'

'She's clever,' Edward sighed. 'Marant even gets me to stop trusting you. What possesses that woman?'

Meanwhile they saw the same Cathy Marant on screen with Danielle.

'We'll begin with the distressing story of the seriously injured boy who was found by former soap actress Angela Faber the other night,' Marant said rather melodramatically. 'Thanks to her quick intervention, our first guest this evening was able to save his life: trauma surgeon, Dr Danielle Bernson.' Polite applause. 'Danielle, how do you think this boy ended up in the Netherlands?'

'I can't tell you everything I know,' a visibly nervous Danielle said. 'It's confidential information. But there are clear indications that we're dealing with the victim of a gang of international child traffickers.'

'You say there are indications,' Marant continued. 'Can you give us a clue?'

Danielle hesitated. 'The boy's clothing was rather unusual,' she finally said. 'He was wearing a traditional Middle-Eastern robe, jewellery, and he was made up to look like a young woman.'

'What does it do to you, seeing a child like that?' Cathy asked with just the right dose of pathos as the camera zoomed in on Danielle who was clearly perspiring.

'It's heart-rending,' Danielle said with a frog in her throat.

Cathy Marant paused briefly while Danielle took a sip of water. Her hand was shaking.

'Let's go back to the boy's appearance,' Marant said, mustering as much empathy as she could. 'It would appear that we're dealing with an ancient tradition from Afghanistan, which has now landed on these shores.'

'That's right.' Danielle sounded less uncertain now. 'Bacha Bazi, it's called. Young boys are dressed as girls and ordered to dance for rich older men.'

'And what happens to them afterwards?' Marant asked in an insinuating tone.

'They're sexually abused.'

A few shots of shocked audience reactions were shown in the ensuing silence. Then it was back to the table, where Marant had assumed a journalistic pose and stared straight into the camera.

'The possession of dancing boys is a status symbol in Afghanistan,' she explained. 'Boys, aged seven, eight, nine, are recruited at markets or on the streets. When they turn eighteen or they're no longer considered attractive, they're at great risk. They must fear for their lives because they know which prominent men have secretly abused them for years. Not infrequently, young men are found with their throats cut. Despite an official ban, the Bacha Bazi ritual is spreading rapidly and now it appears to have reared its illegal head in *our* country.'

Marant then turned demonstratively to Vincent Coronel. Farah saw the bewildered look on Danielle's face.

'Mr Coronel,' Marant said affectedly, 'what do you make of this development?'

'Like everybody else here, I'm shocked,' was Coronel's quick response. 'But you see what foolishly believing in multiculturalism has brought us. I mean, if we tolerate all these Afghans within our borders, we effectively allow these people to bring their reprehensible cultural customs and traditions into our country.'

Farah understood where the conversation was going. Danielle could only watch powerlessly as her story was hijacked to give Vincent Coronel the chance to spout his views on mass immigration to the Netherlands.

Farah swore. In Dari of course.

26

Marouan Diba sauntered past the one-armed bandits lined up in a row in the small pub that was home to a handful of hard-up losers. The sound of the levers being pulled down in different rhythms resembled that of rifles being loaded and unlocked.

The clattering of coins increased the revulsion he felt about his next anticipated loss, yet strongly reinforced his desire to defy fate.

He'd driven downtown, parked the Corolla, and then found a seat in front of a slot machine at Tante Roosje on Rembrandtplein. With a glass of beer in one hand and a cigarette dangling from the corner of his mouth, he fed coins into the machine, practically on autopilot. Marouan's thoughts at this moment were like the fruit symbols on the screen in front of him: they tumbled without the slightest chance of finding each other. The payoff was not a victory, a masterly inspiration, a brilliant idea or a great insight. Zilch, no huge rush of coins, jingling cash flow or silvery climax.

And again and again, his pathetic behaviour kept flashing through his mind: how he'd avoided his partner, how he'd shrunk to the size of Tom Thumb during the conversation with Tomasoa, Park and Calvino. But the thought of the man with the Slavic accent dominated everything. How the hell was he going to make it clear to him that as part of the new MIT his hands would be completely tied?

Then he saw Danielle Bernson on television. Drowned out by the noise of the levers and sporadic ringing. He stumbled towards the television and turned up the sound.

'The boy's clothing was rather unusual' he heard her say. 'He was wearing a traditional Middle-Eastern robe, jewellery, and he was made up to look like a young woman.'

Marouan rubbed his face with both hands. It had become an instinctive habit any time problems arose that were bigger than his own shadow. *Gra, hadchi chhal mqouad!* Shit, what a fucking disaster! He knew it. He was a fucking idiot, the scapegoat, a born loser. If anyone should have kept Danielle Bernson from talking to a Dutch prime-time audience about how much this case really stank, then it should've been him.

A Dutch *hmara*, a stupid chick, who'd studied to be a doctor, now raising a huge hue and cry in millions of homes about an innocent child who was smuggled into the Netherlands.

Danielle Bernson was a *bint el zenqa*. A fucking slag! The sense of his own impotence made Marouan furious. He kicked the slot machine, pounded it with his flat hands, shook the unwieldy thing back and forth and considered giving it a head-butt. Anything to unleash his anger, to severely punish himself.

But he managed to get himself under control and left every-thing for what it was: his beer, the astonished regulars in the pub, the betrayal on television. He stepped outside, pulled the prepaid phone from his coat pocket, and via the speed dial rang the man he hated from the bottom of his heart.

27

Immediately after Joshua Calvino arrived at the WMC's Intensive Care Unit he seized the opportunity to speak to the head nurse in private.

'Not one of my finer moments,' Mariska said candidly, 'but I agreed to keep Danielle in the loop, which I probably shouldn't have. I promised to call her as quickly as possible if there was a problem with the boy.'

'What's wrong with that?' Joshua wanted to know.

'I side-stepped protocol. Once a patient is transferred to us, we are entirely responsible.'

'So why did you agree to keep her in the loop?'

'I know something about Danielle's background. I could see how involved she was with this boy. When complications set in during the night that revealed a ruptured spleen, I immediately called her. She then took it upon herself to come to the OR and against all protocol persuaded the senior trauma surgeon who operated not to remove the boy's spleen.'

'That takes guts,' Joshua said admiringly.

'You don't see the kind of commitment Danielle exhibits very often in our work. So when she called me this morning and asked me to look the other way when she and Angela Faber showed up to visit . . . well, I thought, if it's brief, okay . . .'

'But . . . ?'

'When I saw Dennis Faber and that photographer who was with them, not to mention that TV woman . . . what's her name again?'

'Marant, Cathy Marant.'

'Yes, her. Then I immediately stood my ground, said it was unacceptable.'

'What was her reaction?'

'Danielle wasn't interested in what I had to say. She had the determined look of someone who was going to get what she wanted. At all costs. Once I realized this, I had no choice but to call Hospital Security. But this hospital is pretty big, so before they got here, the whole media circus had already picked itself up and left: in and out in no time.'

'Yet still long enough for an article in *De Nederlander*,' Joshua said.

'I then informed my department about what had taken place,' Mariska said.

'Only then?' asked Joshua, surprised.

'You know, detective, I hate to see someone like Danielle, who hasn't been working here very long and is so dedicated, get into trouble early on. Yes, I hesitated about reporting her, especially because I first saw it as an isolated incident. But once I read the article, I realized how naive I'd been.'

'I'd like to speak to your supervisor,' Joshua said. 'The boy needs police protection. The sooner the better.'

Mariska gave him the number of her supervisor. Joshua got a resolute woman on the phone who told him she'd had men in flak jackets with automatic weapons positioned in front of an ICU room before, so she was used to it. With the promise that she'd cooperate fully regarding the boy's safety in her hospital, Joshua concluded their conversation. He called Tomasoa immediately afterwards to inform him about the latest developments.

Tomasoa preferred short lines of communication and a quick follow-through. As efficiently as he'd put a rush on the forensics investigation, he put things into action now. Normally, if there were indications a witness was in danger, a threat assessment was first made to determine how serious the risk actually was. But after hearing Joshua's account, Tomasoa decided to bypass standard procedure: he made protecting the boy a 'high' priority. In any case, after a short consultation with that evening's chief duty officer, Tomasoa got the go-ahead to post a uniformed police guard at the boy's hospital door. If and when there were signs of an increased threat, for example in response to the TV broadcast this evening, then Tomasoa wouldn't hesitate: he'd ensure that a heavily armed presence was placed right outside the ICU.

Pleased by how swiftly and efficiently Tomasoa had reacted, Joshua went in search of a television. With the help of Mariska, he located one in a day room, where he had to convince a handful of bewildered patients of the importance of switching the channel from the dancing celebrities on ice to the live broadcast of *The Headlines Show*. The Dutch politician Vincent Coronel was already holding forth about the dangers of the multicultural society.

Not much was needed to convince Joshua that once again Farah Hafez had been right. A police investigation that would have benefited from as much media silence as possible was now being broadcast into millions of Dutch living rooms, and was receiving a bleak political dimension as well, thanks to the involvement of Vincent Coronel.

Joshua saw that Danielle was sweating. She could barely find the words to counter Coronel.

'You're talking about contemptible cultural practices and traditions that have been smuggled into our country, but I'm talking about a child, Mr Coronel. A child, you understand?' It looked like she would burst into tears at any moment.

'Dr Bernson,' Coronel replied dismissively, 'you may have saved that boy's life, which is of course praiseworthy – by the way, it's also your medical responsibility – but let's not pretend this boy is just an incident. This isn't an isolated case.'

'What do you mean?'

'More will follow, Dr Bernson. You know it, I know it and our viewer audience knows it.'

'Where are you going with this?' Danielle exclaimed, her voice breaking.

As determined and resolute as Joshua had seen her two nights ago in the middle of the road attending to the boy, so emotional and flustered was she now. Danielle, with all her ideals, had landed in a place where you only got the audience on your side with witty one-liners and populist arguments. With her sincerity, Danielle Bernson had lost the battle in the television arena before she'd even begun.

28

Danielle saw that the conversation was about to go in a completely different direction than she wanted, and she remembered Farah's words, 'It's going to turn against you!' She realized what kind of a trap she'd walked into. She'd thought she'd be able to tell her story here, but now she knew that her appearance was nothing more than a ploy, meant to provide a platform for Vincent Coronel to vent his criticism of the government's current asylum policy.

Coronel, in the meantime, was only too happy to take advantage of this platform.

'We can no longer allow all sorts of foreign practices and above all abuses to be imported into our Dutch society,' she heard him assert in a staccato tone. 'We can no longer accept that Afghan war criminals are eligible to stay in this country. Did you know that the Netherlands currently has I don't know how many ministers, governors, generals and former agents of the feared Afghan secret police, the Khad, living here? All important figures of the former communist regime that terrorized Afghanistan for years! The discovery of a dancing Afghan boy shows that we are dealing with a ring of Afghan criminals who have managed to settle here thanks to Geneva's Refugee Convention and the naivety of the Dutch government.'

Danielle could no longer contain herself and responded sharply.

'Mr Coronel, do you know how many Dutch children are treated every year in hospitals due to abuse? Children who are abused by Dutch people!' she cried angrily.

'I really don't understand the relevance of your question,' Coronel said calmly, but nevertheless he seemed caught off-guard for a moment. Danielle didn't wait for his reply.

'Nearly a hundred thousand!' she cried. 'One hundred thousand! And has anyone ever asked these children what it's like to be beaten, abused or raped?!'

She looked around and saw the expectant faces of the audience in the studio. You could hear a pin drop.

In the heat of the moment, she was no longer afraid of speaking in public.

'Tonight I was going to talk about an Afghan boy, not even ten years old, who was smuggled into the country by an international criminal gang. But that boy could have easily been a Dutch child, or an African child – a child is a child. The real criminals are the bunch who brought him here. But in your hunt for political gain you have the audacity to use child trafficking and child abuse to label refugees and asylum seekers as criminals. Is everything acceptable as long as it wins you votes? Let me tell you this, Mr Coronel: child abuse has nothing to do with politics, nothing to do with immigration and certainly nothing to do with your revolting political views!'

Coronel's comeback to Danielle was weak. He avoided looking at her and alternated his gaze between Cathy Marant and the former footballer's wife.

'In her immense naivety, Dr Bernson doesn't realize that she's saved the life of a boy who's ended up ten thousand miles from his home, precisely because a group of his countrymen are now living here in the Netherlands. And these are people who think they can institute this kind of abuse on a large scale in our country.'

'That doesn't have a damn thing to do with this,' said Danielle, and then she turned towards Marant and took a shot at her, 'Ms Marant, or should I say Ms Manipulator? You should be ashamed of yourself. You lured me here under false pretences.'

'Dr Bernson, you came here of your own free will,' Marant replied arrogantly.

'You're absolutely right, and now I'm going to take advantage of my own free will by leaving.' She immediately acted on her words by getting up and walking away.

'Why don't we break for a commercial; we'll be right back . . .' Danielle heard Cathy Marant say in an icy tone behind her.

29

Anxiously waiting to be connected, Marouan walked along the crowded outdoor terraces of the Rembrandt Bar and Royal Café De Kroon with his phone hugging his ear. He wandered across the tram tracks, lost in thought, causing a dull screeching of brakes and the deafening ring of a bell from the approaching Line 9 tram. Marouan barely noticed.

As he passed a Mariachi band, playing the same tune as always, he was suddenly aware of the growing number of chuckling people standing around and staring, as if his fly were open. When he turned around he saw the reason. A Charlie Chaplin lookalike was walking behind him and mimicking Marouan's every move and facial expression. Marouan waved the street artist away, giving the white-faced Charlie with his elastic body cause to playfully gesture in return. The minute Marouan turned his back on him, the aping pest copied his every movement again.

Before the call was answered, Marouan hung up, abruptly turned and shoved his detective ID under Charlie's nose as he barked 'Police!' On the spot, Charlie mimed how broken-hearted he was. The quickly gathering crowd, who thought they were watching a wonderfully rehearsed performance, gave them a big round of applause. Charlie pretended to cry, started to kneel, and held out both arms to indicate to Marouan that he could handcuff him. Marouan's only escape from the situation was leaving the square as quickly as possible, while the performer, to the great amusement of everybody around, continued his pursuit of Marouan for several metres, like a hungry cat chasing a mouse.

Right in front of Stopera, the city hall, Marouan hit the speed dial on his prepaid phone for the second time. Upon hearing that voice, he related, as if confessing his sins, that a new problem had arisen. He gave his take on the television appearance of the blonde doctor and for a long time only heard white noise on the other end of the line.

'Didn't we agree that you'd handle these sorts of problems yourself?' the haughty voice with that shitty accent finally said. 'So your problems don't become my problems. How can we make this problem yours again, Diva, and the sooner the better?'

'I have no idea,' Marouan answered, sounding like he had cramps in his stomach.

'That's actually the root of all your problems, *kulak*. That you never have a fucking clue.'

Marouan knew he had no choice but to once again submit to insults in the form of a philosophical treatise, hoping there'd be some mercy for him in the end.

'Everything starts with fascination, Diva. Fascination. You're grabbed by something. An idea. An assignment. A goal. Something that gives you direction, that you can build on. Fa-sci-na-tion. Giving you a reason to rise above yourself. But what do you do? You only disappoint . . .'

'Sorry.'

'Go home and wait for my call.'

Click. End of conversation.

Marouan didn't know what to feel: relief or fear. While walking to his car, fear won out. Waiting at home for a call sounded like a cruel euphemism for waiting for inevitable disaster.

As if he was suddenly yesterday's newspaper that unscrupulous angels of revenge would use to wipe their asses.

30

Farah arrived at the entrance of the Zuiveringshal just in time to see Danielle storming out while a girl with milky-white hair and a psychedelic shirt tried to stop her. Danielle shoved the girl aside and made a beeline for her bike.

When she spotted Farah she snapped at her.

'I bet you saw everything. Don't say "I told you so". I don't care!'

'Not at all! You had the courage to say your piece. You gave them what they deserved.'

Danielle didn't react. She leaned over to unlock her bike and as she was fiddling with her key Farah heard her sobbing. The girl with the milky-white hair was suddenly standing between them and gasping that she'd never seen anything like it. Danielle straightened up, her face contorted, and yelled at the girl to piss off. Farah wrapped a comforting arm around Danielle, pulled her close and motioned for the girl to leave.

'Get me out of here,' Danielle muttered in between her tears. 'Away from that stupid cow. That bitch Marant. I want to see the boy.'

'Let's go,' Farah said. 'Leave your bike here. I'll take you.'

A little while later Farah drove the Carrera into the WMC's car park. As they got out, Farah noticed Danielle glancing around anxiously.

'What's the matter?'

'Nothing.'

In the lift there was a long silence.

'Are you okay?'

'No.'

In the corridor outside the ICU Mariska approached them, but Danielle side-stepped her and slipped into the boy's room.

'She's not supposed to go in there,' Mariska said, shaking her head.

'She's upset,' Farah apologized on her behalf. Mariska followed Danielle into the room and gently closed the door behind her. Not long after, Danielle could be heard sobbing again. At the sound of approaching footsteps, as well as male voices, Farah turned around to see Joshua Calvino and a police officer entering the corridor, calmly conferring with one another.

Joshua didn't seem all that surprised to see her again. With a glance at the closed door he asked Farah whether she knew who'd gone in. Meanwhile the sobbing gradually subsided and a moment later the two women came out. Mariska had an arm around Danielle, who was trying to dry her eyes with both hands. 'I'm sorry,' she said, while the tears kept rolling down her cheeks. 'I'm so sorry.'

'You'd better go home, Dr Bernson. We've got everything under control here,' Joshua said kindly.

'Shall I call you a taxi?' Mariska asked.

'There's no need. I'll escort Dr Bernson home myself.' Joshua nodded at the police guard, who introduced himself to Mariska and then accompanied her to the boy's room.

'Thank you,' Danielle said to Farah in passing as she walked to the lift with Joshua. Farah watched them until the doors closed and she was the only one left in the corridor.

Joshua had barely made eye contact with her.

31

While the lights and contours of the city at dusk passed her by, Danielle thought back on what had happened to her since they'd found the boy lying in the middle of the road barely two days ago. Before this incident she'd had the distinct impression that she'd left everything behind, that she'd shaken off Africa and could start over again. But everything she should've forgotten had travelled along beside her like an amorphous shadow that once again had her firmly in its grip.

She longed to forget. Forget that she couldn't escape. Forget that she'd been blind to the errors she'd made, forget that her naivety had turned against her.

She gazed up at the clear sky and despite the dome of reflected light over the city she could still make out a few stars. A bizarre idea that some of the stars had been extinguished long ago – stars that despite their deaths could be seen here light years later. She had the same sort of feeling. Alive, but dead deep within.

She glanced at the man next to her, sitting silently behind the wheel.

'Are you religious, detective?' she asked.

He looked at her in surprise.

'I believe in all kinds of things. As long as it exists and functions,' he said, and when he saw her puzzled look, he tried to clarify. 'I believe in nature, in the cosmos and in the engine of this car.'

'I mean . . . belief in a more abstract sense . . . in a hereafter?' she asked doubtfully.

'I believe I'm able to get you home safely. And I believe in what you've told me. It doesn't get more abstract than that for me, sorry.'

She realized that despite the gravity of the situation a smile had passed her lips.

'Is this how you charm all the girls, detective?'

'So you think somebody's trying to charm the girls if he claims to believe in honesty?'

Yes, I must be crazy, she thought to herself without answering, and then she gazed up at the stars again.

'You mustn't give up, doctor,' said Calvino after a long silence. 'Sleep on it and tomorrow it'll all look a lot different.'

That's the problem, she thought. It might look different, but things don't really change. The same fears and demons always rear their ugly heads and the same mistakes are made over and over again.

They drove into her street and Calvino stopped the car in front of the door she indicated. Before she got out, she thanked him.

'Thanks, not only for the lift, but also for arranging police security for the boy.'

'You're more than welcome.'

There was something about the way he looked at her. As if he expected more. She stumbled out of the car and walked a bit too quickly to her front door, her hand rummaging in her handbag for her keys. All the while, she heard the engine idling and when, with a lot of effort, she finally found her keys and opened the door, she thought she heard him get out of the car. She broke out in a sweat and, despite her fear, turned to see him with his head bent over the steering wheel, looking in her direction. She slipped inside and closed the door while her heart raced like crazy.

In the hall, breathing heavily, she leaned back against the door. Now he knows where I live, she panicked, but then immediately reflected on the absolute absurdity of this thought. After all, this was a detective who had brought her home, a man who seemed reliable and composed, who, acting on his own initiative, had arranged security for the boy.

She heard him slowly pull away and only when the sound of his car was gone did she dare to look out the window. He'd probably waited to make sure she was safely inside and only then drove away. How could she see his concern for her as anything but professional?

Her legs trembled as she mounted the stairs to the living room. The first thing she did was fill a bath and put her phone on silent. After she quickly closed all the curtains, she turned on a few dim lights. She decided to pour herself a whisky, something to relax her while she listened to the bath filling. She found that the safe sounds of home in combination with a drink had a surprisingly calming effect on her.

Even if she had tried, afterwards she wouldn't have been able to remember when she'd fallen asleep. Before she knew it, she was carried off in a warm stream of oblivion.

32

By tearing off from the WMC site and taking the ring road exit at breakneck speed, Farah tried to put the chilly reunion with Joshua out of her mind.

The intensity of her night with him had brought back memories of an early love. At the age of fourteen, Farah had a penchant for lowlifes, because that's how she saw herself. Anyway, she was smitten with the biggest loudmouth in class who wore wellies and drab and dirty clothes whatever the season. He was always spoiling for a fight, covered in bruises and constantly scanning his surroundings like a hunted animal. But when he was with Farah he calmed down and transformed into a gentle lover with infinite patience and hands that made her body tingle.

One day, she impulsively grabbed his pocket knife and carved a superficial cut into the soft inside of his arm, and then asked him to do the same to her. As they had sex their blood intermingled. It had been the most delicious combination of pain and pleasure, blood and ecstasy she had ever experienced. The scars on her arms and on her thighs and stomach were the tangible reminders of this experience.

During later affairs she was always the driving force, the captain of the ship. The only difference was that captains were traditionally the last to leave their ship, whereas she was always the first. None of her conquests had ever inspired in Farah anything remotely like the feelings she'd had for the one-time love of her life.

In ten minutes' time she'd be hearing the crunch of the gravel path beneath her tyres. She knew she would see David's silhouette in the doorway of his welcoming house. He appeared to have developed a sixth sense which told him when she was near, so he would often be waiting for her, even if her visit was unannounced. David never met her halfway – he always stayed where he was. It's what made walking towards him across those pebbles so worthwhile. She longed for the moment she'd be right in front of him and he'd embrace her like someone freshly returned from a trip around the world.

Again, she realized how extraordinary it was that during her six-month relationship with David there had been no other men. Joshua had been the first and, as far as she was concerned, also the last exception. These kinds of escapades had no place in her life any more. If only she could explain it to David. Trying to imagine his reaction, she pictured him looking at her with wild, disbelieving eyes and, while he paced up and down the room, asking why and whether it was his fault, whether he'd done something wrong?

No darling, you did nothing wrong. It's me, me!

She would let him rant and rave before approaching him and touching him tentatively with her fingertips, put up with his resistance and slowly reach for his hands. And then finally, finally David would say with that touching honesty of his that there was no cure for his feelings for her, so she really mustn't hurt him again. This was the moment she would whisper her pledge of faith into his ear, followed by her decision to join him on his big Verne trip. If necessary, she would quit her job for it. Anything to make it up to him. Anything to keep things as they were.

David loved her in a unique way, because he saw something in her that she'd never wanted, or rather, never dared to see in herself. She was only familiar with her fighting spirit. As the child of foster parents in this flat, rainy country where everything was so well organized, she soon discovered that no other girl or boy had a father who was shot by a firing squad, or a mother who perished in the perpetual snow of a mountain pass. Everything about her was different. The way she looked, the way she felt, her past. She never felt truly connected to any-one. Every day, both in and out of school, was one long battle against the jeering, bullying and gossiping of her peers, their parents and even her teachers. She hoped that one day she could accept the unfamiliar, softer side of herself. David would help her.

When, shortly afterwards, she reached the house, she saw to her amazement that he was not waiting for her in the doorway.

33

It was chaos at the gates of St Helen Joseph Hospital. The nursing staff had blocked the access roads to and from the hospital to demonstrate for higher wages, which had been promised by the government but had so far failed to materialize.

'*Amandla*,' chanted the woman Paul recognized as the night nurse who had lovingly cared for him. '*Awethu*,' shouted the protesters. 'Power! To the people!'

The police tried breaking open the locks of the chains some of the demonstrators had used to shackle themselves to the gate, but they were immediately stormed by packs of shrieking nurses. A water cannon was deployed in reaction to this.

Paul climbed over a fence and from beside the road tried several times to hail a passing minibus. For a moment he wondered whether he was using the correct signal. When he caught the eyes of some passengers, he realized that no driver with a minibus full of blacks was prepared to pick him up: a white man with a swollen, purple face, a black eye, a bandaged nose and twenty-four stitches starting at his left eyebrow that made him look like a thug.

A little further down he saw a woman step out of a taxi and he began to wave. He saw the driver sizing him up as he approached the car. He forced a smile in an attempt to break the ice and remarked that he was not nearly as scary as he looked and that he lived downtown at Fifteen Park Street. A very good fare. The driver gestured for him to get in and moments later they were zipping along the gated communities protected by 9,000 volts of electrified barbed wire.

Paul looked at the driver's ID card dangling in front of the windscreen and saw that the man behind the wheel was named Mosi Siluthu. Meanwhile, he also noticed that the garbage alongside the road was piled sky-high. Mosi saw Paul watching and took a good guess that he wasn't aware of the latest developments.

'It's happening all over the place. Everyone is demanding a wage increase. The garbage men have asked for fifteen per cent. So long as they don't get it, they're not going back to work.'

The result of this strike was that the streets of Johannesburg were now filled with splintered glass, old newspapers, huge amounts of plastic, towers of cans, rotting food, and elated rats running among the heaps of garbage and digging tunnels. At this rate they would surpass the number of illegals within a few days' time. Thanks to its sanitation department, Jo'burg was now a rat's paradise.

'The ANC, sir,' Mosi said as he looked at Paul in his mirror, 'governs in the name of big business. And look what happens: repression of labourers. Yesterday garbage men, today hospital staff, tomorrow construction workers, the day after municipal employees, then factory workers. Before you know it, the whole country will be on strike. *Amandla!*'

'*Awethu,*' Paul replied.

'The protests continue to increase,' Mosi said. 'Especially now that Jacob Nkoane has announced his candidacy for the presidency.'

'What?!' exclaimed Paul, shocked.

'Were you cooped up in solitary confinement in that hospital?' Mosi asked and, without waiting for an answer, rambled on. 'The ANC has made reducing poverty a central campaign theme for the upcoming election! But take a good look around you! It's a disgrace that this is what it's come to!'

'How long ago did Nkoane announce?' Paul asked, short of breath.

'Only today,' Mosi replied seriously, and Paul caught his eyes staring at him in the mirror again. The news about Nkoane felt like someone had punched him in the gut. He now realized how much the ANC must have pressured *The Citizen* to make him put aside his corruption investigation and now that same pressure would be exerted tenfold on the Scorpions.

But Paul surmised that Dingane was not a man who succumbed to that kind of pressure.

They silently continued on to Park Street. When they reached his house, Paul was extra generous with his tip and then the man disappeared from sight, mumbling to himself.

It had started raining. The drops clattered in a different key and different rhythm on to the plastic bags, the crumpled boxes and other heaps of rubbish.

With a head full of confused thoughts and haunting images of the condor – his hands gripping him hard and the badly beaten face – Paul opened the creaking door to his flat. For going on six months, it gave off the dismal atmosphere of a 'desperate man alone'. Paul had hoped to leave the jumble of emotions behind him once he'd shut the door, but hopelessness and depression taunted him like demons who'd apparently decided to spend the rest of his life tormenting him.

He walked to the window, behind which a downpour magically transformed the lights of the city into thin vertical beams, and his mobile rang. He thought about Mosi, what he had mumbled to him before he rode away in the taxi amidst the drenched piles of the city's accumulated rubbish: 'This is no longer my world,' and he answered his phone.

34

Edward looked out over the vegetable garden with its aubergines, courgettes and nearly ripe pumpkins. Among the fruit trees further down, startled sheep stared at him in the twilight. He walked over to the herb section, where he picked some mint and let the fresh leaves soften on his tongue before slowly chewing them with his eyes closed. Anything to put off the moment. Anything not to have to key in the Johannesburg number.

Delaying the inevitable, he strolled further into the garden. Past the petunias, the lady's mantel and the yarrow, towards the two centuries-old oak trees that demarcated the land around the farmhouse like gnarled watchmen. He thought back to the years when he met here weekly with the man he was about to phone. The man who'd been no more than a boy back then.

At the time, Edward had recognized the teenager's unbridled curiosity and advised him to keep track of everything he came across in a journal. Thoughts, opinions, random sentences from newspapers or snippets from conversations on television and radio as well as pictures from papers and magazines. He encouraged Paul to identify links between the different elements of his collection and to come up with explanations, hoping to instil in his nephew the desire to develop his own opinion. An opinion he would then have to put to the test. On Paul's seventeenth birthday, Edward agreed with him that they'd meet for weekly debates in which they would differ as sharply as possible on whatever topic Paul chose.

Every Saturday afternoon, Edward would turn up at the farmhouse. In winter they sat in front of the fireplace and wrangled while his sister Isobel prepared a casserole: Dutch-style slow-braised beef served with mashed potato and red cabbage. 'Comfort food' in her words. In summer the two antagonists usually sat facing each other in the front garden, with Isobel serving them iced tea and homemade lemon cupcakes. Edward assumed the role of the steadfast conservative whose take on world politics was informed by self-interest, while Paul argued in favour of his youthful and naive conviction that man was here on earth to rectify everything shattered by previous generations. In the process his nephew branded Edward everything reprehensible under the sun. He was a 'populist idiot', an 'unscrupulous capitalist' or a 'speechifying reactionary'. But with each noxious label Edward felt a growing intimacy between them and saw Paul gradually transform from an introverted kid who had difficulties keeping his aggression in check into a strong-minded young man who had got better at expressing himself. Both Edward and Isobel realized that these weekly sessions were an ideal outlet for a boy who yearned to express his anger about a world that had deprived him of his biggest hero: his father.

During those formative years, Edward taught Paul not only how to navigate the impulses of his personal intuition, but also to trust the accuracy of detached analysis. 'Combine the two and you'll be a great journalist,' he repeatedly told Paul.

Now he stood between the two ancient oak trees, waiting patiently to hear the voice of a once-promising journalist who'd long since lost the ability to combine those two elements.

In the silence that followed after Paul answered, Edward heard it was raining.

'Are you outside?'

'I'm in front of an open window.'

An alarmed Edward pictured Paul jumping and ending up on the street, in the rain. Injured, bleeding and unconscious. Seven or eight storeys below the open window. 'Don't worry,' Paul said, apparently sensing Edward's concerns thousands of kilometres away.

'Should I be worried, Paul?'

'Maybe. If you could see me now.' Paul laughed mirthlessly.

'What happened?'

'Doesn't matter.'

'Everything that happens to you matters to me,' Edward said irritably, like a father reprimanding a wilful son.

'Let's pretend I'm doing well,' Paul said. 'Then at least we can stop talking about that.'

Paul was silent. Edward heard the South African rain tapping in the background and couldn't help but look up.

'I've got a job for you. One you can really sink your teeth into.'

'Sounds good. Tell me more.'

'A young Afghan boy was found in the woods, dressed Bacha Bazi-style. The case appears to have links with Armin Lazonder and a Russian associate of his, Valentin Lavrov.'

All was quiet on the other end of the line. Edward waited for a reaction, but none came.

'You've got my attention,' Paul said eventually.

'I want you to work with Farah Hafez.'

'She's new at investigative journalism?'

'That's why I want you on the job. I've just spoken to her and she's come up with a third name, for what it's worth.'

'All good things come in threes, Ed, so out with it.'

'Grigori Michailov.'

'Since when does the *AND* cover cold cases?'

'What do you mean?'

'Michailov has been dead for quite some time.'

'I know, but he's still claiming victims as one of the walking dead, judging by the latest information we have. Someone tortured by the Khad thought he spotted him.'

'Sounds like the Bermuda Triangle. Lazonder, Lavrov and an undead Michailov.'

'I told you this was a case you'd be able to sink your teeth into.'

'So if I take you up on your offer, I'll be working closely with this woman?'

'Trust me, Paul, she's sharp.'

'What makes you say so?'

'I recognize talent when I see it, remember?'

'I think I get it,' Paul said. 'By hooking her up with me you're turning me into the comeback kid and you give her a leg-up, am I right?'

This time it was Edward who remained silent.

'How's Mum, by the way?'

'I've taken her up to bed. She's sleeping.'

It had stopped raining in Jo'burg.

'Paul?'

'I'll be in touch.'

Edward listened absentmindedly to the dial tone after Paul had hung up. The sheep moved languidly against the purple-red evening sky. In the distance, above the city, he saw an area of low pressure building and heard the distant rumble of thunder.

35

It was dark in the bathroom when Danielle opened her eyes with a start. The water was lukewarm. Had she fallen asleep? It couldn't have been for very long. But she knew one thing for certain. The lights had been on when she got into her bath.

She sat up, feeling slightly dizzy, and while she supported herself on the edge of the tub she searched for a towel in the darkness but couldn't find one. She got out of the bath and reached for the light switch. At that moment she felt a gloved hand cover her mouth before she could scream. She was firmly pressed against the body of a large man, who smelled of leather, mint and a musky aftershave. A man who spoke English with a Russian accent whispered sinisterly in her right ear.

'It's dangerous to fall asleep in a bath. A lot of people drown that way. But it's a peaceful death. You drown without even knowing it. Is that what you'd want?'

He released the pressure on her mouth so she could answer. She shook her head back and forth: no.

'A wise decision. Now you need to tell me what you know,' the man said hoarsely. 'You need to tell me all about the boy. What you didn't get a chance to say on television, you can tell me.'

Again she felt the leather on her mouth loosen its grip. She briefly caught her breath and tried to speak.

'He was used for Bacha Bazi.' She could barely get out the words.

'I know that. But how did he get here?'

Danielle felt a blind panic set in.

'That . . . I don't know.'

She felt herself being lifted up and flung into the bath, her head hitting the edge of the tub. She was immediately pushed under water and felt his other hand grabbing on to her flailing legs. In an attempt to breathe she swallowed water. When the hand unexpectedly pulled her head out of the water she gagged.

He continued to whisper in her ear. 'I don't have to do this, you understand. As long as you tell me what you know. So I'm asking you again. How did the boy get here?'

'I . . . I don't know . . .' she sobbed.

Immediately, the hand pushed her under water again. This time the other gloved hand grabbed her between the legs, causing her mouth to open in a scream and fill with water once more. She felt herself losing consciousness.

That was the moment the hands pulled her up, lifted her out of the bath and pressed her up against a hard male body. As the hands went through her wet hair, down her back and squeezed her buttocks, she tried to stammer a few words through her sobbing.

'He hasn't said anything. He's sedated.'

The hands returned to her head and gripped it tightly. She smelled the mint again as his face appeared close to hers like a dark cloud.

'Listen,' he said. 'What I just did to you is nothing. Nothing compared to what the others will do to you. They will go much further. Silence you for good. Do you understand what I'm saying?'

'You've got the wrong person,' she managed to blurt out.

'No, you're the one who saved his life. That's why I'm saving yours.'

He turned her around.

'Put your hands against the wall.'

She obeyed him.

'Close your eyes.'

She closed her eyes.

'Start counting to sixty, slowly.'

She began to count. When she got to five, he interrupted her. 'Slower . . . If you count slowly, you'll live.'

She started counting again. From one. Slowly. As if she was a dying star light years away. She didn't stop when she reached sixty. Perhaps dying was a little bit like counting for ever.

36

Just before she got to it, the front door swung open and David strode angrily towards her.

'Lies! You can only ignore them for so long!' he shouted agitatedly and grabbed her by the shoulders as though he wanted to give her a good shaking. 'I'm sure you'll work it out. *We'll* work it out! I want you to tell me everything! Everything, you hear me?'

'In a minute, David,' she said, stunned. 'In a minute.'

He wrapped an arm around her and ushered her inside, where the Verne books were scattered about, the malt whisky bottle was three-quarters empty and the air was still thick with the spicy aroma of the meal he'd originally prepared for the two of them.

'You should have warned that doctor about taking her story to Marant,' he said, sounding tense.

The penny dropped. So that's what he was all worked up about. David had watched *The Headlines Show* too.

'I did, darling.'

'So she didn't listen to you. Stupid!'

Farah never thought she'd loathe herself this much. Here she was, with a secret she was dying to confess so her life could go back to normal. A life in which she felt more at home than she'd realized until now.

'Would you please sit down, David?'

'What about you? Don't you want something to eat? And what can I get you to drink?'

'Sit down and listen to me, will you?' she begged.

It did the trick. He grabbed his whisky glass and sat down on the firm designer sofa.

During the long silence, as she searched for the right words, David shifted uneasily in his seat and frowned impatiently.

'You know what kind of life I lived before I met you. You know, right?' she said shakily.

'I've got an idea, yes. That's all I need to know. End of story.'

'I don't want that life any more. Never again.'

'Excellent. Was that it?' He was about to get to his feet again.

'No. I haven't told you everything yet. I mean about last night.'

'You were at the hospital until the early hours.'

'Yes, but after that I went to see someone. A man. And I spent the night there. All night.'

'Who was it? Do I know him?'

'Why do you ask? Does it make a difference?'

'Stayed the night. Does that mean you fucked him?'

'It won't happen again, David. I . . .'

'No,' David said as he got to his feet so unexpectedly it made her start. 'It's already happened!'

He began pacing. No surprises there. He always did when he was trying to find a solution to a problem. Head down, searching for an insight that would restore his grasp of the situation.

'Is it because I'm away too much? Because I've given you too much freedom? Have I been too accepting, is that it?'

She noticed he was losing his temper and involuntarily shrank away.

'I really don't know, David, but you're right.' Yes, that was it. Telling him he was right would calm him down. 'It's happened. But it won't happen again.'

He came to a halt, gave her a sharp look and accentuated his words, which kept coming like the waves of a spring tide, with forceful gestures.

'Okay, it's happened and let's assume it's happened once and it won't happen again . . . that's possible, but who's to say that it was just this once, that you haven't already . . . I mean, has it happened *before*?'

'You'll have to trust me.'

'Trust? You're asking me to *trust* you? After the bombshell you just dropped? What a fucked-up thing to do, Farah!' he fumed. 'First you're a bundle of tears in the shower in the middle of the night, have sex with me like your life depended on it and then you disappear again. Where were you? What were you up to? I've just come back from India, I conclude a world-class deal and instead of wanting to celebrate with me, you turn up here telling me you're screwing other men but that you're thinking of giving it up one of these days . . .'

Halfway through his tirade, she got up to leave.

'Hey, hang on a minute, where do you think you're going?'

'Home. I'll come back once you've calmed down.'

'You won't even let me react to the havoc you've wreaked?! Do you expect me to stick a goddamn flower in your hair and simply forgive you?'

'I'm not expecting anything right now. I'm going, David.'

'Sure, by all means. Brave, very brave. Well, that's you. Don't let anyone get too close. Spend the whole bloody time doing your own thing and remaining elusive. Especially to those who love you. Make me think you're here for me, while you only care about yourself. Make me believe you feel at home here, when in actual fact you're somewhere completely different! You think I don't notice? You're not really here, you're always somewhere else! You've never really been here, you've always been "over there", but you won't tell anyone exactly where that is.'

'No, that's not true, David. I *am* here, I want to be here. I love you.'

'Do you think those are the soothing words I'm waiting for right now?'

'What are you waiting for then?'

'For you to leave. And I mean really leave. Because in the end you'll leave anyway, whether you intend to or not.'

'I don't want to leave.'

'No, but we're not doing this on your terms. You have no right to set the terms. I'm the one setting the terms here, you hear me? This is my house, and in my house I live by my terms! So either you stay and let me finish my rant or you piss off and I'll send you your things!'

'I told you I'm sorry, I love you.'

'But you see, that's the problem. You're not sorry at all and as for the loving, what good does that do me if you go and screw other guys?! What does "loving" mean, for God's sake? I'll tell you what it means? It means fuck all!'

The man facing her was not the David she knew. He was someone else. His evil twin.

After his last few words, Farah walked into the hallway with tears in her eyes, opened the front door and stomped through the gravel back to the Carrera. As she pulled away, she saw his figure in the doorway. The contours of an abrupt ending.

PART THREE
Storm

How did it feel to be dead? It was something he'd asked himself a lot. His granddad said that the gates of heaven would open up. And he'd have a life without end, without pain or hunger.

He'd know that he was in heaven because everybody was dressed in white and they would be singing. But the confusing thing was that he'd seen quite a few people in white lately, and none of them was singing. What's more, he'd seen not one gate open, but lots of them. Gates he was carried through on his back. The other thing his granddad never told him was that heaven was made up of all these different rooms and corridors filled with bright light.

Granddad could tell wonderful stories, but some of his comparisons made him sound like a poet. And he didn't like poems.

He liked games. Especially Aaqab, the eagle game. It went without saying that he would be the eagle sitting on the rock made of gathered timber, tyres and boulders. The other boys would hide and as soon as they emerged like pigeons, he would fly at them, scattering them and giving chase until he'd devoured them all. He hoped that wherever he was, be it heaven or otherwise, he could soon be an eagle again.

But above all he hoped the woman would come again. The woman with the long dark hair, the blue eyes and the gentle voice. The woman who spoke his language and had held his hand. She was like an angel, but dressed in black. That was confusing too, because in heaven nobody wore black.

A face hovered close to him. It was the blonde woman he first saw after he got hit by the light. She was talking to him. But he didn't understand the language they spoke in heaven. The only thing he understood was 'salam'.

She said it no fewer than three times and looked really sad as she did so. She kissed him on the forehead. A sloppy kiss. It made him wonder whether in heaven they were all sad and all gave sloppy kisses.

Then suddenly everybody began to talk at once, in loud, hurried voices, and there was smoke and a smell of burning. The sky was engulfed in flames and everybody was in a rush to get away. Beside him, people were running through the smoke, throwing him worried glances, and after he'd been wheeled through a transparent gate he was slid into a cool cabin with dimmed lighting. He heard an explosion nearby. It reminded him of the thrust of engines during a rocket launch. He felt the entire cabin vibrating and heard the crash of breaking glass and a loud roar. Again, the smell of fire.

All that time he was lying in the iron cocoon. Tied to his bed. Defenceless.

But strangely enough he felt no fear. The last time he'd been afraid was when he was running among the trees. As soon as the white light got hold of him, that fear had evaporated.

What he did feel was regret, since he hadn't had the chance to say good-bye to the angel with her blue eyes and gentle voice.

I

They were built to have the feeling of Manhattan, the lavish penthouses on Amsterdam's Oosterdok where Sasha Kovalev gazed out over the old city from his rooftop terrace as he gulped back a protein shake. Sasha's muscles were throbbing with pain after a less than productive visit to the gym earlier that evening. Normally he did forty-five minutes of dynamic sets with the down moments in between machines as the only time to recover, but since that bullet in the woods had grazed the left side of his chest, he still suffered from considerable pain. The wound stung with every lift, push or pumping motion, so he could barely manage two-thirds of his routine sets. Tonight Sasha had struggled from machine to machine. It seemed that despite his forty-two years of age he was more ready for a retirement home than the prominent position he was used to having in the gym, given his immense height and impressive pecs.

Not only did Sasha's body ache, his head hurt too, all the way to the roots of his jet-black dyed hair. He'd let it hang loose. Wearing it pulled back tightly, like he usually did, was too painful right now.

In his official capacity, Sasha had been employed for years as an interior designer for AtlasNet. In this role, he'd given all of the company's worldwide offices a touch of the avant-garde, with an emphasis on art. Because AtlasNet's big boss, Valentin Lavrov, had a passion for art.

But Lavrov was first and foremost a genius businessman with a Machiavellian instinct for power, a man who used a variety of strategies to continually expand the reach of his influence. During negotiations, Lavrov always made sure he was flanked by an intimidating, silent type. And Sasha had the particular talent of being a threatening presence without uttering a single word or moving a muscle. Sasha was soon Lavrov's favourite companion at business meetings and travelled with him from deal to deal in his boss's private jet. In this way, Sasha acquired a grasp of his employer's business practices.

Needless to say, some of these dealings had a shadier side. Lavrov was used to getting his way. Those who wanted to slow him down or openly contradicted him could count on a surprisingly fierce reaction. But that was only the beginning. Sasha went looking for their darkest secrets and when he found something, those people were put into a position where they could be easily blackmailed. They were left with no other choice but to dance to Lavrov's tune, whether they wanted to or not.

In most cases this blackmail involved sex. That's how Sasha *manoeuvred* the French chairman of the European Commission's Directorate-General for Competition, Nicolas Anglade, into a tight spot. Anglade led the preliminary investigation into the wheelings and dealings of AtlasNet in Europe, and in no time at all he was ranked as one of Lavrov's most hated enemies.

But by now Sasha realized that his own knowledge of Lavrov's deal-making practices, under the cover of AtlasNet, also made him increasingly vulnerable. It was only a matter of time before Lavrov would come to the conclusion that his lieutenant and fixer Sasha knew more than was good for him. He wouldn't be the first, so for some time Sasha had been working on an exit strategy.

He walked to the edge of his expansive rooftop terrace. He knew what they said: pride comes before a fall. But it wasn't really pride that had got the better of him, it was actually impulsiveness. He preferred seeing himself as a brilliant chess player who, unlike others, could determine the outcome of the game before the first move had even been made; someone who'd never let the progress of the game depend on chance.

But this time he'd done just that.

It had happened in the woods, at the moment he'd laid eyes on the Afghan boy with the tinkling jewellery stepping out of the station wagon. The mere sight of the boy hit him like lightning. Such a defenceless child, so pure, and most of all so beautiful. Sasha immediately knew that his exit plan wouldn't be complete if the boy wasn't a part of it. With that insight, he'd spent the last forty-eight hours reviewing all the pieces on the chessboard and deciding that in order to get away with his impulsive manoeuvre in the woods he needed to force the end of the game using a few quick moves. He walked into his flat and made a Skype call to Goa, India.

The man who appeared on screen in front of him spoke English with an Indian accent that Sasha always found amazingly erotic.

'You've made it very difficult, you know,' the man said in a forgiving tone.

'Bikram, my dear,' said Sasha. 'I'm so sorry.'

'Don't call me "dear" now. This is much too serious. You know you've put yourself in a dangerous position. You need to come here as soon as possible.'

'I can't leave him behind.'

Sasha heard Bikram's sigh, a sound of surrender. He'd heard that sigh for the first time during the Amsterdam Art Fair. Bikram, with his dark lashes framing those Indian eyes, was standing in front of a three-metre-high wooden figure of Alcyoneus, the mightiest of Greek mythological giants. The two men had been checking each other out and couldn't contain their laughter upon seeing the Greek hero's humongous circumcized penis.

From that exchange of laughter between two strangers came an insatiable desire that gradually took on another dimension: a monogamous relationship in which their ideals took shape in a masterly plan to start an entirely new life together elsewhere, far away.

Bikram had at that time, as a broker, developed a trusted business relationship with property magnate Armin Lazonder.

Lazonder was an adventurer, who'd started out in the firm of his father John, a manufacturer and supplier of King Vox studio recorders. After taking over the business, the young Lazonder went on to establish a record label of his own, a production company and a software lab. All under the name Dorado Media. But he didn't become truly big until the Iron Curtain came down in Eastern Europe and he took over a large number of privatized metal factories. The small shareholders didn't have a clue how much their companies were worth. But Lazonder did. He sold them on to third parties for enormous sums, and then he invested the money he'd earned in Dutch real estate. After purchasing a few monumental buildings in Amsterdam, he started to work on realizing his dream: the New Golden Age Project.

Bikram mapped out a complex investment plan for the venture and convinced Lazonder it would be better if he put part of his private capital into foreign equities. Lazonder deposited 100 million euros in an account Bikram would manage with a guaranteed profit share of forty to fifty per cent in just six months' time.

However, Bikram didn't buy any foreign equities, but secretly funnelled Lazonder's 100 million euros to an offshore account that he'd opened with Sasha. To keep Lazonder from getting wind of his scheme, Bikram regularly provided him with phoney account statements.

Bikram pulled a few other fast ones with the money too. Finally, Lazonder would realize he'd lost double the amount he'd supposedly invested abroad. The discovery would come to light soon enough: when a few tax inspectors appeared on Lazonder's doorstep.

For his own safety, Bikram had basically disappeared into thin air. Two months earlier he'd gone into hiding in Goa where he'd established himself under a new identity. The plan was for Sasha to join him later so their departures couldn't be connected. False identity papers were also waiting for Sasha at their new luxury seaside villa.

Bikram sighed a second time.

'All that money doesn't mean anything if I can't share it with you. I've arranged an ambulance flight. It can be waiting for you at Schiphol Airport tomorrow evening. But only if you're coming with him.'

Sasha pulled his hair into a ponytail again and smiled.

2

Danielle kept counting until she lost consciousness. When she came to on the tiled floor, her body felt ice-cold. As if she'd been blanketed by snow.

The dimly lit room spun around her as she crawled to the toilet and vomited. On her knees, supporting herself on the rim of the bowl with both hands, she tried pushing her body upright. She took a few deep breaths with her eyes closed. The nausea faded. The spinning gradually stopped.

She then stood up by grasping on to a pipe on the wall and stumbled to the sink where she turned the tap all the way open.

When she bent over to drink the nausea returned for a moment. Bending over further, she let the cold water rush over the bump on the back of her head. She turned off the water. She could taste the salt left by her tears. In the mirror she saw the dark figure of a woman who'd risen from the dead and still couldn't believe she was alive.

She didn't turn on a light. The glare would be unbearable. She knew where to find the paracetamol in the medicine cabinet. She pushed three tablets out of the strip and swallowed them one by one. Then she wrapped a large bath towel around her body and shuffled into the living room where she collapsed on the sofa.

She let herself feel the anger, which had been greater than her fear of dying and stronger than the pain of humiliation. But mainly she was angry at herself, for what she'd put in motion by not listening to Farah Hafez's warnings. Until the absolute last moment Farah had tried to stop her – even made her a new offer. 'An article about you, your motivations, your experience, the injustices you've seen.'

She heard her own distraught response. 'Isn't it a bit late for that?! Let go of my bike!'

She was particularly angry because of her lack of patience. Impatience had always been her downfall.

3

Farah had decided to spend the night holding a vigil in memory of Parwaiz, and had ensconced herself on her old Persian ottoman in the middle of her living room. In recent years she'd been increasingly aware that one day he would no longer be around. When that happened, she knew that the last remaining witness to her childhood, the last remaining link to her family and her past would be gone. It had been unimaginable, but now the unimaginable had suddenly become true.

The melody of a song about eternal longing popped into her head. As she hummed it in the quiet room, noise from the big square filtered through, as the funfair attractions were being quickly and efficiently dismantled.

'Don't know in whose face I smile. Don't know for whom I cry.'

Finally, she picked up the bundle of letters Parwaiz had given her. It was actually more of a parcel, wrapped in some sheets of cardboard, which were covered in red velvet fabric with a gold-and-purple leaf pattern that had become partially unstuck. The cards were held together by two yellowed silk ribbons. For additional protection Parwaiz had wrapped the whole thing in tissue paper and tied it up with string.

Farah unfolded the note Parwaiz had slipped in.

My dear child, the past sneaks up on us like a shadow. But remember that even in the greatest darkness there will always be a pinprick of light, even if it is so small that you can barely see it with the naked eye. You'll see it only once your eyes have become accustomed to the dark. But then you'll know that you've found the power of forgiveness. It is in that tiny pinprick of light. Bear this in mind when you read the letters your mother had wanted to burn out of shame. You must never be ashamed of love. Even when it crosses moral boundaries. Just before the two of you were about to flee, your mother gave me this bundle for safekeeping until she found refuge with you. After her death, I held on to it until I thought the time was ripe to pass it along to you. Seeing as it was your mother who let her heart speak, I mustn't keep the story of this love from you.

Farah read the date on the first letter: *22 August 1977.* Thirty years ago. The letter wasn't from her mother, but a response to what she'd written. It opened with a quote from her mother's favourite poet, the fourteenth-century Persian mystic Hafez, whose last name Farah had taken upon arrival in the Netherlands.

> *O minstrel, sing:*
> *The world fulfilleth my heart's desire!*
> *Reflected within the goblet's ring*
> *I see the glow of my love's red cheek,*
> *And scant of wit, ye who fail to seek*
> *The pleasures that wine alone can bring!*
>
> . . .
>
> *He cannot perish whose heart doth hold*
> *The life love breathes.*

Then her mother's admirer spoke in his own words, in firm handwriting on lined paper.

My dearest, only a great poet can speak his heart in this way. The best I can do is quote Hafez in the hope of giving you a glimpse of my happiness. The joy of having met you and the joy of being allowed to love you.

Unable to cope with the suspense, Farah turned the letter over and looked at the writer's name at the bottom.

Raylan Chapelle.

She stared at the name for ages.

She pictured her mother as she kept vigil by her side for three consecutive nights, while she lay in bed with a fever after meeting Paul.

Farah heard her whisper once more.

'Not you too, sweetie. Not you too.'

She got up and walked across her flat. In front of the open window she watched the Swing being dismantled by a bunch of workmen. Likewise, the old-fashioned Spiegeltent with its colourful stained-glass windows was being taken down panel by panel, while the Ferris wheel with the red bucket seats was lying on its side, stripped of its soul. Small groups of Chinese people were waiting in the wings, poised to start building their own stages, tents and stalls. In the morning, the square would be filled with dancing dragons, Chinese revellers and bewildered tourists.

Suddenly, one of the Chinese pointed up. Cries of surprise followed and in the clear night sky Farah spotted the fiery trail of a falling star, which slowly died out.

There you go, Uncle, she thought to herself. Farewell.

4

A live band was in full swing at the jazz café Casablanca on the Zeedijk when Marouan entered. In a split second he scoured the shady clientele in the room and made a beeline for Sasha Kovalev. With his eyes glued to the blonde female saxophonist in her rhinestone-studded black tuxedo, who'd just begun a spirited solo, Kovalev placed his commanding arm on Marouan's shoulder as if greeting an old friend.

'What are you having, comrade?' Kovalev said in his Slavic-sounding English.

'Listen, Kovalev, I'm not here for small talk or a friendly drink. Let's get down to business,' Marouan replied, irritated.

'You know what's funny,' Kovalev calmly continued, 'you come to live here as an immigrant, or whatever PC term they're using these days. You do your best to contribute, to keep the economy going. Though over time you realize that more and more people would rather see you piss off to your own country. Yet, you decide to swim against the tide. You embrace the language and the customs. The entire time you try to act like a real Dutchman – *BAM* – right to the heart of the matter. Don't kid yourself, Diva. You're not Dutch and neither am I. And let's comfort ourselves with the fact that we'll never be. C'mon, have a drink.'

Marouan was silent. When the bartender looked at him questioningly, he asked for a glass of water. It came with a slice of lemon.

'Do you like jazz, Diva?' Kovalev loved seeing Diba squirm. 'I asked if you like jazz?!'

Marouan knew that Kovalev would use whatever he said to go off on another dubious tangent.

'Only in good company.'

Kovalev laughed aloud. The audience applauded the saxophonist who'd finished her solo. She bowed so deeply Marouan suddenly had a panoramic view of her bronze-coloured breasts. Kovalev whistled on his fingers and turned back to Marouan.

'Make no mistake, my friend. A sax solo like that sounds easy, but it's mighty difficult. You better believe it! Musicians are chosen for their unique ability to improvise.'

'And to bow as deeply as possible,' Marouan sarcastically added.

Kovalev pulled Marouan towards him and started lisping in his ear almost lovingly.

'Look, my dear *durak*, you and I are, in fact, members of the same band, you understand?'

Marouan sipped his water without reacting and kept staring straight ahead at the saxophone player.

'We're a band, Diva, damn it, and you'd better listen up. We've reached a point that demands improvising. Do you hear me?'

'I hear you,' Marouan replied.

'Good. Because the solo is yours. I'm the backup rhythm section. It's your big moment to shine. The grand finale is near.'

Marouan straightened his back.

'You know what they say about Russians, Kovalev? That you're all a bunch of lying thugs.'

'Oh, is that so, Diva?'

'Yes. But it's not entirely correct. You only lie to certain types: to the authorities, to people stuck in the same boat and to the Dutch. So now that you've happily informed me I'm not a Dutchman, I'm certainly not in the same boat as you are and as far as authority is concerned, at the moment I might as well be walking the beat again. And one could ask if I'm even in a position to do that. So tell me more about how you envision this solo of mine?'

Kovalev's grin was now so broad it looked like he'd swallowed a coat hanger.

'You and I, Diva, have developed a relationship. That's important: *blat*, connections, and from that automatically comes *krugovaya poruka*, shared responsibility.'

'I'm not here for a Russian lesson from you, Kovalev.'

'Tomorrow, somewhere in Amsterdam, there'll be a *basran* walking around, a punk piece of shit with a Zastava M57 on him. And believe me, that guy is so trigger happy he even urinates in bursts. He's my gift to you. Bring him in.'

'And then what am I supposed to do with him?'

'Lock him up. Interrogate him. Hassle his Russian rat's ass. I don't know. Whatever detectives like you do with lowlifes you pick up. Impress your chief.'

'By bringing in some guy just because he's packing?'

Kovalev let the ice cubes in the glass clink against his teeth. Marouan could hear Kovalev's grey matter cranking away above the din: I've got this Moroccan chump by the balls. I picked him up out of the gutter, complete with gambling addiction, and patched him up so he'd have no choice but to obey me and now this goat-fucker is acting tough?!

Marouan backed down. 'Is it urgent?'

'Urgent? I'm talking about turbo speed, Diva.'

'Who's the target?'

'The dancing boy.'

'Damn!'

'He needs to be moved from that hospital as quickly as possible.'

'And you think I can just snap my fingers and it's done?'

'With me as inspiration you've been known to work miracles, Diva. Just like that six hundred kilos of cocaine in the belly of a Colombian plane appeared out of nowhere. What was that? Does Detective Diva have special connections? Absolutely, Diva has me! If you can convince your superiors that the boy is in imminent danger and you have the intel from the exact same source as the drug bust, then doors will open to you, you'll be back in the spotlight, the centre of attention: Diva, the sequel!'

'Where does the boy need to go?'

'Doesn't matter. He just can't stay where he is now. Because even with extra security, he still isn't safe. If need be, they'll blow the whole place to smithereens to silence him. Move him and I'll hand you an assassin with mega connections in return. Connections that could topple an entire criminal organization if you play your cards right. But we have to play together, Diva. This needs to be a duet. Our grand finale.'

Marouan gulped back the last of his water, slammed the glass on the counter and looked at Kovalev the way he'd once looked at his Koran teacher before punching him so hard in the face that he gave him a nose bleed.

'Kovalev, as a child I learnt there are no coincidences in the world.'

'Because the Great Creator decides and determines everything,' Kovalev said, grinning.

'Exactly. Coincidence doesn't exist and everything is connected. And so I think those two unidentified corpses in the burnt-out station wagon and that injured Afghan boy all have something to do with you.'

Kovalev looked at Marouan with a cold stare.

'Do you know what it means, Diva, when you accept that man is a product of His Maker?'

'Enlighten me, oh wise Buddha.'

'It means that he can only dance to the whims of His will like a helpless puppet. It's very simple, Diva. You don't dictate to Allah. He dictates to you. See me as a secret agent in His service. As soon as I stop protecting you, your cover will be blown and they'll see you for the compulsive gambling fool you are. You'll immediately be sent back to the Rif Mountains, where you'll spend the rest of your life condemned to sitting on red-hot stones being sucked off by sheep. And what's going to happen to your family then? And how do you think I'm going to get your daughter to repay all the money I've pumped into your pathetic excuse for a life? So do what you do best, Diva, without bothering me with juvenile discussions and childish questions. This will be the last thing.'

'And afterwards?'

'*Que sera, sera*,' said Kovalev with a grin, placing a wad of euros on the bar and slapping Marouan on the shoulder, 'whatever happens, happens.'

When Marouan walked along the Zeedijk moments later, past some late-night partygoers, he knew for sure Kovalev had poor taste in everything. Even his choice of songs. With that less than reassuring thought, and the usual aversion, he walked towards the square behind the Oude Kerk.

The girl with his young Aisha's face and body had her curtain drawn and the windowpane clearly reflected his pitiful image. For the first time he was shocked by the weary, paunchy figure he'd become.

His head was spinning with haunting images and conspiracy theories as he wandered through the streets, finally arriving on Nieuwmarkt, where a crew was dismantling a funfair and arguing with Chinese traders impatient to set up their market stalls.

It was five o'clock in the morning when Marouan pounded on the door of Joshua's houseboat.

5

Danielle had fallen asleep on the sofa out of sheer exhaustion. When she awoke, the towel she'd wrapped around her body earlier was lying crumpled on the floor. She was still cold. She instinctively rubbed the bump on the back of her head, sat up slowly, and stayed in the same position until the pounding in her head subsided. For a moment she thought she might have dreamt it all.

She dragged herself to the kitchen where she drank a large glass of water and swallowed three more paracetamols. She was no longer dizzy or nauseous, but dog-tired. She poured a pint of skimmed milk into a large bowl, added half a pack of cereal, topped it with a big glob of honey and began loudly wolfing down the mixture. After showering, she walked into the living room. She debated whether she should call the detective who'd brought her home last night. Finally she decided not to do it.

Suddenly she noticed a black folder on the table that she didn't recognize. It must have been put there last night. Her heart began to race. She picked up the folder and walked over to the sofa. She opened it and on top of a small stack of papers was a business-class ticket departing from Schiphol Airport with the final destination Toussaint Louverture Airport, Haiti. The ticket was in her name.

Besides the ticket, there was also a letter from Hospital Saint-Michel, in Port-au-Prince, with a request to contact them right away. On an impulse she grabbed her telephone. When she dialled the number and introduced herself, the man on the other end of the line immediately switched to a warm, responsive tone.

'We're pleased that you've called, Dr Bernson. Your reputation precedes you.'

'Is that so?' she replied hesitantly.

'Thanks to you, we've received a donation that, according to current standards, will allow us to pay two licensed physicians for five years and launch a major health programme for the area's poorest children. Given the money will only be transferred once you confirm your arrival, you'll understand that we were anxious to hear from you.'

'Well, eh, here we are . . .' She had to do her very best to keep the confusion she was feeling under control.

'Doctor, you have lots of experience working in Africa,' the man continued, 'so you've seen poverty up close. People here in Haiti are so poor they can't afford a doctor's visit. Our organization is completely dependent on charitable donations from individuals. And nobody has ever given us such a generous gift.'

'No, I can imagine,' Danielle said after an awkward silence.

It was like she'd turned into somebody else and was suddenly staring at the possibility of a whole new life. Far away from this reality where, since last night, her life was in danger.

'When might you be able to come?' the man asked. She could hear him trying not to be too anxious, just like she was trying to hide her bewilderment about this turn of events.

She checked the local arrival time of her flight to Toussaint Louverture Airport. It made her head spin. She suddenly imagined herself strolling around Port-au-Prince while physically she was still here, completely broken.

'Can I call you back?'

She didn't wait for an answer, hung up and wondered if she could manage it again, changing her life overnight. She'd done it before. From Africa to the Netherlands, but it had proven to be a disastrous decision.

The screeching birds coming from her mobile startled her. She gasped when she recognized the voice of the man who'd attacked her last night.

'Did you find what I left for you?'

'I've seen it.'

'It'll save your life. Believe me.'

She had the feeling he meant it. Yet she still asked him why she should believe him.

'You don't have to do it,' he answered calmly. 'It's your choice.' Then he hung up.

She rose to her feet and pressed her body up against the large window. It felt cool to the touch. She could barely think. The only sound she could hear was the whooshing in her ears. Maybe the water of the Gulf of Gonâve, the wide bay of Port-au-Prince, sounded just like this.

6

After Paul Chapelle securely fastened his seatbelt for the flight to Amsterdam that morning, the co-pilot made an announcement requesting that all passengers leave the Boeing 747 because of a mechanical defect they'd just discovered.

It was the drop in the bucket needed to make his deep-seated claustrophobia kick in. In his attempt to be the first of the nearly 500 passengers to exit the airplane, Paul bumped into people who'd quickly stood up to grab their hand luggage from the overhead bins. When he reached the plane's doorway, he leaned against the hull, dizzy and drained. Gasping for air with his mouth wide open, he could barely breathe. It felt like his eyes were about to jump out of their sockets. He thought he'd suffocate. A hand pushed an open paper bag against his mouth. He automatically clutched the bag and started to blow into it.

He looked at the woman who'd helped him. He recognized her face, the sea-blue eyes, straight nose, and lips with the same reassuring smile she'd thrown him when he'd found his seat number twenty minutes earlier. She'd been sitting beside him on the other side of the aisle.

'You'd be a good one for a rugby team,' she said with a wink, as if to put a heroic spin on his frantic struggle forward.

'Forget it,' gasped Paul, 'I'm more like Road Runner, that cartoon character.' He tried to smile.

'You're lucky stewardesses aren't trained to crash tackle their passengers. C'mon, before they change their minds.' Without waiting for a reply, she dragged him down the steps and over to the area where all the passengers were being directed. With one hand guiding Paul's arm, she'd taken control of the situation. The idea that he was being treated like a disobedient little boy brought a stupid grin to his face. He gave her another good look, his strong guardian angel with her dark-blonde hair and classic profile. She was wearing a black linen jacket with a crisp white blouse and high heels, beneath bleached jeans, which made her as tall as Paul. She walked beside him, purposefully yet still elegant, under a gleaming white canopy supported by black pillars. Paul was happy to go on a sightseeing tour of the entire airport in exactly the same way, until he thought again and abruptly stopped her.

'My notebook, my phone, everything is still on the plane.'

'My stuff too,' she said as she turned towards him. Suddenly standing there, kissing distance apart, Paul got the feeling they'd been travelling together for a long time. She looked at him with a welcome mixture of mockery and assurance.

'I'll handle it.'

And off she went. Click-clacking with her heels on the shiny tiles. Paul watched her for a moment and then headed for one of the long waiting-room benches with a view of the runways.

He usually felt at home in airports: places where life stories were collected, where people were weighed down not only by their luggage but also the baggage of the past. He'd always found it something of a sport to make up stories about the people he saw. But now the only story that interested him was his own.

She startled him when she reappeared. She had his hand luggage with her and a plastic cup with water. She sat down beside him.

'Please understand . . . I don't usually react like this,' he mumbled.

'I suspected as much,' she said.

She stuck out her hand.

'Sandrine.'

He dropped the cup he was holding.

'Sorry, Paul.'

'You've got to stop that!'

'What?'

'Constantly saying sorry to me.'

'Okay. Sorry.' He smiled a second time, more effectively than before. Sandrine still had a concerned expression on her face.

'That looked pretty serious out there,' she said.

'It's a long story,' replied Paul.

She nodded. 'It always is.'

7

Waking up was never a slow, slumbering affair for Farah. Usually she propelled herself out of bed as soon as she opened her eyes, pulled on her jogging gear and ran along the canals for forty-five minutes. Back home she'd jump in a cold shower, drop wedges of grapefruit and a banana in the blender, get dressed, down an espresso and leave the house.

This time, however, she'd stayed awake all night. She'd put Raylan Chapelle's love letters away. They overshadowed her memories of Parwaiz.

At the first light of dawn, she retreated into the bathroom and rubbed her body with a sea-salt and coconut-extract cleansing scrub. She wouldn't be drawing a subtle line on her upper eyelid, wearing black mascara or even applying a slick of nude lipstick. Islamic law doesn't allow any form of make-up at a funeral.

Knowing how much Parwaiz appreciated discreet elegance in women, she took a sleeveless jacket out of her wardrobe. It was sober and black and reached way down her thighs. She'd team it with a light-grey silk blouse and loose-fitting black trousers. A coarsely woven black shawl would serve as a headscarf.

She pictured Parwaiz smiling at her proudly, the way he used to do whenever she visited him.

The early-morning TV news blared through the apartment. The meteor shower that had been visible in the night sky received a lot of coverage. A foreign correspondent reported on the election of a new Turkish president, the eleventh in the country's history. This was followed by news of the death of Nicolas Anglade, the French chairman of the European Commission's Directorate-General for Competition. Anglade had taken his own life after a Belgian tabloid published documents and photos linking him to paedophile practices.

Intrigued, Farah walked into the living room. While inserting an earring, she heard that Anglade had been leading a preliminary investigation into potential anti-competitive practices at AtlasNet. The company was suspected of driving up prices and hindering fair competition in Eastern Europe. If found guilty, it could face a penalty of up to ten per cent of its annual turnover. Anglade's death set the investigation back several months. Next up, the weatherman pointed to a storm front heading for the Netherlands from the Atlantic.

Farah heard the procession of dragons approaching from a distance. Eager to be gone before the jumping jacks and firecrackers started going off on the square, she quickly stuck a printed photo of Lavrov in her bag and hurried downstairs. When she swung open the front door, the tantalizing smell of wonton soup, spring rolls and steamed buns wafted towards her. She dashed across the square to the spot where Edward's anthracite-coloured Saab was waiting, double-parked, and ran smack into some kid. It gave her a shock since the young guy, dressed completely in black, stared at her without any hint of emotion. He had a pale, drawn face and a nasty scar across his left cheek. She thought of saying something, but changed her mind and walked off briskly. Some people carry death in their eyes. Establish contact with them and you run the risk of contamination.

Edward drove off as soon as she got in. Farah tried, but failed, to put the kid's cold stare out of her mind.

8

At three o'clock in the morning, after a flight from Russia, a Moscow Fly Airbus landed at Munich Airport. Dimitri was one of the passengers who disembarked. His fake passport got him through Immigration without a problem. At the designated car rental company he was given the keys to a black Volkswagen Touareg with, as promised, a loaded Zastava M57 with silencer under the driver's seat. Dimitri was impressed with the efficiency of the whole operation. His uncle Arseni's anonymous network was a perfectly oiled machine. It was a huge honour for Dimitri that his uncle now thought he was good enough for an assignment.

He set off for Amsterdam. Everything had to be perfect. You only had one debut. He'd prepared the entire operation in minute detail and after studying a map of the Dutch capital he knew exactly where the key downtown locations were. And to top it all, he was rigged out in new clothes. Black jeans. Grey shirt. Charcoal trench coat.

Before getting dressed he'd doused himself with Alain Delon's Shogun eau de toilette. It was more than a symbolic deed, it was an initiation rite. He was about to become somebody, just like the French actor. And all thanks to his uncle Arseni. He'd seen Delon's film *Le Samouraï* nearly a dozen times. What had stuck with him most was the isolation of the contract killer, holed up in a back room where everything was so drab and decrepit that it looked as if the movie had been shot in black-and-white. The samurai's sole companion, the yellow canary bird, hopping apathetically around its cage, was the only thing to suggest otherwise.

Every day, samurai Delon pulled a new pristine white shirt from a warped grey drawer. Even that routine was done with the clinical precision he brought to bear on his job. That precision was also the trademark of the assassin Dimitri would become today.

He habitually raised his right hand to the horizontal scar on his left cheek. It was the outcome of a brawl in Moscow's Poor People nightclub. Dimitri was a regular there, but more importantly he was the nephew of Arseni Vakurov: a name that ought to instil fear and respect in everybody. But for three guys who turned up one night to flaunt their newly acquired wealth, it didn't. They'd shown great contempt for a good-looking guy who happened to have a provincial accent. When they started mocking him he'd beaten them up and eliminated them in cold blood. But not before one of them managed to slice open his cheek with a broken bottle.

Uncle Arseni had said that if he carried on like this his impulsive nature would one day cost him his head. 'Any idiot can kill. You must learn to get rid of your animal instincts and related base passions. Only then will I be able to depend on you.'

Dimitri had done everything he could to encourage his uncle to build on him. He had assisted, learnt and toughened up and his uncle now trusted him to carry out his first job abroad. Unsupervised. Dimitri solo. A master in control.

At an average of 170 kilometres per hour, he zipped along the German motorways. He'd arrive in good time for his morning appointment in Amsterdam.

He left the Touareg in an underground car park and walked along a canal in the direction of the ominous noise of drums.

Dimitri pondered his uncle's words of encouragement spoken to him over the phone. 'This is a one-man mission. Your first. Make me proud.'

He'd been trained to kill. That training started the day he got to be present at one of his uncle's favourite pastimes: taking people who'd tried to screw someone from the organization, who'd been disloyal or tried to steal, and making them talk. Uncle Arseni had told him about the wondrous elasticity of the human skin and demonstrated with clinical precision how to fillet it. This is what he did to those he suspected of disloyalty, thievery and other crimes against the organization. Dimitri thought it was fascinating, apart from the victims' screaming, that is. But his uncle usually stuck some tape across their mouths after he'd suspended them naked from a butcher's hook, and then carefully tackled a particular part of the body with a scalpel.

Following the treatment, Dimitri got to put them out of their misery with a bullet.

The next step in his training was the hunt. It always happened in some forest where men who'd incurred the wrath of the organization were set free. Dimitri had to chase them and shoot from the front, *not* in the back, and from as close as possible. Fatally. With a single bullet. Great exercises in skill they were. Quite different from practising on the shooting range. The ultimate training took place in urban environments and consisted of shooting armed opponents who'd been forewarned he was coming.

And now, having been initiated into all these stages, he was here in the Dutch capital. Get the job done and then get the hell out again before the whole thing blew up in his face.

Someone bumped into him. A fashionable Arab chick with blue eyes. She turned away and hurried off.

Meanwhile the place was teeming with Chinese. Firecrackers were lit. On the off-chance, he turned into a narrow street and a moment later found himself opposite a pagoda-style building. He was staring at the incomprehensible symbols on the ochre-yellow wall when he heard a deep voice behind him speak to him in Russian.

'Going to a funeral, young man?' Dimitri spun on his heels and looked into the steel-blue eyes of a tall man with a steroid-pumped body, which seemed close to bursting out of a light-grey, custom-made Italian suit. He had his left arm in a sling. His head was shaved on both sides, and with the long jet-black strands of hair on top of his crown tied into a ponytail he vaguely resembled a Siberian monk with karate skills.

'Your uncle has called on me to pull you out of the swamp of your ignorance.'

Dimitri felt Ponytail's large hand press against his shoulder blade to indicate he had to walk up the stairs.

'Your first target is a boy. He's in a hospital and probably guarded. I have no further details. Small, Middle-Eastern, dark hair. Once you've dealt with him, you'll continue your work in the medical sector.'

He showed him a photo of the second target. An attractive woman in her mid-thirties with confident grey-blue eyes. Her short blonde hair was fashionably tousled. Dimitri visualized her body as equally firm. With apple-shaped breasts that didn't need a bra, a flat stomach and smooth thighs that would be very accommodating. The fantasy instantly generated a fair bit of testosterone in his body.

'A doctor who needs to be put out of her misery.'

Dimitri took another look at the photo. What could a doctor from the Netherlands have done to attract the evil eye?

'Why kill her?'

The man took a deep breath and sighed in a way to suggest that he'd just committed a serious blunder. Dimitri grew impatient.

'You mean I'm not killing her? Shall I screw her into submission instead?'

Ponytail smiled pityingly.

'How old are you, kid?'

'Eighteen,' Dimitri said with a shrug of his shoulders. 'I know why I'm here,' he added as arrogantly as possible.

The man chuckled.

'You've got a thing about death, my boy. I can tell by looking at you. You even dress like death. In broad daylight!' He wrapped an arm around Dimitri, a seemingly friendly gesture, which was anything but. The steel grip that followed made it clear that the man could crush him on the spot should he wish to.

'Your uncle has sent you to take care of things. But you're taking care of them on *my* turf, and in *my* way. First you deal with the boy. Quickly, efficiently, if you know what I mean. Then it's her turn. The doctor. Do whatever you want with her before you eliminate her. Got it? But take care of the boy first.'

9

Even unshaven and suddenly awoken from a deep sleep, Calvino still looked like a Sunday's child. Marouan saw the surprised face of his partner appear behind the porthole window after he'd banged on the door of his houseboat for several minutes.

'The boy is going to die,' was the first thing he said when Calvino opened the door. The second was, 'tomorrow!' But as he was saying it, he realized he was mistaken. Because 'tomorrow' was actually now today: it was five a.m.

Marouan waddled through the sparsely lit front part of the houseboat examining the meteorological equipment and cloud paintings while Calvino took a few minutes to get dressed.

'Who's your source?' Calvino asked when he reappeared a minute later.

'The same person who tipped me off about the cocaine at Schiphol years ago. I can't say more, only that it's going to happen today and it's a young Russian acting alone.'

'I arranged extra security last night,' Calvino said.

'Police guard at the door?'

'Exactly.'

'Then the threat assessment needs to be updated as soon as possible.'

'What are you saying? That we need to call out a SWAT team? That we should let snipers in bulletproof vests parade around the ICU?'

'No! That's exactly what we shouldn't do.'

Marouan threw Calvino a stern look. Due to lack of sleep he had little patience for Calvino's sarcasm. 'I want the bastard alive, understand? So we can question him. With a bullet through his head, he won't be able to tell us much of anything about who ordered the hit. We need him to talk. His info will also shed more light on the case of the burnt-out station wagon.'

Calvino's expression changed. 'You know more than you're telling me,' he said with a smirk.

Half an hour later they were already sitting down with Tomasoa. Their boss poured them some coffee. In the time that elapsed between Calvino's phone call and the discussion they were now having, Tomasoa had, without any discussion, devised new positions for Marouan and Calvino.

'You'll continue to be part of the MIT, but as a unit within a unit. From now on, you're responsible for everything directly related to the boy. And you report only to me. Clear?'

Marouan felt like a phoenix rising from the ashes.

'What's your plan, Diba?' Tomasoa inquired.

'A trap, chief,' said Marouan. 'A snare, or whatever you want to call it. The police guard stays outside the boy's room. And perhaps some extra hospital security patrolling the main entrances. It should look like the boy has run-of-the-mill protection: that it's a low-priority case. While in reality, there's a cordon of armed men from the arrest team ready to swoop in when necessary.'

'The cop is bait?'

'Exactly.'

'Risky plan, Diba, because what if our guy still manages to get to the boy?'

'We don't run any risk if we secretly move the boy to another location and meanwhile act as if he's still there. If our guy succeeds in getting into the room, he only finds an empty bed.'

Tomasoa had his Yul Brynner-eyes fixed on Marouan the entire time.

It was now 6.30 a.m.

The next time Marouan looked at the clock again was in the office of the head of Intensive Care at the WMC. It was already after seven. The day shift was just coming on. He was practically high on adrenalin. He felt reborn.

'I'm sorry,' he heard Calvino say soothingly to the head of the ICU after he'd briefly explained their plan, 'but for safety reasons it's important that the boy is moved to another hospital as soon as possible.'

Fifteen minutes later the critical care physician on duty had contacted several hospitals and Marouan soon realized their backs were up against a wall. As the clock kept ticking, it became increasingly clear that not one hospital was prepared to take on a patient who from a medical standpoint didn't need to be moved, and who was apparently a criminal target.

While the medical residents did their rounds, the day-shift nurses were brought up to speed about the presence of three armed men from the special squad disguised as ICU staff. It was becoming painstakingly clear to Marouan that without valid medical reasons there was no way the boy would be moved elsewhere.

In the meantime, Calvino had found a spot at police central dispatch in front of a wall of surveillance monitors. From there, he could keep in touch with all the guards stationed at the WMC. Despite the fact that there were no suspicious movements or visitors that morning, Marouan was getting more and more agitated. Following the advice of the special squad he also put on a white doctor's coat and let Mariska convince him to do rounds with her and two of the ICU nurses.

Around midday it became clear that there were slight complications with the boy's spleen. Mariska explained that children's organs, which of course are still growing, react differently to those of adults and that the boy actually needed to be under the care of a paediatric intensive care specialist. That was the key to getting him transferred. Given the expertise that he needed wasn't available at the WMC, he had to be taken to a hospital with a Paediatric ICU.

Within half an hour a new home was found for the boy in the Maaspoort Hospital in Rotterdam. A relieved Marouan asked how soon an ambulance could be arranged, only to be confronted with the next problem. A normal ambulance wasn't a good idea. Given his precarious condition, the boy had to be moved by special transport. It was three o'clock in the afternoon when Mariska phoned the central switchboard to arrange this, and it was five minutes past three when Marouan almost threw a fit upon hearing there were three hospitals with requests for special transport ahead of them, and the boy would have to wait until the early evening.

It was time to call on Tomasoa's services.

10

The sun cast perpendicular strips of light through the windows of the mosque and threw long shadows across the simple coffin in which Parwaiz's ritually washed body had been placed, wrapped in a white linen cloth.

The mullah led the prayer.

'*Innaa liIlayhi Wa Innaa Ilayhi Raaji'oon.*' Verily we belong to Allah and will return to Allah.

Farah looked around. All the women sitting close by were dressed in grey or black. They had wrapped white or grey scarves around their heads and weren't wearing any make-up on their faces. They sat together on one side of the aisle, the men on the other. Farah was pleased that Edward was just across from her and noticed him keeping a watchful eye.

After the final joint prayer, some of the men carried the coffin to the cemetery. The women followed at an appropriate distance, so they wouldn't come in direct contact with the deceased. In this way, the Koran taught, they ran the least risk of emotional damage. From her childhood in Afghanistan, Farah remembered that this is why women there weren't allowed to attend funerals and could only visit the grave a few days after an interment.

The procession came to a halt at the open grave. The final prayer was said. Unlike in the mosque, everybody prayed standing up. This was allowed so the Dutch soil wouldn't stain their mourning clothes. They all raised their hands to just below the chin, their fingertips pressed together to form a small bowl, and said '*Amin*', after which they brushed their hands over their faces. Then the coffin was slowly lowered into the ground.

That's when the mullah nodded to Farah, as agreed. She stepped forward nervously, took a deep breath and to the surprise of those present began to sing a song. It was the song that had popped into her head last night.

'*Namidanam ba ro ki bekhandam. Namidanam ba ro ki begiryaam...*' Don't know in whose face I smile. Don't know for whom I cry...

As she broke into the first chorus, she could hear several women singing along softly in the background. She was touched when she heard male voices joining in too.

Some of those standing around the grave squeezed their eyes shut during the song, but most kept them wide open while singing, allowing the tears to flow freely. They were crying not so much for the man lying in his coffin in the ground, but for their memories, which were slowly curling up and fading like old photographs.

'*Za shahram rafta noor arzo ha. Za bamam morgh dil chonin parida.*' All my dreams have gone. There's no more happiness in my heart.

In her mind Farah walked through the marble halls of the National Museum one last time, hand in hand with Parwaiz. When she opened her eyes again, they fell on a man aiming a zoom lens at her from a couple of graves away. She immediately recognized him as the photographer on the bridge opposite Joshua's canal boat. The 'American tourist' turned out not to be a tourist after all.

Refusing to let it distract her, she closed her eyes and carried on singing. When she looked up again, the man had gone, and for a brief moment she wondered whether she'd imagined him.

On the mullah's instruction, she threw a small shovelful of dark-brown earth on the coffin. The earth hit the wooden lid with short, dry thuds. It struck her as the most dismal sound and she hoped from the bottom of her heart that her nihilist vision of paradise in the hereafter was wrong. She hoped that Parwaiz was now reunited with his wife and their two sons, and that the Eternal had asked him to manage the Heavenly Museum of Angel Art.

'Did you see him?' Edward asked with muted indignation when she rejoined him. Behind them they could still hear the women sobbing.

'Who?'

'Eric Sanders. I don't know what that paparazzo is doing here. Why isn't he in Saint-Tropez snapping half-naked celebrities on their yachts?'

The sobbing of the women gradually turned into a plaintive lament.

'I think he was here for me,' Farah said.

'For you?'

'He had me in his sights yesterday as well,' Farah sighed. 'When I was with Joshua Calvino.'

'What were you doing with Detective Calvino yesterday?'

Farah couldn't help but smile at the thought of the way Edward had tried to impress Joshua during the meeting at *AND* the day before yesterday.

'We were standing on the deck of his canal boat.'

'Work-related?' Edward asked suspiciously.

'Depends on your perspective.'

'Christ Almighty. What's next? Hafez the Heartbreaker strikes again. Does David know about this?'

'He knows,' she said, crestfallen.

'Broken heart, hurt ego, the works?' Edward inquired.

'And a clenched fist,' Farah replied. 'I left.'

'I bet Marant is behind this.'

'But why, Ed?'

'I'm afraid she's embarked on a counter-offensive. I can't think of any other explanation right now.'

They joined the other mourners. Something sweet was passed around. *Halvah*, a jelly-like substance made of toasted semolina and wrapped in bread. 'In the hope that the deceased's spirit is sweet rather than bitter when it enters heaven,' Farah explained to Edward, who looked perturbed as he tried to get it down.

Men and women approached them to thank her for the song. Farah took the printed photo of Lavrov out of her bag and showed it to a couple of men.

'Do you know this man?'

They didn't say anything, just turned away. The mood changed. Here and there small groups with dejected faces were deep in discussion, some people were pointing. Suddenly a man walked up to Farah.

'How dare you?' he yelled angrily. He snatched the photo from her hands and spat on it before tearing it to pieces. 'He was the devil!'

The young mullah tried to calm the situation and took the man aside.

Farah was bewildered.

'Mullah,' she said respectfully when he came back to her. 'I don't know what I've done wrong.'

The mullah gave her a look of reproof.

'Why do you brandish a photo of a man who practically tortured some of my faithful to death?'

'I'm sorry,' Farah said sincerely. 'I apologize for any misunderstanding. The man in the photo is the young director of a large Russian company. The man who is said to have tortured them died a long time ago.'

'Yet I'd still like you to leave,' the mullah said harshly.

'Is that your way of thanking someone for a farewell song beside a grave?' Edward asked tersely. 'I thought your God was one of forgiveness, but apparently I'm mistaken.'

'I'm sorry if you don't like my tone,' the mullah said.

'Never mind,' Farah said. 'My mistake. I should have realized. Thank you for the service, mullah.'

She gave Edward her arm and together they walked back to the car park. If she looked over her shoulder now she'd see men who carried their pasts with them in hearts heavy with hatred.

I I

During the first hour of the flight to Amsterdam, Paul felt too stressed to have a normal conversation. He couldn't call up the necessary arsenal of qualities: spontaneity, vitality, sincerity and his sense of humour, just to name a few. Qualities Sandrine seemed to have in abundance.

She talked passionately about her position on the Amsterdam City Council, about her visit to the first female mayor of Jo'burg, Ashley McLeod. She sang the praises of McLeod's fight against AIDS, corruption and violence against women and children. Paul knew the harsh reality of Jo'burg only too well. But he listened attentively to Sandrine's enthusiastic stories about the city, amazed by the sensuality of her face, the rapidly alternating self-confidence and melancholy.

But he soon felt exhaustion wash over him again. Sandrine was curious about what had happened to his face, but he dodged the subject and grabbed his laptop in an attempt to dispel the fear that had nestled in his body since that thrashing he'd received in Ponte City. Panic surfaced the minute he closed his eyes. Writing had always been quite effective for pushing away neuroses, setbacks and even physical pain for a while.

'Beautiful,' he suddenly heard Sandrine say.

'What?'

'The screensaver on your computer.'

It was a colourful painted scene. In the foreground of a busy market street, two traders rolled out a bright-red carpet. On both sides of the street hung huge pieces of colourful fabric in a myriad of pastel colours, and among the passers-by and gesticulating traders strolled a tanned man in jeans with a blonde woman in a blue kaftan. There was a boy in between them.

'Is it a real place?' Sandrine asked.

'The Char-Chatta bazaar in Kabul.' He pointed at the boy, 'That's me.'

'Really? How amazing! Who painted it?'

'My mother,' said Paul, touching his finger to the blonde woman on the screen. 'In the late sixties she travelled from Amsterdam to Kabul in a bus full of hippies.'

'Then that's your father. He looks like James Dean, but with longer hair.'

Paul smiled. He loved it when people talked that way about his father. 'He was a war correspondent.'

'Unique combination, war correspondent and hippy girl.'

'They say opposites attract. My mother was walking around the bazaar one day and suddenly found herself in the middle of a group of demonstrating students who were being beaten up by riot police. She literally bumped into a man who protected her. That was my dad, Raylan'

'Romantic story.'

'They were really happy together.'

'Were?'

'My father's been dead for nearly thirty years.' Paul gestured with his hand and broke off the conversation. He wanted to tell her everything, but somehow felt uncomfortable, dissatisfied with himself. So he just stared straight ahead.

I2

While Edward accelerated to 120 kilometres in less than ten seconds and sent his Saab 900 hurtling towards Amsterdam-Noord, Farah thought about the man who'd just torn up Lavrov's photo. He'd mistaken the CEO of AtlasNet for an officer in the Russian army who'd died in a bomb attack in the mid-nineties, a certain Michailov. Only now did Farah grasp the full extent of Parwaiz's confusion. Mi-ka-lov. He really had seen a ghost.

A little later Farah sat down in front of her computer and began rereading everything she'd gathered about Michailov, hoping she'd overlooked something, a detail that might provide answers to her question: just how much of a coincidence was the astonishing likeness between him and Valentin Lavrov?

But no answers were forthcoming.

A clip dating from 1994 showed an ageing Michailov, then Defence Minister, addressing the assembled media, shortly before the Russian invasion of Chechnya. 'Give me a parachute battalion and I'll conquer Grozny in two hours.' History had shown that what should have been a two-hour surprise attack turned into a war lasting more than two years, claiming the lives of thousands of young Russian soldiers while tens of thousands of Chechen civilians fell victim to mass cruelty and carpet bombings carried out on the direct orders of Michailov. Responsibility for the bomb attack that put an end to the life of the so-called Hero of the Soviet Union in February 1996 was unanimously claimed by Chechen rebels.

Farah looked up.

'A drum roll would be fitting,' Edward said, giving her a big smile. 'I reckon you deserve something today. Are you ready? I've got surprise for you.'

'If it's a weekend road trip with other vintage Saab enthusiasts, then I must decline the honour,' Farah said with a smile.

'I know there's nothing quite like it, but this is good too, perhaps even better: a meet and greet with Valentin Lavrov.'

'*What?* How did you pull that off?'

'Art,' Edward chuckled. 'Art and Lavrov. Like the Catholic Church and original sin, fatefully entwined. The *AND* international art supplement is scheduled for publication in six weeks' time, and we're still looking for a guest editor. Lavrov is happy to be considered.'

She eyed him suspiciously. 'Ed, are you serious?'

'The most serious excuse I can think of to get close to the man as quickly as possible. That's what we want, right?'

'And when is this supposed to happen?'

'How about this afternoon?'

'You're kidding.'

'Do I look like I'm kidding?'

'I know nothing about art, Ed, I'll be found out in no time.'

'Then you'd better start reading up on things,' Edward said, and put a lavishly illustrated art book the size of a paving slab on her desk. 'I estimate that more than fifty per cent of what's covered in here is in Lavrov's collection, spread across museums and his offices around the world.'

Farah leafed through it. Then she picked up Valentin Lavrov's portrait. The CEO of one of the world's biggest energy firms was mistaken for a Russian brute who used to torture people in underground prisons in Kabul decades ago. The thought of meeting him as early as this afternoon sent shivers down her spine.

13

The former headquarters of the Nederlandsche Handel-Maatschappij was a monumental ten-storey, brick-and-granite building. The main entrance to the erstwhile trading society was flanked by two imposing female statues representing Europe and Asia. Farah arrived on the fourth floor via a marble entrance hall and Venetian-tiled stairwell.

Six months earlier, Lavrov had bought this prestigious floor of old boardrooms from property tycoon Armin Lazonder. The classic interior had since been furiously restyled. The antique, tropical hardwood desks had been replaced with large tables made of recycled wood and both the wainscoting and the walls had been painted off-white to accommodate a range of modern paintings and art objects.

The reception area, where Farah reported, boasted a cannon which once a day fired a red paint bomb against a specially prepared wall. The latter looked like the site of a mass execution. The antique chandeliers that graced the rest of the building had here been replaced – in an apparent ode to the host country – by bundled glass milk bottles filled with clear halogen light.

Farah was ushered into a waiting room where she sat down in one of the round seats with high bamboo backs. Behind the door to Lavrov's office, she heard someone blowing his top. The venomous monologue went on for several minutes. When the door swung open shortly afterwards, Farah instantly recognized the man behind the New Golden Age Project as well as the head honcho of IRIS TV, Armin Lazonder. With a face that spelled trouble, he legged it past Farah without so much as a glance. She watched him go. What was he getting so worked up about, especially in front of Lavrov? The receptionist who'd escorted her to the waiting room approached her.

'Mr Lavrov will see you now.'

Farah got up. Her heart was in her throat. Initially she'd thought it inappropriate to meet the oligarch in the clothes especially selected for Parwaiz's farewell. But at the same time she appreciated the symbolism. The man who employed more than 300,000 people in his global conglomerates was probably also the one who'd – no doubt inadvertently – been the catalyst for Parwaiz's death.

At any rate, the man who now came towards her in his custom-made cashmere suit with his hand outstretched looked eerily like the former commander who'd been the last Russian occupier to leave her country in the late eighties.

Lavrov had a toned body and a sharp, broad-jawed face, thin lips and grey-green eyes. His self-assured handshake betrayed a restless energy. He was a head taller than her and given his greying hair she put him at just over forty.

'The Netherlands never cease to amaze me, Ms Hafez,' Lavrov said in perfect English that betrayed an Oxford education.

'What do you mean?'

'A journalist with a passion for art who looks like she has just stepped out of the Elysian Fields. Where have you been hiding all this time?'

'We like to keep a low profile in this country,' she replied while trying to mask her discomfort by peering around the gigantic boardroom. Low profile – not a label she'd ever attach to this interior.

Most striking were two gigantic panels attached to the walls. One was covered in inch-thick splodges of blue and white oil paint and littered with shards of smashed terracotta vases. The other showed a naked blue man with a sword balancing on top of two pillars, surrounded by the remnants of what must have been Victorian crockery. She quickly checked the label for the artist's name. Julian Schnabel.

'I see you're quite taken by my two most recent acquisitions, Ms Hafez.'

'I love Schnabel's work.' She turned back to Lavrov, with a beaming smile that she hoped would camouflage her nerves. 'I'm particularly fond of action painting. And please call me Farah.'

Lavrov nodded in agreement. 'Only if you call me Valentin.'

And then, in an illuminated alcove, she spotted a small statue of an elegant woman in a transparent gown, which did little to conceal her voluptuous breasts, with a slender waist that gave way to broad hips. Farah's heart skipped a beat.

'Sharada,' she whispered. Spellbound, she walked over to the statue. 'The river goddess.'

'I love contrasts. And I couldn't think of a greater contrast with Schnabel's masculine swagger,' she heard Lavrov say.

'From the treasures of Begram, first century AD,' Farah said as she tried to recover from the shock. The statue which Parwaiz had shown her in Kabul's National Museum decades ago now stood in the Amsterdam office of a Russian tycoon. She had to carry on talking to take hold of herself.

'Did you know this figurine has its origins in Indian Gandhara art?'

'No, I didn't know,' Lavrov said, sounding intrigued.

'Similar statues have been found in Swat in Northern Pakistan,' she resumed nervously. 'The same wide-open eyes. If you look carefully, you can even see the iris.'

Lavrov walked up to her and leaned in close to the statue. She could smell his musky body odour, a combination of mint, lavender and bergamot.

'You're right,' he said in awe.

She didn't want to leave a silence. She had to keep talking.

'Do you know the story of the soldier and the river goddess, Mr Lavrov?'

'No, but something tells me that you'd like to tell me it. And please stop calling me "Mister". You're making me feel very old.'

'That's the last thing I want to do,' she said with a smile.

'Excellent. I'm all ears, Farah.'

'The story goes that, centuries ago, Alexander the Great's youngest soldier was standing on the bank of the Amu Darya, just as the river goddess emerged. It was love at first sight for both of them. The young man jumped into the water to be with her but, delirious with love, he'd forgotten he couldn't swim.'

'So he drowned?'

'The river goddess let him drown.'

'A cruel thing for a goddess to do.'

'Yes, but it was the only way for them to be together.'

Lavrov gestured invitingly to the Mies van der Rohe sofa. 'Would you say that the moral of this story is that the end justifies the means, however cruel they are?'

'On the contrary,' Farah said. 'Rather that love flourishes in the underworld.'

They were sitting close together. Keep talking, she reminded herself. Don't allow any silences.

'You're aware that the figure used to be in the National Museum of Kabul?'

'No, I didn't know that. I bought it off a private collector. Where did you get that information?'

She fell silent, lost for words.

'I beg your pardon, I forgot to ask: would you like something to drink?' He rose to his feet.

'Mineral water, please,' she said, somewhat relieved.

Lavrov ordered mineral water via the intercom. Then he paused briefly in front of the statue before he sat down again. 'As you probably know, I'm working on an energy project in Indonesia that should make the country self-sufficient.'

'No,' she said, surprised. 'I didn't know that.'

They were interrupted by the arrival of the receptionist who put down a tray with two glasses of water.

'To our collaboration,' Lavrov said. The clinking of their crystal glasses resonated in her ears.

'How long has it been since you were in the country of your birth?' Lavrov suddenly asked.

Farah was startled. She wanted to ask how he got that information, but immediately realized he must have done a background check. Nobody entered this space without having been properly screened.

'It's been so long I barely remember it.'

'But you do remember the statue.'

'The river goddess?' she said, trying to stay calm. 'Yes, I remember it. I was very young at the time. A child.' She looked at him, feeling exposed, stripped bare. She was naked beside a man in a suit of armour. 'But we're not here to talk about me, Valentin. Let's discuss the art supplement.'

'Of course. Shoot,' Lavrov said. He leaned back, provocatively relaxed.

'Six times a year our paper publishes an international, high-end luxury lifestyle magazine, with prominent guest editors determining both form and content. In consultation of course.'

'A very Dutch way of doing things, the consultation bit.' He produced a stiff smile.

'The idea is that you'll select a few topics with a clear emphasis on contemporary art and lifestyle. Your choices. We'll provide assistance.'

'When's the publication date?'

'In six weeks' time.'

'That's quite soon. We'll definitely have to include the opening of a very special exhibition at the Pushkin Museum on the occasion of your prime minister's visit to Moscow the day after tomorrow.'

'Talk about soon,' Farah commented.

'A couple of contemporary Russian artists have created impressions of Dutch classics, including *The Night Watch*, *The Garden of Earthly Delights* by Hieronymus Bosch and Vermeer's *Girl with a Pearl Earring*. I insist that you come to Moscow as soon as possible, Farah. At my expense, of course. Or does that jeopardize your objectivity as a journalist?' he asked with a sly smile.

'When it comes to art, you can never be objective. You either love it or hate it. Needless to say, I'll have to consult with my boss first. In a very Dutch way.'

'When in Rome . . .' He put down his glass. 'If you'll excuse me now, I have another appointment.' He said it calmly enough, but underneath she sensed a sudden urgency to bring their talk to an end.

'Of course,' she said, and got up. Too fast. She felt dizzy.

'Are you okay?' he asked out of politeness.

'Yes. But tell me, Valentin . . .' She looked at him as if she'd suddenly remembered something. 'Is it possible that I saw you in The Hague yesterday?'

'The Hague?' He regarded her suspiciously.

'In a silver-coloured Bentley, I believe.'

Feeling uncomfortable under his piercing gaze, she took a step back.

'I'd have to check my diary, Farah,' he said with a forced smile. 'I've been out and about a lot in recent days.'

'Of course,' she said. She allowed herself to be escorted to the door. Once there, she turned to face him.

'Oh, and one other thing.'

'Something that can't wait?'

'There's a remarkable resemblance.'

'Resemblance?'

'Between you and former commander Grigori Michailov. I've seen a photo of him from 1989. You're his spitting image.'

Although he was standing close to her, she was acutely aware of the icy distance.

'Imagine, Farah, that Alexander the Great's young soldier from your charming story had been able to take a picture of his river goddess. And imagine I'd seen that photo. In that case, I'd undoubtedly have thought that Sharada herself had just walked into my office.' He shook her hand. 'Please let my PA know as soon as possible when you're coming to Moscow. She'll arrange everything.'

'All right,' Farah said, feeling tense. 'Thank you for meeting me.'

'No,' Lavrov replied. His mouth was smiling, but his eyes weren't. 'Thank *you*, Farah.'

Just as she was walking back to the lobby, the cannon fired a bright-red paint bullet against the wall. It was hard not to interpret it as a warning sign.

14

Dimitri was thoroughly fed up with Amsterdam. As far as he was concerned, the three Xs in the municipal coat of arms stood for Small, Crowded and Dirty. On the canals, countless small boats got in each other's way, in the street cyclists were intent on knocking down disoriented tourists, the taxi drivers were all Arabs who fleeced their passengers and the tram drivers acted like they drove tanks. He could see the towering WMC building rising up in the distance. Thank God.

He was the Angel of Death and not a soul knew he was coming. They wouldn't know what hit them until he was gone again. As he stood on the plaza in front of the hospital, he saw an ink-black rain front advancing from the west. A medevac helicopter landed on the roof. Sauntering people, acutely aware of their mortality, looked up in awe. Typical, Dimitri thought to himself. The minute they feel death snapping at their heels, people suddenly invest all their hope in heaven.

Something was bothering him. A premonition. But he couldn't put his finger on it. It wasn't because this was his first 'baby'. His uncle had taught him to think objectively. It wasn't about lives, however young they were. It all revolved around a higher purpose. Eliminating targets to achieve objectives. And objectives didn't benefit from emotions.

Beside the enormous revolving door stood a huge rent-a-cop with an afro wearing an earpiece. Talk about conspicuous security, Dimitri thought. Why not plant a Royal Guard's fur hat on his 'fro and tell him to parade up and down with a fake gun. The looming fellow was a preposterous piece of window dressing.

Smiling broadly, Dimitri held out his arm to an elderly lady, who was trundling along with a stick and a tatty bag. The woman took his arm and started babbling nineteen to the dozen in that weird guttural language they spoke here and let him carry her bag. The rent-a-cop with the earpiece smiled at them. Dickhead, Dimitri thought. Once inside the lobby he callously left the woman to fend for herself again.

He hated hospitals, especially the smell, that foul, sickly stench of sweat mixed with antiseptic. After scanning the signs with indecipherable lettering he ducked into a side wing, walked through a few swing doors and ended up in a staff toilet. There he stuck a flesh-coloured plaster on his scar, fastened a thin moustache to his upper lip and donned nerdy specs. Efficient actions, resulting in an instant metamorphosis.

15

Danielle had walked around her house for hours that morning with the slums of Port-au-Prince swimming in her thoughts. She pulled her favourite T-shirts out of the wardrobe, along with her underwear, jeans, and the little make-up she owned. Every item she picked up and packed made her in turn feel confused, sad, relieved and anxious. A whole range of emotions: apparently part of the most primal form of self-preservation. Fleeing.

Then the birds, which thank goodness had been quiet all morning, screeched again. The voice of her superior at the hospital sounded stern. An urgent meeting was in order. Could she come to the WMC immediately? Of course. But she'd visit for an entirely different reason. The last things she threw into her suitcase were her flip-flops. She stuck the airline ticket at the very bottom of her handbag.

With a moment of silence, she bid her house farewell.

She was about to knock on the Head of Trauma Surgery's door when she saw Detective Calvino approaching her in the corridor.

'Thanks for coming so quickly.' He seemed nervous. When he shook her hand, he noticed something was up. 'Are you okay?'

'I slept badly.' Without thinking, she ran her hand over the painful bump on her head. 'How's the boy?' she asked anxiously.

'I'm told he's stable, medically speaking. I can't say more now. We'll discuss it in a moment,' he said with an apologetic smile. 'Shall we go?'

As they entered the room, Danielle's immediate supervisor Alexandra Plein came out from behind her desk. She was tense.

'I'll keep this very brief,' she said curtly. 'As you may know, Danielle, immediately after the broadcast of *The Headlines Show* last night, Detective Calvino arranged a police guard for the boy. But of course the issue is: if there hadn't been an article in the newspaper, and if you hadn't appeared on TV this wouldn't have been necessary.'

'I understand,' said Danielle. She wasn't intent on defending her actions.

'Listen,' said Alexandra. 'I know how passionate you are about your work. But it isn't a reason for an MMT doctor to single-handedly start operating on a victim of a hit-and-run without consulting anyone. The MMT was out of service for an hour due to this. Then you forced your colleague Dr Radder to stand idly by in the OR instead of allowing him to do what he does best, namely trauma surgery! And I haven't even mentioned the fast one you pulled on the ICU head nurse by whisking a few TV celebrities inside for a quick visit. And last but not least, you didn't consult with hospital management before bandying words about on that dodgy talk show.'

Danielle heard Detective Calvino cough.

'If I may interrupt you, Dr Plein? I didn't come here to listen to a staff reprimand. I'm here to inform you that the threat to the boy has become much greater than previously assumed. The boy is in immediate danger. We're working on moving him to another hospital as quickly as possible.'

'But . . . you can't put this all on me?' Danielle said, taken aback. 'I saved his life.'

'Saving lives is your job, Danielle. That's what we pay you to do. Not to launch media campaigns!'

'Dr Bernson,' Calvino said in a soothing tone. 'I'd like you to keep doing your work as well and as uninterrupted as possible. And I don't doubt your professionalism. But I hope you realize that by seeking publicity you've seriously compromised this boy's life.'

'Hospitals are not supposed to be the focus of media atten- tion,' added Alexandra Plein in an irritated tone. 'Under no circumstances. We're here to make people better, not to make them celebrated causes.'

'That wasn't my intention,' Danielle curtly replied.

'Whatever your intentions were, you'll have every opportunity to explain in an upcoming hearing. Until further notice, Danielle, you're suspended.'

She hadn't expected this. What she'd done, after all, had been justified. She'd thought about it. Everything she'd done, she'd done for a reason. But she'd overshot her mark. Apart from the fact that she hadn't actually come to the hospital to have this talk, there was no point in protesting Alexandra's decision or entering into any further discussion with her.

'Is it possible for me to see him for a moment? If the boy is going to be transferred, I'd like to say goodbye to him.'

'Only ICU staff are allowed into the room since last night,' Alexandra said coldly.

'I can assure you,' Detective Calvino said apologetically, 'that the boy's in good hands and that you don't have to worry. Hopefully that's some comfort.' Before leaving the room, he shook her hand, glancing at her a bit too conspicuously. Was there more going on? Danielle wondered. He'd been so formal to her during the talk, it hardly seemed genuine. Ill at ease, Danielle stood in front of Alexandra who attempted to steer her out of the office with a misplaced casual tone. 'Take it easy. Go away for a while.'

I'm certainly going to do that, Danielle thought as she walked into the corridor.

Detective Calvino was waiting for her a short distance away. 'Dr Bernson, can you keep a secret?' he whispered in a conspirational tone.

16

By chance, Dimitri discovered a storage room with wooden shelves stacked with neatly folded workwear. A minute later he was wearing a hospital coat and walking past tumble driers and washing machines so big you could fit in at least two rent-a-cops. He routinely grabbed one of the metal carts with clean linen and calmly wheeled it away. He followed some women in rumpled white outfits into the staff lift, where he recognized the letters ICU alongside one of the push buttons.

At the entrance to Intensive Care a security guard rummaged through the contents of his linen cart. Like he'd be stupid enough to hide something there. Why don't you frisk me, you prick? Dimitri thought. Let's see who pulls the Zastava first, you or me. But the man waved him through without so much as another glance.

In the corridor Dimitri spotted a policeman sitting in front of one of the doors like a pathetic museum attendant. Target located. But Dimitri didn't like the look of things. The amateur security guards, the dozy policeman at the door, the figure behind the counter who looked up just a bit too long and appeared to be on duty for the first time – it all felt like they were expecting him. Or was he imagining things?

Still pushing his cart, he saw a wide door that opened on to a storage room. He went in, looked around and was pleased with what he saw. Uncle Arseni had introduced him to chaos theory, telling him that order and chaos are flipsides of one and the same coin. Chaos was apparent disorder. Apparent, because it was brought about in an orderly way, by a so-called attractor. And today Dimitri was the attractor. With his Zippo lighter, a cart full of linen and a battery of stored oxygen tanks he was about to create total chaos.

17

'What just happened couldn't be helped,' Detective Calvino said apologetically. 'I saw what you did for that boy. I'm happy to take you to him. After all, you saved his life.'

A moment later, Danielle was leaning over the child. Although she knew he couldn't understand her, she still wanted to tell him he'd be safe, safer than if she stayed around.

'I hope,' she whispered, forcing a smile, 'you have a long and healthy life and who knows . . .' Then she faltered. She wanted to say something like 'Who knows, perhaps we'll see each other soon,' but she knew there'd be no reunion. In place of him, there'd only be other boys and girls. Also uprooted, desperately poor and helpless. And they would be followed by others. Port-au-Prince wouldn't be her last stop, not by a long shot.

As she gave him a kiss goodbye, tears fell on to his face.

'We should go,' Detective Calvino softly said.

They stood together in the lift, silent, staring at their shoes. Just before Detective Calvino stepped out on the ground floor, she gave him a quick kiss on his cheek. It was just as clumsy as the first time she'd kissed a boy in the playground. He hesitated for a second in between the open lift doors and turned towards her. She caught his surprised smile and then the doors closed.

Her hand impulsively reached for the stop button. She saw the scene unfold: the doors opened again and she threw her arms around Calvino's neck, told him everything that had really happened the night before. 'Protect me,' she whispered loudly. 'Protect me.'

The lift doors opened. She stared into the neon-lit concrete car park. Didn't move. Felt paralysed. The doors closed. Opened. Closed again. And then the fire alarm went off.

She was running through the dark: gunshots rang out, the rustle of knee-high grass along her legs, the screams of the children she'd left behind.

'Protect me.'

She stepped into the car park, blinded by the neon light, pursued by the ringing alarm that worked on her nerves. She couldn't stop. She couldn't go back. Fleeing was her only protection. Consumed by fear, in a panic, she waved her keys at every car she walked past.

The fire alarm clattered like a machine gun against her eardrums. She heard the screams of people running. Between two cars she leaned forward, terribly nauseous but unable to vomit. For a while she leaned against the bonnet of a convertible, then she took a few deep breaths and waved her keys in every direction again. She heard an unexpected click and turned. Her red Fiat was right behind her.

She got in as fast as she could. She started the engine, pushed down firmly on the accelerator and shot out of the parking space. A large car approaching from the left screeched to a halt. A black Volkswagen Touareg had nearly rammed her. Because of the bright lights, she could barely see the driver. She made an apologetic gesture. The Touareg blinked its lights to indicate she could proceed.

As she drove out of the car park, she saw that a heavy cloud cover had practically wiped out all the sunlight. It looked like the evening had fallen half a day too early. She had to turn on her headlights in order to see better. Leaving the hospital grounds, she passed three fire engines with their sirens blaring, but she was now breathing more calmly.

It was almost all behind her, she assured herself.

18

Marouan surveyed the situation. He knew where the special squad in their medical getups had stationed themselves: one was acting as a desk clerk and the other was supposedly keeping a close eye on the patient monitors. The only clearly identifiable security was the uniformed policeman at the door. It was his task to be noticed. He was probably dripping with sweat with that bullet-proof vest under his uniform.

All of them were wearing an earpiece. There had been rather frequent communication in the first few hours. But this had tapered off. No suspicious movement. No conspicuous visitors, except for the disheartened blonde critical-care physician who appeared at the ICU escorted by Calvino. Marouan noticed she'd been crying. Apparently, she wanted to see the boy. Marouan thought he'd give them a moment to get this emotional bullshit over with.

In the meantime, a failed suicide was brought in. Within minutes Calvino returned to the lift with the blonde doctor. A nerdy type was pushing a linen cart along the corridor. The patient in Room 3 went into septic shock. All this misery and woe got on Marouan's nerves.

In the last hour, Marouan had started to doubt Kovalev's prediction. He'd been given a description of the probable hitman, but it was as vague as the average weather forecast. Young, noticeable scar on his left cheek, dressed all in black. Existentialist type. All well and good, but the guy wasn't going to walk into the ICU smoking a pipe and quoting Sartre.

Shortly thereafter, Calvino checked in via his earpiece. He'd returned to Hospital Security and been told the MICU, the mobile intensive care unit, would arrive in about ten minutes. The plan was for Marouan to head to the inner courtyard where he'd meet the arriving MICU team to finalize the transfer, while Calvino would hand over the monitoring task to a colleague.

Marouan had a bad feeling. 'Can't we wait with the transfer until we have this guy in custody?'

'I understand what you're saying, partner,' Calvino said. 'But our instructions are clear. You and I are responsible for the boy. We'll accompany the MICU to Rotterdam. The rest of the team hauls in the Russian the minute he shows his face.'

Marouan would have done anything to get away from the ICU as quickly as possible. Together with Mariska, he sped to the ground floor in the staff lift. He felt his ears pop and that sick feeling in his stomach returned. It was like when you dropped something breakable and knew you'd be too late to catch it. He pinched his nose and popped his ears open. Had he overlooked something? He had no idea. Hospital Security, a police guard and armed undercover agents were all on standby.

Everything under control, you'd think.

Maybe it was the messy cramped courtyard that worked on his nerves.

'The ambulance entrance of the underground car park is too low for the MICU,' Mariska said, sensing his anxiety. 'That's why we always receive it here.'

Marouan nodded. Then he heard an alarm. At first he thought it was the siren of an approaching ambulance. But Mariska looked up, equally startled.

'What is it?' Marouan asked.

'There must be a fire on one of the wards,' Mariska replied.

At that moment, Marouan knew he'd let something slip out of his hands, and it was probably already too late to catch it.

Fire.

Why hadn't this ploy crossed his mind?

'You meet the MICU!' shouted Marouan at Mariska as he ran back into the building.

The practical shoes with the steel toecaps she wore underneath her ambulance uniform always made Vera Hendrix feel like a construction worker. But they were a bitter necessity, those shoes. The stretcher they used on these special transports, the so-called MICU trolley, was fitted with lots of equipment and weighed a couple of hundred kilos. You wouldn't want the wheels to accidentally land on your toes.

The MICU itself was a twelve-ton container, built on a Volvo lorry undercarriage and set up as an intensive care unit on wheels providing inter-clinical transport of ICU patients. Together with driver Harold Jacobs and IC specialist Ewald Jong, Vera made up the team accompanying this evening's transport.

It was rare for the timetable to be revised last minute and the team to be personally briefed about the next transport. Both had happened today. The original transports had been postponed with immediate effect. The MICU coordinator on duty told them the patient in question was a boy of around seven, the victim of a hit-and-run. It had required two surgical interventions to stop the internal bleeding, reset a broken pelvis and a leg fracture, remove part of his spleen, attend to a head trauma, lung injuries and internal bruising and stabilize the boy so he could be transferred to the children's ICU at the Maaspoort Hospital in Rotterdam. Secrecy was of the essence.

After the briefing they hurried back to the MICU. Normally they always checked their equipment prior to departure, but given the urgency of the transport they decided to do so en route to the WMC. Vera checked the trolley with the attached IC equipment to see if it had sufficient battery life. Properly charged batteries were crucial, because in between loading and unloading a patient, the respirator, monitor, controls and infusion pumps had to keep working. Vera remembered that one time they got stuck in a hospital lift for almost ninety minutes because the trolley turned out to be too heavy. The batteries started draining like mad, but when they were freed after what had felt like an eternity the patient was still stable because the batteries had been charged in full on departure.

A check revealed that the batteries were at seventy per cent capacity. She glanced at Ewald. 'Acceptable risk,' he said. She disagreed, but given the situation there was no use arguing. The respirator's automatic control system indicated that everything else was fine.

Because of the thick partitioning wall between the driver's cab and the IC unit, she and Ewald could only communicate with Harold via the intercom. But a monitor connected to a camera inside the cab gave them a view of the road. Vera tended to get carsick if she couldn't look at the road every now and then.

Harold informed them that their planned arrival time at the WMC would be in ten minutes, and that after loading the boy they'd receive a police escort. When they drove on to the WMC site soon after, they were overtaken by two fire engines with blaring sirens.

'What's going on?' Ewald yelled through the intercom. They could hear Harold urgently conferring with the WMC over the radio.

'Fire in the ICU!'

20

Sasha Kovalev got out of his car just before the large plaza in front of the WMC. Menacing grey clouds loomed overhead.

No matter where he went, he felt like a stranger. He'd spent his entire life on the move, so no place felt like home. It suited him just fine. He felt privileged to have experienced how a lavish nomadic existence transcended borders and time zones. How often had he gazed out the window of Lavrov's private jet at the world below and fought the seductive notion that he was a demigod who could triumph over time and space: master of his own destiny. An illusion, of course. People were made to fail. You had to do your best to stay one step ahead of that failure.

Especially now.

Before leaving his flat half an hour earlier, he'd given the skyline of Amsterdam one last look, knowing that an anonymous life awaited him in Goa. But a life where he would put down roots: a life with the three of them.

They would walk on the beach together, Bikram at his side, with the boy between them. They would each hold one of his small hands. The boy would be up and about again. Unsteady on his feet at first, but they had all the time in the world. The boy would be hesitant about walking into the sea at low tide. They wouldn't let him go too far. They would stay right beside him: quickly lift him out of the water if he got frightened.

Sasha could have never imagined himself thinking this way. It was a curious development. As if he'd been a stranger to himself for many years and could finally see what was important in this life. He was now happy to trade his fantasy of dominating time and space for the illusion of family happiness.

He left the key in the ignition and walked on to the plaza. Three fire engines with their sirens blaring raced passed him. Helmeted men with oxygen masks stormed into the hospital lobby. Sasha calmly walked via a side wing of the building towards the inner courtyard.

21

The staff lift must have been blocked. Marouan decided he'd better take the stairs. By the third floor he was completely out of breath and his heart was racing, and not only due to his poor condition. Dark-grey smoke from a few floors higher blanketed the stairwell. Panicked people bumped against him. They screamed and pushed each other. Someone fell and someone else stumbled over them.

On the ICU floor, shadows ran back and forth in the scorching mist. Marouan searched for the special squad men. He bumped into a patient's bed being pushed towards the blocked lift by two nurses wearing surgical masks. A pointless endeavour.

Suddenly he saw the policeman lying on the ground in the doorway of the room he'd been guarding. A nurse was bent over him, desperately trying to revive him. Marouan saw where he'd been hit. Double tap to the heart. He entered the boy's room and saw, to his immense dismay, the damage the other bullets had done.

22

The linen draped over the tanks muffled the explosion. But the oxygen fanned the flames in no time. The resulting smoke was so heavy that within minutes the entire ward was enveloped in a bank of thick fog. Total panic ensued. Nurses outscreamed the alarms. Dimitri watched it all with great satisfaction. He was a master of chaos.

In the corridor he kept the police officer in his sights. When the man left his post in response to cries for help further down, Dimitri quickly slipped into the room and at point-blank range fired two shots at the motionless boy. One to the head and one to the heart. The silencer was hardly necessary, given the infernal din in the corridor.

When he turned around, he saw the police guard in the doorway. The man shouted something unintelligible and aimed his gun at him with a trembling hand. Quick as a flash, Dimitri shot him twice in the chest. The policeman fell backwards into the thick smoke, as if he was suddenly yanked offstage with a hook. There was loud screaming everywhere.

Dimitri hurried over to the stairwell. It was pandemonium there too, full of screeching and screaming people pushing and shoving one another, all trying to be the first to make it downstairs. He stuck close to the wall and walked down calmly. Among the people jostling and stumbling over one another he spotted the Arab doctor he'd seen at the ICU front desk earlier, struggling against the flow of traffic in the stairwell.

Dimitri didn't put up any resistance and allowed himself to be carried along by the crowd, by the avalanche of panic, which eventually brought him to the main lobby where he darted into a stairwell to the car park.

Starting the Touareg marked the end of his first mission. Having to suddenly brake for a red Fiat turned out to be the beginning of his second. To his immense surprise, Dimitri recognized the blonde driver who nervously waved to apologize as his next victim.

23

When the MICU's tailgate was unlocked and the two doors swung open, the noisy fire alarm reverberated inside the vehicle. Vera and Ewald quickly wheeled the trolley on to the loading ramp. On the advice of the critical care nurse who introduced herself as Mariska, they took an alternative route via the goods lift. While in transit they discussed the boy's condition. There had been some problems with his spleen this morning.

When the lift doors opened they all clasped a hand to their mouth and pushed the trolley into the ICU corridor through the smoke and confusion of the ongoing evacuation. Firefighters with oxygen masks charged on to the unit and ran past them. At the end of the corridor, they saw flames coming out of a storage room. At the word go, one of the firefighters hurled a Fire Knock Out in the room. Firehoses were unrolled. A large ventilator was set up.

A Moroccan-looking man in a white coat confronted them. 'Police, follow me.'

They ended up in a remote corner of the unit where a man with an oxygen mask and a machine gun was waiting for them. 'It's okay,' they heard the detective shout. 'The boy's transport!' Then he turned to Vera and Ewald. 'We brought him here this morning,' he said in between gasping breaths. 'And thank God we did.'

'Why's that?'

'Someone just entered his first room and pumped two bullets into a nursing doll.'

24

The storm front was now hanging directly above her. Danielle was finally composed enough to realize the weather might impact her departure from Schiphol. She was ready for her next journey. Somehow she'd been leaving her whole life. Always in transit. No one could burn their bridges behind them better than she could. The Netherlands was about to be a distant memory.

She kept her eyes on the road and thought of what she'd be leaving behind. A life without friends that mainly consisted of work. Her brand new Ikea furniture and second-hand Fiat Punto had offered her little pleasure. Temporary possessions that she hadn't even had time to get used to.

She heard the birds screeching. She couldn't contain her curiosity and answered. The man's voice at the other end of the line was agitated.

'Danielle Bernson?'

'Speaking.'

'I'm calling you because . . . I saw you on television and I have information about the boy in the woods.'

'The boy? How did you get my number? '

'Via the hospital.'

'What do you know about the boy?'

'I can't say, not on the phone, that is.'

'Why don't you call the police?'

'I'll tell you that too, when I see you.'

'I'm sorry, but I can't meet with you.'

'You have to see me. I know what happened.'

She hesitated.

'You need to call someone else. A journalist. Her name is Farah Hafez. She works for the *AND*.'

'Do you have her number?'

'No. She should be easy enough to find.'

25

Vera deftly manoeuvred the trolley beside the boy's bed. Together with Ewald she began to disconnect him before hooking him up to the trolley equipment. They switched the ventilator tube and then swapped over the heart-rate and blood-pressure monitor. Tugging at the bottom sheet, they slid the boy on to the trolley.

The return route was risky. However advanced their equipment might be, in the midst of this pandemonium anything was possible. The fire was under control now, and the immense ventilator in the corridor was steadily dispersing the smoke, but there was still a lot of distress. People were running up and down the corridor. An unexpected emergency stop, or worse, a collision, could cause the boy serious harm. Every single step in this corridor was fraught with risk.

They'd been joined by a second detective. He and his older colleague cleared the way for the trolley, their hands hovering above their service guns. The man with the machine gun brought up the rear, his eyes darting from left to right.

In the goods lift Vera learnt what had been arranged. Because of the very real threat of an attack, the boy had been moved in the morning. A stand-in, a nursing doll with brown skin and black hair, was fitted with an oxygen mask and nicely tucked into his bed. Following a recent training course, Vera had some experience with those dolls and knew how lifelike they looked. The police had truly done everything they could to trap the attacker, to the point of deploying snipers disguised as doctors. But the chaos of a fire on the unit had taken them by surprise.

The young detective said that guarding every single entrance and exit would be pointless. Half the hospital was emptying out. Stopping the flow of fleeing people would claim victims and only increase the panic. The main thing now was to get the boy to safety as quickly as possible.

When they reached the courtyard and wheeled the boy into the MICU under the watchful eye of the man with the machine gun, Vera heaved a sigh of relief. She secured the trolley to the anchoring points inside the ambulance as fast as she could. Then the tailgate was closed and soon after they drove out of the yard, towards the car park exit where the detectives would be waiting for them in their car.

She was concentrating on the boy's breathing and on the heart-rate monitor when the vehicle suddenly braked and stopped. On the screen she saw a man in black walking towards the MICU. The detectives were nowhere to be seen. Via the intercom she heard the door of the driver's cab open and slam shut again. A male voice barked orders in English.

'What's going on, Harold?' she yelled into the intercom. No response. The MICU accelerated again. 'Harold? Is everything all right?'

She took out her mobile phone, keyed in Harold's number and cursed when she got through to his voicemail. She looked at the screen and saw that they'd turned on to the slip road leading to the ring road, without their police escort. Then she heard the voice of the unknown man over the intercom. He spoke English with a thick Eastern European accent.

'One more phone call and you'll be scraping your driver's brain off this partition.'

As they gathered speed, Vera felt the same fear bubbling up as that time when they got stuck in the lift.

26

Constantly checking her rear-view mirror, after the light turned green, Danielle kept close watch of the black Touareg tailing her. He also took the route over the viaduct. At the end, she merged into the left lane. The Touareg followed her like a shadow. Just before the exit, she made a sharp right, hit the gas and drove as hard as she could.

Her heart stopped for a moment when the Touareg's lights appeared again in her mirror. She pressed down hard on the accelerator again and suddenly realized she was entering the Amsterdamse Bos. She raced along a narrow tarmac road beside a wide ditch.

When, after several sharp turns, she saw a dark lane to her right, she quickly turned off the main road. After a hundred metres she braked and turned off the engine and headlights. Holding her breath, she watched in her rear-view mirror as the Touareg sped past at full speed.

She waited until she'd calmed down; grabbed the wheel to steady her hands. She was shivering, as if it was suddenly a few degrees colder. In the distance she heard the dull thud of an approaching thunderstorm.

She started the car again. Cautiously and without lights she backed up on to the tarmac road. Just before she turned, the Touareg reappeared out of nowhere from the other direction. Her right hand gripped the gearstick and she stamped on the accelerator. The speedometer read eighty when she realized she was going to hit the row of trees at the end of the road like a brick wall. She turned the wheel so quickly that the Fiat flipped over twice and then came to a halt standing on its wheels again.

Smoke. Hissing. Torn metal. The dust from the exploding airbag filled her nose and mouth. The unmistakable smell of leaking gasoline. The bittersweet taste of blood gushing from a wound on her forehead. Impending nausea. She pushed the door open, rolled out on to her hands and knees, and sat up. She somehow managed to stand and stumbled into the woods. Bright flashes of lightning distorted her vision. Trees suddenly reached diagonally into the sky. Branches were arms that wanted to grab her. Tree roots turned into traps.

She recognized the airport's runway marker lamps in the distance and convinced herself that it was the finish line of this sinister chase. She would shake him off. The lights would save her life. She was home free.

She ran right into him.

As if he'd been waiting for her all along.

27

Farah loved the smell of old leather that greeted her every time she opened the door of her Porsche Carrera. She relished the deep throbbing of the air-cooled engine whenever she accelerated and the intimation of power as she felt the tyres grip the tarmac. Like no other, she understood why people went for a drive when they had something on their mind. The more she let her classic muscle machine rip, the clearer things became in her head.

She sped over the ring road with the sole aim of driving as long and as fast as it took to get some sort of handle on the meeting with Valentin Lavrov. What intrigued her most, strangely enough, was how the statue of the river goddess had ended up in Lavrov's office among all those modern monstrosities, and so prominently displayed too. Lavrov had done his homework on Farah. But since he couldn't have possibly known about her emotional bond with the figurine, it had to be a coincidence. That said, there were three things Farah didn't believe in. Marriage, heaven and coincidence.

Had she disclosed something she shouldn't have with her question about the Bentley? And what about the way Lavrov looked at her after she mentioned his resemblance to former commander Michailov? She could drive for days, but this time the answers wouldn't just present themselves. She'd have to go to Moscow. She'd have to capitalize on the position of trust which she appeared to have acquired this afternoon.

With her speedometer now indicating 150 kilometres per hour, she felt the urge to call David. She usually phoned him when she'd experienced something remarkable or she was worked up about something. David was an excellent listener and great at dispensing constructive advice. But she didn't miss him just for that. The thought that an intense six months together had simply evaporated, just because of a single slip-up, was unbearable.

Fifteen minutes later she drove up the driveway of the house by the pond. The front door swung open and the sight of David standing there, laidback as ever while he waited for her, made her feel both warm and guilty. It would take quite a few awkward words, lots of evasive answers before their first tentative touch. But eventually they'd hug and she'd push him up the stairs to the bedroom.

That course of events seemed unlikely when she got closer. The look in his eyes suggested that his antagonism had only increased. It had been encapsulated, that was all, the way burning hot uranium is contained by a shield of reinforced concrete.

'Come in,' he said without touching her. 'I want to show you something.'

She followed him inside. In passing she spotted a few boxes in the hallway. On the table inside lay today's copy of *De Nederlander*. David picked it up and opened it to the page that featured paparazzo Eric Sanders' most recent shots. A photo picturing her beside Parwaiz's grave was accompanied by the screaming headline: FARAH H. SINGS ISLAMIC BATTLE HYMN AT FUNERAL. Another photo, which showed her kissing Joshua on his canal boat, was captioned with words that left a bad taste in her mouth. *In her leisure time Farah H. does not adhere to the letter of Islamic law. Dressed only in a T-shirt, she spends her mornings on the canal boat of a handsome detective for whom she recently left well-known documentary filmmaker David van Rhijn.*

'How long has this been going on?' David asked.

'This hate campaign? A couple of days.'

'No, Farah, I mean this!' David practically stabbed his finger through the photo of the canal boat flirtation. 'How long has *this* been going on? You sneaking around with this detective?'

'Do you actually believe what it says?'

'So it didn't happen? This was Photoshopped?'

'It happened once.'

'And this one time was captured by a photographer?'

His suppressed anger flared up.

'Why didn't you want me to come to the funeral?' he asked unexpectedly.

'After what happened last night?'

'I've got a good headline for what happened last night,' he hissed. 'Woman owns up to persistent cheating, man gets angry, woman runs off to cry on new boyfriend's shoulder.'

'That's not what happened and you know it. Allow me some dignity.'

'And what do you allow me?' He brandished the newspaper. His ultimate piece of evidence.

'It's simple, David. Either you believe these lies, or you believe me.'

'It's that simple, is it?'

'It's that simple, yes.'

'As simple as putting stuff in boxes,' he said without any emotion. 'They're in the hallway. Take them and get lost.'

All of a sudden she felt pity for the man opposite her. But it wasn't the sort of pity that included compassion. It amazed her just how badly she'd misjudged this man. Warm-hearted, intelligent and funny, he now seemed adrift in his hostility and was desperately digging in his heels.

She walked back to the hallway and quickly glanced in the boxes. They were filled with her jeans, trainers, knickers, bras, T-shirts, make-up and books. She hesitated briefly before picking up the first box and carrying it to the Carrera. Perhaps it really is that simple, she thought as she walked back and forth. The end of a relationship made tangible by a handful of boxes. Just like the end of a life is sealed in a coffin.

28

As the KLM Boeing 747 from Johannesburg touched down on the Buitenveldert runway at Schiphol Airport, Paul was busy blowing into the paper bag Sandrine had handed him. Twenty minutes later, they faced each other again beside the luggage carrousel. She had her suitcase, he was still empty-handed.

'Thank you.'

'You're welcome,' Sandrine said. 'All the best, Paul.'

He tried to smile, but it made him feel like a second-rate actor in a low-budget film. She rubbed his shoulder and kissed him on the cheek.

As soon as she disappeared behind the frosted glass windows of the arrivals hall, he felt a pang of loneliness. He picked up his bag and shuffled through the doors past the customs official, who looked straight through him. He was back in the Netherlands. Home. But it didn't feel like it. In the huge hall, he watched the anticipating faces of the people waiting.

As a boy he'd stood here with his mother, waiting for his father, who'd travelled to Cambodia a month earlier. Every morning for weeks, he'd lit a tea light in front of the wooden statuette of a small Thai angel with outstretched hand. Then he and his mother had breakfast together, and every morning she promised to come and pick him up from school the minute she received word of Dad's homecoming. As the days went by, he noticed his teachers were watching him with ever greater concern while the other kids at school were doing their best to be nicer to him than usual. During the weekly football game, his team mates were clearly making a point of passing him the ball and putting him in a position to score. In the weeks that his father was missing, Paul became top scorer of his team.

On a Wednesday afternoon, when he was not at school, a car pulled up outside. A black Chevrolet with a CD licence plate. *Corps Diplomatique.* A uniformed driver got out and opened the rear door for a tall man with glasses wearing a dark suit. The man stared impassively at the farm while a young woman carrying a large bag got out of the other side of the car. Together they walked to the front door.

His mother opened it without uttering a word and was equally reticent throughout the man's faltering monologue. Every now and then he took his glasses off to clean them, which Paul understood to be a ploy to give his mother time to process the news.

Human remains had been found. Somewhere in an isolated location north of the Cambodian capital Phnom Penh. It had been virtually impossible to identify the body, but perhaps Mrs Chapelle might recognize a few items of clothing, a shoulder bag, a writing pad with notes? His mother had nodded quietly. Her subsequent question had sounded chilling.

'When is he coming back?'

The man put his glasses back on. 'This evening.'

For the first time in his life Paul saw a lead-lined coffin. His mother broke down completely when they were told the coffin couldn't be opened.

'Please bear in mind, Mrs Chapelle, that your husband was dead for some time before the body was found . . . You're better off remembering him the way he was when you last saw him.'

Paul placed his hand on his heart and then reached for the cold lid of the coffin, hoping to bring his father back to life in this way. But whether it was his mother's sobbing, the soldiers' pitying looks or his lack of conviction, nothing happened. No tingling sensation. No resurrection. Only a crushing emptiness.

Whenever he was at Schiphol, these memories came rushing back. In places where people bid each other farewell for longer or shorter periods of time, or fell into one another's arms again, he could only think of his father, the man he'd never been able to say goodbye to.

Then he heard his name being called.

29

Dimitri remembered the name he'd given the goose he once caught as a little boy: *Snegurochka*, the Snow Maiden. She put up a fight and threatened to bite, hissing frightfully all the while. But as soon as he had a firm hold on her, with one hand around her neck and the other around both her legs, the creature appeared to freeze.

He knew it was an instinctive reaction, the brain transmitting to all muscle groups that escape from this grip was impossible. It would be better to remain in a state of wakeful, feigned sleep and wait for that split-second weakening of the grip that might offer the chance of fighting back.

It was just like this with the woman he'd seen crawling out of her spinning car and staggering into the forest. By drawing an imaginary line, he made an outflanking manoeuvre. He'd done so very calmly, paying close attention to the tree stumps and roots that might trip you up when you walked too fast, like she did. When he heard her approach, he waited, very quietly, for the moment she'd be really close. And then she bumped into him. As if he was a walking magnet.

Now, as he carried her out of the woods, she lay outwardly submissive in his arms. And although deep down in her subconscious she must have realized escape was impossible at this point, he knew that if his grip weakened for just a second, every last instinct, muscle and organ in her body would rally to force an escape.

He put her down on the bonnet of the Touareg and touched her head wound. She began to groan softly. She opened her eyes and gave him a distant look. He smiled at her as he unbuttoned her blouse, and lapped up the trickle of blood that oozed out of her head wound, down her chin and over her right breast.

She whispered something. He couldn't understand her. She was whispering in her own language. She was a stranger and yet she felt familiar. Then she switched to English. He caught the word '*boy*'. It sounded loving, as if she was trying to reassure him. He leant over and licked and bit her nipples which stiffened while she sobbed and carried on whispering in English. He picked up '*please*' and realized she was surrendering. He felt the fear of the goose which was about to die as he yanked off her knickers under her skirt.

Her body tensed as if some electrical pulse shot through it when he thrust inside her. He tried to control himself and moved his pelvis in a measured way. With each thrust he heard her body underneath him banging dully against the metal bonnet. He was aware of her flailing arms and pressed his face against her breasts.

The moment he came inside her he stood up straight, in glorious ecstasy. At that same moment he heard the shot from his Zastava and felt the pain flare up in his right shoulder. He was flung off her as though hit by lightning, and as he fell to the ground bleeding he saw her dark silhouette merging with the black of the Touareg.

30

The last time Edward had seen his nephew cry was at Raylan's funeral. He remembered standing beside Isobel and holding her. But Isobel had been in a different world. One in which she was trying to swim against the current of time in the hope of somehow reviving the love of her life. Little Paul had joined them and taken his mother's hand. And so, locked in grief and longing, the three of them had slowly turned to stone.

Edward thought back to when he and Isobel and a seven-year-old Paul had waved goodbye to Raylan at Schiphol on his way to Cambodia thirty years ago. He wondered whether his brother-in-law had known deep down what fate awaited him when he went through Security and, contrary to habit, turned around and stood for ages, without calling out, without waving, like a living statue, as if he wanted to take one last look before turning away and disappearing for ever.

Paul looked just as lost among the crowd in Schiphol's arrivals hall, Edward noticed, as his father in the departure lounge all those years ago. The same drawn features in a face that remained attractive despite stress and fatigue, despite being unshaven and sallow. Like father, like son.

He strode up to Paul, threw both arms around him and pressed him close. Paul extricated himself from the embrace with some difficulty and wiped his tears on his sleeve.

'Haven't you got something better to do than to reduce a man who's just flown for twelve hours to tears?'

'If I'd known you'd become such a softie, I'd have had a ball pit installed for you here. Looks good, the bandaging. And the stitches. What happened?'

'Later, Ed.'

'Is that all you've brought?' Edward pointed to Paul's small suitcase.

'I'm here too. And I come with lots of baggage.'

31

From the moment he laid her over the bonnet of the Touareg, Danielle could no longer think, no longer react. All she could do was accept what was coming. She was in a kind of sleep state where she could only whisper – beg for mercy. When he entered her with his hard, muscular body, she weakly tried pushing him away with her arms.

How she did it, she no longer knew, but all of a sudden she felt the metal in his coat pocket and she clasped her hand around it. She had gathered all the strength she could muster and shot at the grunting silhouette hanging over her. The impact threw him off of her, and she slid off the bonnet. The gun fell out of her hands.

Reeling with dizziness, she staggered into the woods. She couldn't remember the number of times she'd almost collapsed. It didn't matter. She had to disappear among the trees. Low hanging branches whipped against her face, but she tried to stay on her feet and to keep going; Just keep going, she thought, hoping against her better judgement that somewhere a kind of salvation lay ahead.

Until she suddenly saw all the trees in front of her falling and realized that she was the one taking the fall.

32

A large video screen in Schiphol's arrivals hall was showing a live broadcast of *The Headlines Show*. Paul saw footage of a young and attractive Middle Eastern woman wearing a black headscarf and standing beside a grave.

'Oh no,' Edward sighed next to him. 'This can't be true. Dear God, tell me this isn't happening . . .' Meanwhile, the voice of the presenter with the cherry-red mouth echoed through the arrivals hall.

'This is a side to Farah H. we haven't seen before,' she crowed triumphantly. 'Here she is at a funeral, singing an Islamic battle hymn.'

'Your new colleague,' Edward said dully. He nodded at the screen.

'Who? That twat with the cleavage?'

'No. Her.' Edward pointed to the screen. Paul realized it was the same woman from the funeral, except this time she was on the deck of a houseboat, dressed in only a T-shirt and kissing a man who clearly had his hand between her legs.

'Jesus on a stick,' Edward muttered. 'I didn't realize it was this type of photo.'

'What's this all about?' Paul asked.

The presenter reappeared on screen. 'But in her leisure time, Farah H. tends to flout Islamic law. Here she is in a different capacity, that of a man-eater.'

'This is about Farah,' Edward clarified. 'They're throwing mud at her. Don't ask me why. I was at the funeral this morning. Just about everybody was in tears while she sang that song. What times are we living in, for God's sake?'

'In times of cheap sensation, Ed,' said Paul. 'And plenty of media outlets thrive on it.' With fascination Paul stared at the pictures of Farah. The girl from the butterfly garden in Kabul had become a Dutch journalist. However big he'd thought his world was, a twist of fate had reduced it and brought them back together again after nearly thirty years.

'She said she'd be here.' Edward looked around. 'Something must have come up. She had a meeting with Lavrov today. We've got a brilliant scheme. Lavrov is prepared to contribute to a special art edition.'

'A bold move,' Paul said. Meanwhile, he kept half an eye on the screen, which now showed the presenter in the studio talking via a video link to the Dutch Prime Minister, who was about to travel to Russia for a five-day visit, together with Finance Minister Lombard and a bevy of successful businesspeople. 'Prime Minister, what are you hoping to achieve?' he heard her booming voice as they walked through the revolving doors.

Outside, in the large plaza, the wind was gathering strength. In the distance, a huge black storm front was approaching.

'How's Mum?' Paul asked.

'She needs you.'

At that moment, Paul spotted Sandrine at the nearby taxi stand.

'Just a second, Ed.'

He called her name. She didn't hear him, but when she saw him trotting towards her she seemed unsure what to do.

'There's no such thing as coincidence.' Paul thought it sounded silly, but he couldn't think of anything else to say.

'Sure there is,' she replied cheerfully. 'It just depends on who orchestrates it.'

'Can we offer you a lift?'

'It's nearly my turn. Thanks, anyway.'

'Travel safely,' he intoned a little sadly, at which he promptly turned around and walked away. Looking up, he saw jet-black billows rapidly obscuring the twilit sky.

33

Dimitri must have been out cold for a moment. The searing heat where the bullet had entered brought him to again. He pressed his hand to the bloody wound and crouched down on his knees to search for the Zastava. As soon as he'd found it, he pulled himself up on the car and looked around to see where the woman had gone.

He caught a glimpse of her lurching between the trees. He squeezed his eyes to slits to take aim.

The shot rang out and she fell instantly. As if her legs were snapping twigs. She writhed in the grass. He hobbled towards her and when he stood beside her she looked up and begged him.

'*Please . . .*'

Dimitri hated it when women begged. Begging was like signing a non-existent truce.

He shook with anger as he aimed his Zastava. He had allowed himself to be caught off-guard by her and it infuriated him. Now he had to wait until he was calm again, his emotions frozen. He had to shut himself off from all the distracting noise that was intruding on the moment he would cut short her life. He wanted to kill her in the only proper way: with clinical precision. The way a surgeon removes a growth from an otherwise healthy body.

He heard the monotonous roar of distant traffic, but above all he heard the ominous growl of the approaching storm. Raindrops fell from the jet-black sky like molten lead.

He saw the woman opening her mouth wide. It became a sound hole for the death scream that rose up from her stomach like an unstoppable eruption. Her entire body resonated with the scream.

The silence that fell after he'd emptied the magazine in her was so overwhelming that it felt as if her death had sucked up all the sound.

Dimitri was shaking on his legs, as his finger kept pulling the trigger.

34

As Paul, who'd offered to drive, manoeuvred the Saab from the airport on to the ring road, Edward put Farah on speaker phone. She sounded dejected, but Paul still recognized the proud girl of yesteryear in her voice.

'Sorry that I'm late,' he heard her say. 'It's already in *De Nederlander*, Ed.'

'And it was just on *The Headlines Show*,' Edward replied. 'I see that I've got a nymphomaniac journalist with a penchant for singing jihadist battle hymns on my payroll. Good to know for future staff parties.'

'I don't think it's funny, Ed.'

'Me neither. Marant's playing a very nasty game here.'

'But why?'

'I suspect we'll find out soon enough.'

A bolt of lightning shot through the sky. Its echo could be heard over the connection with Farah. At the same time Paul spotted a tired-looking Sandrine in the taxi overtaking them.

'Where are you now?' Edward asked.

'Heading towards Schiphol. I was hoping Paul might be delayed. Is he with you?'

'He's sitting next to me. Insisted on parking his arse on the driver's seat of the Saab. And forget what I said about that handsome face of his,' Edward chuckled. 'He looks a mess.'

'Hello, Paul,' came through the speakers.

Paul took a while to react. 'Funny to hear your voice again, Farah. After all these years,' he finally said.

'Funny? You seem to have the same sense of humour as your uncle.'

Paul sighed. Yup, and she was as stubborn as ever, he thought to himself.

'How was Lavrov?' Edward asked impatiently.

'Bizarre story, Ed. He wants me to go to Moscow.'

'Moscow?'

A second lightning strike was immediately followed by a loud thunderclap. Paul heard Farah's startled shriek through the speakers.

All the cars ahead of them switched on their full beams and slowed as a thick sheet of rain reduced visibility. A couple of cars swerved unexpectedly on to the hard shoulder, which only made things worse. Paul turned the windscreen wipers to their fastest setting, but that didn't help much. With his gaze fixed on the road ahead, he gradually reduced his speed, but carried on driving. If he stopped, the oncoming cars would crash into them.

The connection with Farah appeared to be broken. The noise from the speakers was drowned out by the leaden drops that beat out a deafening crescendo on the car roof.

35

Dimitri had crawled inside the Touareg. The blood that seeped from the wound in his shoulder now covered his entire upper body. It felt as if he had a high fever. Sweat gushed out of his pores. Sharp pains shot through his torso and his head was throbbing so badly he thought it might burst at the temples. Everything he looked at was shrouded in a woolly fog and the tiniest movement, like turning the ignition, caused him almost unbearable pain.

Relying on his instincts, he focused on the narrow, winding road ahead, hoping to end up at the motorway approach.

He had trouble seeing and narrowly missed a tree, but with the Touareg's windscreen wipers sweeping back and forth he finally arrived at a paved road that took him across a wide concrete bridge from where, to his right, he caught a glimpse of the motorway.

The motorway was a pandemonium of honking cars and blinding headlights that appeared to be heading straight towards him through the rain. Driven by pain, Dimitri pressed down on the accelerator as hard as he could.

Along with the increase in speed and the adrenalin coursing through his veins, his thoughts returned. He'd explain to Uncle Arseni what had happened. That he'd made it. And that's when he saw the bright light looming up in front of him. As if he'd driven through a tunnel and had now reached the other side, where everything was overwhelmingly, blindingly white.

36

The MICU seemed to have vanished from the earth. Even the coordination centre couldn't reach the unit. All the lines were dead. Mobiles weren't answered. But thanks to the vehicle-tracking system aboard, the ambulance could be located. The MICU was driving on the A9 towards Schiphol.

Marouan pushed the Corolla as hard as he could. Within minutes, they shot on to the A9. Bright bolts of electricity sparked in the night sky. The accumulating mass of heavy clouds above them finally broke open. Once they had the MICU in sight, an incredible downpour flooded the ring road in seconds.

Marouan could just make out a large tanker in front of the MICU suddenly hitting its brakes while trying to pass another vehicle on the right. He heard the impact of a collision and immediately saw a black four-wheel drive sail over the railing. On the other side of the motorway, it plunged into oncoming traffic, and landed on top of a taxi.

The tanker jackknifed and in a sea of sparks smashed through the railing, headed directly for the middle pillar of the flyover. Marouan hit the brakes hard, skidded on to the hard shoulder on the right and shouted at Calvino to duck.

Seconds later he heard the immense crash of the tanker hitting the pillar, immediately followed by the explosion.

When Marouan sat up and looked around, it seemed like a vengeful God had chosen to commence Judgement Day on the Amsterdam ring road.

37

In the oncoming lane of the dual carriageway, Paul saw a large tanker in the process of overtaking another vehicle suddenly start flashing its lights while frantically honking its horn.

Across the barrier on the left, a black Touareg going the wrong way appeared from under the flyover and drove straight at the tanker. Behind the tanker, the blue lights of a large ambulance could be seen.

Paul heard the booming crash as the Touareg hit the tanker head on and was catapulted across the barrier. The tanker began zigzagging as it drove towards the flyover in a sea of sparks. It ploughed into the central pillar.

An explosion followed seconds later.

In the next few minutes, Paul could barely move, but saw everything in crystal-clear detail: the flames shooting out of the tanker, the cars colliding, the passengers crawling out in a daze or staring in shock through their shattered windows while the rain continued to pelt the motorway and everything on it.

He saw it all without hearing the sounds that went with it, as if he was under a glass bell jar. He felt comfortably numb, so he could process everything without panicking. And so he calmly touched the bloodied head of his uncle who was lying unconscious beside him amidst shards of glass. Paul leaned over to see if he was still breathing, undid the seatbelt and checked his pulse.

When Edward opened his eyes, he gazed at Paul with a distant look. Unable to understand what he was trying to say, Paul put his finger on Edwards's lips and spoke in his ear.

'Don't move, Ed, until the ambulance gets here.'

That's when he became aware of his own body, of his ragged breathing, and felt a rush of panic. Everything that had happened right before the accident came back in flashes.

He remembered the downpour and seeing Sandrine's taxi passing by as the first lightning struck. And then: the black Touareg flying through the air and landing on top of the taxi.

Suddenly his hearing returned.

Paul opened the car door and ran.

38

The force of the explosion shattered the MICU's windscreen just after Harold ducked down under his wheel. He saw the flying shards of glass hitting the man beside him in the face, while the pressure of the explosion threw him against the metal rear partition of the cab. The man who'd held him at gunpoint for the past few minutes, demanding that the MICU be driven to Schiphol Airport, was out cold.

Harold immediately grabbed the gun. He yelled into the intercom microphone that the situation was under control again and he steered the MICU backwards on to the hard shoulder, but during that manoeuvre the man with the face peppered with glass began to come to. Harold left the MICU idling, while holding the gun aimed at him.

'Out!' Harold shouted above the noise.

The man stared hard at Harold. 'You, don't shoot,' he said, which sounded less like an observation than an order.

'You, don't shoot!'

Harold felt the man's iron grip around his hand and dropped the gun. Immediately after, a fist slammed into his face, throwing him against the door. The man spat Russian expletives at him and kicked him out of the cab.

He couldn't have been unconscious on the wet tarmac for more than a couple of seconds, but when he opened his eyes he saw the man aiming the barrel of the gun at him.

Harold heard the shot.

He was amazed that dying was so quick and easy.

39

As the torrential rain beat down harder and harder on the car roof, Farah took the first available exit. She decided to park at a carpool location near the flyover until the storm had passed.

In the distance she heard the warning signals of a heavy lorry. Lightning appeared to strike close by the flyover, followed by a fearsome screeching noise like that of a crashing plane. Instinctively she ducked down.

The terrible explosion seemed to bathe everything in broad daylight for a moment.

When she raised her head again she saw towering flames shooting through the rain. She got out of the car and, trembling all over, began walking. With each step closer to the flyover, she could feel the searing heat of the fire and the smell of burning oil. The flames came from a tanker, which had just rammed the central pillar of the flyover.

All hell had broken loose. A black SUV looked like it had plunged from a great height. Only metres away, a taxi had rolled over and landed diagonally on the hard shoulder. The driver of a large ambulance fell out of his vehicle.

She watched it all, cemented to the spot, until she felt the first tremor ripple through the concrete. The flyover shuddered, shook and appeared to collapse on to the motorway.

In the other lane she saw a man with a bandaged face running towards the collapsing flyover as though wishing to be buried underneath. She yelled at him, but he didn't hear her.

40

Paul was oblivious to any obstacles. As he ran underneath, he didn't even realize that part of the flyover was crashing down around him. His fear was gone. His whole being was focused on the task at hand.

The taxi's wheels were spinning in the air. He knelt down in front of one of the windows and, still panting, forced himself to look inside. He saw the mangled body of the man at the wheel.

Then he saw Sandrine. Strapped in her seatbelt, she was dangling from the back seat upside-down and unconscious. As Paul crawled in through the shattered window, shards of glass lacerated his body.

He heard someone yelling something unintelligible. A hand stuck an object through a crushed door. Paul instinctively reached for what the hand was offering him. It was the handle of an opened pocket knife.

He began to cut through the seatbelt holding Sandrine, but the knife felt blunt and he failed to get a grip on the material.

Sandrine's face lit up fiery red when the Touareg's petrol tank exploded and caught fire. Small blue flames raced along a trail of leaked petrol, greedily seeking their next target, and reached the taxi within seconds.

That's when the seatbelt ripped in two.

Sandrine's head landed on Paul's stomach. Just then someone began pulling at his legs to get him out. With Sandrine on top of him, it was impossible. The glass cut deeper into his body. Paul howled in pain. He tried to straighten out Sandrine's body on top of his, so the unconscious woman could be slid out over him.

'The woman first!' he yelled. 'The woman first!'

Her head lay on his chest when he felt her slowly sliding away, out of the car. As Sandrine slid away, so too did his strength. There was no more searing heat, no more dust that made breathing all but impossible, no more people to be rescued. Only a calm, quiet darkness.

41

Marouan sprung out of the Corolla and ran to the MICU, which was about a hundred metres from the flyover – among the other cars with their shattered windows and injured passengers – standing diagonally in the road. The first thing he saw was the driver being thrown from the ambulance and landing dazed on the ground. Then Marouan thought his eyes were deceiving him: Kovalev's looming shape appeared in the doorway of the vehicle. He was holding a gun.

Marouan didn't believe in mirages. He immediately knew that this was what he'd always been waiting for.

A way out of all his misery.

His entire life seemed to come together in this single moment. All his suffered defeats and humiliations fused in his body like atoms in a nuclear reactor. Clogged arteries opened wide to let his seething hatred gush through; all his muscles were fired up from years of pent-up resentment.

Marouan was about to free himself from his chains by the simple act of pulling the trigger. He pointed his Walther P5 at the right side of Kovalev's chest and fired. The impact of the bullet threw Kovalev on to the tarmac like a rag doll. He no longer moved.

42

From the flyover Farah saw how the man with the bandaged head re-emerged from the collapsing concrete on the other side and carried on running. Then, above all the other noise, she heard a gunshot, a sharp cymbal crash amidst the infernal din.

On the far side of the lane she saw Detective Diba with a gun in his hand, leaning over the motionless body of a man. The driver she'd seen tumbling out of the ambulance earlier scrambled to his feet. There was a quick exchange of words between the two. Diba gestured for the driver to get out of the way. A moment later, the ambulance turned on to the hard shoulder and drove off in the opposite direction, weaving its way through the stranded cars.

That's when Farah spotted Joshua. He was walking on the motorway in a daze. She shouted his name and gesticulated wildly with both arms, but he neither saw nor heard her.

The running man had now reached a taxi and kneeled down to peer inside. He must have seen something or someone, because he frantically tried to squeeze into the wreckage.

Farah didn't want to just stand there and watch. She wanted to help. She hurried back to her car, drove a couple of hundred metres away from the flyover and made a U-turn.

Keeping the clutch depressed, she put one foot firmly on the brake and pushed the other down hard on the gas. The Carrera's tachometer was going crazy. Then she released the clutch.

The concrete construction she was driving towards at more than 100 kilometres per hour in less than ten seconds began to crumble and fall away on to the tanker.

And as the Carrera sped across the middle of the flyover at 150 kilometres per hour, the road completely collapsed.

43

As Marouan watched the MICU pull away, Calvino stumbled into view. He didn't seem able to grasp the full extent of this apocalypse. Marouan shouted into his police radio for emergency assistance. Meanwhile, he stared at Kovalev, the man who had facilitated his gambling addiction for years in return for 'mutual' services, lying there lifeless, no longer a threat to him. Marouan had never thought shooting somebody would give him so much pleasure. With that one shot he'd not only repaid his debt and purged his conscience, but it seemed like life had taken on an entirely new perspective in a single blink. It felt like new blood was rushing through his veins.

The intensity of every minute sound, both near and far, penetrated his being. With crystal clarity, he took in each and every movement in the chaos around him. Like the sound of boots running on the tarmac and the image of a man with a bandaged head who was crawling into a taxi lying upside down on the other side of the road.

Marouan shouted commands to Calvino and then as quickly as he could climbed over the double barrier to the other side of the motorway. In the wreck of the Touareg, he saw the badly mutilated driver. The metal was folded around him, infused with the smell of spilled petrol. There was no escape possible. The leaking fuel streamed in a thin trail towards the taxi. Marouan followed the trail, crouched and discovered the silhouette of a woman, trapped by her seatbelt, hanging upside down in the back, while the man with the bandaged head tried everything he could to free her. Marouan took out his pocket knife and holding the blade, offered it to him through the shattered window. It was pulled from his hand so hard that the knife cut into his palm. With a cry of pain, he pulled his bloodied hand back.

Kneeling on the wet tarmac, he tried to keep track of what was happening inside the taxi. He saw the woman, finally freed from her seatbelt, fall on top of the man. He ran to the other side of the taxi to help her out. He stuck his arms inside, and badly cut his other hand as he tried to protect the woman's head from the shards still stuck in the window groove. A vessel was severed, causing blood to spurt everywhere and mix with the rain.

Marouan took the woman in his arms, lifted her up and looked around, searching for help. But all he saw were panicked people running all over the motorway.

44

The Carrera had flown across the gaping hole in the middle of the collapsing flyover. On the other side Farah raced down the ramp, zigzagging among the stranded cars to get to the taxi. Why? She couldn't really say. All she knew is that she had to do it.

When she got to the taxi, she was stunned to see Detective Diba with a seriously injured woman in his arms. She braked, jumped out, ran around the Carerra, yanked open the passenger door, flipped the seat forwards, threw the boxes out and helped Diba gently place the woman on the back seat.

Then she followed Diba to the taxi which had large blue flames dancing around its frame.

She and Diba each began tugging at one of the man's feet, but failed to get him moving. Meanwhile the taxi caught fire, bringing with it the risk of imminent explosion. Farah caught a singeing smell and pulled at the foot again with all her might. And then he suddenly emerged from the distorted doorway like a lugubrious newborn, looking into his saviours' faces, bewildered.

For a moment everything was blurred, the only focus was that of his eyes on hers.

'Farah?!'

She stared back.

'It's me, Paul.'

She was still speechless. He grabbed hold of her and demanded to know: 'Where is she?'

Diba helped him up and together they hobbled over to the Carrera. Impatiently, he directed Farah to the driver's seat and slapped the roof. 'Don't wait for an ambulance. Head straight to the WMC!'

Farah weaved her way around the stranded cars. The man beside her leaned over his backrest to the woman in the back of the Carrera and took her hand.

Only then did she realize who was sitting next to her. She yelled above the din.

'Paul Chapelle!'

On his distorted face she saw a smile she hadn't seen in thirty years, but would recognize anywhere.

Before long, the contours of the WMC appeared above the landscape. Fire engines and ambulances sped past them in the oncoming lane.

Farah struggled to breathe. *Concentrate. Focus on your breathing. Calm down now.*

Less than three minutes later she pulled up outside the Emergency Department and helped Paul lift the woman out of the car. Then she ran inside, where she found doctors and nurses getting ready for the imminent deluge of injured people. They looked up as a limping and bleeding Paul carried in the unconscious woman.

45

Diba had shouted at him to stay with the body of the man who'd been downed. Before Joshua was fully aware of what was going on, he saw his overweight partner jump the barrier as light as a deer and run to the overturned taxi on the other side of the road.

A shattered Joshua looked around. There was nothing that could've prepared him for such a disaster. Compared to this inferno, the panic during the fire in the hospital was a calm prelude. And it was not even the soaring flames, the wounded crawling from their cars, the desperate yelling for help, the collapsing flyover and the raging panic that upset him. It was the complete absence of what gives life meaning, what makes you get up every morning and face another day.

In the midst of this futility, his staggeringly spry partner had ordered him to keep watch over a corpse? As if there weren't any living beings who could better use his help right now. He looked at the man who'd been shot and was surprised by the absence of blood from the gunshot wound. Only his face was injured by splintered glass. When he leaned over him, he got the shock of a lifetime.

The dead man had opened his eyes and was now staring right at him.

PART FOUR
Fallen

The mist around him was beginning to dissolve. He was surprised to find that he could walk again and felt curiously happy and relieved. As if nothing had happened. He was back in the orphanage courtyard, with boys excitedly running away to hide from him. Two men entered the courtyard. They weren't an uncommon sight here. Whenever they came they'd talk to some of the boys and occasionally take one with them. That boy would be going to new parents, it was said, making everybody envious.

Now the men were back. They were looking around and talking. Then they pointed to him. The orphanage director approached him. 'Go and collect your things, Sekandar, you're leaving.' He wanted to know where he was going, but the director didn't answer his question. He only repeated what he'd just said. 'Collect your things, Sekandar.'

When he said goodbye, the director had tears in his eyes. He didn't like it. He couldn't stand men who cried. He was only a boy, yet he wasn't crying, was he?

The two men took him in a car with a back seat made of smooth black leather and cold air blowing about constantly. When the car started moving he felt as if he was taking off. He heard a woman singing, her voice coming from all possible corners of the car, while the men talked softly over it and patted him on the head. One of them kept looking and smiling at him, telling him he was a handsome boy.

He'd been too afraid to ask where they were going. It would have been impolite and at the orphanage they'd taught him never to be impolite to grown-ups if somebody came for him.

The car journey took a very long time and when they finally arrived at the big house, the sun was already setting. They drove through a gate that was guarded by two men who immediately closed it again. Then he was given food. And since he'd gone without meat for the longest time, he ate till his tummy ached.

It struck him that there was no woman in the house and he didn't have the nerve to ask if he'd be living here from now on. He hoped not, because as beautiful as the house was, it felt like a prison. He wasn't allowed out.

Then one of the men told him to come along. He had to take off his clothes and stand under the water, which he refused to do. That was the first time he was hit. The blow hurt a lot, because the big ring on the man's fat finger struck his forehead. When he finally stood under the shower, the man who'd hit him started removing his clothes too. He came and stood beside him and rubbed him with soap. As he felt the man's hands move over his body, his mind separated from his body and flew away from where he was standing. Away from the shame and fear.

The city looked so dark from above. He was afraid to land anywhere, preferring instead to hover high in the sky. But a gust of wind blew him off-balance, his wings stopped working and he was pulled down, back into that tiled prison cell.

Something strange had happened to the man who'd joined him under the water. His eyes were gleaming as he towelled him dry, and when he rubbed him with oil that smelled of coconut he told him, in a voice that was gentler than before, that he was a sweet boy, a good boy.

Then the man showed him his new clothes.

They were women's clothes. He'd seen them in films on television in which dancing women with big smiles and really high voices sang about love, and made eyes at men who'd brushed their pearly whites so they could smile back nicely. Now he was being transformed into one of those women, and not just because of the clothing. The man also blackened his eyes, put red lipstick on his mouth and draped him in jewellery with bells.

'You're a girl now, a beautiful little dancer. Look how beautiful you are,' the man said, holding up a mirror.

I

Sasha Kovalev was lying on the wet tarmac. *Diva's* shot had hit his bullet-proof vest with such an unexpected force that this was his second knockout in one night. He opened his eyes. An unfamiliar man was hanging over him with his gun drawn. A jumble of sounds entered his head. While the sharp pain of splintered glass seared his face, in his mind he saw the black Touareg shooting by again and the jackknifing tanker ramming the flyover pillar. The explosion blew him against the partition of the ambulance. That had been his first knockout in years.

His breath caught in his throat. The man with the gun was yelling at him in Dutch. A siren blared in his ears, brakes were screeching. Two policemen pulled him to his feet, slapped on handcuffs and frisked him. Suddenly Diva was standing in front of him again. With bleeding hands this time. And with far too big a mouth, given the pathetic figure he was.

'Who do you think you are, goddammit? Fucking Rasputin or what?'

Although it had stopped raining, the sky above was still pitch black. An army of firefighters was spraying foam at the jack-knifed tanker. The air was teeming with trauma helicopters.

Diva gave Sasha a hard shove into the police van, deliberately knocking his head against the doorframe. Sasha clenched his teeth to cope with the searing pain in his face, while fighting the tightness in his chest and the growing anger at his own recklessness. An ashen-faced Diva, with a worryingly blank look on his face, sat down beside him clutching a cocked Walther P5 in his bloody hands. The barrel was aimed at Sasha's right temple. A tiny bump in the road and a bullet would 'accidentally' burrow itself in Sasha's cortex. The policemen objected to the weapon, leading to a sharp exchange of words between them and Diva. Thankfully the gun disappeared back in its holster.

Sasha looked out across the poorly lit, soaking wet roads. The cogs in his head were whirring feverishly. He should have left the boy to his own devices. Bikram had been right. He should never have allowed himself to be guided by something as woolly as emotion. They'd landed him in this mess, in the back seat of an erratically accelerating police car next to a detective who'd been his lapdog for years but was now throwing his weight about like a Doberman.

At the Emergency Department, a doctor injected him with a painkiller. His face now felt like a tightly stretched pig's bladder, fingers sliding across, scalpels making delicate incisions and pincers removing minuscule glass shards. When he exited, Sasha caught his reflection in a glass door and winced in pain.

The interrogation room at the police station was as bare and solid as the interior of a bunker. He'd been handcuffed to his seat. It took ages for his interrogators to arrive and in the meantime the painkillers were wearing off.

The Indian medics hired by Bikram wouldn't wait for the MICU forever. By now the ambulance flight from Goa must have left the hangar and taken off from Schiphol empty. If everything had gone to plan, he'd be soaring somewhere over Europe now, brushing his hand over the boy's forehead and saying a few reassuring words.

'It's all over now. You're safe.'

At that thought, his body shuddered with anger again. The handcuffs rattled, the table shook. Goa was further away than ever.

After some time, the man who'd been watching him when he'd come around on the tarmac walked in. Besides a substantial dose of fatigue, his young face also betrayed a strong sense of purpose. He was followed by Diva, with a face like a death mask and both hands bandaged. It looked like he was wearing mittens at the height of summer. Despite everything

424

that had happened, Sasha couldn't help but smile at this observation.

The young detective switched the recording device on, spoke a few words of Dutch into the microphone, sat opposite Sasha and introduced himself in English.

'Italian?' Sasha asked.

Calvino ignored the question and nodded at Diva who'd taken a seat in a corner with his death mask and mittens.

Sasha looked over at Diva, saw the fury in his eyes and grinned. Diva must bitterly regret not aiming at his head.

'You were read your rights during your arrest,' Calvino said.

'Could be,' Sasha replied. 'But I don't understand Dutch.'

'We appointed you a lawyer.'

'Who I refused.'

'I've informed the Public Prosecutor.'

'Excellent.'

'He's given me permission to question you.'

'Then, by all means, begin,' Sasha said, still with a smirk.

'Mr Kovalev, you are accused of violent abduction and attempted murder. As a suspect, you're under no obligation to answer. Is that clear?'

Sasha nodded. He liked this goombah. The guy had flair.

'Excellent, Mr Kovalev,' Calvino said, to signal he was kicking off properly now. 'Sorry for the delay. We were waiting for the initial forensic results from the assault on a policeman at the Waterland Medical Centre. It turns out the bullet isn't from the weapon you were carrying.'

Sasha looked from Calvino to Diva, who avoided his gaze. That's when he realized something must have gone wrong. That pimply debutant from Moscow must have been at the hospital, but apparently the trap hadn't snapped shut in time and he got away. Diva had messed up. What else was new?

'I don't know about any policeman. I never set foot in that hospital.'

'You deny any involvement in the assault or the arson in the ICU?'

425

'Arson? Detective, I'm not a pyromaniac and certainly not a cop killer. I deny any direct involvement.'

'Any *direct* involvement?'

'That's what I said.'

'What about indirect?'

Sasha glanced at Diva again, who was shifting nervously in his seat.

'Several parties are interested in the boy, Mr Calvino.'

'You mean besides you and me?'

'That's right. And they don't all have the best intentions.'

'But you do?'

'I'll happily explain it to you, Detective Calvino, provided you get me a glass of water and some painkillers. It's a long story.'

Calvino looked at Diva, who got up agonizingly slowly and shuffled out of the room like a pensioner. When he returned a little later, it was without water of course. The sheep-fucker liked a practical joke. Meanwhile, Detective Calvino was pacing the room. He wasn't a brilliant interrogator, or at least he was playing the part. In that case he was a fine actor.

'To be honest, I don't mind a bit of silence, Mr Kovalev,' Calvino stated. 'When others are silent, it gives me space to think. And then, I think: It's the boy. You're only interested in the boy. In the boy and nothing else. And then I think, isn't that great? Isn't that a remarkable coincidence?' Calvino stood still and leaned towards Sasha. 'Because we're interested in him too.'

'So we have mutual interests,' Sasha said, grinning.

A policeman walked in with a bottle of water and a blister pack of tablets, which he handed to Calvino. Calvino poured the water into a plastic cup, pressed an effervescent tablet from the strip, tossed it in and pushed it all over to Sasha, who had just enough slack in his handcuffs to pick up the cup and pour its contents down his throat.

'Tell me, Mr Kovalev, when did you first see him, the boy?'

Heaving a sigh of relief, Sasha put the cup back on the table. Water trickled down his chin. He could smell the forest air when he thought back to the moment, three days ago now. It had been a clear night, the moon bright, with the heat of the day lingering among the trees. A young, Middle-Eastern-looking girl got out of the station wagon. She looked Sasha straight in the eyes and at that moment he felt something deep within break, something that could never be repaired again. Never before had a child's eyes had such an impact on him. It was like he'd looked deep inside his own soul.

'I first saw him a few days ago.'

'Where?'

'In the Amsterdamse Bos, near the old villa.'

'What were you doing there?'

'Arranging a meeting.'

'A meeting between whom?'

'Between the child and . . . someone else. The villa was the meeting place.'

'Someone else, you say? And who might this someone else be?'

'A man in a custom-made suit, too heavy for his age, no doubt a husband and father. A man of stature who thinks he's above the law. A power-hungry man without morals.'

'The mind boggles, Mr Kovalev. I ask you about the identity of the man who was supposed to be meeting the boy and you quote *Reader's Digest* to me.'

'Because I'm trying to explain something to you, detective. We're talking about a man who's so power hungry that he's crossed boundaries that you and I didn't even know existed. A man who's discovered power as the ultimate form of pleasure. There's no greater pleasure for this man than having control over the life of a helpless child.'

There was a sinister silence in the interrogation room.

'Who is he?' Calvino asked in a hoarse voice.

'Before I tell you that, I'd prefer to tell you about what took place before the meeting, if you don't mind.'

Calvino looked astonished, rubbed his face and then snarled at him.

'I've got a better idea. Why don't we schedule a break, take a holiday. Saunter along a boulevard, lounge on the beach, ponder our sins and when we've all had a good rest and got ourselves a nice suntan, filled our bellies with good food and emptied all the wine cellars, we'll get back to this.' Meanwhile, he pulled photos out of a folder and slammed them one by one on the table. 'Or we review the chronology of events,' he said hoarsely. 'I suspect we'll get some names that way.'

Sasha looked at the photos. They showed numbered locations in and around the villa, a close-up of a bloodstained earring and a child's slipper partially concealed by undergrowth.

'Shots were fired both inside and outside the villa,' Calvino said. 'Bullet casings, blood and drag marks were found at both locations. Can you tell me what happened, or is that something else you want to get back to later? After the summer recess?'

Sasha stared stoically at Calvino and relived the moment he'd followed the boy and his guard into the villa. With his gun drawn but without a plan. To begin with, everything had gone fairly smoothly. He'd screwed on the silencer, waited until the boy was out of his field of fire and then pulled the trigger.

'I went inside, detective, and I eliminated the first man.'

'And then what?'

'Then I took the boy outside.'

'What went wrong?'

'Everything. I used my silencer, but the man outside must have heard something. He was waiting for me. The bullet grazed my chest.'

'You weren't wearing a bullet-proof vest, for a change?'

Sasha sighed. The sarcasm was too much for him right now.

'What about the boy?'

'He ran into the woods. I told him to.'

'And this all happened before the man, whose identity you still won't reveal, arrived on the scene, I presume?'

'During the altercation I saw his car approaching. He made a U-turn at once. He was gone by the time I'd taken out the second guy. That's when I heard the bang.' Sasha fell silent and took a few deep breaths. 'It doesn't matter how small or skinny a body is, even hitting a hare on a road produces a hell of a lot of noise. I knew it was the boy.'

'Did you go and check?'

'I walked into the woods, down the hill, towards the road. I must have been halfway when I heard another car brake, followed by a dull thud. As I approached the road, I saw a woman frantically yelling into her mobile phone as she got out of the car she'd crashed into a tree. The boy lay motionless on the road.'

'Why didn't you go to him?'

'I thought he was dead.'

Calvino looked at him, stunned. 'What happened next?'

Sasha was silent. He was searching for words to describe the moment, but none came. There were probably no words for what he'd felt seeing the boy lying there.

'Let me help you,' Calvino said, and Sasha saw that the detective meant it this time. 'There was a dead man inside the villa, a dead man outside, and now there was a dead child on the road as well. You knew that before long there'd be police cars and an ambulance on the scene. All you managed to do within that short space of time was eradicate as many traces as possible in and around the villa. Am I warm?'

Sasha nodded. He'd dragged both men into the station wagon, had driven it to the clearing, unscrewed the number plates, doused the car in a jerry can of petrol and set it alight. The fire-spitting station wagon had illuminated the first part of his route back.

A second series of photos followed, which Calvino slapped on the table like before. Sasha saw the burnt-out shell of the station wagon. And then the pictures from the local cabinet of horrors: two charred corpses on the pathologist's chrome slab.

'Based on the casings found outside the villa, the autopsy has established a match with the calibre bullet in the sternum of the one of the bodies from the burnt-out station wagon.'

'Impressive job, detective.'

'But the circle isn't complete until we compare the casings with the type of gun you were carrying this evening.'

Sasha couldn't help it; he tried to applaud with his cuffed hands.

Calvino regarded him impassively. 'But there's one thing I still don't get, Mr Kovalev. To what in God's name do I owe your willing cooperation?'

Sasha produced a faint smile. 'I tried to save a child and in the process killed two men to whom a human life means nothing more than a stack of banknotes. What's the point of keeping that a secret?'

'Sure,' Calvino said. 'Just like you don't need to keep the identity of the man the boy was intended for a secret.'

'As I said, I'm happy to give it to you. But I think we'd better formalize our mutual interests first.'

'I didn't realize we had any.'

'More than you think. I don't just have one name for you, I have several. And I've got information. Valuable information.'

'How valuable?'

'By Dutch standards, enough to bring down your government. By international standards, enough to raise serious questions about a billion-dollar empire. So, valuable enough, I should think.'

'How do I know you're not bluffing?' Calvino asked.

'The organization I work for must know I'm here by now, and no doubt they'll be aware of the reason. Needless to say, they won't be pleased with my actions. Especially not when they realize I'm thinking of airing some of their dirty laundry. Since tonight, I'm living on borrowed time, Detective Calvino. I'm not exactly in a position to bluff.'

'What do you want in return for all this info?'

'An international witness protection programme.'

For the first time, Diva, still sitting in the corner, uttered a guttural sound – like a fuse being blown.

'Mr Kovalev,' Calvino said, outwardly unmoved, 'even if we managed to get you into such a programme, you're still our suspect, and you still have to be tried and punished for your crimes.'

'I don't doubt it,' Sasha said. 'But when the Public Prosecutor hears what I've got to say, his demands will drop even faster than the price of the euro.'

'If your information is that valuable, Mr Kovalev, you're going to have to come up with more than you just gave me. You see, I've got to convince certain people of the need to offer you witness protection. I can only do that if I've got concrete information, not a vague promise you can bring down our government. Plenty of people in this country think they can do the same.'

'I can tell you who my boss is and how corrupt his global empire is.'

'So which boss and which company are we talking about, Mr Kovalev?'

'Valentin Lavrov, CEO of AtlasNet.'

'Go on.'

'I can tell you which Dutch businessmen and politicians have been bribed by my boss.'

'Names, please.'

'Armin Lazonder.'

'Explain.'

'The New Golden Age Project is a large-scale money-laundering scheme operated by Lavrov in exchange for concessions to build Europe's largest gas storage facility. Nicolas Anglade stumbled across it during his investigation and now he's dead.'

'Anglade killed himself.'

'That's what we've all read in the paper and seen on television, sure. But the thing about killing yourself, as the words suggest, is you have a big hand in it. In Anglade's case, it was mostly others who were involved.'

'And you've got proof of that?'

'Of course I've got proof. And, by the way, I thought you wanted to know who the boy was intended for?'

'Who?' Calvino asked, beginning to run out of patience. 'Who was it?'

Sasha said the name.

Calvino looked at him as if he saw water burn.

2

Marouan had done his best to keep a low profile all through the interrogation. By exerting an immense amount of effort, he'd managed to restrain his anger. But his desire for revenge ran deep. He knew better, but couldn't stop wishing for a miracle: a sudden fit of madness that would incapacitate Kovalev for life, acute heart failure or a fatal epileptic seizure. And if all this wishful thinking didn't help, he would pin his last hope on the Hand of God. Because Marouan, a weak man who'd made an error of judgement, had failed to kill Kovalev on the motorway.

Then again, given the creative slant of Kovalev's 'open-hearted' story, there probably wasn't an inkling of hope. With his testimony, Kovalev had portrayed himself as a tireless crime-fighter. It was an epic tale verging on the heroic. *Criminal sees the light! Shoots down two human traffickers to rescue a defenceless child from their clutches.*

Besides, his story indicated he was willing to cooperate. He masterfully played his joker; revealed he was in possession of valuable information. The whole interrogation was nothing more than a crash course in 'how to kiss ass to get into witness protection'.

And Calvino fell for it hook, line and sinker.

Marouan was only a stone's throw away from being unmasked as the compulsive gambler he was. Thanks to years of financial support from top criminal Kovalev, he'd led a double life in which he'd deliberately misled his colleagues and superiors.

No way that was happening: not over his dead body!

'I've been paying close attention, Cal,' Marouan volunteered, after they'd stopped the recorder and gone out into the corridor to digest what they'd just heard. 'One of us needs to, right?'

'What are you talking about?'

'The bastard is fucking with us. Kovalev's lying through his teeth, trying to make us believe he's got important information to save his own skin. But he doesn't have anything. He's only pretending. Stalling for time.'

Calvino stared at him.

'Do you two know each other?'

'What do you mean?'

'The way you look at each other. And you talk about him like you've known him forever.'

'What are you getting at?'

'On the motorway tonight you immediately addressed him in English.'

'He's Russian, goddamn it.'

'How did you know that? Was he waving a Russian flag?'

'Did you hear what I just said? That man's fucking us where we breathe. And if my ears don't deceive me, he's already convinced you that your partner is a liar.'

'Why did you call him a "Fucking Rasputin"?'

'I aimed and fired. He should have stayed dead.'

There was an awkward silence. Joshua gave him a probing look.

'Why did you want him dead so badly?'

Marouan was shitting himself. He had to be careful about what he said to Calvino.

'You're twisting my words, Cal. Don't! I shot him in the chest. It happened in a split second.'

'We'll come back to this, okay?'

'Come back to what? We've got a guy in custody who tried to gun down an ambulance driver and you've been completely taken in by him. Let's talk about that!'

'Give me one good reason, Diba, just one, why this man isn't a valuable witness? Given what he's told us about the shooting at the villa, the station wagon: it all fits. Then there's also his connection to AtlasNet, as well as what he knows about Anglade's suicide. If it's all true, the Minister of Economic

Affairs will soon have to step down. And yes, Kovalev is still a suspect, but as far as I see it, also a key witness.'

'Do you hear yourself, Cal? "If it's all true." I'm telling you it isn't. It's a bullshit story. Told by a ruthless criminal who's totally taken with a small Afghan boy. What is this, a Disney film?'

'As soon as we get Tomasoa's approval, we'll hand our Russian friend over to the Special Witness Team. Whether he's talking crap or not.'

Calvino stomped off, stopped abruptly and turned.

'Do you want me to sort this out alone?'

'Go ahead. I'll stay here. I don't really trust the guy.'

'Whatever works for you.'

Joshua Calvino proceeded down the corridor. Marouan watched him go and then returned to the interrogation room, where he asked the policeman present to go get some coffee. Once the policeman had left, Marouan closed the door and went and stood across from Kovalev, who had a sinister look on his face.

'You shitting in your pants yet, Diva?'

'What do you mean?'

'Because of what's going to happen if I start spilling the beans? Or are you hoping I'll spare you? Is that it? Remind me why I should, given you tried to kill me?'

Marouan went to the table and leaned forward.

'Because I'm your only way out, that's why.'

Marouan reached into his pocket, took out the handcuff key and waved it in front of Kovalev's face, like an altar boy swinging an incense burner during High Mass.

'We'll make it look like a struggle.'

Kovalev stared. First in disbelief, but that disbelief quickly turned to anger.

'I was going to go away with the boy, remember? Vanish into thin air. Then you would've been rid of me. And vice versa. We were supposed to improvise, you and me. Our last performance. And the solo was yours. Did you forget that, asshole? You were going to shine again with that trigger-happy hitman from Moscow, who I offered up on a silver platter. But no, you let him get away! He shoots a cop and you let him get away!'

Marouan felt the blood draining from his face. He hurled the key into a corner and grasped the edge of the table. Kovalev raged on.

'I'll tell you what you are, Diva. You're a dog, a flee-ridden stray who doesn't recognize a bone when it's being tossed right at him. You thought you'd kill me. I'm going to make sure you're flushed through the sewer like the pile of shit you are. You disloyal mongrel!'

Marouan was amazed at the slowness with which he – despite his festering rage – approached Kovalev on the other side of the table. As he did so, he suddenly saw something in Kovalev's eyes that he'd never seen in all those years.

Fear.

Fear of death, to be exact.

Marouan saw that Kovalev knew all too well what was awaiting him in this locked interrogation room.

3

'What a mess,' said a visibly stressed Tomasoa as he sat down and nobly tried not to jump to his feet immediately. Calvino had never seen his boss so agitated.

'We're going to have to hand over the case to the National Crime Agency. They have a special team for at-risk witnesses. They'll do the follow-up interrogations. It's out of our hands.'

'But why can't we do it ourselves, chief?' Joshua could hardly contain his frustration.

'Did you hear me say that we can't? We're simply no longer allowed. Their team will thoroughly investigate everything Kovalev comes up with. Painstaking work that you and I aren't cut out for, believe me. Only once they've finished checking all the filth that our Russian friend spews up will they put a deal on the table. Until then we're on the sidelines watching. Not only good things come in threes, Calvino, also the bad ones. We almost lost a colleague, we let the perpetrator escape from the hospital, and now we have to hand over our suspect as a key witness. I've had better days.'

'There's probably more, chief,' Joshua said hesitantly.

'More misery, Calvino?'

'Something that's been bothering me for a while.'

'If this is about emotions, you're better off somewhere else. You know I'm not much of a shoulder to cry on.'

'I have a feeling that Diba knows him.'

'Who?'

'Kovalev. The way the two interact with each other without saying a word. They know each other. I'm sure.'

Tomasoa didn't reply. He stood up, slowly, much too slowly for him, and went to the window. He stood there, not moving a muscle, his hands in his pockets.

'Do you know what you're starting, Calvino?' he finally said.

'I think so.'

'And you're absolutely sure this isn't personal?'

'Of course it's personal, chief. I've admired the guy for years, always wanted to work with him. But somewhere something went wrong. And every day I see it getting worse. Tonight was the last straw. I'm sick and tired of covering for him.'

Tomasoa turned. Joshua saw the deep lines in his face, his almost leering frown.

'Facts, Calvino? Besides being disappointed in your partner, do you have any facts?'

'Diba knocked on my door late last night and said he knew with one hundred per cent certainty that an attack on the boy was imminent. When he wouldn't tell me who'd given him the info, I knew something was seriously wrong. After all, why keep your source a secret from your partner? During Kovalev's interrogation I suddenly got my answer. Oddly enough, without even asking.'

Tomasoa listened without interrupting and gestured with a simple hand motion for Joshua to continue.

'After Kovalev told me how he'd tried to save the boy's life at the villa, how he thought he was dead at first, but because of all the publicity knew he was still alive – that's when I knew. The media hype woke the sleeping dogs. Kovalev was the one who tried to protect the boy from those dogs. He tipped Diba off about the attack.'

All of Tomasoa's anxiety seemed to disappear, replaced by a fatalism that now weighed him down. He sunk deep into his chair.

'Once I connected the dots,' Joshua said, 'I suddenly had the answer to how the hell Kovalev knew about the secret MICU transport.'

'Fine,' Tomasoa muttered. 'If you're right, we have a mole in our corps. It seems sensible for you to go back to the interrogation room and question Kovalev further about this. And tell Diba I want to see him.'

Joshua hesitated.

'Could you leave me out of this for now, chief?'

Tomasoa nodded.

With the weight of the world on his shoulders, Joshua walked back through the canteen where, momentarily abandoning his routine, he pushed the espresso button on the coffee machine. He took a sip, then immediately dropped the cup into the rubbish bin.

As he approached the interrogation room, he heard an agitated man talking into a police radio. A policeman came out of the room. His face was drained of all colour. Joshua went inside. Diba's white-bandaged hands were covered with the blood seeping from Kovalev's bandaged head into a big red puddle on the table.

'I tried to stop him,' stammered Diba. 'He started banging his head, just like that. I tried to stop him . . .'

Joshua put two fingers against Kovalev's carotid artery and thought he felt a faint pulse.

When he looked up, Diba was gone.

4

Farah was standing on the deserted promenade deck of a hideous construction on posts that stretched far out into the sea. She was aware of ominous dark seawater calmly splashing against the stone pillars metres below her.

With every move she'd made since the pile-up on the ring road, it felt as if gravity had begun to tug harder at her. Even her thoughts were more sluggish than usual. But it wasn't just the accident and its aftermath that were to blame. It was everything that had happened in the past few days.

Only an hour ago, she'd been in the Emergency Department, sitting at the head of Paul's bed while a nurse removed the glass shards from his back, disinfected the wounds and stitched them up again. Paul, who was lying on his stomach, was putting a brave face on it while he asked Farah non-stop questions about her meeting with Lavrov and told her with something akin to pride how he'd come by his other injuries in Ponte City. Boys will be boys. Then she'd accompanied him to the ward where Edward was being treated for airway complications and an irregular heartbeat. Lung X-rays and an ECG had been made, but he'd have to spend the night in hospital for observation.

Farah had gone to the ICU as soon as she could, totally unprepared for what she was about to hear. Mariska filled her in. The fire, the assault, the shot policeman, the MICU transport. Apparently the boy had arrived safely at the children's ICU at the Maaspoort Hospital in Rotterdam.

That's when she received the phone call.

'Ms Hafez, the doctor said I should phone you.'

'What doctor?'

'Dr Bernson. It's about the boy from the hit-and-run.'

'What about him?'

'I know what's going on . . . what happened.'

'I'm all ears.'

'Not over the phone. That's impossible.' The man sounded worn out, angst-ridden.

'When can I speak to you then?' she asked.

So here she was. Late at night, gazing at the lights of the seaside resort Scheveningen from a deserted pier.

'Ms Hafez?'

Farah turned around and saw a man whose thin face she would have forgotten tomorrow. That's how nondescript he looked. In fact, everything about the man – his posture, appearance and clothes – exuded detachment, but not the kind people from well-to-do circles sometimes projected. This detachment was one of servility. The man now standing before her appeared to be made to linger on a rainy dyke in grey October weather without being noticed.

'I saw you on television,' he said with a voice that betrayed two packs of cigarettes a day. 'That was you, wasn't it, at the martial arts gala?'

'If you're referring to Carré, then yes, that was me.'

'Did you tell anyone you were meeting me?'

'My boss knows about it.'

'I don't want to draw attention to myself, you see. I just want to put things right. Nobody's ever had an inkling. Not even my wife.'

'What kind of inkling?'

'Of the double life I've led. For years.'

The man seemed neurotic. A miserable wretch who had nowhere to go to unburden his troubled mind.

'What kind of double life are you talking about?'

He didn't seem to hear her, too caught up in the story he needed to get off his chest.

'In both lives I've been loyal, you know. But there comes a point when you have to choose. If you don't choose, choices are made for you. I wish I'd made mine sooner. Now it's too late. Obedience is your greatest virtue. That's what my father used to say. That's how I was raised. With immense respect for authority. I always believed that people got their just desserts if they'd been obedient.'

'Not any more?'

'Faith keeps a man going, Ms Hafez. Start doubting and you're done for. I no longer believe in anything. Not after what happened to the boy.'

The man looked away from Farah, ashamed it seemed, and stared at the irregular pattern of the waves for a while without a word.

'I was always curious to know what lay beneath. Beneath the water, I mean. But I'm not a diver. I'm even too scared to go snorkelling. At home I've got a couple of aquariums. When my wife's in front of the telly, I look at what's happening underwater.'

His doleful, somewhat bloodshot eyes turned back to Farah. He pulled out a packet of Marlboro. 'Do you mind?' he asked. Farah shook her head. He coughed and flashed her an apologetic grin. 'The doctor told me to stop ages ago. But yeah, those choices again.' He blew out the smoke in a straight line.

'We all hide things, Ms Hafez. Because we're ashamed of them, or because they make us smaller. Or else we run away from them. Until they catch up with us.'

Farah scrutinized him. She wasn't scared; the man didn't seem to pose a threat. In fact, she felt a growing irritation at his grovelling banality. But she also knew that the greatest psychopaths were often the most unobtrusive types. Trapped in their parochial lives, they could only escape through heinous deeds that momentarily restored part of their lost identity. This man fit that description.

'You should know, Ms Hafez, that I acted under coercion. I didn't do it out of free will. But I don't want my wife to suffer as a result. I don't want anything to happen to her. I've got savings. There's money for her. I hope she'll forgive me for never telling her about my other life. But I fear she won't. That's not who she is.'

442

He fell silent again. Farah couldn't tell whether he was relishing his moment or stalling because he was too scared to say what he had to say.

'Are you religious?' he asked.

'I try to be,' Farah replied.

'You know there's nothing and that's why you want to believe in something,' the man said.

'You contacted me,' Farah said coldly. 'You wanted to tell me something. What is it you wanted to share with me?'

Some ten metres below, the waves were starting to beat harder against the pillars. The man was clutching the railing so tightly, it looked like he was afraid of falling.

'I've been driving him for three years now, my boss. When I first laid eyes on him, I thought he was that chancellor from Germany, what's his name again? Helmut Kohl. Tall, fat and used to ordering people around. The kind of man you think knows what's what, otherwise he wouldn't have such a high position. The kind of man you obey. I was sworn to secrecy. I know the rules of the game. Loyalty and confidentiality. It wasn't hard for me. Lombard was the kind of person who inspired it.'

'Are you talking about Finance Minister Lombard?'

'I was keen to be of service to him. To be more than just a driver who ferried him from A to B. Someone he could rely on. We were a good team, Lombard and I. But always with the necessary distance. Although you develop a personal bond, we never became friends. I didn't want to either. It would've only muddied the water.'

He lit a second cigarette and inhaled, perhaps trying to muster the courage to continue his story.

'The first time he called me late at night, he told me not to forget my promise. "Promise is debt," he said. I wondered why he was so emphatic about that. After all, I'd been driving him around for months. He wanted me to take him to a park. I remember the place, it had those trees with the enormous trailing branches, what do you call 'em?'

'Weeping willows,' Farah said, thinking to herself: how appropriate.

'He asked me to wait. A moment later he returned, with a boy, an Asian kid, young.'

'How young?'

'Very young. Definitely underage. "Just drive around," Lombard said, which I did, watching in my rear-view mirror what was happening, what they were doing.'

He took a couple of deep puffs and began to cough his lungs out. 'Sorry,' he said, after he'd caught his breath again. 'There are things I can tell you, Ms Hafez, things that happened in the back seat of that car you wouldn't think possible. It didn't always happen in the car, sometimes in hotels too, but never the expensive ones he usually stayed in, as you can imagine. It's as if he liked to slum it when he was messing with those boys.'

'Were you there the night the Afghan boy was hit?'

The man seemed to flinch at that. 'In the past year I've often had to drive Lombard to certain locations in the middle of nowhere. Usually a wooded area somewhere. Sometimes on an industrial estate, or the Port of Antwerp. Always in isolated places and always in the dead of night. I was told to wait somewhere, somewhere inconspicuous. On his return he always looked agitated. Once he had blood on his hands and clothes. He was crying. I didn't ask anything. I didn't want to know. I cleaned the car later that night.'

'What happened in the Amsterdamse Bos?'

'Just before we got to the villa, I saw a man running. I knew something was wrong. I heard shots. Lombard started panicking. With considerable difficulty, I managed to turn the car. Then, when we got back to the road . . .' He faltered.

Farah saw he was crying. But he didn't make a sound and looked like he was about to choke. She didn't intervene, but waited until he'd calmed down again.

'I keep seeing her fly across the bonnet.'

'It was a boy.'

'I didn't know that then. She appeared out of nowhere. Completely out of the blue. Like she had wings. I keep seeing her face before me. Her eyes as she hit the windscreen.'

He looked away, staring out across the sea like he was somewhere else entirely. Back in the woods, Farah suspected.

'It all happened in a flash. I slammed on the brakes, but it was too late. She bounced off the car like she was made of rubber. But the blow, the blow was *so* hard. It's stuck in my head. It won't budge. I can't sleep any more. Whenever I close my eyes, I see those eyes. Hear that thud again.'

His voice trembled. He clutched the railing even tighter, as if they were standing on a rolling ship about to sail into a storm. Farah felt no pity whatsoever.

'I wanted to stop, but Lombard yelled at me to carry on driving. He kept yelling. I stepped on the gas. It must have all happened in seconds.' He looked at her like a fearful child who'd run out of excuses.

'Strange to think how many thoughts you can have in the space of a few seconds, Ms Hafez. The thoughts I had, I can't remember them all . . .'

'You didn't stop,' Farah said icily.

'The whole time he was yelling at me from the back seat. "Faster, faster," he kept yelling.'

'You should take your story to the police.'

'I know,' the man said. 'I know. After seeing that doctor on television, I tried to get her phone number. I wanted to tell her. She cared so much.'

'Then why are you telling me?'

'For years I've kept quiet about the filthy goings-on right before my eyes. I colluded. I'm guilty. But I'm not the only one who's guilty, you know what I mean?'

'I think I do,' Farah said. 'That's why you should come with me.'

She saw him leaning forward, his hands folded over the railing. Like a believer who's just been to confession and is now saying the Lord's Prayer in penance.

5

He no longer cared if they found him. Marouan needed this shower to wash everything away. The temperature of the water as hot as possible, the jet as hard as could be: measures to remove every last bit of Kovalev. But there wasn't much time – the man's evil had permeated every pore of Marouan's body like nuclear particulates.

After rubbing himself dry, he sprinkled so much cologne on his body that he got dizzy. He pulled on clean underwear and a crisply ironed shirt. He chose his best suit, bought less than a month ago for a wedding celebration.

Remorse and regret are no more than the torment of the non-believer. The time that is given to us always comes to an end. And we are powerless to save ourselves from death. As it is God who creates all life and death.

He'd turned on hardly any lights and walked through the empty house in the darkness, touching everything: the sofa, the table, the chairs, even the lifeless fake marble kitchen counter, which still smelled of Dettol.

Everything he touched reminded him of another time, another life in which everything had made sense, where things had a purpose, where everything was connected, seemed to complement each other.

He looked out over the dark garden, withered bushes, the patio stones plagued by weeds. Every year he promised himself he'd tidy it up, and every year nothing came of his plans.

With barely a glance, he pulled a CD by Oum Kalthoum from a rickety shelving unit.

The Corolla stank of food, sweat and frustration. He started the car, gave the dark house one last look glance and pulled away. A few streets further, two police cars going in the opposite direction passed at high speed.

In the historic city centre, he found a cramped parking space along a canal and walked to the familiar cobblestone square.

To his own amazement, it merely took a smile to gain Marouan access behind the glass door. The girl looked at him as if she was seeing him for the first time. He took out his wallet, and as he put three one-hundred-euro notes on the table told her that she need not let anybody else in for the next hour.

'I can't,' she said, startled. 'It's too long.'

'Then tell me how long we have together,' Marouan said.

'Fifteen minutes, tops.'

He left the money and said, 'Then this is for fifteen minutes.'

She looked at him suspiciously. 'What do I have to do?'

Softly, from deep down in his throat, came Marouan's answer. 'Dance for me.'

She looked at the bills on the table.

'That's what you'll give me if I dance for you?'

He saw her hesitate.

'Here? Now?'

'Here. Now. For me.' He gave her the CD. 'To the most beautiful music I could find for you.'

With her back to him, she put the CD into the player and when she heard the first drawn-out note of the orchestra introducing the song *Alf Leila wa Leila*, a change came over her. She looked at him as if he'd just given her a gift.

She pulled her hair loose and tied a shawl around her hips to cover her legs. She stood before him. Her body moved to the rhythm of the *guembri*, the Arabic lute. And when Oum Kalthoum started to sing 'Let us live in the eyes of the night,' Marouan saw that she wasn't dancing for him alone. The other man in the room was the music.

He abandoned himself to her movements, as if he were being swept away by the sea, and he knew that this moment would never return, that it would pass and he would hardly be able to believe it had happened. It filled him with indescribable gratitude and deep sorrow at the same time.

She stretched out her arm in a wave that seemed to flow down to her hips, the undulating movements taking possession of her body, all of it coming together in her belly, where it rippled further.

The regal movement of her arm as she turned her head was followed by a veil of hair – like the echo of a gong being struck.

Oum Kalthoum's last words hung in the silent room.

'Let us live in the eyes of the night and tell the sun come over, come after one year, not before.'

She still had her eyes closed. Marouan couldn't find the right words to break the silence; he didn't want to see her open her eyes again and take the money off the table; it was perfect as it was. He slipped away without a sound.

6

Joshua Calvino didn't know what he was thinking or feeling, he just knew he had to put one foot in front of the other, keep on going. And so he dragged himself to his desk, where he collapsed on his chair like a boxer who'd taken a succession of punches in a much too long match.

Kovalev was whisked away in an ambulance. Diba had vanished in the chaos, and there were police cars en route to his home. The bell for the next round sounded. It was the phone on his desk.

'Joshua?' He recognized the voice of Ellen Mulder, the pathologist. 'I understand that you guys are working on the Afghan boy's case?'

'Right. Why?'

'A woman was brought in tonight. The doctor who was on television.'

Less than fifteen minutes later, Joshua was in the chilly tiled room staring down at the naked and violated body of Danielle Bernson. The hum of the air conditioning was drowned out by a pulsing throb. It took a while before he realized it was the pounding of his own heart reverberating against his eardrums. He'd entered the room without putting up his professional guard. Defenceless. Just as defenceless as Danielle must have felt when she stared into the barrel of the gun.

Ellen Mulder spoke to him in a quiet voice.

'The cause of death was a bullet to the back that went right through her left lung and aorta. A second bullet pierced her forehead, entered her brain and exited just above the second cervical.'

Joshua looked at her blankly.

449

'She was dead after the first shot,' Ellen said, as if to reassure him. Then she pointed at the wound on Danielle's forehead.

'The surrounding skin is scorched. The bullet came from close by.'

'From how far away?'

'It was up close and personal.'

Joshua could hardly suppress his desire to let out a barrage of obscenities.

'How well did you know her?' she asked.

Joshua was silent. He wanted to shake Danielle awake, but could only passively watch.

'We're not like the gods, Joshua. We all have our faults, we can't control everything,' she said. 'We don't know ourselves, hardly understand what others are capable of. To make all of this a bit more bearable, we alleviate our guilt by getting really good at something. Specializing. I do dead people. You do the guilty ones. But we often forget that reality is much more complex than what our specialty entails.'

He looked at her, pained.

'Don't beat yourself up. Concentrate on collecting the facts so you can catch the lowlife who did this.'

'What else can you tell me?' Joshua asked hoarsely.

With mathematical precision, her rubber-gloved fingertips touched the bullet wounds in Danielle's upper and lower body and came to rest on her right thigh.

'She was raped, Joshua.'

He turned and walked over to the window with the opaque plexiglass, somehow thinking there'd be a gust of fresh air to alleviate his nausea. Behind him Ellen covered Danielle Bernson's body again with the sheet. She pulled off her rubber gloves and dropped them in a bin. Then she walked towards him. He could feel her warm breath as she stood behind him. Then he started talking. And the words just poured out.

'You set certain boundaries for yourself when you start out in this profession. But over time those boundaries are crossed.

You don't notice it. Until you realize . . .' He turned around '. . . you've overextended yourself, and not for the first time.'

'There's always a way back, Joshua.'

'When will your report be finished?'

'I'm going to start straight away.'

'If I can get a copy tomorrow, I'd appreciate it. Thank you, Ellen.'

He felt her eyes as he disappeared through the swinging doors. He wanted to go home, crawl into bed, sleep and wake up next to Farah, who would then persuade him to lift anchor, start the engine and head for the horizon with the swans trailing behind them. Oh Farah. His mobile rang and when he looked at the screen, he saw her name.

'Joshua?'

'What is it?'

'I've got someone here I think you should speak to.'

7

The airplanes landing at Schiphol Airport were coming in low. Marouan thought back on the time when he was still only a policeman and wanted to be a detective. But they were determined to keep him on the street. After all, he was the one who kept the Moroccan bad boys in check. Outraged, he filed a complaint. Of course there was denial all around. Even the newspapers came to report on it. Suspicions of discrimination. It pissed off the brass.

He thought back on cruising around with his Belmondo bravado once he'd made detective and had returned home for a holiday. Driving under the starry Marrakech sky while his brother accused him of being a *Khilqa*. He lay there that night with his weary head between Aisha's breasts. Back home beside the woman he'd fallen in love with so very long ago.

Even now he wanted to lie with her, wanted to make love to her, fill their jaded existence with cries that would arouse hope: they could still be happy. He would go to the dusty field right beside the family home to give his son a piece of his mind. Why couldn't he learn to give the ball a good kick with the side of his foot, so the ball stopped spinning out of control nowhere near the goal? He would lay his hand on Jamila's shoulders and reassure her. She was already aware of how beautiful she was, but oblivious to how threatening and unscrupulous the pockmarked losers that buzzed around her were.

He stopped the car right in front of the Rembrandttoren. He left the engine idling, keyed in the number and a moment later heard her sleepy, surprised voice.

'It's me,' he softly said, and he realized his eyes were stinging.

'I know,' she replied. Her voice was caring.

'Were you sleeping?'

'What is it?'

He heard a hint of panic in her voice. Normally he never called her at this time of night, and when he did he usually kept it short, only asked a few questions to show some interest. It gave her time to routinely sum up the events of that day into a meaningless story, before he'd say he wouldn't be long now. And then they could both hang up, relieved. And everything would be okay again, for the time being anyway.

But now it was different.

Despite the fact that she'd been woken out of a deep sleep, she immediately knew it was him, and for a split second he even thought he heard a muffled sort of joy in her voice. He thought of the many times he'd lain awake listening to her breathing, how it regularly turned into soft snoring, sometimes faltered; and then he would stroke her and her breathing would calm down.

'What is it?' she repeated.

'Don't worry. Everything is fine. How would you like to stay a little longer?' He said it as calmly as possible, and took her silence as confirmation.

'Aisha?' He swallowed a few times before he continued. 'Kiss Jamila and Chahid for me. Tell them I love them.'

When he hung up, he stepped out of the car and approached the large glass entranceway of the Rembrandttoren. He flashed his ID at the guard behind the desk. The guard came to the door, distrustfully gazed at Marouan's bandaged hands and then his ID.

'Police investigation,' Marouan cried. He knew how to exploit his authority and signalled to the man to open the door. 'We think there's a problem with your alarm system,' he said, standing in the vast marble lobby. 'Police central dispatch says there's something wrong in the penthouse boardroom. For fuck's sake, hasn't anyone noticed anything?'

Without waiting for an answer, Marouan continued. 'We've got to get to the bottom of this quickly,' he said as he pressed the lift button. 'Planning on joining me?'

He leaned against the chrome lift walls, and he could feel the sweat trickling down his back. The security guard was wearing a badge with his name and the City Secure logo.

'Good company. Perhaps the best. How long have you been working for them, Clive?'

'Six months or so.'

'And before that?'

'Why?'

'You're lucky, at CS they only hire the best.'

Clive gave him a guarded smile. Marouan pulled out a pack of chewing gum and offered him a piece. Clive hesitated, but then pressed one out of the strip.

'Big plans for the future, Clive? Or do you want to stay in security?'

'Detective. Maybe.'

'Ah, now you're talking. Detective, really?'

Clive nodded.

'Fine profession.'

The lift doors slid open. Marouan spotted a frosted glass corridor that held promises of a boardroom. 'Let's do this quickly,' he said. 'I have lots of other things to do.'

They walked through the corridors, and through two large rooms with glass walls, oval conference tables, chairs and video screens. Nothing special, except the breathtaking view from 150 metres above Amsterdam. After checking three rooms, one in each corner of the building, they were now in the fourth space among large white leather sofas, a Steinway grand piano and a bar. The power boardroom.

Marouan could see Schiphol in the distance. An airplane glided by. He imagined the passengers pressing their noses against the porthole windows, watching a mosaic of bright lights increase in size.

'You don't need to be a detective, Clive,' he said, smiling. 'With a job in this building, you're the king of the hill.' Marouan casually glanced around. 'The windows don't open?'

Clive shook his head. 'Safety reasons.'

They walked back to the main corridor where Clive pressed the lift button and then rang his colleague via his security radio to say that everything looked okay. Then Marouan noticed stairs behind a glass door.

'Where does that go?'

'It's the door to heaven.'

'Then I'd better give that a quick check too.' He said it with a grin and took the steps two at a time, released the safety lever and was suddenly standing in a circular cage with the night sky and the stars almost within reach.

The structure's door wasn't secured with a lock. A flat roof without a railing stretched out in front of him. He felt strangely calm as he walked towards the edge. King of the hill.

Then he took the plunge.

Aisha was waiting for him. How long had it been since she'd done this? She stood in the doorway, as if she sensed something special was going to happen today. As if she knew that this time he was coming home for real. She smiled at him and he could smell the garlic, ginger, toasted almonds and orange blossom honey she'd put in the meal cooking in the tagine. He tried to find the words to tell her how happy he was that she'd been waiting for him tonight. She just smiled in reply; words weren't necessary. She understood.

She welcomed him home and shut the door.

8

Radjen Tomasoa knew that if you wanted to stay the course in this line of work, you had to be prepared for everything. You had to let as little as possible get to you. But how could he have anticipated what was now coming? It hit him like a sledgehammer. He'd downplayed all the warning signs. An immense feeling of guilt hung over him like a cloud.

He helplessly stared upwards to where Detective Marouan Diba's broken body was lying on the steel points of the five-centimetre-thick glass entranceway canopy. The glass had cracked in a random pattern from the force of the fall, like a thick layer of ice shattered by the impact of a large stone.

The Oracle. That's what Diba had been called, because of the mysterious manner in which he knew all those years ago exactly where he needed to be to find 600 kilos of raw cocaine in the belly of a cargo plane. Thanks to this amazing discovery, Tomasoa suddenly had in Diba an investigator of national renown.

But then wild rumours started making the rounds. The finding of this cocaine had the smell of an inside job, a shady job behind the scenes. The night before the confiscated load would have been officially destroyed, a switch had taken place. The real stuff had disappeared out the back door only to be traded again.

There were persistent rumours, but not a shred of evidence. Diba seemed to have lost his focus and more often than not seemed distracted and gruff. Colleagues started to distance themselves from him. Eventually Diba had only one man left who openly stood behind him. But earlier that evening Calvino had made it clear that he'd had enough too.

If you believed the other rumours, Diba's marriage was also on the rocks. And apparently he was regularly spotted in the casino alone. True or not, Diba had functioned just fine all those years. Anyway, Radjen Tomasoa didn't believe in discussing personal problems with his people. What he believed in was discipline, perseverance and self-reliance. Tomasoa stood by the theory that men were created to face the fiercest storms, and never lose their bearings.

Of course he'd noticed that Diba was no longer the same old detective who, bursting with ambition, was always in overdrive. Diba had turned into a fat man with a very short fuse who always got into arguments around the coffee machine. The last time the newspapers wrote about Diba was to tar and feather him because of the clumsy way he'd handled Dennis Faber's arrest.

What Tomasoa blamed himself for was that he'd spoken to Diba about all these matters, but had missed the fact that Diba's problem ran considerably deeper, too deep to ease with a few kind words or even a harsh reprimand.

Nobody had dared speak to Diba, nobody had realized what might have kept the Oracle from taking the free fall that landed him on the Rembrandttoren's glass canopy. All Tomasoa could still do was swear to the City Secure guard Clive Trustfull that he'd personally see to it that after tonight he'd never have a job with a shred of responsibility.

The first TV truck had already arrived on the scene. Tomasoa saw the IRIS TV logo and shouted to the officer by the barrier tape not to let anyone through. It was nevertheless unavoidable that plenty of people would begin their morning with an article or a short TV item devoted to the tragic death of a once-celebrated detective. And that would be followed by the most speculative stories in the media over the course of the day.

The infamous drug bust from years ago would be raked up again. New life would be blown into the rumours of shady deals and secret contacts with the underworld. The police station in Amsterdam would be besieged by journalists, photographers and camera crews. Every cop, detective and employee coming and going to work would get a microphone stuck in their face. Hadn't they noticed anything? Reporters would take up strategic positions with the Amsterdam police station looming behind them like some eerie backdrop. From that vantage point, they would report as seriously as possible, rattle off an account of the events, while throwing the building a glance over a shoulder now and again.

What had played out behind the walls of the police station? That same night a suspect had been whisked off to hospital with serious injuries after being interrogated, and a detective who'd been present at that questioning had taken his own life.

Whatever strategy Tomasoa devised to control the fallout today, his whole team would be damaged. Calvino would have a particularly hard time of it. After all, he'd been the suicidal detective's partner. Hadn't he noticed anything?

As he drove back at high speed to the station, Tomasoa was already calling in his first tactic. The number of Diba's wife in Marrakesh had to be traced. Their home had to be searched for any clues as to his motives. All contact with the media would now have to go through him. Not a single employee was allowed to speak to the press. He would prepare the press release himself. Normally a job for the Public Relations department, but he chose not to let this one out of his hands. And right after Detective Calvino had questioned the driver, he had to report directly to him, hopefully before the news of Diba's death reached him. Tomasoa wanted to tell him in person.

After he'd passed all that along, Tomasoa began to formulate the content of the press release in his head. He wanted to focus on stress, problems in Diba's private life, even if his gut feeling told him there had to be more. If Kovalev survived his injuries, hopefully he'd be able to shed some light on what had happened.

But that hope was short-lived. Before he even reached the office, Tomasoa received a call confirming that Kovalev had died of a cerebral haemorrhage.

Back at the office, he racked his brain about how best to inform the Internal Investigations Unit about what had gone down during the interrogation. Suddenly Calvino appeared in his doorway, looking like he'd just finished a week-long round-the-clock shift of duty.

'Here you go. The driver's full confession. Complete with exact dates, descriptions of people and locations, with the villa in the Amsterdamse Bos as the last nasty bit of business.'

'Good work,' Tomasoa said, 'where is he now?'

'In the canteen, drinking a coffee and eating biscuits with a police guard at his side.'

'Okay,' Tomasoa said absentmindedly. He'd rarely felt so ill at ease as today. Calvino had already had quite a rough night, but still he continued. Calvino was a man capable of weathering a storm. A man after his own heart.

'Joshua, Diba is dead.' There was no other way to put it. The cold, hard facts were all he had to offer Calvino, as if this made the message less awful. 'He threw himself off the roof of the Rembrandttoren.'

In the ensuing silence Tomasoa imagined Detective Diba taking the plunge again, but this time through Calvino's eyes.

His long-time idol had fallen.

9

Joshua Calvino felt a wave of nausea rush over him. He leaned against the doorframe. 'I should have seen it coming,' he said in a flat voice.

Tomasoa got up and walked to the window. 'I don't know where it went wrong, Cal, or when it started: if he was indeed a mole, had debts, was having an affair or had a drinking problem. But apparently there was a lot going on and none of us saw it.'

'I saw it.'

'I don't know what you saw but I know you made a big effort to protect him. You shouldn't blame yourself for anything.'

'Has his family been informed?'

'Not yet. I'll call his wife in Marrakech as soon as I get her number.'

Joshua had met Diba's wife on a few occasions. A timid woman who must have been beautiful in her youth. But worries and body fat had added an impenetrable layer, making sure that her beauty had become practically invisible. It was as if she was a Matryoshka doll who'd been hidden in a fatter, uglier version.

'Take a few days off, Calvino. That's an order,' Tomasoa said. He turned around and walked back to his desk. 'There'll be an internal investigation into what went on in the interrogation room, they're going to dig into Diba's life and no doubt yours as well.'

'Who's going to round off the boy's case, handle the follow-up on the driver's statement?'

'The Lombard case is a matter for the national guys.'

'All well and good,' Joshua replied, exceptionally irritated. 'But I'm not going home as long as there's a guy walking around who leaves a trail of abused and possibly dead children. I want to put this one to bed.'

Tomasoa slammed his hand on the desk.

'Let me rephrase this, Calvino. *We've* got it covered! Don't see it as a personal vendetta, a way to avenge Diba's death.'

'We can arrest Lombard now, just based on his driver's confession,' Joshua said, as restrained as possible.

'Lombard is in Moscow with a trade delegation. We have no jurisdiction there.'

'We have a liaison officer in Moscow. He works at the Dutch embassy. We can turn to him for legal assistance.' Joshua wasn't going to let this case be hampered by mourning the loss of Diba for too long. Stagnation was decline. Joshua wanted to plough ahead. Throw himself into the eye of the storm. And it looked like Tomasoa was still willing to help him.

'Okay, Joshua, there's a few things we can do before we turn everything over to the national guys. If we can get our hands on substantial evidence that verifies the driver's statement, then Lombard goes down for the count.'

'Lombard also rents lodgings in The Hague,' Joshua said. 'We need to get into his computer.'

'Why there? Why not the one at his home?'

'Home computers have shared files. He'd be crazy to keep photos and films on there. If we want to find something, it's going to be on his computer in The Hague.'

Tomasoa called the Public Prosecutor and dragged him out of bed to issue an emergency search warrant: a very reliable witness from the minster's inner circle had substantiated that there had been systematic child abuse for years. Proof of this would likely be found in the computer files of the accused, who was currently in Moscow. The officer hesitated. He first had to consult with the National Crime Agency.

It took Tomasoa and Joshua less than an hour to get to The Hague. Thanks to a handy device to disable the alarm, within minutes they were standing on the fortieth floor of the

Kroontoren, where large rectangular tilting windows offered a spectacular view of the city at night. The white walls, the blinds, the sofa and furniture contrasted with the black chandelier, chairs, benches and the explicit modern art on the walls.

They proceeded quickly and quietly, as if they regularly broke into the pieds-à-terre of government ministers. All the rooms and cupboards were searched with flashlights. They found nothing. The place was clean as a whistle.

Then they lowered the blinds in the office and someone from the Dutch Forensic Institute took a seat at Lombard's computer.

It was quiet in the apartment, except for the hum of the air conditioning. The Forensic Institute's expert began to crack codes and checked if all the programs had been installed intentionally or were possibly the result of some virus. If they found anything suspicious in Lombard's files, it was crucial for them to prove he'd downloaded it himself.

The nervous tapping on the keyboard made everyone uneasy. There were brief, repeated moments of silence filled with expectation, followed by a new series of lightning-fast keystrokes.

'He might be active on the anonymous Tor network,' said the forensics guy in hushed tones. 'IP addresses can't be traced there. The network is intended to allow information to be shared anonymously.'

The tapping went on and on; the silences in between got shorter. Joshua and Tomasoa felt less motivated by the minute. Their eyes met, they silently assessed each other's level of fatigue, and grimly looked away. The tapping continued.

All of a sudden, there was an unexpectedly long silence followed by mumbled swearing. They perked up, bent over the screen and saw images being extracted from a zip file. Joshua's relief soon gave way to deep disgust. Nothing could prepare you for seeing images of child abuse.

'That's him,' Joshua cried. He pressed his finger against the touch screen, on the video file of a very young dancer in a light-blue robe.

The music sounded tinny. A shaky camera recorded a heavily made-up boy, awkwardly shaking his hips, raising his arms and stamping his feet, causing small bells to tinkle. The camera jerked towards the boy. A male voice said something off-screen. The boy hesitated, stopped moving. A hand began to pull at the boy's robe, which made him stumble. The camera zoomed in further; it was right above him now.

The boy lay on the ground and Joshua saw the fear in his eyes.

'Stop right here.' Tomasoa's voice trembled with anger. 'Can you tell where this was sent from?'

The forensics guy needed several minutes to trace the IP address of the sender's server.

Once he found it, he whistled softly through his teeth.

The file was sent from the Dutch embassy in Kabul.

10

Farah threw her body weight against the front door of her apartment. When the mercury rose in summer, the wood expanded so she had to grab the doorknob and wrench and tug like mad. By now she hadn't slept for two nights, couldn't remember the last time she'd had any food and was unsteady on her legs.

As soon as she got in she fell backwards on her bed, assuming she'd be overcome by all-obliterating sleep before she'd even hit the mattress. Instead she spent many long minutes staring at the ceiling with her thoughts churning and adrenalin jolting through her body. This is what it must feel like to be in freefall and to keep falling and falling . . .

She remembered Parwaiz's hand restraining her and wondered what might have happened had he not done that. The Bentley might have knocked her down. In that case, would Parwaiz still be alive?

Only this morning she'd stood by his grave. But now he was beyond the reach of the living.

She recalled leaving David's house with a load of boxes only a few hours ago. Why had she resigned herself to the idea that David was now beyond her reach? What would have happened if she'd simply carried the boxes upstairs again, unpacked them, put her clothes back in the wardrobe, her books on the old pile and returned all her make-up to the bathroom cabinet?

Now the boxes sat rain-drenched on the blackened ring road. She'd chucked them out so Detective Diba could place the badly injured woman on the back seat. And then Paul Chapelle sat down next to her. This wasn't her imagination running away with her, ghosts and memories that got the better of her. These were facts. She'd managed to free a man from a burning taxi and he turned out to be the boy who'd made her feverish with infatuation thirty years ago.

The facts had brought a long-hidden story to light. She'd listened to that story on a deserted pier, late at night, before driving its narrator to the police station in Amsterdam where she'd introduced him to Joshua Calvino.

The facts had brought her this evening to the office of Chief Inspector Tomasoa, a tall Indonesian with a strikingly bald head who told her he'd seen her fight in Carré. He asked how she'd come into contact with the driver, and when she explained that he'd originally wanted to talk to Danielle Bernson, she'd caught the meaningful look exchanged between Calvino and Tomasoa.

The next fact had blown her sideways. Danielle was in the mortuary. She'd been murdered in the Amsterdamse Bos that evening. And then, when Tomasoa answered the phone, his confident face turned ashen grey. Without a word about what he'd just been told, but with a shadow clouding his face, he asked Joshua to question the driver. He escorted Farah to the lobby and told her he wanted to speak to her again later.

The proud Chief Inspector was a broken man – that too was a fact. She watched him step into his car and drive off. She longed for home, for bed, for a couple of hours of sleep before it was time to check in at the Aeroflot business-class desk for her flight to Moscow.

But sleep wouldn't come.

Staring at the ceiling, she relived the past forty-eight hours in fifteen one-minute segments. Then she got up and walked over to the window, opening it wide to let in the fresh night air. Nieuwmarkt was deserted. The Chinese had already cleared the square.

She took a shower and as the warm water ran over her body she pictured Sharada, the river goddess, in the middle of Lavrov's office. The river goddess belonged to Parwaiz's world, not to that of Valentin Lavrov.

How come the past was suddenly so terrifyingly close? There was Raylan Chapelle and his love letters to her mother Helai,

Paul suddenly jumping into the Carerra next to her after three decades – the many thoughts, memories and images were jostling each other, demanding her attention, and all the while the warm water gushed over her body.

She wished she were standing under a waterfall that would not only wash her body but the world around her clean of all its misery. A waterfall that would push the hands of the clock backwards, bring Danielle Bernson back to life and let Parwaiz dart across the square in The Hague again, pointing at the kites in the sky like a little boy. A waterfall that would enable her to drive back to David's house, where he'd be waiting for her in the doorway with a broad smile on his face. A waterfall that could heal wounds.

Such a waterfall didn't exist.

She turned off the tap, dried herself, rubbed her body with lotion and put her necklace back on, followed by the three silver rings, one on each ring finger and the third on her right thumb. She didn't get dressed yet, but started laying out her clothes for Moscow on the bed. When she was done she put the paper butterfly and the bundle of letters from Raylan Chapelle next to them, alongside a collection of Rumi poems.

She dreaded leaving, for fear she might never return. Moscow felt like an ominous, alien world. But she had to go to find what she was looking for – an explanation for what had happened, a deeper meaning for this inexplicable sequence of events, which, by the looks of it, all led to a single man.

Valentin Lavrov.

PART FIVE
Home

The men who'd picked him up from the orphanage had made him wear really fancy robes and jewellery this time. By now he'd learnt how to make up his eyes, put on lipstick and powder his face. They'd brought him to a large house surrounded by a high wall. This was an important appointment, they told him.

He had to do his best.

The room he was standing in was so high and so badly lit that the ceiling was barely visible. The man who entered had pink puffy skin and pale-blond hair, and he wore a light-coloured suit. He was sweating and just stared at him for a while without a word.

He was told to dance and pretend to be a singing woman without a voice. Then the two men were dismissed. He never saw them again. Meanwhile the man in the suit had taken a seat and was smiling and watching him quietly. The flushed cheeks and blond hair were something he'd never forget; nobody had ever looked at him like this before. So quietly and so long. Finally the man asked him in a whisper to dance as best as he could.

He imagined he was an actress in a romantic film, swathed in thin veils and swirling around to the strains of a beautiful song only he could hear. Then he noticed that the man had taken off his jacket and was coming towards him with a camera. His smile now gone, the man yanked at him so hard he lost his balance and fell down hard on the floor. When he looked up, he saw what the man was doing to himself. Instantly he felt the eagle wings emerge from his body. He spread them and flew out of the large, dark room, and once outside he soared so high he could no longer see the city lights. The air was cool and dark this far above the clouds.

I

After the Ilyushin Il-96 had landed at Domodedovo Airport, Farah saw it was 39 degrees Celsius. She entered a kiosk. The *Moscow Times* reported on the attack in the metro that morning. It had taken thirty-five lives, and at least three times that number had been injured. Chechen rebels had claimed responsibility. The Dutch trade delegation couldn't have picked a worse time for its visit, nor could Farah.

The taxi to the city centre cost 2,800 roubles and took more than three hours. They crawled along the six-lane motorway, through the vast suburbs, past huge housing blocks built during the Cold War.

As they neared central Moscow, she saw fewer messy building sites and dug-up pavements. The shops began to look more luxurious and the boulevards lined with limos, Lexuses and Porsches were being kept squeaky clean by a small army of street cleaners with dustpans and brooms. Looming up at the end of Tverskaya Ulitsa, the main artery into the heart of the city, was her final destination, the Hotel National, where Lenin once had his office.

When she finally got to her room, Farah was so exhausted all she could do was peel the clothes off her overheated body before falling into the profound sleep she'd been craving for almost three days.

When she opened her eyes again, a throbbing headache had nestled between her temples.

In the bathroom she drained a large glass of water and swallowed two ibuprofen and then staggered across the garish carpet to the two windows. When she finally managed to open them, the city noise flew in on the muggy air. Despite the late hour, she saw black Mercedes cars with blue flashing lights coming out of the Kremlin across the street.

More than twelve hours ago she'd stood in much the same way, with her eyes trained on Nieuwmarkt, her hands resting on the windowsill, her body leaning forward and her head tilted back the way wolves do when they howl at the moon.

Farah was howling too, inside, that is. She'd lost her sense of self after everything that had happened. She was a journalist, not even a remarkable one. And while she could boast nearly ten years of experience, hardly any of it was as an investigative journalist. The issues she'd investigated had been social ones. She'd never covered a criminal case and never had cause to probe the life of a particular individual.

Now she suddenly found herself dealing with an international network of criminals that was as big as it was inscrutable, and looking into a case that had already claimed several lives in a short amount of time. She didn't have a clue how to proceed. All she knew was that having plucked her 'expertise' from a handful of art books, she was now passing herself off to the prime suspect as a cultural reporter. Having stupidly agreed to Edward's plan, she currently found herself playing an altogether unfamiliar game.

During the flight to Moscow she realized she'd been wrong to accept Lavrov's invitation. It was naive to think she could prise potentially incriminating information from a global tycoon. First thing this morning she'd phone Edward and tell him they were on a hiding to nothing. But the more she thought about it, the greater her suspicion there was no way back.

As she pondered all this and stared across the city, she saw a flash of light followed by a large column of fire shooting up above the blocks of flats in the distance. Shortly afterwards she heard the dull thud of the explosion that must have caused it. The vibrations even made the window frames shake. Farah was frozen to the spot. The entire city seemed to hold its breath. Then the first sirens could be heard in the distance. A low-flying helicopter sped towards a bright orange-red cloud of dust shot through with flames.

The realization hit her like lightning. Here in Moscow she was no longer the cosmopolitan citizen she imagined herself to be when basking in the safety and security of Amsterdam. Now she was one of millions of anonymous, disaffected people in an overcrowded city that seemed to be closing in on her.

2

The morning after the accident on the motorway, Paul and Edward took a taxi to the family farm. As he walked through the garden towards the house, Paul saw the fragile figure of his mother in the doorway. Isobel was, as always, wearing eccentric make-up and wrapped in batik cloth with oriental floral designs. When they embraced he caught a whiff of the patchouli oil she always dabbed on her neck. It smelled like long ago, like home.

That same evening he was going to hop on a plane and follow Farah to Moscow. He thought the pretext of the *AND* publishing an art supplement was an idiotic plan.

Given Moscow was his next destination, it was high time to recontact his main source there, a female journalist who always had inside information on Russia's business and political elite.

Anya Kozlova worked for the *Moskva Gazeta*, a liberal weekly that followed and critically commented on Russia's President Potanin's every step and outspokenly opposed mafia organizations, corruption and conflicts of interest between politicians and businessmen. Not only did the Russian government consider the *Moskva Gazeta* a giant pain in the ass because of all of this, but it was one of the few papers that pressed for a peaceful solution to the unending conflict in Chechnya. 'Haven't we learned anything from Afghanistan?' Anya had written years ago when the Russians brutally invaded the breakaway province.

Since going off to Johannesburg three years earlier, Paul hadn't spoken to Anya. He knew the reunion wouldn't be easy. She'd undoubtedly rub his nose in the fact he was unable to maintain relationships because he was socially and emotionally inept. Anything to make it clear she still held a grudge because he'd never fallen for her charms. Anything to have the last word.

Anya Kozlova had chosen journalism because of her intense need to prove a point. The greater the resistance of others, the harder she went up against them. This, and her innate hatred of anything that even carried a whiff of authority, had solidified her reputation of being a hard-hitting journalist. It gave many people reason to dislike her.

'I knew one day you'd come knocking on my door again,' she said when she heard his voice. 'Rumour has it that things aren't going so well with you.'

'That's right,' Paul said, indulging her. 'I need your help.' Finally, he heard her thinking.

'How can I be of service?'

He explained in detail the connection between the Dutch finance minister, the entrepreneur Armin Lazonder and industrialist Valentin Lavrov. It hadn't made much of an impression on her, but when he talked about how it was all linked to an Afghan boy, he knew he'd hit a nerve. Anya had a weak spot for children.

She picked him up from the airport in her rattling Skoda Garde and took him to the Tsvet Nochi Club, once Paul's favourite nightspot, where without even asking she ordered him beef stroganoff.

'You look as lousy as you sounded on the phone,' she said a bit harshly. 'You should start eating your greens.'

Nothing had changed: her dark, boyish haircut and that devious glance she gave him, as if he'd come back to Moscow for her.

'Johannesburg, Amsterdam, Moscow. And all because of one Afghan boy. How did you actually make all these connections?'

'A colleague of mine discovered the links. My former boss wants me to help her.'

473

'If you already have her, why do you need me?'

'She's a rookie and she doesn't know Russia.'

'If she's so inexperienced, why is she on the case?'

'Right from the start she got very involved with the Afghan boy. A combination of circumstances led her to the connection with Lavrov.'

'Clever for such an inexperienced person. What's her name?'

'Farah Hafez.'

'Sounds like the name of an exotic princess.'

'She's Afghan.'

'But she isn't with you now?'

'She flew in earlier. And why are you so interested in her?'

'I'm interested in how the two of you are going to approach this, is that so strange?'

Paul took a piece of his beef stroganoff and chewed it thoroughly. Anya gave him a patronizing smile.

'You don't have a clue how you're going to go about this, right? No idea?'

With a sigh he placed his knife and fork beside his plate and took a sip of red wine. 'First explain to me how AtlasNet managed to grow from a small enterprise into an international conglomerate in such a relatively short time.'

'If you give me a bite,' Anya said, teasing him. Paul pushed the plate towards her. Everything had a price for Anya, and it was usually much higher than she first let on. After stuffing her face with three forkfuls of his stew, she slid Paul's plate back to him like it was a grand gesture.

'It started three years ago, right after you left without warning. Potanin locked up Aleksandr Zyuganov, the owner of the NovaMost energy company, for fraud,' she said, washing down his stroganoff with a big gulp of wine. 'But of course the real reason was that Zyuganov had plans to run in the next year's presidential election. Zyuganov's pockets were lined with roubles and this would've allowed him to buy a lot of power. So a mock trial was organized and Zyuganov was exiled to Siberia. End of Zyuganov.'

'And what happened to NovaMost?'

'All of NovaMost's shares went to the fledgling company AtlasNet, owned by the then unknown Valentin Lavrov.'

'Why Lavrov?'

'It was a public secret that Valentin Lavrov was already the President's protégé. Rumours at the time suggested that Lavrov only set up AtlasNet because he'd been instructed to do so, if you know what I mean.'

'So almost overnight, AtlasNet became a major player, thanks to the shares of the exiled Zyuganov.'

'Exactly. Yet another example of powerful people dividing and conquering with the loser known from the outset.'

'Did all the shares go to Lavrov?'

She slowly drained her glass of wine, deliberately, as if she was trying to buy time.

'As CEO, Lavrov obviously held a controlling interest in those shares. However, there was also a shadow shareholder. Except nobody on the financial markets actually knew who it was.'

'But you found out,' Paul said.

Anya leaned forward and whispered, 'It's explosive.'

'You're not saying that the Presi—' But Paul didn't get any further. Anya held her hand over his mouth.

'Didn't you hear me? It's explosive,' she whispered again.

'How long have you all known?'

'Not long.'

'And when are you going to make it public?'

'The question is whether we're going to disclose it at all. If we publish what we know, we reveal that we have access to secret matters of state. And with this we'd sign our own death warrants. Two of our journalists have already been killed in the past year. There's a law that authorizes the President to deploy special units for the liquidation of enemies, or extremists, as they call them, inside of Russia but also abroad. I'm not planning on dying any time soon.'

'Do you think you can help me, Anya?'

Suddenly she was serious. 'I can do a lot more than that.' She grabbed the knife and fork, pulled the plate towards her, wolfed down three more big bites and stood up.

'Let's go!' she said.

Paul knew it was useless to resist.

3

The Skoda Garde beamed bright strips of light through the smoky haze that hung all through the city. 'Forest fires,' Anya said with a quick glance at Paul. 'If we have a north-easterly wind, even briefly, we're covered in smoke.' The radio reported an attack on an apartment building in the outskirts of the city. 'The latest offensive by the Chechens,' Anya said. 'They're bringing the war to our doorsteps.'

They drove on to Yauzskiy Bul'var. Rescue helicopters flew over low and on the other side of the grassy divide fire engines with emergency lights and sirens shrieking raced towards the suburbs.

Moments later they turned on to Ulitsa Pokrovka, where editor-in-chief Roman Jankovski of the *Moskva Gazeta* had already been awakened by a call from Anya. 'Can't it wait until tomorrow?' he'd mumbled into the phone. Yet he also knew that once Anya got an idea in her head, it simply couldn't wait. 'I have the perfect fellow for us,' she said. More wasn't needed to convince Roman.

She found a parking spot for the Skoda right across from the old apartment building where Jankovski lived.

'It must be very important,' Paul sighed.

'Believe me,' said Anya, 'when Roman Jankovski gets out of bed for you at three a.m. then it's very important indeed.'

In front of the monumental entrance, Anya was just about to ring the brass doorbell of number 187 when the heavy front door swung open and two men in dark overalls came bolting outside. Anya was thrown off balance by their speed. Paul caught her. The two men ran diagonally across the street to a grey Lada station wagon. A third man came out and collided with Paul. The man took a swing at Paul, but Paul blocked it, got him in an arm lock and jabbed his knee hard into the man's right side. The guy collapsed with a loud groan. Hearing this, the other two stopped and turned around. One of them pulled a gun. The door hadn't fallen shut yet, and Anya gave it a shove with her shoulder. She pulled Paul inside and then kicked the door closed with a loud bang.

'We're not rid of them yet,' she said in a loud whisper.

The elevator would take too long, the stairwell galleries were too exposed. They fled into the basement. Behind them they heard the heavy door open again, men's muffled voices, commands exchanged, footsteps in the entry hall and on the gallery stairwell and the steps to the basement. Anya pushed Paul into a dark alcove which reeked of urine and rubbish. They held their breath as they heard footsteps approaching. In the corridor leading to the basement, they saw the flickering of a flashlight. Something rustled in the alcove. Paul felt a rat brush past his boots. The footsteps in the corridor stopped. The light returned, shot past the alcove. The sound of footsteps disappeared into the distance.

They could hear muffled male voices again coming from the entry hall, brusque and decisive. The door fell shut. Only after the longest time did Anya and Paul dare to move again. On their guard, they left the alcove. Paul grabbed his mobile phone to light the basement corridor and walked towards where he'd heard the footsteps going.

Anya hissed, 'Come back.'

He pretended not to hear her, walked on and pulled the handle of each basement storage room.

Anya was pissed off. Fear made her furious. When she saw Paul go into a storage room, she swore under her breath. She went after him, wanted to punch him, kick him, anything to fight off her fears. He stood motionless just inside the door. Then, in the bluish glow cast by his phone, she saw what he'd discovered.

4

Farah woke up slowly to banging on her door. The traffic noise that came in through the open windows bounced off the walls and there was a veil of smog in the room. On the other side of the door a male voice called her name. With a sheet wrapped around her sweaty body she unlocked the door and found herself staring into Paul Chapelle's roughed up face.

'Strange room service they've got here,' she said and yawned.

'Are you coming?'

'Where?'

'The *Moskva Gazeta*. It's important.'

'Give me ten.'

Fifteen minutes later she was downstairs in the lobby shaking hands with a pretty, tomboyish woman with a short bob and piercing grey-blue eyes.

'Anya Kozlova. And you must be the princess.'

'Princess?'

'From the East.'

'I'm nobody's princess,' Farah said curtly, which produced a broad smile on Anya Kozlova's face.

'Are we going in that?' she asked Paul as the three of them walked towards a dented Skoda.

'I'm sure I'd put on airs and graces too if I were staying at the Hotel National,' he laughed.

Farah settled in the back seat. 'What's on the agenda?'

Paul was about to respond when Anya accelerated unexpectedly, only to join the busy traffic, cursing all the while.

'Paul told me about some stupid plan to convince Lavrov you're an art journalist,' Anya shouted while giving Farah a cynical look in the rear-view mirror.

Weirdly enough, Farah kind of liked her. 'She's right, that girlfriend of yours,' she said to Paul.

'She's not my girlfriend.'

'Whoever she is, she's right. It's a hopeless plan. I'm a journalist, not a spy. I may have an exotic name, but that hardly means I should follow in Mata Hari's footsteps.'

'Did you tell her about last night?' Anya asked Paul.

'Should I be interested?' Farah said.

Paul nodded seriously. 'It's the reason we're going to their offices.'

Farah was told the story about the planned three a.m. meeting with editor-in-chief Roman Jankovski, the unplanned confrontation with the three men who came running out of the building and the wholly fortuitous discovery of five large bags of RDX in a storage space in the basement. Enough to blow up the whole building.

'The bags were connected with wires and attached to a detonating device that indicated a remaining time of twenty-three minutes,' Paul explained calmly. By the time the bomb disposal unit arrived, of those twenty-three minutes there were exactly five left. Thanks to Paul's description of the man he'd fought with, all three men were traced and brought in for questioning by morning.

'So why are we going to their editorial offices now?' Farah wanted to know.

Anya acted like she understood Dutch. 'They were probably from the FSB,' she replied.

'The Russian security services,' Paul clarified. 'We reckon they wanted to make it look like a Chechen attack and kill two birds with one stone: sway public opinion even further in favour of a war in Chechnya while blowing the editor-in-chief of Russia's most critical weekly paper to smithereens.'

'But what's that got to do with *us*?' Farah asked irritably.

'They want to share state secrets with us,' Paul said. 'They're going to make us an offer.'

Anya grinned at her in the mirror. 'An offer you can't refuse.'

5

The very first moment Joshua Calvino shook Liaison Officer Max Berger's hand in the stately Dutch embassy on Kalashny Pereulok, he felt an instinctive dislike for the man. With his pseudo-aristocratic appearance and carefully composed sentences, Berger reminded him of an actor in a British TV series about the tragic downfall of an old blue-blooded family. If anyone deserved the term 'haughty' then it was Berger. Joshua had to dig deep to hide his aversion to the man. He needed Berger's help.

'Quite a delicate matter, to put it mildly,' Berger said as he escorted Joshua to his office through the attractively lit corridors hung with old Dutch Masters. 'All the more since we have not received an official request for legal assistance from the Public Prosecutor back home. And, of course, Detective Calvino, you understand that without such a request, it is hopeless to count on any help from the Russian authorities.' He graciously offered Joshua the black leather chair facing his polished desk.

'The Public Prosecutor's office is working on it,' Joshua said as he sat down. 'They were the ones who advised me to touch base with you in advance, so we can take immediate action once the official request for legal assistance arrives.'

'Let me reiterate, Detective Calvino,' Berger emphasized, 'we have not received an official request.' Joshua was not going to let himself be brushed off by a man wearing a cravat and a silk shirt. He gave Berger a determined look.

'The Public Prosecutor has insisted that while we're waiting for the wheels to be set in motion, everything must be done to unofficially notify the Russian authorities of the impending arrest, along with an express request to cooperate.'

'Well, well,' said Berger. He seemed somewhat amused by Joshua's grandstanding. 'Are those the instructions the Public Prosecutor gave you?'

'Or perhaps you think I'm here without official orders, without a solid plan?'

Berger raised his hand imploringly while pressing the telephone to his ear. 'Marianne? Could you please check if in the last hour the Public Prosecutor has blessed us with a request for legal assistance?'

Awaiting Marianne's answer, Joshua absently gazed at the photo of the Dutch queen just above Berger's head. He knew that the matter was actually somewhat different than he'd just portrayed it. Despite Tomasoa's insistence, the Public Prosecutor wasn't prepared to move on this quickly. Joshua and Tomasoa had discussed the matter at length. The term 'class justice' had come up. Once the intention to arrest Lombard became common knowledge among the ranks of the trade delegation – which wouldn't take long among that tight-knit clique – then Lombard and his associates would do everything in their power to avert disaster.

Even though Tomasoa admitted he was powerless to do more, Joshua wasn't prepared to wait for anything official. He'd taken it on himself to book a round-trip flight Amsterdam–Moscow, hoping that with the necessary bluffing he could convince Berger to take action. But from the very start in the embassy's foyer, Berger behaved so uncooperatively that Joshua feared his trip to the Russian capital might be pointless.

'No?' Berger cried theatrically into the phone. 'Are you quite sure, Marianne? Well, thank you.' He hung up the receiver as if it were a costly relic.

'There has been no call for assistance,' Berger said, as if he were reciting the closing line of a Greek tragedy. He got up, walked over to an antique-looking cabinet and opened a hatch door to reveal a collection of colourful bottles. Joshua had the fleeting thought that he'd just landed in a lavish cocktail bar.

'What'll it be, detective?' Berger asked.

'Water, please,' Joshua said.

'Permit me to be candid, detective,' Berger said moments later when he placed a glass of Perrier in front of Joshua, 'is this your first "mission" abroad?'

'What do you mean?' Joshua gulped back the sparkling water. The walk to the embassy in the heavy smog had made his throat feel like he'd smoked an entire pack of cigarettes. A miserable feeling for a non-smoker.

'Let me explain: the field of diplomacy is an extremely sensitive one,' Berger said as he slowly took the seat behind his desk again. 'It is often a matter of walking on eggshells, operating with immense tact, choosing the right words, slowly manoeuvring and then closing in when you want to score a point. And you, detective, just barged in with a bomb in your hands. If you understand what I'm saying.'

'I do,' Joshua calmly replied, 'Then again, it's not every day that we expose a Dutch minister as a paedophile.'

'You also understand that the Russian authorities will do everything possible to protect their good relations with the Netherlands by not rushing into anything,' Berger replied in a condescending tone. 'And even when the Public Prosecutor submits an official request, then there's another reason the Russian authorities will not be eager to arrest a Dutch minister here in Moscow: economic motives. With import figures of around fourteen billion euros, the Netherlands is the largest destination for Russian goods and produce. Need I say more?'

'So you're telling me that economic motives sometimes outweigh the law?' Joshua heard how sharply the words rolled off his tongue. He saw the icy look in Berger's eyes. Joshua now knew one thing for certain: he wasn't cut out for diplomacy. He wondered if there was even the slightest chance of still convincing Berger to help him.

'What I am saying, Detective Calvino, is that even with a formal request from the Public Prosecutor, we would have to move heaven and earth to get the Russians to initiate an arrest.

But nothing is impossible. In your opinion, how conclusive is the evidence against Lombard?'

'We have a full confession from Lombard's driver, complete with dates, locations and the names of others involved. And we found extremely damaging material on Lombard's computer. I don't want to boast, but I think it's a watertight case. For all intents and purposes.' Joshua had never used this expression. *For all intents and purposes.* He had to laugh. Apparently Berger's pretentiousness was starting to wear off on him.

'And you are certain this material was obtained lawfully?' Berger asked with a mouth as narrow as the stripes of his shirt.

'We had a search warrant from the Public Prosecutor to enter his lodgings and we confiscated his computer once we found the incriminating files. Could it be any more legitimate in your opinion?'

Berger swivelled back and forth in his office chair. 'Incriminating files, what do they indicate exactly?'

'I'd really prefer not to go into detail at this moment. Besides I can't,' Joshua brusquely said. 'It's too gruesome. But what I can say is that the files indicate that Minister Lombard is actively involved in a paedophile network that, as far as we can presently tell, reaches deep into the heart of the Dutch embassy in Kabul.'

His last words definitely hit a nerve. Joshua had managed to arouse Berger's interest. Waiting to play your trump card often worked wonders. Berger sat up even straighter behind his desk.

'As I said, detective, nothing is impossible. A new diplomatic officer was recently posted here from Kabul. If what you are saying ends up being true, it is not good. Not good at all. We have to uphold a high standard overseas. On the phone your boss Tomasoa mentioned a possible connection between Lombard and Lavrov. Can you tell me anything more about that?'

'We interrogated a key witness who was on AtlasNet's payroll. His statement suggests that Lavrov bribed businessmen and politicians to acquire the concession in the Netherlands to build Europe's largest gas storage facility.'

'So this is about more than the minister? If I understand you correctly?'

'Minister Lombard is our priority. But once he starts talking, we have no doubt others will be named and Lavrov will certainly be among them.'

'And who is this key witness, if I may ask?'

Joshua thought for a moment. He'd agreed with Tomasoa to leave the events surrounding Kovalev's death out of it for now. 'I'm presently not at liberty to say because of security reasons.'

Berger got up and walked to the window, where he pulled up the blinds. The smog seemed even thicker than earlier. 'This misery just continues,' he said, disheartened. 'Forest fires outside the city. That's what the north-easterly wind brings us these days: plenty of filth.' He walked back to his desk. 'Your boss also told me that the doctor involved in the boy's case was murdered.'

'Danielle Bernson.' Joshua said her name as if he still couldn't believe it himself. 'Apparently they suspected she knew too much. The bullets came from a Zastava that was later found on a young Russian who died in a car accident in Amsterdam. Besides the Zastava, the man was wearing a locket. With a photo of three men. One we've identified as Arseni Vakurov. Another as Valentin Lavrov.'

The look on Berger's face suggested he'd really dropped a bombshell this time.

Joshua continued. 'There are more than enough indications that Lavrov is somehow involved in the whole affair, Mr Berger. But, as I already said, at this moment the minister is our priority.'

Berger nodded approvingly. 'I also understand you received unexpected assistance?'

'Sorry?'

'A journalist who is looking into this case.'

'You mean Farah Hafez?'

'Your boss did not mention her name. Farah Hafez, you say?' Joshua immediately regretted his impulsive reaction. 'She works for the *AND*,' he said, regaining his self-control.

'How did she get involved in this case?'

'Personal motives. She was the first to have contact with the Afghan boy when he was brought into the hospital. She felt drawn to him, so she started to investigate the case. She was also the one who gave us Lombard's driver.'

'So she knows about the damaging material you have on Lombard.'

'We've agreed she won't publish anything until Lombard is arrested.'

'And she is also aware of the possible connections with Lavrov?'

'Yes, that's right.'

Berger clasped his hands together, rested his chin on them and looked at Joshua intently.

'I take this seriously, detective. Very seriously. Such a sensitive case with so many implications. I'm glad you shared the details with me. I know what I have to do now. I am going to exert my influence to have the Public Prosecutor file a formal request for legal assistance as quickly as possible and I am going to informally share with the authorities what they can expect.' He stood up demonstratively, as if to indicate that as far as he was concerned, the conversation had come to an end.

'We are going to get to the bottom of this,' Berger said, escorting Joshua to the door as politely as he'd invited him to take a seat earlier. In the hall he gave Joshua the unsolicited advice to visit a museum and get a feel for the city, after which he said, undoubtedly to reassure him, 'I will be in touch,' and then he returned to his office and shut the heavy door behind him.

Joshua looked back at the stately building displaying the Dutch coat of arms and wished he was back in the smelly Corolla alongside his partner Diba. Anything rather than being here alone in this immense city of millions surrounded by uncertainty, doubt and a haze of windblown ash.

6

Moscow's streets were clogged with cars, all seemingly intent on thwarting Anya Kozlova's efforts to steer her dull yellow Skoda to Ulitsa Vorontsovo Pole where the *Moskva Gazeta* had its offices.

'We're here for Lavrov. Where do the terrorist bombings and the security services come in?' Farah asked while feverishly rummaging around in her handbag for more painkillers.

'There are fresh elections in a year's time,' Paul said. 'And the president is seeking re-election. So he creates mayhem.'

'Right, by the looks of it he's not the only one,' Farah said with a brief glance at Anya who yanked angrily at the wheel, accelerated, braked again, and appeared to be wishing all Russian drivers a single ticket to hell. 'And why would a president create chaos? Doesn't that work against him?'

'He's not supposed to be seen as the instigator, but as the one combatting it.'

'I still don't see the point. Surely you're not going to have buildings blown up by supposed terrorists if it means killing innocent civilians?'

'If you believe the end justifies the means, then that's *exactly* what you do,' Anya yelled while crossing a chaotic junction with her hand glued to the horn. 'In that case you blow up a building and blame the Chechens. And you don't get public opinion on your side unless lots of civilians die!'

In the meantime cars kept approaching from all sides so the Skoda suddenly came to a complete standstill.

'Violence is part and parcel of Russian culture,' Paul said. 'You can't seize power here without using force.'

'And your horn!' Anya said furiously as she abruptly slipped between two oncoming cars and manoeuvred the Skoda perilously close around a bus full of stunned tourists before pulling into a side street, where she parked so swiftly that the contents of Farah's handbag went flying through the car and Paul banged his head against the windscreen. 'We're here.'

The *Moskva Gazeta* was located on the second floor of a grey, five-storey building. In the lobby, which was full of campaign posters in Cyrillic print, a man was waiting for them with his arms open wide. With his full beard and convivial nature, Roman Jankovski looked like a younger version of Tevye, the Jewish milkman from Anatevka, the Russian village in *Fiddler on the Roof*. The editor-in-chief hugged Paul like a prodigal son before kissing Farah on the hand with an unexpected flourish.

'Welcome, Farah. Paul has told me a lot about you,' he said courteously. 'And from now on I'll believe every word he says. What else can I do? He saved my life last night!' His laughter thundered through the lobby. Given the enthusiasm with which he slapped himself on the thigh, Farah half expected him to break into a Cossack dance. But instead Roman took her graciously by the arm and escorted them down a drab corridor that called to mind an old school with high ceilings and spiderwebs in the corners. Through the tall windows she saw *Moskva Gazeta* journalists busily conferring with one another.

'Moscow is experiencing another wave of terror,' a serious-looking Roman said to explain the buzz of activity in the offices.

'I understand it isn't always entirely clear who the terrorists are,' Farah replied.

'Which makes it all the more worrying.'

They passed a large glass display case containing portraits of young men and women, a Macintosh Classic computer, a purple scarf with dark-red bloodstains, a Christmas card from Bill Clinton and a well-preserved copy of the book *Weapons and Fighting Arts of the Indonesian Archipelago*.

'Who's the martial arts fan here?' asked Farah, who'd halted in front of the display case, pleasantly surprised at what she saw.

'She was.' Roman pointed to the photo of a young woman. 'Elena Vertinski.'

'Was?'

'This is our remembrance corner. Our modest mausoleum. These are photos of the *Moskva Gazeta* journalists murdered over the past few years. Elena was working on a large-scale investigation into the arms trade and money laundering. She stumbled across evidence that implicated the Russian security services. Shortly after, she became seriously ill. The doctors said she was suffering from a rare allergy. Three days later she was dead. Nobody was allowed to see her medical records. Not even her family. We suspect she was poisoned.'

'And who's that?' Farah asked, pointing to a handsome man with a vague resemblance to Joshua Calvino.

'Semyon Domnikov,' Roman said. 'He was a freelancer. Gunned down after he penned a piece about a Russian commander who was suspected of having summarily executed all the male inhabitants of a Chechen village.' He gave her an apologetic look. 'But please excuse me. Here I am welcoming you and the first thing I do is regale you with tales of death.'

'Sounds like a Russian to me,' Anya grunted.

'Sounds like a bad host,' Roman said with a smile, offering Farah his arm again and ushering her into his office.

'I've come close to shutting down the *Moskva Gazeta*,' Roman said after the four of them sat down at a large oval table. Family photographs adorned the walls alongside black-and-white snaps of the editor with a variety of statesmen, including Bill Clinton and Mikhail Gorbachev. 'But Anya and her colleagues have managed to convince me that if we shut the paper down, there'll be nobody to do our job. We're the last of the Russian free press Mohicans.'

Meanwhile he handed around some cups. Anya brandished a thermos flask of coffee.

'Or do you guys fancy something stronger?'

'Water,' Farah said. 'With an aspirin, if you have one.'

Anya popped out and returned with a large glass of water and a strip of aspirin.

'What I still don't get, to be honest,' Farah said, after she'd drained the contents of the glass in a couple of gulps along with three aspirin, 'is that your journalists are threatened or murdered as soon as they stick their noses in too deep, and yet *Moskva Gazeta* is allowed to carry on. How do you explain that?'

Roman pointed to a framed photograph on the wall. It showed a smartly suited man demonstratively reading a copy of the *Moskva Gazeta* together with Potanin. 'Our main financial backer, Vasili Nevinny, with our beloved president,' he said with a liberal dose of irony. 'However illogical it may sound, Farah, the continued existence of our paper is essentially a PR matter for the men at the Kremlin. "Look," they say to their foreign detractors, "those rebellious boys and girls at the *Moskva Gazeta* can publish whatever they want. And yet you claim we don't have press freedom here in Russia?"'

'Bizarre,' Farah said.

'It is indeed. But there's another reason, an equally bizarre one,' Roman said. 'Our critical reporting inadvertently informs those very same figures at the Kremlin what the man in the street really thinks about them. You can bet the *Moskva Gazeta* is read by the government's most powerful advisors and by the *siloviki,* the FSB guys. Most of the information they receive from their own agents is wide of the mark. We tell them what's really going on in society. Let me tell you a secret.' Grinning broadly, Roman leaned across the table towards Farah and said in a conspiratorial whisper, 'We're actually on the FSB's payroll.' His roaring laughter filled the room.

'Roman will soon be awarded a medal by our president to mark his twelve-and-a-half years in the business,' Anya said with a chuckle.

'Congratulations,' Farah said, 'but I'm sure that's not why you invited us here.'

'True.' Roman looked at Paul. 'What have you told her?'

'Not much,' Paul replied.

'Right. As you may already know, Farah, in recent years Potanin has been trying to curb the power of the rich industrialists who oppose him. The most prominent among them was Aleksandr Zyuganov. Three years ago, after a show trial for tax evasion and fraud, he was sent to a Siberian labour camp. All the shares in Zyuganov's energy company NovaMost were transferred to the then newly founded AtlasNet, which was headed by the up-and-coming Valentin Lavrov. Are you still with me?'

'I think so,' Farah said. She noticed that her headache was finally beginning to subside. 'Sounds like a brilliant plan to me. You eliminate your most powerful opponent and acquire a rich ally in the process. I bet Lavrov reckons his president is a pretty good guy?'

'He and Lavrov get on like a house on fire,' Roman responded. 'That's why we started looking into this diversion of stocks. We kept a very low profile and the progress was slow. It's a diffuse network, but not long ago we stumbled across documents proving that while the president passed more than half of those shares to Lavrov at the time, he kept more than forty-five per cent for himself.'

'In other words,' Farah said in disbelief, 'your president not only eliminates his opponents, but he also lines his pockets with their shares.' She looked sharply at Roman Jankovski. 'Would you guys publish that?'

'Place our findings next to what I just told you about Elena Vertinski, Semyon Domnikov and the other murdered journalists and you'll understand that we've got a dilemma. And that's exactly why I've asked you and Paul to come here.'

'You've got incriminating documents that may be perceived as a danger to the state,' Farah concluded. 'So now you're looking for a foreign paper to publish them, because it would be too dangerous for you. Am I right?'

Roman nodded solemnly. 'In our line of work you've got to hope for the best, but with Lavrov, and even more so Potanin, definitely be prepared for the worst. Add our findings to Paul's recent discovery – the murky deals that Lavrov appears to have concluded behind the scenes with members of the South African government in exchange for concessions for the expansion of his mining corporations. Then add all this to the trail that takes us from the Afghan boy via your minister, perhaps indirectly, to AtlasNet. These three cases really require the intervention of Interpol specialists. Then again, if we join forces and get to the bottom of this fiendishly complicated case, we journalists will be doing the world a damn good service, right? But the question is: are we prepared to go that far? Are we up for it?'

'You're forgetting a fourth point,' Anya said. 'AtlasNet has a monopoly on gas supplies. For years now it's been using gas as a means of blackmail. Former Eastern bloc countries that are getting too chummy with the West suddenly have their gas cut off. They're even going as far as sabotaging attempts by EU nations to tap into alternative energy sources. Nicolas Anglade was investigating those practices. According to your media, he committed suicide after files containing indecent images of children were found on his computer.

'But strangely enough, those files were found on his home computer. However obsessive paedophiles may be, they'll think ten times before they download films and photos at home, where their wife and children or other housemates could come across them. Someone planted those files in Anglade's computer and made sure they were discovered. And you can certainly ask yourself if he really committed suicide.'

Each word seemed to affirm Farah's premonition of the night before. The treacherous complexity of the case was increasing by the hour and wrapping its tentacles ever tighter around her. She felt apprehensive. 'We'll have to consult our editor-in-chief,' she said in a hoarse voice. 'There are quite a few security risks involved with this, and that's putting it mildly.'

'That's another thing I'd like to talk to you about,' Roman said. 'I understand that you've asked Lavrov to be the guest editor of your special art edition.' There was a moment's silence in the room. Roman Jankovski rubbed his beard. 'Look, there's no doubt Lavrov already knows a lot more about you than you'll ever find out about him. It's a mistake to think you could get anywhere near him or catch him saying something incriminating in this way.'

'What's the alternative?'

'There isn't one. It would be unwise to withdraw at this stage. Make the supplement. But leave out the critical questions. Don't act the spy. Once the supplement is finished, you should see it as a done deal. When we come out with our evidence later, you can always say that while working on the supplement you stumbled across some facts that you went on to investigate further. In reality, it's the other way around, but here in Russia the facts are falsified on a daily basis, so why wouldn't you do the same for once?'

At that moment a young woman came in. She said something in Russian to Roman before switching on the large television in the corner of the room. A stocky man in a grey suit appeared on the screen. He held a large shiny bag in his hands and addressed the viewers in a condescending tone.

'The mayor of Moscow,' Paul clarified. 'He says they've discovered that the incident last night, in the building where Anya and I discovered the bags, wasn't an act of terrorism, but an exercise. The bags weren't filled with RDX.'

'Then what do they claim it was?' asked Farah, watching the mayor triumphantly holding up the bags in front of the camera.

'Sugar!' Anya said with a sardonic smile.

7

As if the End of Days was nearing, Anya Kozlova sped through Moscow towards the Pushkin Museum. Their meeting at the *Moskva Gazeta* had taken up more time than expected. Paul and Farah had needed to consult at length with their editor in the Netherlands.

A deal seemed possible from what they'd been told, but the final details still had to be ironed out with *AND*'s management.

But deal or no deal, being late for this social event was not an option. The Dutch trade delegation's tightly organized programme had begun in the morning with a wreath-laying ceremony at the Tomb of the Unknown Soldier. Seventy-five thousand tulip bulbs had been planted in Gorky Park and in about ten minutes' time the gala in the Pushkin Museum would begin.

Anya ignored an ENTRY FORBIDDEN sign and raced into a one-way street in the wrong direction. Barely five minutes later, waving their press credentials and the VIP card that had been bestowed on Farah, they were being ushered through the security check at the top of the grand staircase. They entered a magnificent ballroom where a starry starry night à la Vincent van Gogh was being projected on the ceiling at that moment. As Farah approached the entourage hovering around Valentin Lavrov, Paul unexpectedly ducked behind a marble pillar.

'What's got into you?' Anya asked.

'See that guy with the bald head?' Paul said. Anya looked around and saw a man at Lavrov's side. He had the nose of a hawk and the face of a wizened vulture.

'Arseni Vakurov,' muttered Paul. 'My plastic surgeon. He gave me a hell of a facelift in Jo'burg recently. Once these last bandages and stitches are removed, I'll look twenty years younger.'

Suddenly a slew of mobile phones in the room began to ring, zoom and resound as though an invisible conductor had struck up a digital orchestra. Anya's phone also went off. It was Roman, who told her that a large group of masked men and women had entered the Mass Media Centre of Moscow State University and taken two hundred International Summer School students hostage.

There was a huge commotion in the ballroom: apparently a number of the students being held were Dutch. Amidst the chaos of emotions, Anya saw Lavrov talking to Farah with seeming calm, after which she accompanied him through the crowd. Bodyguards led by the vulture shielded them completely.

Anya hurried down the wide staircase with Paul. Outside by the main entrance columns they saw Lavrov and Farah get into the second of two black Falcon four-wheel drives, which then sped off.

'Oh, just our luck,' Anya sighed as they ran to her double-parked car.

8

Farah was sitting next to Lavrov in the back seat of the Falcon, fighting her growing fear. They were driving through the city's fringes, an area marred by drab high-rises.

'Dreadful news, that hostage-taking,' Lavrov said in a reassuring tone. 'But I'm sure the authorities will do everything they can to resolve the situation. We won't let it spoil our lovely evening.'

'You wanted to show me something special?' Farah said guardedly.

'A special woman deserves something special,' Lavrov said with a smile. An enigmatic smile.

Outside the city, they passed army trucks parked by the side of the road and columns of soldiers digging fire trenches. She thought of Roman Jankovski's words: when dealing with Lavrov you could hope for the best, but you'd better be prepared for the worst. She also thought of her father's advice: you need to feel the fear to go through it. She was busy arming herself for a fight, when Lavrov noticed she was tensing up.

'Are you all right, Farah?'

'I don't like surprises,' she said. 'Not even when they're special.'

'True, I'm not giving you much of a choice,' he replied. Had she been more naive, she might have interpreted his smile as charming, but her intuition told her it was the smile of a man with a cold heart. She ought to try to escape – as soon as possible. She was prepared for the worst.

A firefighting plane flew low overhead, its engines roaring. The haze of smoke appeared to be thinning. For what seemed like several kilometres, they drove past a green fence before coming to a halt at a wide entrance gate where they were met by security guards emerging out of a glass booth.

Then the two Falcons proceeded up a hill to a sleek post-modern house with enormous windows.

When Farah stepped out of the car, she caught the scent of pine trees. The wind was south-westerly and the air was clear, not a hint of smog here. Via a maze of wide wooden staircases, Lavrov escorted her through the enormous house full of modern art directly up to the third floor.

'Are you ready?'

'As I said, I don't like surprises.'

'You'll love this one, Farah,' he said with a smile. 'You'll love it.' Glass doors slid open and they entered a pleasantly cool, dim room where the sound of running water could be heard. Then, slowly, a spotlight came on. A narrow strip of light revealed the statue of Sharada, the river goddess.

'I know how much this statue means to you,' Lavrov said. 'I saw how moved you were when you spotted it in my office in Amsterdam. That's when I got this idea. I'm sorry, the exhibition at the Pushkin Museum was just an excuse. I hope you'll forgive me.'

Farah glared at him. She was bamboo now. Strong and flexible.

'No,' she said calmly. 'I won't.'

'I hope what I'm about to tell you will change your mind,' Lavrov said, unmoved. 'I told you we're working on a special project in Indonesia. It has the potential to lift the lives of millions of Indonesians to a higher level. The moment I saw your fascination with this statue, I dubbed the project "Sharada".'

Farah took another look at the statue. Seeing it again caused her physical pain. The sadness over Parwaiz's death suddenly came rushing to the surface.

'Some thirty small, floating nuclear power stations are being built off the coast of Java. We opted for small installations because their limited capacity poses less of a safety threat. We're further developing the concept of underwater power stations from the 1960s, which is when the initial experiments with nuclear reactors on board submarines took place. In fact, the current Sharada design even looks like a submarine, but without the screw propeller and the weapons. Each Sharada power station will be installed on the seabed at a depth of 100 metres. Beyond the reach of terrorists, pirates, hurricanes and tsunamis. And there's a crucial role for you in all this.'

'How's that?' she asked, surprised.

'Let me explain. Come with me.' He ushered her to the enormous patio from where they looked out across a tree-lined lake. A champagne cooler and two glasses were waiting on a table.

'This project needs not only a symbol, but also a face. Somebody to spread its philosophy. To visit locations, speak to government leaders, bring fellow investors on board. And that person, Farah, is you.'

Lavrov gently popped the cork from the bottle and filled the two glasses with sparkling champagne. Farah was completely taken aback and struggled for breath. She saw that Lavrov wanted to hand her a glass and had to resist the urge to ward off that gesture the way she'd do in a fight.

'Why me?'

'You're intrepid, intelligent, passionate and extremely presentable as well.' Lavrov was still holding out the glass to her.

'No, thanks,' she said firmly. 'What's the real reason?'

'The real reason?' He raised an eyebrow. 'I'm not a philanthropist, I'm a businessman. I can offer you a share of the profit. Come and work for me. Better than writing phoney art supplements about dodgy oligarchs, right, Farah Gailani?'

She looked at him, unsure what to say. Roman Jankovski had been right. This man knew everything about her.

'Let me be frank, Farah. In Amsterdam you asked me how I came by the statue. Well, I inherited it from my biological father. Grigori Michailov.'

'Michailov was your father?'

'You didn't make the connection because of the different surname. You're not the only one. I'm what you'd call the bastard son.'

Now she understood what had happened in The Hague when the Bentley drove by. Lavrov's shocking resemblance to his father had been too much for Parwaiz's heart. From beyond the grave Michailov had claimed another life.

'Bastard son or not,' she said. 'I can't work for you, Lavrov. Sharada belongs in an Afghan museum. She shouldn't be misused by a criminal investor who's only interested in making other countries energy-dependent, because that's what this is all about. You said so yourself. You're not a philanthropist, but a businessman. And if the facts are anything to go by, a ruthless one too.'

Lavrov put the champagne glasses back on the table. The look in his eyes had changed. He regarded her coldly.

'Now that we know who our real fathers are, let's stop all this pretending.'

'Please,' Farah said.

'I know your real reason for coming to Moscow,' Lavrov said. 'It was a disappointing realization, in more ways than one. I would have enjoyed being involved in a beautiful art special with you, but I'm afraid that's out of the question now.'

Farah felt her breath catch in her throat, but she still didn't think she was in real danger. Outside the Pushkin Museum she'd got into the Falcon before lots of witnesses. Paul and Anya must have seen her leave. If anything were to happen to her, the trail would lead straight to this house. Lavrov was far too cunning for that. He had something else up his sleeve.

'We have some good contacts at the Dutch embassy,' Lavrov resumed. 'This morning a certain Detective Calvino dropped by with some rather incriminating information. I understand you're on quite intimate terms with him?'

'Leave Calvino out of this.'

'Of course. The man's just doing his job.'

'So am I.'

'No, Farah. You're doing more than that. You've thrown yourself heart and soul into this case. And you've already unearthed more than is good for both of us. That's why I hope you'll reconsider and accept my offer. I'm throwing you a life-line, Farah, do you understand?'

'Throw whatever you want, but I'm not a woman who betrays her principles. And now I'd like to leave, if you don't mind.'

'One final question then,' he said firmly. 'And I'd like you to think about this carefully. Right now, not far from here, hundreds of students are being held hostage. With some luck, most of them will survive. But my question is this: are you, like those black widows walking around there in suicide vests, prepared to sacrifice your life for an unattainable ideal?'

'Only if I'm forced to.'

'In that case, I suggest you reconsider and raise a glass with me after all.'

'Not in a million years,' she said. 'I'll take my chances.'

'Oh, will you . . . ?'

He accompanied her downstairs and shook her hand at the front door. 'We could have gone far together, you and me. Not as adversaries but as allies. That's what I was hoping. But you've made your decision, Farah. I'm very sorry to see it end like this.'

'I'm not. Goodbye.'

She breathed a sigh of relief as she walked to the waiting Falcon. But the chauffeur beside the car showed no intention of opening the door. Then she heard footsteps behind her on the gravel. Turning around she saw two men coming towards her from either side, followed by two more behind them. Now she understood the ramifications of her decision and heard her father's voice.

'Remember what you did when you first felt the fear?'

She assumed her starting position. With her right hand opened up and held out. The first man grabbed her left arm and shoved her back with full force. She absorbed the blow and landed a right hook on his chin, rammed him in the ribs with a left and threw him against the car with a right kick. She had no time to think. Her whole being was now geared towards the next opponent she glimpsed from the corner of her eye.

Her body was taken over by the ancient spirit of dead warriors preparing for a controlled and rapid counter-offensive. Standing with her legs aligned, she kicked the right one at the second man's thigh while at the same time absorbing his blow by grabbing his arm and using the momentum to plant the knuckles of her fist extra hard in his Adam's apple.

She averted the third man's low kick with a scooping motion. As she caught his outstretched leg, she rotated 180 degrees, brought her elbow to crotch level and rammed it straight in.

Then there was the unmistakable sound of an automatic weapon being cocked. In a split second she realized she'd never be able to floor her fourth opponent, a bald man with the eyes of a vulture, because he'd blow her brains out first.

9

Paul had been consumed by an intense hatred since that beating he'd taken in Ponte City. He'd felt the adrenalin surge through his body again after spotting the condor at the Pushkin Museum. His need for revenge was so overpowering that for a moment he lost sight of the fact it was Farah who now needed help. He tried reaching her by phone, but there was no answer.

In the Skoda they could hardly keep up with the two black Falcons that raced through the suburbs at top speed, but Anya had a hunch where they were going.

'Lavrov has a large villa on Lake Glubokoe,' she said, driving purposefully on, despite losing the Falcons when they were delayed by a procession of army trucks full of soldiers being brought in to fight the forest fires.

'There's Lavrov's estate!' Anya cried suddenly.

She pointed to the left side of the road, where Paul saw an endlessly long, undoubtedly electrified fence delineating an artificial boundary between the asphalt and pine woods. They drove past an entryway with a black metal gate guarded by broad-shouldered men in dark suits. From behind the bullet-proof glass of their booth, they spotted the Skoda immediately.

Anya stepped on the gas. 'I know a safer way,' she said with a devilish smirk.

Moments later, she turned left on to a bumpy dirt road. The Skoda hobbled over the gravel along the green metal mesh until they were close to the edge of the lake. Paul suspected they were driving around the lake. Anya kept glancing left out her window. Paul looked at her apprehensively, but she wasn't saying anything. After a few minutes she pointed through the trees.

'Lavrov's villa!'

She slowed down and manoeuvred the Skoda behind a large shrub, quickly grabbed her camera and lens case and ran up a steep hill, which turned out to be higher than the fence. Paul followed, hot on her heels.

'We have to be careful. Lavrov's guards patrol this area in their jeeps,' she said, out of breath.

Across the lake Paul saw a large post-modern villa with huge windows. The two Falcons were parked in the driveway. Nearby stood a man casually smoking a cigarette. There was little other movement.

'I see them,' Anya exclaimed, keeping the long telephoto lens pointed at the villa. Paul saw two small figures on a pano-ramic terrace and heard an audible clicking sound. Anya used the Nikon like a sharpshooter. 'Dammit! I think something's wrong,' she muttered as she watched Farah and Lavrov go back into the house.

There was the roar of an engine. In the distance a jeep approached along the fence.

'We've got to go,' Anya said. She was about to return to the car when Paul stopped her. He took the Nikon from her and through the viewfinder saw Farah in front of the villa sur-rounded by a few men, including the one he wanted dead, the condor. Meanwhile, the jeep patrolling the fence kept getting closer.

'We really need to go, Paul,' Anya snarled but Paul kept tak-ing pictures. Within seconds, Farah took out the three men who were guarding her.

'My God,' Paul said 'that woman's a lioness!' But when the condor aimed his weapon at her head, the lioness froze. Handcuffed and with a sack over her head, Farah was then shoved into the boot of one of the Falcons.

Anya dragged Paul away. They jumped back into the Skoda. Thanks to the curves along the fence they weren't spotted by the jeep. Shortly afterwards, having reached the paved road again, Paul saw the black Falcon speed through the gate with Vakurov at the wheel.

Anya soon lost the Falcon again, but just kilometres away, due to the threat of the rapidly spreading fire, the flow of vehicles was stopped by military personnel. From afar they saw that the Falcon was singled out and allowed to leave the line of traffic and drive along the hard shoulder. While scorching ashes were spewed across the road by the fire they saw raging to their left, Anya pulled her steering wall to the right and put her foot down hard on the accelerator. Paul couldn't help but shut his eyes as they too sped along the hard shoulder past the angry soldiers.

Because of the red-hot rain of ashes and the thick, dirty smoke that drifted over the road, the Falcon also had to slow down. Anya managed to keep up until they reached the outskirts of Moscow.

'*Chyort voz'mi!*' she cried as they approached downtown. 'Shit, they must be headed to the Seven Sisters!' Paul was familiar with the seven skyscrapers – built by Stalin – where Moscow State University was located, where hundreds of students were now being held hostage by Chechen rebels.

They managed to get within a hundred metres of the large complex before they encountered the tanks and vehicles of the Russian army that had sealed off the grounds. To their amazement, they saw the Falcon being allowed through the barricade.

10

Chalim Barchayev, brigadier general of the Smertniki suicide squad, looked around the auditorium and liked what he saw. He'd gathered the vast majority of the students in the large lecture theatre and distributed the others across three adjacent seminar rooms. He'd also ordered the strategic placement of several booby traps. On his command, the fourteen black widows in the unit would immediately blow themselves up. Chechen women were prepared to do everything for some money, a one-way ticket to paradise and the honour of revenging husbands who'd been killed by the Russians.

They'd arrived in the capital at different times and at different locations. Some had spent days travelling. This morning they'd all driven in from the suburbs in separate minivans and had gathered at the time agreed. They crossed the park in front of the Seven Sisters, like so many tourists and students did on a daily basis. It all looked perfectly normal. Young people with large bags and rucksacks walking over to the university to attend a range of summer school courses.

They hadn't spoken much. There was no need to talk; everybody knew what the mission was about and what was expected of them. Most of the women had little or no experience of hostage-taking, but they'd been given clear instructions, trained for days and had the protocol drilled into them. They knew they were going to die. After one of these operations you didn't live to tell the tale. Unless your name was Chalim Barchayev and Moscow had declared you dead on more than one occasion, but at the next fatal hijacking, kidnapping or hostage-taking you seemed to rise from the ashes like a phoenix.

Further down the corridor he saw the man with the head of a vulture. He was pushing a handcuffed woman with long black hair ahead of him. For a moment, Barchayev thought she was a sister-in-arms. If so, he wouldn't have wanted her to die. He'd have taken her as his fifth wife and kicked out the other four.

'She's going to be the main attraction,' Vulture Head said in Russian. 'The grand finale. But first we'll turn her into a film star.'

She's too beautiful, Chalim thought to himself. But he knew he had no choice. The financial backer, who'd rewarded him so handsomely for this action, was too powerful.

I I

On the other side of the digital camera, which was mounted on a slender tripod, the condor casually held a gun to the head of a young student begging for her life. From that position he looked at Farah with an almost bored grin.

'Now say what I want you to say, bitch. And do it convincingly. You can save this girl's life.'

'What do you want me to say?' Farah murmured. She was trembling with despair.

'Repeat after me!' the condor said. 'I, Farah Hafez . . .'

'I, Farah Hafez . . .'

'. . . support the jihad against President Potanin's criminal regime.'

Suddenly she saw her father standing in a corner. '*Padar*,' she begged in silence. 'Please help me. Give me the wisdom to do what I have to do.'

'Give them what they want,' her father said. 'You'll save a life by doing so, *bachem*.' But when Farah repeated what the condor primed her to say, he only pressed the gun tighter against the whimpering girl's temple and threatened to pull the trigger.

'The jury thought your performance was rather, let's say, amateurish. You'll have to do better – with more feeling this time,' he snarled.

Farah took a deep breath. She was on the verge of hyperventilating. She thought of the way she'd flung her Russian opponent on to the mat in Carré, and fired her text at the camera.

'I, Farah Hafez, support . . .'

No shot rang out. Instead the condor slapped her in the face with the flat of his hand.

'Don't overdo it, bitch.'

12

Chaos abounded in the crisis centre: it was a pandemonium of Babylonian proportions with a room full of know-it-alls shouting at and through each other, each believing they had the best solution for the hostage crisis.

Amid the bedlam, Paul was acutely aware that there was no government representative present, while Chalim Barchayev had made it more than clear he was only prepared to deal with Kremlin officials. The result: a stalemate because Potanin's people didn't negotiate with terrorists, even if most of the two hundred hostages were foreign students. Thus the area was teeming with staff from different international embassies.

'C'mon,' Anya said. 'We're of no use here.'

Once outside, she walked up to an ambulance, where she spent some time whispering with two nurses outside Paul's earshot. Then she motioned to him. A few minutes later, wearing white coats and carrying medical supplies, they approached the military cordon surrounding the building. Anya explained, and clearly successfully, that they'd just got word some of the hostages needed immediate medical attention. Once they neared the building, she also knew exactly where they had to go.

'I went to university here, remember?' Via the basement door they headed up two flights of stairs.

'But if we can do this, why isn't the army doing anything?' Paul whispered, agitated.

'It's happening,' Anya said. 'Apparently Alpha Spetsnaz is assembled right around the corner. But top officials in the Kremlin have a vested interest in letting this boil over. A few hostages might even have to be sacrificed; it's hard to know. Ditch the white jacket!'

'*Zhurnalisti!*', she shouted as they walked through a dark-tiled corridor. She pushed the Nikon into Paul's hands. In a few seconds they were surrounded by three women with black headscarves clad in bomb vests.

'Anya Kozlova, from the *Moskva Gazeta*. I'm here for Chalim Barchayev.'

In the improvised command centre in the cafeteria, Paul saw a menacing-looking man who reminded him of a radical imam. But this man wasn't wearing the prescribed long robe, the *mustahab*, but wore camouflage fatigues, was hung with grenades and had an automatic weapon within reach. Barchayev began to smile broadly when he saw Anya, grabbed his AK-47 and pointed it at her.

'You know what we do with Russian infiltrators?' he said, laughing.

'It's not funny, Chalim, you don't want to know what tricks I had to pull this time to get inside,' Anya said.

To Paul's shock, they embraced. But he realized she was bluffing. He could hear it in her voice. She was pretending to be the defiant terrorist sweetheart and it worked.

'And who's he?' Barchayev casually asked, pointing the barrel of his weapon at Paul.

'My photographer.'

'Looks like he pissed off a whole lot of people.'

'Right you are,' she replied. 'He's the worst photographer ever.'

Their laughter belonged in a pub at last orders, not in this cafeteria with the sobbing of female hostages in the background.

'What's your plan now, Chalim?' Anya asked, displaying little emotion.

'Simple: to die,' he said with a grin.

'Again?'

'Yes. And all the hostages die with us. Because I don't expect the Kremlin guys to show.'

'But you're at war with Russia, not the rest of the world. Most of these students aren't Russian.'

Suddenly Barchayev sounded very calm. 'It's time to show the world that no life is sacred to those Kremlin bastards.' To Paul it sounded like a line someone else had thought up for him.

'May we take some photos?' Anya asked. 'The world always wants to see faces.'

The auditorium stank of sweat and urine: the smell of fear. The stench made it hard for Paul to breathe. There was a large black flag with Arabic writing on it. When Paul discovered Farah amongst the hostages, he felt his heart skip a beat. She was handcuffed to a chair, with a wide piece of tape across her mouth. An explosive was strapped to her chest. The wires were connected to a laptop, with a digital clock ticking down the last thirty minutes. Farah was sweating profusely and her body was trembling all over, despite the stifling heat.

'A gift from our client,' Barchayev proudly mocked.

'Who gave you her?' Anya asked as Paul walked towards Farah, holding his Nikon. He didn't hear Barchayev's reply. He was only focused on Farah's huge terrified eyes. She wasn't looking at him, but at something behind him. Before Paul could turn around, a rifle butt cracked his skull.

He woke up in the corridor with Arseni Vakurov looming over him.

'*Pentimento, pentimento.* Repentance, repentance!' Vakurov echoed as if he were singing the lead in Wagner's *Ring of the Nibelung.* 'Haven't you learned anything, Chapelle?!'

Vakurov's kick hit him in the midriff, cutting off his breath. The boot rested on Paul's left arm. He feebly resisted with his right hand but couldn't prevent the other boot from kicking his head like a football.

He realized he was going to be stomped to death. He vomited blood. Lay there motionless. Heard the sound of heavy panting above him.

Vakurov was staring at him.

'This is no fun. What are you, a faggot? Get the fuck up!'

Paul pulled himself up on his hands and knees. He grabbed on to a door handle, rose to his feet unsteadily only to be met by a karate kick to the chest that propelled him backwards right through a stained-glass door. Paul landed on the floor amidst the broken glass and could barely hear what Vakurov said next, 'Now it's over.' Prophetic words to say the least. When the condor kicked what was left of the door out of its frame and stepped through it to finish Paul off, he tripped a booby trap wire.

Before Paul even realized it, Arseni Vakurov had been blown to bits, his body parts flying in every direction.

13

Major Sergey Boldyrev was thirty-six and a staff officer of the Alpha Spetsnaz anti-terror unit in charge of special operations. He and his commandos had rolled out of the hold of a Flying Tank, a MI-24 helicopter that had landed not far from the Seven Sisters earlier in the day.

He'd spent years fighting in Chechnya as a member of the Seventh Novocherkassk Special Force, during which he'd managed to kill both of Barchayev's infamous brothers, Abdul and Movsar. Eliminating the most feared scion of the Barchayev clan, Chalim, would be the crowning glory of his career.

Sergey had gathered together his men in the building next to the Mass Media Centre. The commandos had been trained to force their way into occupied buildings and to quickly eliminate their opponents with precision shots. Sergey had been given the green light by his superiors and after the explosion he'd just heard he didn't want to wait a second longer.

He'd shown his men the floor plans. 'This is where we are. The terrorists are over in this sector. We suspect they've installed booby traps at the entrances, there and there. So that's why we're entering here – where they'll least expect us. It's a narrow passage. I want five scouts to take the lead. Watch out for explosives. Marksmen close behind. As soon as we're in, deploy stun grenades. The back-up team provides cover. Stick close to the marksmen. Ready?'

'*Deystviye!*'

Thirty commandos ran, stooped down, across the grass towards the auditorium. They broke the windows and glass doors with the backs of their automatic weapons, then threw the stun grenades, whose furious thunder and lightning effect disorientated the terrorists who were then shot in the head with silenced hand guns. In that way Sergey managed to free all the hostages from the three seminar rooms within the space of a few minutes and break through to the auditorium, where he eliminated the remaining black widows. There was no trace of Barchayev.

Suddenly a man with a ravaged face appeared in front of him. His clothes were splattered with blood and, by the looks of it, pieces of human skin and tissue. He frantically pointed to a young Middle-Eastern-looking woman who'd had her mouth taped shut and was strapped to a chair. With his ear protectors on Sergey struggled to understand what the man was saying, but he instantly knew what was going on. He yelled into his microphone for assistance with an improvised explosive device.

Then he ordered the immediate evacuation of the building.

He knelt down beside the woman. He recognized the army-green casing in front of her belly by its inscription: FRONT TOWARD ENEMY. It was a M18A1 Claymore, filled with hundreds of steel bullets which, upon ignition, would be expelled at more than 1,000 kilometres per second. Two wires were connected to a laptop that showed a digital clock counting down.

Sergey noticed they had seven minutes left. He took off his ear protectors and spoke briefly with the man who'd been badly beaten. He turned out to be a Dutch journalist. The woman in the chair was his colleague. Sergey had received basic training in disconnecting timers, but didn't know how to do this on a laptop. There was no guarantee he'd manage to save the woman's life – and with that all of theirs. He told the man to talk to her, to keep her calm.

14

Paul could immediately tell from Farah's eyes that she was somewhere else, far away, hiding behind a curtain of fear. They were surrounded by noise, screaming, orders being shouted in Russian, students fleeing through the exits. It was total mayhem. He knelt beside her and began talking as calmly as he could manage.

'Farah, it's me, Paul. Do you recognize me? Farah, can you hear me?'

The Alpha commander instructed him to take hold of her shoulders to stop the trembling. It would be best if she moved as little as possible.

'Stand next to her. Try to keep her focused!'

Paul did what he was told, leaned over her caringly and continued talking.

'I . . . you know what it is, I haven't seen you in over thirty years . . . but I've never forgotten you . . . did you know that? And after all that time, you saved my life in a car accident! Do you know how that feels? Listen to me, it feels brilliant. It feels amazingly brilliant. You hear what I'm saying, brilliant! And you didn't fucking pull me out of that wreck to . . .'

She was breathing too rapidly. The commander now had two others assisting him. They deliberated in a feverish tone as one of them was about to cut a wire attached to the timer. The other man stopped him because he discovered something on the laptop screen.

Paul was still talking. 'We're going to be okay, you hear me, you and I. So stay with me. Look at me, Farah! I'm here with you, don't give up!' He was handed a bottle of water and put it against her mouth. She drank instinctively.

'We're going to take care of everything. Look . . . look at me . . .' And he bent slightly forward to look into her eyes.

'The first time . . . Do you remember the first time? The butterflies in the garden? Can you see me . . . ? Farah, do you see me standing here?' For a moment he thought he caught a glint of recognition in her eyes.

'Farah . . . !'

15

The Fokker Executive Jet 70 taking off from Domodedovo International Airport bound for Schiphol was only half full. The Dutch prime minister and his staff had immediately cancelled the rest of the planned visit, but part of the trade delegation had chosen to stay despite the hostage crisis.

Thanks to the connections of a former detective colleague, who now worked for State Security back home, Joshua had managed to get a seat on the private government plane. Before taking off, he'd called Tomasoa and explained the situation to him. Tomasoa had the impression that the Public Prosecutor was stalling on the Lombard matter, but he'd had contact with the National Department of Criminal Investigations. The plan was for a team to be waiting at the gate when Lombard landed and to detain him for questioning.

But Joshua had an uneasy feeling, especially since Tomasoa had told him that the preliminary investigation into Kovalev's death had stirred up trouble. 'It's all getting rather complicated.' Joshua couldn't get those words out of his head. Tomasoa was not a man who easily labelled things 'complicated'.

Once the Fokker had landed and was hooked up to the gangway, Joshua felt his heart throbbing in his throat. He followed closely on the heels of the security men escorting Lombard. As they approached the gate, there were indeed two men from Criminal Investigations waiting, accompanied by two military policemen.

He felt a moment of quiet triumph. He made eye contact with the national guys. After the arrest, he'd compliment them and perhaps even give them a comradely slap on the shoulder. But his joy gave way to disbelief when he saw that the detectives didn't stop Lombard and his party. All four of them were now staring at him with taut faces. A detective a head taller approached him.

'Detective Calvino,' he calmly said, 'in connection with an investigation into the death of a man in custody and violation of diplomatic law, you are hereby under arrest.'

16

The butterflies scattered because the boy suddenly came and stood in front of her. His face looked like he'd just been in a fight. He was sweating and he gazed at her intently with his bright-blue eyes. He knew her name, he knew who she was. He asked her if she could see him. He asked in Dari.

'Farah, do you see me?'

She said she could see him, he mustn't think she was blind, but she didn't hear herself speaking. Her voice was lost somewhere. No sound came out of her mouth. Still, she carried on talking to him.

'I can see you, Paul. I know who you are.'

She wished she could calm his nerves, because he was sweating and talking too fast. She herself was calm; she was where she wanted to be: in the garden, among the butterflies that were fluttering all around her. She wanted to reassure him.

'There's no scaring me.'

She said it with as much persuasion as she could muster, but it didn't get through to him. He came really close, his face hovering right in front of hers. Then she noticed that the droplets running down his cheeks weren't sweat. She'd never been this close to a boy before. She could hear his breath in her ear. Felt herself growing light. Her heart was beating so fast now she thought it might burst.

'Farah?'

Her father's voice. This was confusing.

'It's time, Farah.'

She saw her father, looking at her like he'd done before he drove off in the black Borgward for the last time.

'*Padar!*' She yelled at the top of her lungs.

And then the sun broke into a thousand fiery pieces and the butterfly garden turned as white as snow.

Acknowledgements

Dad for all your travels and Mum for being his rock.

Marianne for your faith in me.

Jihane for your beautiful stories.

Tom for your inspirational guidance and support.

Patricia for your take on Farah and your help building her world.

Diana for your surprising insights and incisive analyses.

Perry, Susan, Basir, Lola, Tuba and Shahiera for the patience and respect with which you initiated me into so many aspects of your native country.

Sehnaaz and Julian for the introduction to Pencak Silat.

Ton for your dedicated coaching on detective matters. Stefan for your invaluable assistance.

Erik, Tessa, Lizenka, Ad and Frodo for the medical underpinnings.

Lidy, John and Annieke for your tales from the world of journalism.

Paul for your monetary expertise and Nico for your advice.

Everyone who read and commented during the various stages of the book: Josje, Michael, André, Henk, Bernique, Lilian, Donat, Bas, Lamia, Mo, Roel, Jan, Meike, Clemence, Ivar, Annet. And anyone I may have forgotten . . .

My heartfelt thanks!